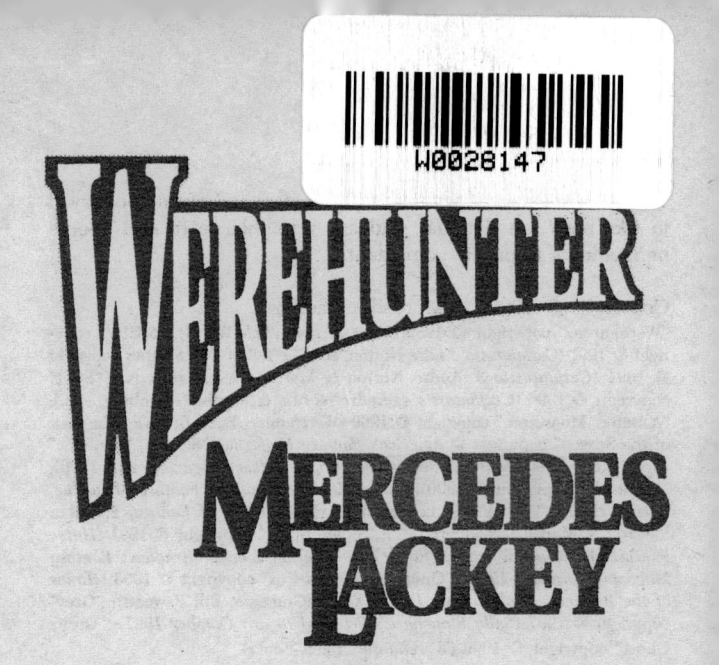

WEREHUNTER

MERCEDES LACKEY

WEREHUNTER

This is a work of fiction. All the characters and events portrayed in this book are fictional, and any resemblance to real people or incidents is purely coincidental.

Copyright © 1999 by Mercedes Lackey
"Werehunter" copyright © 1989 (*Tales of the Witch World*); "SKitty" copyright © 1991 (*Catfantastic*, Andre Norton, ed.); "A Tail of Two SKitties copyright © 1994 (*Catfantastic 3*, Andre Norton & Martin Greenberg, eds.); "SCat" copyright © 1996 (*Catfantastic 4*, Andre Norton & Martin Greenberg, eds.); "A Better Mousetrap" copyright © 1999 (*Werehunter*, Baen Books); "The Last of the Season" copyright © *American Fantasy Magazine*; "Satanic, Versus ..." copyright © 1990 (*Marion Zimmer Bradley's Fantasy Magazine, Fall 1990*); "Nightside" copyright © 1990 (*Marion Zimmer Bradley's Fantasy Magazine, Spring 1990*); "Wet Wings" copyright © 1995 (*Sisters of Fantasy 2*, Susan Shwartz & Martin Greenberg, ed.); "Stolen Silver" copyright © 1991 (*Horse Fantastic*); "Roadkill" copyright © 1990 (*Marion Zimmer Bradley's Fantasy Magazine, Summer 1990*); "Operation Desert Fox" copyright © 1993 (*Honor of the Regiment: Bolos, Book I*, eds. Keith Laumer & Bill Fawcett); "Grey" copyright © 1997 (*Sally Blanchard's Pet Bird Report October 1997*); "Grey's Ghost" copyright © 1999 (*Werehunter*, Baen Books)

All rights reserved, including the right to reproduce this book or portions thereof in any form.

A Baen Books Original

Baen Publishing Enterprises
P.O. Box 1403
Riverdale, NY 10471

ISBN: 0-671-57805-7

Cover art by Bob Eggleton

First printing, April 1999

Distributed by Simon & Schuster
1230 Avenue of the Americas
New York, NY 10020

Typeset by Windhaven Press, Auburn, NH
Printed in the United States of America

TWO OUT OF THREE AIN'T BAD...

Something very large occluded the light for a moment in the next room, then the lights went out, and Diana Tregarde distinctly heard the sound of the chandelier being torn from the ceiling and thrown against the wall. She winced.

There go my Romance Writers of the World dues up again, she thought.

"I got a glimpse," Andre said. "It was very large, perhaps ten feet tall, and—*cherie,* looked like nothing so much as a rubber creature from a very bad movie. Except that I do not think it was rubber."

What shambled in through the door was nothing that Diana had ever heard of. It was, indeed, about ten feet tall. It was covered with luxuriant brown hair—all over. It was built along the lines of a powerful body-builder, taken to exaggerated lengths, and it drooled. It also stank, a combination of sulfur and musk so strong it would have brought tears to the eyes of a skunk.

Di groaned, putting two and two together and coming up with—*Valentine Vervain cast a spell for a tall, dark and handsome soul-mate, but she forgot to specify "human."* "Are you thinking what I'm thinking?"

The other writer nodded. "Tall, check. Dark, check. Long hair, check. Handsome—well, I suppose in some circles." Harrison stared at the thing in fascination.

The thing saw Valentine and lunged for her. Reflexively, Di and Harrison both shot. He emptied his cylinder and one speed loader. Di gave up after four shots. No effect. The thing backhanded Andre into a wall hard enough to put him through plasterboard. Andre was out for the count. There are some things even a vampire has a little trouble recovering from.

"Harrison, distract it, make a noise, anything!" Diana pulled the atheme from her boot sheath and began cutting Sigils in the air with it, getting the Words of Dismissal out as fast as she could without slurring the syllables.

The thing lunged toward Harrison, missing him by inches, just as Di concluded the Ritual of Dismissal.

To no effect. . . .

—from "Satanic, Versus..."

BAEN BOOKS by MERCEDES LACKEY

BARDIC VOICES
The Lark & the Wren
The Robin & the Kestrel
The Eagle & the Nightingales
The Free Bards
Four & Twenty Blackbirds
Bardic Choices: A Cast of Corbies
(with Josepha Sherman)

The Fire Rose
Fiddler Fair
Werehunter
The Ship Who Searched
(with Anne McCaffrey)
Wing Commander: Freedom Flight
(with Ellen Guon)
If I Pay Thee Not in Gold
(with Piers Anthony)

URBAN FANTASIES
Bedlam's Bard
(with Ellen Guon)
The SERRAted Edge:
Born to Run (with Larry Dixon)
Wheels of Fire (with Mark Shepherd)
When the Bough Breaks (with Holly Lisle)
Chrome Circle (with Larry Dixon)

THE BARD'S TALE NOVELS
Castle of Deception (with Josepha Sherman)
Fortress of Frost & Fire (with Ru Emerson)
Prison of Souls (with Mark Shepherd)

Contents

Introduction 1
Werehunter 12
SKitty 38
A Tail of Two SKitties 56
SCat 72
A Better Mousetrap 92
The Last of the Season 110
Satanic, Versus 126
Nightside 143
Wet Wings 164
Stolen Silver 170
Roadkill 186
Operation Desert Fox 194
Grey 222
Grey's Ghost 237

Introduction

Those of you who are more interested in the stories than in some chatty author stuff should just skip this part, since it will be mostly about the things people used to ask us about at science fiction conventions.

For those of you who have never heard of SF conventions (or "cons" as they are usually called), these are gatherings of people who are quite fanatical about their interest in one or more of the various fantasy and science fiction media. There are talks and panel discussions on such wildly disparate topics as costuming, propmaking, themes in SF/F literature, *Star Wars*, *Star Trek*, *Babylon 5*, *X-Files*, SF/F art, medieval fighting, horse-training, dancing, and the world of fans in general. There are workshops on writing and performance arts. Guests featured in panels and question and answer sessions are often featured performers from television and movies along with various authors and the occasional professional propmaker. Larry and I no longer attend conventions for a number of reasons, not the least of which is that we have a great many responsibilities that require us to be home.

Some of those responsibilities are that we are volunteers for our local fire department. Larry is a driver and outside man; I am learning to do dispatch, and hopefully will be able to take over the night shift, since we are awake long after most of the rest of the county has gone to sleep. Our local department is strictly volunteer and works on a very tight budget. Our equipment is old and needs frequent repair, we get what we can afford, and what we can afford is generally third or fourth-hand, having passed through a large metropolitan department or the military to a small municipal department to the Forestry Service and finally to us. In summer I am a water-carrier at grass-fires, meaning that I bring drinking-water to the overheated firefighters so they don't collapse in the 100 plus degree heat.

Another duty is with the EOC (formerly called the Civil Defense Office). When we are under severe weather conditions, the firefighters are called in to wait at the station in case of emergency, so Larry is there. I go in to the EOC office to read weather-radar for the storm-watchers in the field. Eventually I hope to get my radio license so I can also join the ranks of the storm-watchers. We don't "chase" as such, although there are so few of the storm-watchers that they may move to active areas rather than staying put. Doppler radar can only give an indication of where there is rotation in the clouds; rotation may not produce a tornado. You have to have people on the ground in the area to know if there is a funnel or a tornado (technically, it isn't a tornado until it touches the ground; until then it is a funnel-cloud). Our area of Oklahoma is not quite as active as the area of the Panhandle or around Oklahoma City and Norman (which is why the National Severe Storms Laboratory is located there) but we get plenty of severe, tornado-producing storms.

In addition, we have our raptor rehabilitation duties.

Larry and I are raptor rehabilitators; this means that we are licensed by both the state and the federal government to collect, care for, and release birds of prey that are injured or ill. Occasionally we are asked to bring one of our "patients" for a talk to a group of adults or children, often under the auspices of our local game wardens.

I'm sure this sounds very exciting and glamorous, and it certainly impresses the heck out of people when we bring in a big hawk riding on a gloved hand, but there are times when I wonder how we managed to get ourselves into this.

We have three main "seasons"—baby season, stupid fledgling season, and inexpert hunter season.

Now, injuries—and victims of idiots with guns—can come at any time. We haven't had too many shooting victims in our area, thank heavens, in part because the cattle-farmers around our area know that shooting a raptor only adds field rats and mice to their property. But another rehabber gave up entirely a few years ago, completely burned out, because she got the same redtail hawk back *three times*, shot out of the sky. Injuries that we see in our area are most often the case of collision— literally—with man's environmental changes. Birds hit windows that seem to them to be sky, Great Blue Herons collide with power-lines, raptors get electrocuted by those same lines. But most often, we get birds hit by cars. Owls will chase prey across the road, oblivious to the fact that something is approaching, and get hit. Raptors are creatures of opportunity and will quite readily come down to feed on roadkill and get hit. Great Horned Owls, often called the "tigers of the sky," are top predators, known to chase even eagles off nests to claim the nest for themselves—if a Great Horned is eating roadkill and sees a car approaching, it will stand its ground, certain that it will get the better of anything daring to try to snatch its dinner! After all, they have been developing and evolving for millions of years, and swiftly moving vehicles have only been around for about seventy-five years; they haven't had nearly enough time to adapt to the situation as a species. Individuals *do* learn, though, often to take advantage of the situation.

Kestrels and redtails are known to hang around fields being harvested to snatch the field-rats running from the machinery, or suddenly exposed after the harvesters have passed. Redtails are also known to hang about railway right-of-ways, waiting for trains to spook out rabbits!

Our current education bird, a big female redtail we call Cinnamon, is one such victim; struck in the head by a CB whip-antenna, she has only one working eye and just enough brain damage to render her partially paralyzed on one side and make her accepting and calm in our presence. This makes her a great education-bird, as nothing alarms her and children can safely touch her, giving them a new connection with wild things that they had never experienced before.

But back to the three "seasons" of a raptor rehabber, and the different kinds of work they involve.

First is "baby season," which actually extends from late February through to July, beginning with Great Horned Owl babies and ending when the second round of American Kestrels (sparrowhawks, or "spawks" as falconers affectionately call them) begins to push their siblings out of nests. The first rule of baby season is— try to get the baby back into the nest, or something like the nest. Mother birds are infinitely better at taking care of their youngsters than any human, so when wind or weather send babies (eyases, is the correct term) tumbling, that is our first priority. This almost always involves climbing, which means that poor Larry puts on his climbing gear and dangles from trees. When nest and all have come down, we supply a substitute, in as close to the same place as possible; raptor mothers are far more fixated on the kids than the house, and a box filled with branches will do nicely, thank you.

Sometimes, though, it's not possible to put the eyases back. Youngsters are found with no nest in sight, or the nest is literally unreachable (a Barn Owl roost in the roof of an institution for the criminally insane, for instance), or worst of all, the parents are known to be dead.

Young raptors eat a lot. Kestrels need feeding every hour or so, bigger birds every two to three, and that's from dawn to dusk. We've taken eyases with us to doctor's appointments, on vacation, on shopping expeditions, and even to racing school! And we're not talking Gerber's here; "mom" (us) gets to take the mousie, dissect the mousie, and feed the mousie parts to baby. By hand. Yummy! Barred Owl eyases are the easiest of the lot; they'll take minnows, which are of a size to slip down their little throats easily, but not the rest. There's no use thinking you can get by with a little chicken, either—growing babies need a lot of calcium for those wonderful hollow bones that they're growing so fast, so they need the whole animal.

Fortunately, babies do grow up, and eventually they'll feed themselves. Then it's just a matter of helping them learn to fly (which involves a little game we call "Hawk Tossing") and teaching them to hunt. The instincts are there; they just need to connect instinct with practice. But this is *not* for the squeamish or the tender-hearted; for the youngsters to grow up and have the skills to make them successful, they have to learn to kill.

The second season can stretch from late April to August, and we call it "silly fledgling season." That's when the eyases, having learned to fly at last, get lost. Raptor mothers—with the exception of Barn Owls—continue to feed the youngsters and teach them to hunt after they've fledged, but sometimes wind and weather again carry the kids off beyond finding their way back to mom. Being inexperienced flyers and not hunters at all yet, they usually end up helpless on the ground, which is where we come in.

These guys are actually the easiest and most rewarding; they know the basics of flying and hunting, and all we have to do is put some meat back on their bones and give them a bit more experience. We usually have anywhere from six to two dozen kestrels at this stage every year, which is when *we* get a fair amount of exercise, catching grasshoppers for them to hunt.

Then comes the "inexpert hunter" season, and I'm not referring to the ones with guns. Some raptors are the victims of a bad winter, or the fact that they concentrated on those easy-to-kill grasshoppers while their siblings had graduated to more difficult prey. Along about December, we start to get the ones that nothing much is wrong with except starvation. Sometimes starvation has gone too far for them to make it; frustrating and disappointing for us.

We've gotten all sorts of birds over the years; our wonderful vet, Dr. Paul Welch (on whom may blessings be heaped!) treats wildlife for free, and knows that we're always suckers for a challenge, so he has gotten some of the odder things to us. We've had two Great Blue Herons, for instance. One was an adult that had collided with a powerline. It had a dreadful fracture, and we weren't certain if it would be able to fly again (it did) but since we have a pond, we figured we could support a land-bound heron. In our ignorance, we had no idea that Great Blues are terrible challenges to keep alive because they are so shy; we just waded right in, force-feeding it minnows when it refused to eat, and stuffing the minnows right back down when it tossed them up. This may not sound so difficult, but remember that a Great Blue has a two-foot sword on the end of its head, a spring-loaded neck to put some force behind the stab, and the beak-eye coordination to impale a minnow in a foot of water. It has *no* trouble targeting your eye.

We fed it wearing welding-masks.

We believe very strongly in force-feeding; our experience has been that if you force-feed a bird for two to three days, it gives up trying to die of starvation and begins eating on its own. Once again, mind you, this is not always an easy proposition; we're usually dealing with fully adult birds who want nothing whatsoever to do with us, and have the equipment to enforce their preferences. We very seldom get a bird that is so injured that it gives us no resistance. Great Horned Owls can exert pressure of 400 ft/lbs per talon, which can easily penetrate a Kevlar-lined welding glove, as I know personally and painfully.

That is yet another aspect of rehabbing that most people don't think about—injury. Yours, not the bird's. We've been "footed" (stabbed with talons), bitten, pooped on (okay, so that's not an injury, but it's not pleasant), gouged, and beak-slashed. And we have to stand there and continue doing whatever it was that earned us those injuries, because it certainly isn't the *bird's* fault that he doesn't recognize the fact that you're trying to help him.

We also have to know when we're out of our depth, or when the injury is *so* bad that the bird isn't releasable, and do the kind and responsible thing. Unless a bird is *so* endangered that it can go into a captive breeding project, or is the rare, calm, quiet case like Cinnamon who will be a perfect education bird, there is no point in keeping one that can't fly or hunt again. You learn how to let go and move on very quickly, and just put your energy into the next one.

On the other hand, we have personal experience that raptors are a great deal tougher than it might appear. We've successfully released one-eyed hawks, who learn to compensate for their lack of binocular vision very well. Birds with one "bad" leg learn to strike only with the good one. One-eyed owls are routine for us now; owls mostly hunt by sound anyway and don't actually need both eyes. But the most amazing is that another rehabber in our area has routinely gotten successful releases with owls that are minus a wingtip; evidently owls are such strong fliers that they don't need their entire wingspan to prosper, and *that* is quite amazing and heartening.

We've learned other things, too; one of the oddest is that owls by-and-large don't show gradual recovery from head-injuries. They will go on, day after day, with nothing changing—then, suddenly, one morning you have an owl fighting to get out of the box you've put him in to keep him quiet and contained! We've learned that once birds learn to hunt, they prefer fresh-caught dinner to the frozen stuff we offer; we haven't had a single freeloader keep coming back long after he should be independent. We've learned that "our" birds learn quickly not to generalize about humans feeding them— once they are free-flying (but still supplementing their hunting with handouts) they don't bother begging for food from anyone but those who give them the proper "come'n'get it" signal, and even then they are unlikely to get close to anyone they don't actually recognize.

We already knew that eyases in the "downy" stage, when their juvenile plumage hasn't come in and they look like little white puffballs, will imprint very easily, so we quickly turn potentially dangerous babies (like Great Horned Owls) over to rehabbers who have "foster moms"—non-releasable birds of the right species who will at least provide the right role-model for the youngsters. Tempting as the little things are, so fuzzy and big-eyed, none of us wants an imprinted Great Horned coming back in four or five years when sexual maturity hits, looking for love in all the wrong places! Remember those talons?

For us, though, all the work is worth the moment of release, when we take the bird that couldn't fly, or the now-grown-up and self-sufficient baby, and turn him loose. For some, we just open the cage door and step back; for others, there's a slow process called "hacking out," where the adolescent comes back for food until he's hunting completely on his own. In either case, we've performed a little surgery on the fragile ecosystem, and it's a good feeling to see the patient thriving.

Those who have caught the raptor-bug seem like

family; we associate with both rehabber and falconers. If you are interested in falconry—and bear in mind, it is an extremely labor-intensive hobby—contact your local Fish and Wildlife department for a list of local falconers, and see if you can find one willing to take you as an apprentice. If you want to get into rehab, contact Fish and Wildlife for other rehabbers who are generally quite happy to help you get started.

Here are some basic facts about birds of prey. Faloners call the young in the nest an eyas; rehabbers and falconers call the very small ones, covered only in fluff, "downies." In the downy stage, they are very susceptible to imprinting; if we have to see babies we would rather they were at least in the second stage, when the body-feathers start to come in. That is the only time that the feathers are not molted; the down feathers are actually attached to the juvenile feathers, and have to be picked off, either by the parent or the youngster. Body-feathers come in first, and when they are about half-grown, the adults can stop brooding the babies, for they can retain their body-heat on their own, and more importantly, the juvenile feathers have a limited ability to shed water, which the down will not do. If a rainstorm starts, for instance, the downies will be wet through quickly before a parent can return to the nest to cover them, they'll be hypothermic in seconds and might die; babies in juvenile plumage are safe until a parent gets back to cover them.

When eyases never fight in the nest over food this means both that their environmeent provides a wealth of prey and that their parents are excellent hunters. If they are hungry, the youngest of the eyases often dies or is pushed out of the nest to die.

Redtails can have up to four offspring; two is usual. Although it is rare, they have been known to double-clutch if a summer is exceptionally long and warm. They may also double-clutch if the first batch is infertile.

Redtails in captivity can live up to twenty-five years;

half that is usual in the wild. They can breed at four years old, though they have been known to breed as young as two. In their first year they do not have red tails and their body-plumage is more mottled than in older birds; this is called "juvenile plumage" and is a signal to older birds that these youngsters are no threat to them. Kestrels do not have juvenile plumage, nor do most owls, and eagles hold their juvenile plumage for four years. Kestrels live about five years in the wild, up to fifteen in captivity, eagles live fifty years in captivity and up to twenty-five in the wild.

Should you find an injured bird of prey, you need three things for a rescue: a heavy blanket or jacket, cohesive bandage (the kind of athletic wrap that sticks to itself), and a heavy, dark-colored sock. Throw the blanket over the victim, locate and free the head and pull the sock over it. Locate the feet, and wrap the feet together with the bandage; keep hold of the feet, remove the blanket, get the wings folded in the "resting" position and wrap the body in cohesive bandage to hold the wings in place. Make a ring of a towel in the bottom of a cardboard box just big enough to hold the bird, and put the bird in the box as if it was sitting in a nest. Take the sock off and quickly close up the box and get the victim to a rehabber, a local game warden or Fish and Wildlife official, or a vet that treats injured wildlife. Diurnal raptors are very dependent on their sight; take it away and they "shut down"—which is the reason behind the traditional falcon-hood. By putting the sock over the head, you take away the chief source of stress, the sight of enormous two-legged predators bearing down on it.

Andre Norton, who (as by now you must be aware) I have admired for ages, was doing a "Friends of the Witch World" anthology, and asked me if I would mind doing a story for her.

Would I mind? I flashed back to when I was thirteen or fourteen years old, and I read Witch World and fell completely and totally into this wonderful new cosmos. I had already been a fan of Andre's since I was nine or ten and my father (who was a science fiction reader) loaned me Beast Master because it had a horse in it and I was horse-mad. But this was something different, science fiction that didn't involve thud and blunder and iron-thewed barbarians. I was in love.

Oh—back in "the old days" it was all called "science fiction." There was no category for "fantasy," and as for "hard s/f," "sword and sorcery," "urban fantasy," "high fantasy," "cyberpunk," "horror," "space-opera"—none of those categories existed. You'd find Clark Ashton Smith right next to E. E. "Doc" Smith, and Andre Norton and Fritz Leiber wrote gothic horror, high fantasy, and science fiction all without anyone wondering what to call it. Readers of imaginative literature read everything, and neither readers nor writers were compelled by marketing considerations to read or write in only a single category.

At any rate, many years later, my idol Andre Norton asked me for a story set in one of my favorite science-fiction worlds. Somehow I managed to tell Andre that I would be very happy to write a story. This is it. In fact, this is the longer version; she asked me to cut some, not because she didn't like it the way it was, but because she was only allowed stories of 5,000 words or less; here it is as I originally wrote it.

Werehunter

It had been raining all day, a cold, dismal rain that penetrated through clothing and chilled the heart to numbness. Glenda trudged through it, sneakers soaked; beneath her cheap plastic raincoat her jeans were soggy to the knees. It was several hours past sunset now, and still raining, and the city streets were deserted by all but the most hardy, the most desperate, and the faded few with nothing to lose.

Glenda was numbered among those last. This morning she'd spent her last change getting a bus to the welfare office, only to be told that she hadn't been a resident long enough to qualify for aid. That wasn't true—but she couldn't have known that. The supercilious clerk had taken in her age and inexperience at a glance, and assumed "student." If he had begun processing her, he'd have been late for lunch. He guessed she wouldn't know enough to contradict him, and he'd been right. And years of her aunt's browbeating ("Isn't one 'no' good enough for you?") had drummed into her the lesson that there were no second chances. He'd gone off to his lunch date; she'd trudged back home in the rain. This afternoon she'd eaten the last packet of cheese and crackers and had made "soup" from the stolen packages of fast-food ketchup—there was nothing left in her larder that even resembled food. Hunger had been with her for so long now that the ache in her stomach had become as much a part of her as her hands or feet. There were three days left in the month; three days of shelter, then she'd be kicked out of her shoddy efficiency and into the street.

When her Social Security orphan's benefits had run out when she'd turned eighteen, her aunt had "suggested" she find a job and support herself—elsewhere. The suggestion had come in the form of finding her belongings in boxes on the front porch with a letter to that effect on top of them.

So she'd tried, moving across town to this place, near the university; a marginal neighborhood surrounded by bad blocks on three sides. But there were no jobs if you had no experience—but how did you get experience without a job? The only experience she'd ever had was at shoveling snow, raking leaves, mowing and gardening; the only ways she could earn money for college, since her aunt had never let her apply for a job that would have been beyond walking distance of her house. Besides that, there were at least forty university students competing with her for every job that opened up anywhere around here. Her meager savings (meant, at one time, to pay for college tuition) were soon gone.

She rubbed the ring on her left hand, a gesture she was completely unaware of. That ring was all she had of the mother her aunt would never discuss—the woman her brother had married over her own strong disapproval. It was silver, and heavy; made in the shape of a crouching cat with tiny glints of topaz for eyes. Much as she treasured it, she would gladly have sold it—but she couldn't get it off her finger, she'd worn it for so long.

She splashed through the puddles, peering listlessly out from under the hood of her raincoat. Her lank, mouse-brown hair straggled into her eyes as she squinted against the glare of headlights on rain-glazed pavement. Despair had driven her into the street; despair kept her here. It was easier to keep the tears and hysterics at bay out here, where the cold numbed mind as well as body, and the rain washed all her thoughts until they were thin and lifeless. She could see no way out of this trap—except maybe by killing herself.

But her body had other ideas. *It* wanted to survive, even if Glenda wasn't sure *she* did.

A chill of fear trickled down her backbone like a drop of icy rain, driving all thoughts of suicide from her, as behind her she recognized the sounds of footsteps.

She didn't have to turn around to know she was being followed, and by more than one. On a night like tonight, there was no one on the street but the fools and the hunters. She knew which she was.

It wasn't much of an alley—a crack between buildings, scarcely wide enough for her to pass. *They* might not know it was there—even if they did, they couldn't know what lay at the end of it. She did. She dodged inside, feeling her way along the narrow defile, until one of the two buildings gave way to a seven-foot privacy fence.

She came to the apparent dead-end, building on the right, a high board fence on the left, building in front. She listened, stretching her ears for sounds behind her, taut with fear. Nothing; they had either passed this place by, or hadn't yet reached it.

Quickly, before they could find the entrance, she ran her hand along the boards of the fence, counting them from the dead-end. Four, five—when she touched the sixth one, she gave it a shove sideways, getting a handful of splinters for her pains. But the board moved, pivoting on the one nail that held it, and she squeezed through the gap into the yard beyond, pulling the board back in place behind her.

Just in time; echoing off the stone and brick of the

alley were harsh young male voices. She leaned against the fence and shook from head to toe, clenching her teeth to keep them from chattering, as they searched the alley, found nothing, and finally (after hours, it seemed) went away.

"Well, you've got yourself in a fine mess," she said dully. "Now what? You don't dare leave, not yet—they might have left someone in the street, watching. Idiot! Home may not be much, but it's dry, and there's a bed. Fool, fool, fool! So now you get to spend the rest of the night in the back yard of a spookhouse. You'd just better hope the spook isn't home."

She peered through the dark at the shapeless bulk of the tri-story townhouse, relic of a previous century, hoping *not* to see any signs of life. The place had an uncanny reputation; even the gangs left it alone. People had vanished here—some of them important people, with good reasons to want to disappear, some who had been uninvited visitors. But the police had been over the house and grounds more than once, and never found anything. No bodies were buried in the back yard—the ground was as hard as cement under the inch-deep layer of soft sand that covered it. There was nothing at all in the yard but the sand and the rocks; the crazy woman that lived here told the police it was a "Zen garden." But when Glenda had first peeked through the boards at the back yard, it didn't look like any Zen garden *she* had ever read about. The sand wasn't groomed into wave-patterns, and the rocks looked more like something out of a mini-Stonehenge than islands or mountain-peaks.

There were four of those rocks—one like a garden bench, that stood before three that formed a primitive arch. Glenda felt her way towards them in the dark, trusting to the memory of how the place had looked by daylight to find them. She barked her shin painfully on the "bench" rock, and her legs gave out, so that she sprawled ungracefully over it. Tears of pain mingled with the rain, and she swore under her breath.

She sat huddled on the top of it in the dark, trying to remember what time it was the last time she'd seen a clock. Dawn couldn't be too far off. When dawn came, and there were more people in the street, she could probably get safely back to her apartment.

For all the good it would do her.

Her stomach cramped with hunger, and despair clamped down on her again. She shouldn't have run—she was only delaying the inevitable. In two days she'd be out on the street, and this time with nowhere to hide, easy prey for them, or those like them.

"So wouldn't you like to escape altogether?"

The soft voice out of the darkness nearly caused Glenda's heart to stop. She jumped, and clenched the side of the bench-rock as the voice laughed. Oddly enough, the laughter seemed to make her fright wash out of her. There was nothing malicious about it—it was kind-sounding, gentle. Not crazy.

"Oh, I like to make people think I'm crazy; they leave me alone that way." The speaker was a dim shape against the lighter background of the fence.

"Who—"

"I am the keeper of this house—and this place; not the first, certainly not the last. So there is nothing in this city—in this world—to hold you here anymore?"

"How—did you know *that*?" Glenda tried to see the speaker in the dim light reflected off the clouds, to see if it really was the woman that lived in the house, but there were no details to be seen, just a human-shaped outline. Her eyes blurred. Reaction to her narrow escape, the cold, hunger; all three were conspiring to make her light-headed.

"The only ones who come to me are those who have no will to live *here*, yet who still have the will to live. Tell me, if another world opened before you, would you walk into it, not knowing what it held?"

This whole conversation was so surreal, Glenda began

to think she was hallucinating the whole thing. Well, if it was a hallucination, why not go along with it?

"Sure, why not? It couldn't be any worse than here. It might be better."

"Then turn, and look behind you—and choose."

Glenda hesitated, then swung her legs over the bench-stone. The sky was lighter in that direction—dawn was breaking. Before her loomed the stone arch—

Now she *knew* she was hallucinating—for framed within the arch was no shadowy glimpse of board fence and rain-soaked sand, but a patch of reddening sky, and another dawn—

A dawn that broke over rolling hills covered with waving grass, grass stirred by a breeze that carried the scent of flowers, not the exhaust-tainted air of the city.

Glenda stood, unaware that she had done so. She reached forward with one hand, yearningly. The place seemed to call to something buried deep in her heart—and she wanted to answer.

"Here—or there? Choose now, child."

With an inarticulate cry, she stumbled toward the stones—

And found herself standing alone on a grassy hill.

After several hours of walking in wet, soggy tennis shoes, growing more spacey by the minute from hunger, she was beginning to think she'd made a mistake. Somewhere back behind her she'd lost her raincoat; she couldn't remember when she'd taken it off. There was no sign of people anywhere—there were animals; even sheep, once, but nothing like "civilization." It was frustrating, maddening; there was food all around her, on four feet, on wings—surely even some of the plants were edible—but it was totally inaccessible to a city-bred girl who'd never gotten food from anywhere but a grocery or restaurant. She might just as well be on the moon.

Just as she thought that, she topped another rise to find herself looking at a strange, weatherbeaten man standing beside a rough pounded-dirt road.

She blinked in dumb amazement. He looked like something out of a movie, a peasant from a King Arthur epic. He was stocky, blond-haired; he wore a shabby brown tunic and patched, shapeless trousers tucked into equally patched boots. He was also holding a strung bow, with an arrow nocked to it, and frowning—a most unfriendly expression.

He gabbled something at her. She blinked again. She knew a little Spanish (you had to, in her neighborhood); she'd taken German and French in high school. This didn't sound like any of those.

He repeated himself, a distinct edge to his voice. To emphasize his words, he jerked the point of the arrow off back the way she had come. It was pretty obvious he was telling her to be on her way.

"No, wait—please—" she stepped toward him, her hands outstretched pleadingly. The only reaction she got was that he raised the arrow to point at her chest, and drew it back.

"Look—I haven't got any weapons! I'm lost, I'm *hungry*—"

He drew the arrow a bit farther.

Suddenly it was all too much. She'd spent all her life being pushed and pushed—first her aunt, then at school, then out on the streets. This was the last time *anybody* was going to back her into a corner—this time she was going to fight!

A white-hot rage like nothing she'd ever experienced before in her life took over.

"Damn you!" she was so angry she could hardly think. "You stupid clod! I *need help!*" she screamed at him, as red flashes interfered with her vision, her ears began to buzz, and her hands crooked into involuntary claws, *"Damn you and everybody that looks like you!"*

He backed up a pace, his blue eyes wide with surprise at her rage.

She was so filled with fury that grew past controlling—she couldn't see, couldn't think; it was like being possessed. Suddenly she gasped as pain lanced from the top of her head to her toes, pain like a bolt of lightning—

—her vision blacked out; she fell to her hands and knees on the grass, her legs unable to hold her, convulsing with surges of pain in her arms and legs. Her feet, her hands felt like she'd shoved them in a fire—her face felt as if someone were stretching it out of shape. And the ring finger of her left hand—it burned with more agony than both hands and feet put together! She shook her head, trying to clear it, but it spun around in dizzying circles. Her ears rang, hard to hear over the ringing, but there was a sound of cloth tearing—

Her sight cleared and returned, but distorted. She looked up at the man, who had dropped his bow, and was backing away from her, slowly, his face white with terror. She started to say something to him—

—and it came out a snarl.

With that, the man screeched, turned his back on her, and ran.

And she caught sight of her hand. It wasn't a hand anymore. It was a paw. Judging by the spotted pelt of the leg, a leopard's paw. Scattered around her were the ragged scraps of cloth that had once been her clothing.

Glenda lay in the sun on top of a rock, warm and drowsy with full-bellied content. Idly she washed one paw with her tongue, cleaning the last taint of blood from it. Before she'd had a chance to panic or go crazy back there when she'd realized what had happened to her, a rabbit-like creature had broken cover practically beneath her nose. Semi-starvation and confusion had kept her dazed long enough for leopard-instincts to take over. She'd caught and killed the thing and had half eaten it before the reality of what she'd done and become broke through her shock. Raw rabbit-thing tasted *fine* to leopard-Glenda; when she realized that, she finished it, nose to tail. Now for the first time in weeks she was warm and content. And for the first time in years *she* was something to be afraid of. She gazed about her from her vantage-point on the warm boulder, taking in the grassy hills and breathing in the warm, hay-scented air with a growing contentment.

Becoming a leopard might not be a bad transformation.

Ears keener than a human's picked up the sound of dogs in the distance; she became aware that the man she'd frightened might have gone back home for help. They just *might* be hunting her.

Time to go.

She leapt down from her rock, setting off at a right angle to the direction the sound of the baying was coming from. Her sense of smell, so heightened now that it might have been a new sense altogether, had picked up the coolth of running water off this way, dimmed by the green odor of the grass. And running water was a good way to break a trail; she knew that from reading.

Reveling in the power of the muscles beneath her sleek coat, she ran lightly over the slopes, moving through the grass that had been such a waist-high tangle to girl-Glenda with no impediment whatsoever. In almost no time at all, it seemed, she was pacing the side of the stream that she had scented.

It was quite wide, twenty feet or so, and seemed fairly deep in the middle. Sunlight danced on the surface, giving her a hint that the current might be stiffish beneath the surface. She waded into it, up to her stomach, hissing a little at the cold and the feel of the water on her fur. She trotted upstream a bit until she found a place where the course had narrowed a little. It was still over her head, but she found she could swim it with nothing other than discomfort. The stream wound between the grassy hills, the banks never getting very high, but there rarely being any more cover along them than a few scattered bushes. Something told her that she would be no match for the endurance of the hunting pack if she tried to escape across the grasslands. She stayed in the watercourse until she came to a wider valley than anything she had yet encountered. There were trees here; she waded onward until she found one leaning well over the streambed. Gathering herself and eying the broad branch that arced at least six feet above the watercourse, she leaped for it, landing awkwardly, and having to scrabble with her claws fully extended to keep her balance.

She sprawled over it for a moment, panting, hearing the dogs nearing—belling in triumph as they caught her trail, then yelping in confusion when they lost it at the stream.

Time to move again. She climbed the tree up into the higher branches, finding a wide perch at least fifty or sixty feet off the ground. It was high enough that it was unlikely that anyone would spot her dappled hide among the dappled leaf-shadows, wide enough that she could recline, balanced, at her ease, yet it afforded to leopard-eyes a good view of the ground and the stream.

As she'd expected, the humans with the dogs had figured out her scent-breaking ploy, and had split the pack, taking half along each side of the stream to try and pick up where she'd exited. She spotted the man who had stopped her easily, and filed his scent away in her memory for the future. The others with him were dressed much the same as he, and carried nothing more sophisticated than bows. They looked angry, confused; their voices held notes of fear. They looked into and under the trees with noticeable apprehension, evidently fearing what might dwell under their shade. Finally they gave up, and pulled the hounds off the fruitless quest, leaving her smiling catwise, invisible above them in her tree, purring.

Several weeks later Glenda had found a place to lair up; a cave amid a tumble of boulders in the heart of the forest at the streamside. She had also discovered why the hunters hadn't wanted to pursue her into the forest itself. There was a—thing—an evil presence, malicious, but invisible, that lurked in a circle of standing stones that glowed at night with a sickly yellow color. Fortunately it seemed unable to go beyond the bounds of the stones themselves. Glenda had been chasing a half-grown deer-beast that had run straight into the middle of the circle, forgetting the danger before it because of the danger pursuing it. She had nearly been caught there herself, and only the thing's preoccupation with the first prey had saved her. She had hidden in her lair, nearly paralyzed with fear, for a day and a night until hunger and thirst had driven her out again.

Other than that peril, easily avoided, the forest seemed safe enough. She'd found the village the man had come from by following the dirt road; she'd spent long hours when she wasn't hunting lurking within range of sight and hearing of the place. Aided by some new sense she wasn't sure that she understood—the one that had alerted her to the danger of the stone circle as she'd blundered in—she was beginning to make some sense of their language. She understood at least two-thirds of what was being said now, and could usually guess the rest.

These people seemed to be stuck at some kind of feudal level—had been overrun by some higher-tech invaders the generation before, and were only now recovering from that. The hereditary rulers had mostly been killed in that war, and the population decimated; the memories of that time were still strong. The man who'd stopped her had been on guard-duty and had mistrusted her appearance out of what they called "the Waste" and her strange clothing. When she'd transformed in front of his eyes, he must have decided she was some kind of witch.

Glenda had soon hunted the more easily-caught game out; now when hunger drove her, she supplemented her diet with raids on the villager's livestock. She was getting better at hunting, but she still was far from being an expert, and letting leopard-instincts take over involved surrendering herself to those instincts. She was beginning to have the uneasy feeling that every time she did that she lost a little more of her humanity. Life as leopard-Glenda was much easier than as girl-Glenda, but it might be getting to be time to think about trying to regain her former shape—before she was lost to the leopard entirely.

She'd never been one for horror or fantasy stories, so her only guide was vague recollections of fairy-tales and late-night werewolf movies. She didn't think the latter would be much help here—after all, she'd transformed into a leopard, not a wolf, and by the light of day, not the full moon.

But—maybe the light of the full moon would help.

She waited until full dark before setting off for her goal, a still pond in the far edge of the forest, well away from the stone circle, in a clearing that never seemed to become overgrown. It held a stone, too; a single pillar of some kind of blueish rock. That pillar had never "glowed" at night before, at least not while Glenda had been there, but the pond and the clearing seemed to form a little pocket of peace. Whatever evil might lurk in the rest of the forest, she was somehow sure it would find no place there.

The moon was well up by the time she reached it. White flowers had opened to the light of it, and a faint, crisp scent came from them. Glenda paced to the poolside, and looked down into the dark, still water. She could see her leopard form reflected clearly, and over her right shoulder, the full moon.

Well, anger had gotten her into this shape, maybe anger would get her out. She closed her eyes for a moment, then began summoning all the force of that emotion she could—*willing* herself back into the form she'd always worn. She stared at her reflection in the water, forcing it, angrily, to be *her*. Whatever power was playing games with her was *not* going to find her clay to be molded at will!

As nothing happened, her frustration mounted; soon she was at the boiling point. Damn everything! She—would—not—be—played—with—

The same incoherent fury that had seized her when she first changed washed over her a second time—and the same agonizing pain sent blackness in front of her eyes and flung her to lie twitching helplessly beside the pool. Her left forepaw felt like it was afire—

In moments it was over, and she found herself sprawling beside the pond, shivering with cold and reaction, and totally naked. Naked, that is, except for the silver cat-ring, whose topaz eyes glowed hotly at her for a long moment before the light left them.

The second time she transformed to leopard was much easier; the pain was less, the amount of time less. She decided against being human—after finding herself without a stitch on, in a perilously vulnerable and helpless form, leopard-Glenda seemed a much more viable alternative.

But the ability to switch back and forth proved to be very handy. The villagers had taken note of her raids on their stock; they began mounting a series of systematic hunts for her, even penetrating into the forest so long as it was by daylight. She learned or remembered from reading countless tricks to throw the hunters off, and being able to change from human to leopard and back again made more than one of those possible. There *were* places girl-Glenda could climb and hide that leopard-Glenda couldn't, and the switch in scents when she changed confused and frightened the dog-pack. She began feeling an amused sort of contempt for the villagers, often leading individual hunters on wild-goose chases for the fun of it when she became bored.

But on the whole, it was better to be leopard; leopard-Glenda was comfortable and content sleeping on rocks or on the dried leaves of her lair—girl-Glenda shivered and ached and wished for her roach-infested efficiency. Leopard-Glenda was perfectly happy on a diet of raw fish, flesh and fowl—girl-Glenda wanted to throw up when she thought about it. Leopard-Glenda was content with nothing to do but tease the villagers and sleep in the sun when she wasn't hunting—girl-Glenda fretted, and longed for a book, and wondered if what she was doing was right . . .

So matters stood until Midsummer.

Glenda woke, shivering, with a mouth gone dry with panic. The dream—

It wasn't just a nightmare. This dream had been so real she'd expected to wake with an arrow in her ribs. She was still panting with fright even now.

There had been a man—he hadn't looked much like any of the villagers; they were mostly blond or brown-haired, and of the kind of hefty build her aunt used to call "peasant-stock" in a tone of contempt. No, he had resembled her in a way—as if she were a kind of washed-out copy of the template from which his kind had been cut. Where her hair was a dark mousy-brown, his was just as dark, but the color was more intense. They had the same general build: thin, tall, with prominent cheekbones. His eyes—

Her aunt had called her "cat-eyed," for she didn't have eyes of a normal brown, but more of a vague yellow, as washed-out as her hair. But *his* had been truly and intensely gold, with a greenish back-reflection like the eyes of a wild animal at night.

And those eyes had been filled with hunter-awareness; the eyes of a predator. And *she* had been his quarry!

The dream came back to her with extraordinary vividness; it had begun as she'd reached the edge of the forest, with him hot on her trail. She had a vague recollection of having begun the chase in human form, and having switched to leopard as she reached the trees. He had no dogs, no aid but his own senses—yet nothing she'd done had confused him for more than a second. She'd even laid a false trail into the stone circle, something she'd never done to another hunter, but she was beginning to panic—he'd avoided the trap neatly. The hunt had begun near mid-morning; by false dawn he'd brought her to bay and trapped her—

And that was when she'd awakened.

She spent the early hours of the morning pacing beside the pond; feeling almost impelled to go into the village, yet afraid to do so. Finally the need to *see* grew too great; she crept to the edge of the village past the guards, and slipped into the maze of whole and half-ruined buildings that was the village-proper.

There was a larger than usual market-crowd today; the usual market stalls had been augmented by strangers with more luxurious goods, foodstuffs, and even a couple of ragged entertainers. Evidently this was some sort of fair. With so many strangers about, Glenda was able to remain unseen. Her courage came back as she skirted the edge of the marketplace, keeping to shadows and sheltering within half-tumbled walls, and the terror of the night seemed to become just one more shadow.

Finally she found an ideal perch—hiding in the shadow just under the eaves of a half-ruined building that had evidently once belonged to the local lordling, and in whose courtyard the market was usually held. From here she could see the entire court and yet remain unseen by humans and unscented by any of the livestock.

She had begun to think her fears were entirely

groundless—when she caught sight of a stranger coming out of the door of what passed for an inn here, speaking earnestly with the village headman. Her blood chilled, for the man was tall, dark-haired, and lean, and dressed entirely in dark leathers just like the man in her dream.

He was too far away for her to see his face clearly, and she froze in place, following him intently without moving a muscle. The headman left him with a satisfied air, and the man gazed about him, as if looking for something—

He finally turned in her direction, and Glenda nearly died of fright—for the face was that of the man in her dream, and he was staring directly at her hiding place as though he knew exactly where and what she was!

She broke every rule she'd ever made for herself—broke cover, in full sight of the entire village. In the panicked, screaming mob, the hunter could only curse—for the milling, terror-struck villagers were only interested in fleeing in the opposite direction from where Glenda stood, tail lashing and snarling with fear.

She took advantage of the confusion to leap the wall of the courtyard and sprint for the safety of the forest. Halfway there she changed into human for a short run—there was no one to see her, and it might throw him off the track. Then at forest edge, once on the springy moss that would hold no tracks, she changed back to leopard. She paused in the shade for a moment, to get a quick drink from the stream, and to rest, for the full-out run from the village had tired her badly—only to look up, to see him standing directly across the stream from her. He was shading his eyes with one hand against the sun that beat down on him, and it seemed to her that he was smiling in triumph.

She choked on the water, and fled.

She called upon every trick she'd ever learned, laying false trails by the dozen; fording the stream as it threaded through the forest not once but several times; breaking her trail entirely by taking to the treetops on an area where she could cross several hundred feet without once having to set foot to the ground. She even drove a chance-met herd of deer-creatures across her back-trail, muddling the tracks past following. She didn't remember doing any of this in her dream—in her dream she had only run, too fearful to do much that was complicated—or so she remembered. At last, panting with weariness, she doubled back to lair-up in the crotch of a huge tree, looking back down the way she had passed, certain that she would see him give up in frustration.

He walked so softly that even *her* keen ears couldn't detect his tread; she was only aware that he was there when she saw him. She froze in place—she hadn't really expected he'd get *this* far! But surely, surely when he came to the place she'd taken to the branches, he would be baffled, for she'd first climbed as girl-Glenda, and there wasn't any place where the claw-marks of the leopard scored the trunks within sight of the ground.

He came to the place where her tracks ended—and closed his eyes, a frown-line between his brows. Late afternoon sun filtered through the branches and touched his face; Glenda thought with growing confidence that he had been totally fooled by her trick. He carried a strung bow, black as his clothing and highly polished, and wore a sword and dagger, which none of the villagers ever did. As her fear ebbed, she had time to think (with a tiny twinge) that he couldn't have been much older than she—and was very, very attractive.

As if that thought had touched something that signaled him, his eyes snapped open—and he looked straight through the branches that concealed her to rivet his own gaze on *her* eyes.

With a mew of terror she leapt out of the tree and ran in mindless panic as fast as she could set paw to ground.

The sun was reddening everything; she cringed and thought of blood. Then she thought of her dream, and the dweller-in-the-circle. If, instead of a false trail, she laid a *true* one—waiting for him at the end of it—

If she rushed him suddenly, she could probably startle him into the power of the thing that lived within the shelter of those stones. Once in the throes of its mental grip, she doubted he'd be able to escape.

It seemed a heaven-sent plan; relief made her light-headed as she ran, leaving a clear trail behind her, to the place of the circle. By the time she reached its vicinity it was full dark—and she knew the power of the dweller was at its height in darkness. Yet, the closer she drew to those glowing stones, the slower her paws moved; and a building reluctance to do this thing weighed heavily on her. Soon she could see the stones shining ahead of her; in her mind she pictured the man's capture—his terror—his inevitable end.

Leopard-Glenda urged—kill!

Girl-Glenda wailed in fear of him, but stubbornly refused to put him in the power of *that*.

The two sides of her struggled, nearly tearing her physically in two as she half-shifted from one to the other, her outward form paralleling the struggle within.

At last, with a pathetic cry, the leopard turned in her tracks and ran from the circle. The will of girl-Glenda had won.

Whenever she paused to rest, she could hear him coming long before she'd even caught her breath. The stamina of a leopard is no match for that of a human; they are built for the short chase, not the long. And the stamina of girl-Glenda was no match for that of he who hunted her; in either form now, she was exhausted. He had driven her through the moon-lit clearings of the forest she knew out beyond the territory she had ranged before. This forest must extend deep into the Waste, and this was the direction he had driven her. Now she stumbled as she ran, no longer capable of clever tricks, just fear-prodded running. Her eyes were glazed with weariness; her mind numb with terror. Her sides heaved as she panted, and her mouth was dry, her thirst a raging fire inside her.

She fled from bush to tangled stand of undergrowth, at all times avoiding the patches of moonlight, but it seemed as if her foe knew this section of the wilderness as well or better than she knew her own territory. She could not rid herself of the feeling that she was being driven to some goal only he knew.

Suddenly, as rock-cliff loomed before her, she realized that her worst fears were correct. He had herded her into a dead-end ravine, and there was no escape for her, at least not in leopard-form.

The rock before her was sheer; to either side it slanted inward. The stone itself was brittle shale; almost impassable—yet she began shifting into her human form to make that attempt. Then a sound from behind her told her that she had misjudged his nearness—and it was too late.

She whirled at bay, half-human, half-leopard, flanks heaving as she sucked in pain-filled gasps of air. He blocked the way out; dark and grim on the path, nocked bow in hand. She thought she saw his eyes shine with fierce joy even in the darkness of the ravine. She had no doubts that he could see her as easily as she saw him. There was nowhere to hide on either side of her.

Again leopard-instinct urged—kill!

Her claws extended, and she growled deep in her throat, half in fear, half in warning. He paced one step closer.

She could—she could fight him. She could dodge the arrow—at this range he could never get off the second. If she closed with him, she could kill him! His blood would run hot between her teeth—

Kill!

No! Never, never had she harmed another human being, not even the man who had denied her succor. No!

Kill!

She fought the leopard within, knowing that if it won, there would never be a girl-Glenda again; only the predator, the beast. And that would be the death of her—a death as real as that which any arrow could bring her.

And he watched from the shadows; terrible, dark, and menacing, his bow half-drawn. And yet—he did not move, not so much as a single muscle. If he had, perhaps the leopard would have won; fear triumphing over will. But he stirred not, and it was the human side of her that conquered.

And she waited, eyes fixed on his, for death.

:*Gentle, lady.*:

She started as the voice spoke in her head—then shook it wildly, certain that she had been driven mad at last.

:*Be easy—do not fear me.*:

Again that voice! She stared at him, wild-eyed—was he some kind of magician, to speak in her very thoughts?

And as if that were not startlement enough, she watched, dumbfounded, as he knelt, slowly—slowly eased the arrow off the string of his bow—and just as slowly laid them to one side. He held out hands now empty, his face fully in the moonlight—and *smiled*.

And rose—and—

At first she thought it was the moonlight that made him seem to writhe and blur. Then she thought that certainly her senses were deceiving her as her mind had—for his body *was* blurring, shifting, changing before her eyes, like a figure made of clay softening and blurring and becoming another shape altogether—

Until, where the hunter had stood, was a black leopard, half-again her size.

Glenda stared into the flames of the campfire, sipping at the warm wine, wrapped in a fur cloak, and held by a drowsy contentment. The wine, the cloak and the campfire were all Harwin's.

For that was the name of the hunter—Harwin. He had coaxed her into her following him; then, once his camp had been reached, coaxed her into human form again. He had given her no time to be shamed by her nakedness, for he had shrouded her in the cloak almost before the transformation was complete. Then he had built this warming fire from the banked coals of the old, and fed her the first cooked meal she'd had in months, then pressed the wine on her. And all with slow, reassuring movements, as if he was quite well aware how readily she could be startled into transforming back again, and fleeing into the forest. And all without speaking much besides telling her his name; his silence not unfriendly, not in the least, but as if he were waiting with patient courtesy for her to speak first.

She cleared her throat, and tentatively spoke her first words in this alien tongue, her own voice sounding strange in her ears.

"Who—are you? *What* are you?"

He cocked his head to one side, his eyes narrowing in concentration, as he listened to her halting words.

"You speak the speech of the Dales as one who knows it only indifferently, lady," he replied, his words measured, slow, and pronounced with care, as if he guessed she needed slow speech to understand clearly. "Yet you do not have the accent of Arvon—and I do not think you are one of the Old Ones. If I tell you who and what I am, will you do me like courtesy?"

"I—my name is Glenda. I couldn't do—this—at home. Wherever home is. I—I'm not sure what I am."

"Then your home is not of this world?"

"There was—" it all seemed so vague, like a dream now, "A city. I—lived there, but not well. I was hunted—I found a place—a woman. I thought she was crazy, but—she said something, and I saw this place—and I had to come—"

"A Gate, I think, and a Gate-Keeper," he nodded,

as if to himself. "That explains much. So you found yourself here?"

"In the Waste. Though I didn't know that was what it was. I met a man—I was tired, starving, and he tried to drive me away. I got mad."

"The rest I know," he said. "For Elvath himself told me of how you went *were* before his eyes. Poor lady—how bewildered you must have been, with no one to tell you what was happening to you! And then?"

Haltingly, with much encouragement, she told him of her life in the forest; her learning to control her changes—and her side of the night's hunt.

"And the woman won over the beast," he finished. "And well for you that it did." His gold eyes were very somber, and he spoke with emphasis heavy in his words. "Had you turned on me, I doubt that you would ever have been able to find your human self again."

She shuddered. "What am I?" she asked at last, her eyes fixed pleadingly on his. "And where am I? And why has all this been happening to me?"

"I cannot answer the last for you, save only that I think you are here because your spirit never fit truly in that strange world from which you came. As for where—you are in the Dale lands of High Halleck, on the edge of the Waste—which tells you nothing, I know. And what you are—like me, you are plainly of some far-off strain of Wereblood. Well, perhaps not quite like me; among my kind the females are not known for being able to shape-change, and I myself am of half-blood only. My mother is Kildas of the Dales; my father Harl of the Wereriders. And I—I am Harwin," he smiled, ruefully, "of no place in particular."

"Why—why did you hunt me?" she asked. "Why did they want *you* to hunt me?"

"Because they had no notion of my Wereblood," he replied frankly. "They only know of my reputation as a hunter—shall I begin at the beginning? Perhaps it will give you some understanding of this world you have fallen into."

She nodded eagerly.

"Well—you may have learned that in my father's time the Dales were overrun by the Hounds of Alizon?" At her nod, he continued. "They had strange weapons at their disposal, and came very close to destroying all who opposed them. At that time my father and his brother-kin lived in the Waste, in exile for certain actions in the past from the land of Arvon, which lies to the north of the Waste. They—as I, as you—have the power of shape-change, and other powers as well. It came to the defenders of the Dales that one must battle strangeness with strangeness, and power with power; they made a pact with the Wereriders. In exchange for aid, they would send to them at the end of the war in the Year of the Unicorn twelve brides and one. You see, if all went well, the Wererider's exile was to end then—but if all was not well, they would have remained in exile, and they did not wish their kind to die away. The war ended, the brides came—the exile ended. But one of the bridegrooms was—like me—of half-blood. And one of the brides was a maiden of Power. There was much trouble for them; when the trouble was at an end they left Arvon together, and I know nothing more of their tale. Now we come to my part of the tale. My mother Kildas has gifted my father with three children, of which two are a pleasure to his heart and of like mind with him. I am the third."

"The misfit? The rebel?" she guessed shrewdly.

"If by that you mean the one who seems destined always to anger his kin with all he says and does—aye. We cannot agree, my father and I. One day in his anger, he swore that I was another such as Herrel. Well, that was the first that *I* had ever heard of one of Wereblood who was like-minded with me—I plagued my mother and father both until they gave me the tale of Herrel Half-blood and his Witch-bride. And from that moment,

I had no peace until I set out to find them. For surely, I thought, I would find true kin-feeling with them, the which I lacked with those truly of my blood."

"And did you find them?"

"Not yet," he admitted. "At my mother's request I came here first, to give word to her kin that she was well, and happy, and greatly honored by her lord. Which is the entire truth. My father—loves her dearly; grants her every wish before she has a chance to voice it. I could wish to find a lady with whom—well, that was one of the reasons that I sought Herrel and his lady."

He was silent for so long, staring broodingly into the flames, that Glenda ventured to prompt him.

"So—you came here?"

"Eh? Oh, aye. And understandably enough, earned no small reputation among my mother-kin for hunting, though they little guessed in what form I did my tracking!" He grinned at her, and she found herself grinning back. "So when there were rumors of another Were here at the edge of the Waste—and a Were that thoughtlessly preyed on the beasts of these people as well as its rightful game—understandably enough, I came to hear of it. I thought at first that it must be Herrel, or a son. Imagine my surprise on coming here to learn that the Were was female! My reputation preceded me—the headman begged me to rid the village of their 'monster'—" He spread his hands wide. "The rest, you know."

"What—what will you do with me now?" she asked in a small, fearful voice.

"Do with you?" he seemed surprised. "Nothing— nothing not of your own will, lady. I am not going to harm you—and I am not like my father and brother, to force a one in my hand into anything against her wishes. I—I go forward as I had intended—to find Herrel. You, now that you know what your actions should *not* be, lest you arouse the anger of ordinary folk against you, may remain here—"

"And?"

"And I shall tell them I have killed the monster. You shall be safe enough—only remember that you must *never* let the leopard control you, or you are lost. Truly, you should have someone to guide and teach you, though—"

"I—know that, now," she replied, very much aware of how attractive he was, gold eyes fixed on the fire, a lock of dark hair falling over his forehead. But no man had ever found her to be company to be sought-after. There was no reason to think that he might be hinting—

No reason, that is, until he looked full into her eyes, and she saw the wistful loneliness there, and a touch of pleading.

"I would be glad to teach you, lady," he said softly. "Forgive me if I am over-forward, and clumsy in my speech. But—I think you and I could companion well together on this quest of mine—and—I—" he dropped his eyes to the flames again, and blushed hotly "—I think you very fair."

"Me?" she squeaked, more startled than she had been since he transformed before her.

"Can you doubt it?" he replied softly, looking up eagerly. He held out one hand to her. "Can I hope— you *will* come with me?"

She touched his fingers with the hesitation of one who fears to break something. "You mean you really want me with you?"

"Since I touched your mind—lady, more than you could dream! Not only are you kin-kind, but—mind-kin, I think."

She smiled suddenly, feeling almost light-headed with the revelations of the past few hours—then giggled, as an irrelevant though came to her. "Harwin—what happens to your clothes?"

"My *what*?" he stared at her for a moment as if she had broken into a foreign tongue—then looked at her, and back at himself—and blushed, then grinned.

"Well? I mean, I left bits of jeans and t-shirt all over the Waste when *I* changed—"

"What happens to your ring, lady?"

"It—" her forehead furrowed in thought. "I don't know, really. It's gone when I change, it's back when I change back." She regarded the tiny beast thoughtfully, and it seemed as if one of its topaz eyes closed in a slow wink. But—no. That could only have been a trick of the firelight.

"Were-magic, lady. And magic I think I shall let you avail yourself of, seeing as I can hardly let you take a chill if you are to accompany me—" He rummaged briefly in his pack and came up with a shirt and breeches, both far too large for her, but that was soon remedied with a belt and much rolling of sleeves and cuffs. She changed quickly under the shelter of his cloak.

"They'll really change with me?" she looked down at herself doubtfully.

"Why not try them?" He stood, and held out his hand—then blurred in that disconcerting way. The black leopard looked across the fire at her with eyes that glowed with warmth and approval.

:*The night still has time to run, Glenda-my-lady. Will you not run with it, and me?*:

The eyes of the cat-ring glowed with equal warmth, and Glenda found herself filled with a feeling of joy and freedom—and of *belonging*—that she tossed back her head and laughed aloud as she had never in her life done before. She stretched her own arms to the stars, and called on the power within her for the first time with joy instead of anger—

And there was no pain—only peace—as she transformed into a slim, lithe she-leopard, whose eyes met that of the he with a happiness that was heart-filling.

:*Oh yes, Harwin-my-lord! Let us run the night to dawn!*:

The four SKitty stories appeared in Cat Fantastic *Anthologies edited by Andre Norton. I'm very, very fond of SKitty; it might seem odd for a bird person to be fond of cats, but I am, so there it is. I was actually a cat-person before I was a bird-mother, and I do have two cats, both Siamese-mix, both rather old and very slow. Just, if the other local cats poach too often at my bird feeders, they can expect to get a surprise from the garden-hose.*

SKitty

:*Nasty,*: SKitty complained in Dick's head. She wrapped herself a little closer around his shoulders and licked drops of oily fog from her fur with a faint mew of distaste. :*Smelly.*:

Dick White had to agree. The portside district of Lacu'un was pretty unsavory; the dismal, foggy weather made it look even worse. Shabby, cheap, and ill-used.

Every building here—all twenty of them!—was offworld design; shoddy prefab, mostly painted in shades of peeling grey and industrial green, with garish neon-bright holosigns that were (thank the Spirits of Space!) mostly tuned down to faintly colored ghosts in the daytime. There were six bars, two gambling-joints, one

38

chapel run by the neo-Jesuits, one flophouse run by the Reformed Salvation Army, five government buildings, four stores, and once place better left unnamed. They had all sprung up, like diseased fungus, in the year since the planet and people of Lacu'un had been declared Open for trade. There was nothing native here; for that you had to go outside the Fence—

And to go outside the Fence, Dick reminded himself, *you have to get permits signed by everybody and his dog.*

:*Cat*,: corrected SKitty.

Okay, okay, he thought back with wry amusement. *Everybody and his cat. Except they don't have cats here, except on the ships.*

SKitty sniffed disdainfully. :*Fools*,: she replied, smoothing down an errant bit of damp fur with her tongue, thus dismissing an entire culture that currently had most of the Companies on their collective knees begging for trading concessions.

Well, we've seen about everything there is to see, Dick thought back at SKitty, reaching up to scratch her ears as she purred in contentment. *Are you quite satisfied?*

:*Hunt now?*: she countered hopefully.

No, you can't hunt. You know that very well. This is a Class Four world; you have to have permission from the local sapients to hunt, and they haven't given us permission to even sneeze outside the Fence. And inside the Fence you are valuable merchandise subject to catnapping, as you very well know. I played shining knight for you once, furball, and I don't want to repeat the experience.

SKitty sniffed again. :*Not love me.*:

Love you too much, pest. Don't want you ending up in the hold of some tramp freighter.

SKitty turned up the volume on her purr, and rearranged her coil on Dick's shoulders until she resembled a lumpy black fur collar on his gray shipsuit. When she left the ship—and often when she was in the ship—that was SKitty's perch of choice. Dick had finally prevailed on the purser to put shoulderpads on all his shipsuits—sometimes SKitty got a little careless with her claws.

When man had gone to space, cats had followed; they were quickly proven to be a necessity. For not only did man's old pests, rats and mice, accompany his trade—there seemed to be equivalent pests on every new world. But the shipscats were considerably different from their Earth-bound ancestors. The cold reality was that a spacer couldn't afford a pet that had to be cared for—he needed something closer to a partner.

Hence SKitty and her kind; gene-tailored into something more than animals. SKitty was BioTech Type F-021; forepaws like that of a raccoon, more like stubby little hands than paws. Smooth, short hair with no undercoat to shed and clog up airfilters. Hunter second to none. Middle-ear tuning so that she not only was not bothered by hyperspace shifts and freefall, she actually enjoyed them. And last, but by no means least, the enlarged head showing the boosting of her intelligence.

BioTech released the shipscats for adoption when they reached about six months old; when they'd not only been weaned, but trained. Training included maneuvering in freefall, use of the same sanitary facilities as the crew, and emergency procedures. SKitty had her vacuum suit, just like any other crew member; a transparent hard plex ball rather like a tiny lifeslip, with a simple panel of controls inside to seal and pressurize it. She was positively paranoid about having it *with* her; she'd haul it along on its tether, if need be, so that it was always in the same compartment that she was. Dick respected her paranoia; any good spacer would.

Officially she was "Lady Sundancer of Greenfields"; Greenfields being BioTech Station NA-73. In actuality, she was SKitty to the entire crew, and only Dick remembered her real name.

Dick had signed on to the CatsEye Company ship *Brightwing* just after they'd retired their last shipscat to spend his final days with other creaky retirees from the spacetrade in the Tau Epsilon Old Spacers Station. As junior officer Dick had been sent off to pick up the replacement. SOP was for a BioTech technician to give you two or three candidates to choose among—in actuality, Dick hadn't had any choice. "Lady Sundancer" had taken one look at him and launched herself like a little black rocket from the arms of the tech straight for him; she'd landed on his shoulders, purring at the top of her lungs. When they couldn't pry her off, not without injuring her, the "choice" became moot. And Dick was elevated to the position of Designated Handler.

For the first few days she was "Dick White's Kitty"— the rest of his fellow crewmembers being vastly amused that she had so thoroughly attached herself to him. After a time that was shortened first to "Dick's Kitty" and then to "SKitty," which name finally stuck.

Since telepathy was *not* one of the traits BioTech was supposedly breeding and genesplicing for, Dick had been more than a little startled when she'd started speaking to him. And since none of the others ever mentioned hearing her, he had long ago come to the conclusion that he was the only one who could. He kept that a secret; at the least, should BioTech come to hear of it, it would mean losing her. BioTech would want to know where *that* particular mutation came from, for fair.

"Pretty gamy," he told Erica Makumba, Legal and Security Officer, who was the current on-watch at the airlock. The dusky woman lounged in her jumpseat with deceptive casualness, both hands behind her curly head—but there was a stun-bracelet on one wrist, and Erica just happened to be the *Brightwing*'s current karate champ.

"Eyeah," she replied with a grimace. "Had a look out there last night. Talk about your low-class dives! I'm not real surprised the Lacu'un threw the Fence up around it. Damn if *I'd* want that for neighbors! Hey, we may be getting a break, though; invitation's gone out to about three cap'ns to come make trade-talk. Seems the Lacu'un got themselves a lawyer—"

"So much for the 'unsophisticated primitives,'" Dick laughed. "I thought TriStar was riding for a fall, taking that line."

Erica grinned; a former TriStar employee, she had no great love for her previous employer. "Eyeah. So, lawyer goes and calls up the records on every Company making bids, goes over 'em with a fine-tooth. Seems only three of us came up clean; us, SolarQuest, and UVN. We got invites, rest got bye-byes. Be hearing a buncha ships clearing for space in the next few hours."

"My heart bleeds," Dick replied. "Any chance they can fight it?"

"Ha! Didn't tell you *who* they got for their mouthpiece. Lan Ventris."

Dick whistled. "*Somebody's* been looking out for them!"

"Terran Consul; she was the scout that made first contact. They wouldn't have anybody else, adopted her into the ruling sept, keep her at the Palace. Nice lady, shared a beer or three with her. She likes these people, obviously, takes their welfare real personal. Now—you want the quick low-down on the invites?"

Dick leaned up against the bulkhead, arms folded, taking care not to disturb SKitty. "Say on."

"One—" she held up a solemn finger. "Vena—that's the Consul—says that these folk have a long martial tradition; they're warriors, and admire warriors—but they admire honor and honesty even more. The trappings of primitivism are there, but it's a veneer for considerable sophistication. So whoever goes needs to walk a line between pride and honorable behavior that will be a *lot* like the old Japanese courts of Terra. Two, they are very serious about religion—they give us a certain amount of leeway for being ignorant outlanders, but if you transgress too far, Vena's not sure what the penalties may be. So you want to watch for signals, body-language from the priest-caste; that could warn you that you're on dangerous ground. Three—and this is what may give us an edge over the other two—they are very big on their totem animals; the sept totems are actually an important part of sept pride and the religion. So the Cap'n intends to make you and Her Highness there part of the delegation. Vena says that the Lacu'un intend to issue three contracts, so we're all gonna get one, but the folks that impress them the most will be getting first choice."

If Dick hadn't been leaning against the metal of the bulkhead he might well have staggered. As most junior on the crew, the likelihood that he was going to even go beyond the Fence had been staggeringly low—but that he would be included in the first trade delegation was mind-melting!

SKitty caroled her own excitement all the way back to his cabin, launching herself from his shoulder to land in her own little shock-bunk, bolted to the wall above his.

Dick began digging through his catch-all bin for his dress-insignia; the half-lidded topaz eye for CatsEye Company, the gold wings of the ship's insignia that went beneath it, the three tiny stars signifying the three missions he'd been on so far. . . .

He caught flickers of SKitty's private thoughts then; thoughts of pleasure, thoughts of nesting—

Nesting!

Oh *no!*

He spun around to meet her wide yellow eyes, to see her treading out her shock-bunk.

SKitty, he pled, *Please don't tell me you're pregnant—*
:*Kittens,*: she affirmed, very pleased with herself.

You swore to me that you weren't in heat when I let you out to hunt!

She gave the equivalent of a mental shrug. :*I lie.*:

He sat heavily down on his own bunk, all his earlier excitement evaporated. BioTech shipscats were supposed to be sterile—about one in a hundred weren't.

And you had to sign an agreement with BioTech that you wouldn't neuter yours if it proved out fertile; they wanted the kittens, wanted the results that came from outbreeding. Or you could sell the kittens to other ships yourself, or keep them; provided a BioTech station wasn't within your ship's current itinerary. But of course, only BioTech would take them before they were six months old and trained. . . .

That was the rub. Dick sighed. SKitty had already had one litter on him—only two, but it had seemed like twenty-two. There was this problem with kittens in a spaceship; there was a period of time between when they were mobile and when they were about four months old that they had exactly two neurons in those cute, fluffy little heads. One neuron to keep the body moving at warp speed, and one neuron to pick out the situation guaranteed to cause the most trouble.

Everyone in the crew was willing to play with them—but no one was willing to keep them out of trouble. And since SKitty was Dick's responsibility, it was *Dick* who got to clean up the messes, and *Dick* who got to fish the little fluffbrains out of the bridge console, and *Dick* who got to have the anachronistic litter pan in his cabin until SKitty got her babies properly toilet trained.

Securing a litter pan for freefall was not something he had wanted to have to do again. Ever.

"How could you *do* this to me?" he asked SKitty reproachfully. She just curled her head over the edge of her bunk and trilled prettily.

He sighed. Too late to do anything about it now.

" . . . and you can see the carvings adorn every flat surface," Vena Ferducci, the small, darkhaired woman who was the Terran Consul, said, waving her hand gracefully at the walls. Dick wanted to stand and gawk; this was *incredible!*

The Fence was actually an opaque forcefield, and only *one* of the reasons the Companies wanted to trade with the Lacu'un. Though they did not have spaceflight, there were certain applications of forcefield technologies they *did* have that seemed to be beyond the Terran's abilities. On the other side of the Fence was literally another world.

These people built to last, in limestone, alabaster, and marble, in the wealthy district, and in cast stone in the outer city. The streets were carefully poured sections of concrete, cleverly given stress-joints to avoid temperature-cracking, and kept clean enough to eat from by a small army of street-sweepers. No animals were allowed on the streets themselves, except for house-trained pets. The only vehicles permitted were single or double-being electric carts, that could move no faster than a man could walk. The Lacu'un dressed either in filmy, silken robes, or in more practical, shorter versions of the same garments. They were a handsome race, upright bipeds, skin tones in varying shades of browns and dark golds, faces vaguely avian, with a frill like an iguana's running from the base of the neck to a point between and just above the eyes.

As Vena had pointed out, every wall within sight was heavily carved, the carvings all having to do with the Lacu'un religion.

Most of the carvings were depictions of various processions or ceremonies, and no two were exactly alike.

"That's the Harvest-Gladness," Vena said, pointing, as they walked, to one elaborate wall that ran for yards. "It's particularly appropriate for Kla'dera; he made all his money in agriculture. Most Lacu'un try to have something carved that reflects on their gratitude for 'favors granted.'"

"I think I can guess that one," the Captain, Reginald Singh, said with a smile that showed startlingly white teeth in his dark face. The carving he nodded to was a series of panels; first a celebration involving a veritable kindergarten full of children, then those children—now sex-differentiated and seen to be all female—worshiping at the alter of a very fecund-looking Lacu'un female, and finally the now-maidens looking sweet and demure, each holding various religious objects.

Vena laughed, her brown eyes sparkling with amusement. "No, that one isn't hard. There's a saying, 'as fertile as Gel'vadera's wife.' Every child was a female, too, that made it even better. Between the bride-prices he got for the ones that wanted to wed, and the officer's price he got for the ones that went into the armed services, Gel'vadera was a rich man. His First Daughter owns the house now."

"Ah—that brings up a question," Captain Singh replied. "Would you explain exactly who and what we'll be meeting? I read the briefing, but I still don't quite understand who fits in where with the government."

"It will help if you think of it as a kind of unholy mating of the British Parliamentary system and the medieval Japanese Shogunates," Vena replied. "You'll be meeting with the 'king'—that's the Lacu'ara—his consort, who has equal powers and represents the priesthood—that's the Lacu'teveras—and his three advisors, who are elected. The advisors represent the military, the bureaucracy, and the economic sector. The military advisor is always female; all officers in the military are female, because the Lacu'un believe that females will not seek glory for themselves, and so will not issue reckless orders. The other two can be either sex. 'Advisor' is not altogether an accurate term to use for them; the Lacu'ara and Lacu'teveras rarely act counter to their advice."

Dick was paying scant attention to this monologue; he'd already picked all this up from the faxes he'd called out of the local library after he'd read the briefing. He was more interested in the carvings, for there was something about them that puzzled him.

All of them featured strange little six-legged creatures scampering about under the feet of the carved Lacu'un. They were about the size of a large mouse, and seemed to Dick to be wearing very smug expressions . . . though of course, he was surely misinterpreting.

"Excuse me Consul," he said, when Vena had finished explaining the intricacies of Lacu'un government to Captain Singh's satisfaction. "I can't help wondering what those little lizard-like things are."

"Kreshta," she said, "*I* would call them pests; you don't see them out on the streets much, but they are the reason the streets are kept so clean. You'll see them soon enough once we get inside. They're like mice, only worse; fast as lightning—they'll steal food right off your plate. The Lacu'un either can't or won't get rid of them, I can't tell you which. When I asked about them once, my host just rolled his eyes heavenward and said what translates to 'it's the will of the gods.'"

"Insh'allah?" Captain Singh asked.

"Very like that, yes. I can't tell if they tolerate the pests because it is the gods' will that they must, or if they tolerate them because the gods favor the little monsters. Inside the Fence we have to close the government buildings down once a month, seal them up, and fumigate. We're just lucky they don't breed very fast."

:*Hunt?*: SKitty asked hopefully from her perch on Dick's shoulders.

No! Dick replied hastily. *Just look, don't hunt!*

The cat was gaining startled—and Dick thought, appreciative—looks from passersby.

"Just what is the status value of a totemic animal?" Erica asked curiously.

"It's the fact that the animal can be tamed at all. Aside from a handful of domestic herbivores, most animal life on Lacu'un has never been tamed. To be able to take a carnivore and train it to the hand implies that the gods are with you in a very powerful way." Vena dimpled. "I'll let you in on a big secret; frankly, Lan and I preferred the record of the *Brightwing* over the other two ships; you seemed to be more sympathetic to the Lacu'un. That's why we told you about the totemic animals, and why we left you until last."

"It wouldn't have worked without Dick," Captain Singh told her. "SKitty has really bonded to him in a remarkable way; I don't think this presentation would come off half so impressively if he had to keep her on a lead."

"It wouldn't," Vena replied, directing them around a corner. At the end of a short street was a fifteen foot wall—carved, of course—pierced by an arching entranceway.

"The palace," she said, rather needlessly.

Vena had been right. The kreshta were *everywhere*.

Dick could feel SKitty trembling with the eagerness to hunt, but she was managing to keep herself under control. Only the lashing of her tail betrayed her agitation.

He waited at parade rest, trying not to give in to the temptation to stare, as the Captain and the Negotiator, Grace Vixen, were presented to the five rulers of the Lacu'un in an elaborate ceremony that resembled a stately dance. Behind the low platform holding the five dignitaries in their iridescent robes were five soberly clad retainers, each with one of the "totemic animals." Dick could see now what Vena had meant; the handlers had their creatures under control, but only barely. There was something like a bird, something resembling a small crocodile, something like a snake, but with six very tiny legs, a creature vaguely catlike, but with a feathery coat, and a beast resembling a teddybear with scales. None of the handlers was actually holding his beast, except the bird-handler. All of the animals were on short chains, and all of them punctuated the ceremony with soft growls and hisses.

So SKitty, perched freely on Dick's shoulders, had drawn no few murmurs of awe from the crowd of Lacu'un in the Audience Hall.

The presentation glided to a conclusion, and the Lacu'teveras whispered something to Vena behind her fan.

"With your permission, Captain, the Lacu'teveras would like to know if your totemic beast is actually as tame as she appears?"

"She is," the Captain replied, speaking directly to the consort, and bowing, exhibiting a charm that had crossed species barriers many times before this.

It worked its magic again. The Lacu'teveras fluttered her fan and trilled something else at Vena. The audience of courtiers gasped.

"Would it be possible, she asks, for her to touch it?"

SKitty? Dick asked quickly, knowing that she was getting the sense of what was going on from his thoughts.

:Nice,: the cat replied, her attention momentarily distracted from the scurrying hints of movement that were all that could be seen of the kreshta. *:Nice lady. Feels good in head, like Dick.:*

Feels good in head? he thought, startled.

"I don't think that there will be any problem, Captain," Dirk murmured to Singh, deciding that he could worry about it later. "SKitty seems to like the Lacu'un. Maybe they smell right."

SKitty flowed down off his shoulder and into his arms as he stepped forward to present the cat to the Lacu'teveras. He showed the Lacu'un the cat's favorite spot to be scratched, under the chin. The long talons sported by all Lacu'un were admirably suited to the job of cat-scratching.

The Lacu'teveras reached forward with one lilac-tipped finger, and hesitantly followed Dick's example. The Audience Hall was utterly silent as she did so, as if the entire assemblage was holding its breath, waiting for disaster to strike. The courtiers gasped at her temerity when the cat stretched out her neck—then gasped again, this time with delight, as SKitty's rumbling purr became audible.

SKitty's eyes were almost completely closed in sensual

delight; Dick glanced up to see that the Lacu'teveras' amber, slit-pupiled eyes were widened with what he judged was an equal delight. She let her other six fingers join the first, tentative one beneath the cat's chin.

"Such soft—" she said shyly, in musically-accented Standard. "—such nice!"

"Thank you, High Lady," Dick replied with a smile. "We think so."

:Verrry nice,: SKitty seconded. :Not head-talk like Dick, but feel good in head, like Dick. Nice lady have kitten soon, too.:

The Lacu'teveras took her hand away with some reluctance, and signed that Dick should return to his place. SKitty slid back up onto his shoulders and started to settle herself.

It was then that everything fell apart.

The next stage in the ceremony called for the rulers to take their seats in their five thrones, and the Captain, Vena, and Grace to assume theirs on stools before the thrones so that each party could present what it wanted out of a possible relationship.

But the Lacu'teveras, her eyes still wistfully on SKitty, was not looking where she placed her hand. And on the armrest of the throne was a kreshta, frozen into an atypical immobility.

The Lacu'teveras put her hand—with all of her weight on it—right on top of the kreshta. The evil-looking thing squealed, squirmed, and bit her as hard as it could.

The Lacu'teveras cried out in pain—the courtiers gasped, the Advisors made warding gestures—and SKitty, roused to sudden and protective rage at this attack by *vermin* on the nice lady who was *with kitten*—leapt.

The kreshta saw her coming, and blurred with speed—but it was not fast enough to evade SKitty, gene-tailored product of one of BioTech's finest labs. Before it could cover even half of the distance between it and safety, SKitty had it. There was a crunch audible all over the Audience Chamber, and the ugly little thing was hanging limp from SKitty's jaws.

Tail high, in a silence that could have been cut up into bricks and used to build a wall, she carried her prize to the feet of the injured one Lacu'un and laid it there.

:*Fix him!*: Dick heard in his mind. :*Not hurt nice-one-with-kitten!*:

The Lacu'ara stepped forward, face rigid, every muscle tense.

Spirits of Space! Dick thought, steeling himself for the worst, *that's bloody well torn it*—

But the Lacu'ara, instead of ordering the guards to seize the Terrans, went to one knee and picked up the broken-backed kreshta as if it were a fine jewel.

Then he brandished it over his head while the entire assemblage of Lacu'un burst into cheers—and the Terrans looked at one another in bewilderment.

SKitty preened, accepting the caresses of every Lacu'un that could reach her with the air of one to whom adulation is long due. Whenever an unfortunate kreshta happened to attempt to skitter by, she would turn into a bolt of black lightning, reenacting her kill to the redoubled applause of the Lacu'un.

Vena was translating as fast as she could, with the three Advisors all speaking at once. The Lacu'ara was tenderly bandaging the hand of his consort, but occasionally one or the other of them would put in a word too.

"Apparently they've never been able to exterminate the kreshta; the natural predators on them *can't* be domesticated and generally take pieces out of anyone trying, traps and poisoned baits don't work because the kreshta won't take them. The only thing they've *ever* been able to do is what we were doing behind the Fence: close up the building and fumigate periodically. And even that has problems—the Lacu'teveras, for instance, is violently allergic to the residue left when the fumigation is done."

Vena paused for breath.

"I take it they'd like to have SKitty around on a permanent basis?" the Captain said, with heavy irony.

"Spirits of Space, Captain—they think SKitty is a sign from the gods, incarnate! I'm not sure they'll let her leave!"

Dick heard that with alarm—in a lot of ways, SKitty was the best friend he had—

To leave her—the thought wasn't bearable!

SKitty whipped about with alarm when she picked up what he was thinking. With an anguished yowl, she scampered across the slippery stone floor and flung herself through the air to land on Dick's shoulders. There she clung, howling her objections at the idea of being separated at top of her lungs.

"What in—" Captain Singh exclaimed, turning to see what could be screaming like a damned soul.

"She doesn't want to leave me, Captain," Dick said defiantly. "And I don't think you're going to be able to get her off my shoulder without breaking her legs or tranking her."

Captain Singh looked stormy. "Damn it then, get a trank—"

"I'm afraid I'll have to veto that one, Captain," Erica interrupted apologetically. "The contract with BioTech clearly states that only the designated handler—and that's Dick—or a BioTech representative can treat a shipscat. And furthermore—" she continued, halting the Captain before he could interrupt, "it also states that to leave a shipscat without its designated handler will force BioTech to refuse anymore shipscats to *Brightwing* for as long as you are the Captain. Now I don't want to sound like a troublemaker, Captain, but I for one will flatly refuse to serve on a ship with no cat. Periodic vacuum purges to kill the vermin do *not* appeal to me."

"Well then, I'll order the boy to—"

"Sir, I *am* the *Brightwing*'s legal advisor—I hate to say this, but to order Dick to ground is a clear violation of *his* contract. He hasn't got enough hours spacing yet to qualify him for a ground position."

The Lacu'teveras had taken Vena aside, Dick saw, and was chattering at her at top speed, waving her bandaged hand in the air.

"Captain Singh," she said, turning away from the Lacu'un and tugging at his sleeve, "the Lacu'teveras has figured out that something you said or did is upsetting the cat, and she's not very happy with that—"

Captain Singh looked just about ready to swallow a bucket of heated nails. "Spacer, *will* you get that feline calmed down before they throw me in the local brig?"

"I'll—try sir—"

Come on, old girl—they won't take you away. Erica and the nice lady won't let them, he coaxed. *You're making the nice lady unhappy, and that might hurt her kitten—*

SKitty subsided, slowly, but continued to cling to Dick's shoulder as if he was the only rock in a flood.
:*Not take Dick.*:

Erica won't let them.

:*Nice Erica.*:

A sudden thought occurred to him. *SKitty-love, how long would it take before you had your new kittens trained to hunt?*

She pondered the question. :*From wean? Three heats,*: she said finally.

About a year, then, from birth to full hunter. "Captain, I may have a solution for you—"

"I would be overjoyed to hear one," the Captain replied dryly.

"SKitty's pregnant again—I'm sorry, sir, I just found out today and I didn't have time to report it—but sir, this is going to be to our advantage! If the Lacu'un insisted, *we* could handle the whole trade deal, couldn't we, Erica? And it should take something like a year to get everything negotiated and set up, shouldn't it?"

"Up to a year and a half, standard, yes," she confirmed. "And basically, whatever the Lacu'un want, they get, so far as the Company is concerned."

"Once the kittens are a year old, they'll be hunters just as good as SKitty is—so if you could see your way clear to doing all the set up—and sort-of wait around for us to get done rearing the kittens—"

Captain Singh burst into laughter. "Boy, do you have any notion just how *many* credits handling the entire trade negotiations would put in *Brightwing's* account? Do you have any idea what that would do for *my* status?"

"No sir," he admitted.

"Suffice it to say I *could* retire if I chose. And—Spirits of Space—kittens? Kittens we *could* legally sell to the Lacu'un? I don't suppose you have any notion of how many kittens we can expect this time?"

He sent an inquiring tendril of thought to SKitty. "Uh—I think four, sir."

"Four! And they were offering us *what* for just her?" the Captain asked Vena.

"A more-than-considerable amount," she said dryly. "Exclusive contract on the forcefield applications."

"How would they feel about bargaining for four to be turned over in about a year?"

Vena turned to the rulers and translated. The excited answer she got left no doubts in anyone's mind that the Lacu'un were overjoyed at the prospect.

"Basically, Captain, you've just convinced the Lacu'un that you hung the moon."

"Well—why don't we settle down to a little serious negotiation, hmm?" the Captain said, nobly refraining from rubbing his hands together with glee. "I think that all our problems for the future are about to be solved in one fell swoop! Get over here, spacer. You and that cat have just received a promotion to Junior Negotiator."

:Okay?: SKitty asked anxiously.

Yes, love, Dick replied, taking Erica's place on a negotiator's stool. *Very okay!*

A Tail of Two SKittys

The howls coming from inside the special animal shipping crate sounded impatient, and had been enough to seriously alarm the cargo handlers. Dick White, Spaceman First Class, Supercargo on the CatsEye Company ship *Brightwing*, put his hand on the outside of the plastile crate, just above the word "Property." From within the crate the muffled voice continued to yowl general unhappiness with the world.

Tell her that it's all right, SKitty, he thought at the black form that lay over his shoulders like a living fur collar. *Tell her I'll have her out in a minute. I don't want her to come bolting out of there and hide the minute I crack the crate.*

SKitty raised her head. Yellow eyes blinked once, sleepily. Abruptly, the yowling stopped.

:*She fine,*: SKitty said, and yawned, showing a full mouth of needle-pointed teeth. :*Only young, scared. I think she make good mate for Furrball.*:

Dick shook his head; the kittens were not even a year old, and already their mother was matchmaking. Then again, that *was* the tendency of mothers the universe over.

At least now he'd be able to uncrate this would-be "mate" with a minimum of fuss.

The full legend imprinted on the crate read "Female Shipscat Astra Stardancer of Englewood, Property of BioTech Interstellar, leased to CatsEye Company. Do not open under penalty of law." Theoretically, Astra was, like SKitty, a bio-engineered shipscat, fully capable of handling freefall, alien vermin, conditions that would poison, paralyze, or terrify her remote Terran ancestors, and all without turning a hair. In actuality, Astra, like the nineteen other shipscats Dick had uncrated, was a failure. The genetic engineering of her middle-ear and other balancing organs had failed. She could not tolerate freefall, and while most ships operated under gravgenerators, there were always equipment malfunctions and accidents.

That made her and her fellows failures by BioTech standards. A shipscat that could not handle freefall was not a shipscat.

Normally, kittens that washed out in training were adopted out to carefully selected planet- or station-bound families of BioTech employees. However, this was not a "normal" circumstance by any stretch of the imagination.

The world of the Lacu'un, graceful, bipedal humanoids with a remarkably sophisticated, if planet-bound, civilization, was infested with a pest called a "kreshta." Erica Makumba, the Legal Advisor and Security Chief of Dick's ship described them as "six-legged crosses between cockroaches and mice." SKitty described them only as "nasty," but she hunted them gleefully anyway. The Lacu'un opened their world to trade just over a year ago, and some of their artifacts and technologies made them a desirable trade-ally indeed. The *Brightwing* had been one of the three ships invited to negotiate, in part because of SKitty, for the Lacu'un valued totemic animals highly.

And that was what had led to Captain Singh of the

Brightwing conducting the entire trade negotiations with the Lacu'un—and had kept *Brightwing* ground-bound for the past year. SKitty had done the—to the Lacu'un—impossible. She had killed kreshta. She had already been assumed to be *Brightwing*'s totemic animal; that act elevated her to the status of "god-touched miracle," and had given the captain and crew of her ship unprecedented control and access to the rulers here.

SKitty had been newly-pregnant at the time; part of the price for the power Captain Singh now wielded had been her kittens. But Dick had gotten another idea, and had used his own share of the profits *Brightwing* was taking in to purchase the leases of twenty more "failed" cats to supplement SKitty's four kittens. BioTech cats released for leases were generally sterile, SKitty being a rare exception. If these twenty worked out, the Lacu'un would be very grateful, and more importantly, so would Vena Ferducci, the attractive, petite Terran Consul assigned to the new embassy here. In the past few months, Dick had gotten to know Vena very well—and he hoped to get to know her better. Vena had originally been a Survey Scout, and she was getting rather restless in her ground-based position as Consul. And in truth, the Lacu'un lawyer, Lan Ventris, was much better suited to such a job than Vena. She had hinted that as soon as the Lacu'un felt they could trust Ventris, she would like to resign and go back to space. Dick rather hoped she might be persuaded to take a position with the *Brightwing*. It was too soon to call this little dance a "romance," but he had hopes. . . .

Hopes which could be solidified by this experiment. If the twenty young cats he had imported worked out as well as SKitty's four half-grown kittens, the Lacu'un would be able to import their intelligent pest-killers at a fraction of what the lease on a shipscat would be. This would make Vena happy; anything that benefited her Lacu'un made her happy. And if Dick was the cause of that happiness. . . .

:*Dick go courting?*: SKitty asked innocently, salting her query with decidedly *not*-innocent images of her own "courting."

Dick blushed. *No courting,* he thought firmly. *Not yet, anyway.*

:*Silly,*: SKitty replied scornfully. The overtones of her thoughts were—why waste such a golden opportunity? Dick did not answer her.

Instead, he thumbed the lock on the crate, a lock keyed to his DNA only. A tiny prickle was the only indication that the lock had taken a sample of his skin for comparison, but a moment later a hairline-thin crack appeared around the front end of the crate, and Dick carefully opened the door and looked inside.

A pair of big green eyes in a pointed gray face looked out at him from the shadows. "Meowrrrr?" said a tentative voice.

Tell her it's all right, SKitty, he thought, extending a hand for Astra to sniff. It was too bad that his telepathic connection with SKitty did not extend to these other cats, but she seemed to be able to relay everything he needed to tell them.

Astra sniffed his fingers daintily, and oozed out of the crate, belly to the floor. After a moment though, a moment during which SKitty stared at her so hard that Dick was fairly certain his little friend was communicating any number of things to the newcomer, Astra stood up and looked around, her ears coming up and her muscles relaxing. Finally she looked up at Dick and blinked.

"Prrow," she said. He didn't need SKitty's translation to read that. He held out his arms and the young cat leapt into them, to be carried in regal dignity out of the Quarantine area.

As he turned away from the crate, he thought he caught a hint of movement in the shadows at the back. But when he turned to look, there was nothing there, and he dismissed it as nothing more than his imagination. If there *had* been anything else in Astra's crate, the manifest would have listed it—and Astra was definitely sterile, so it could not have been an unlicensed kitten.

Erica Makumba and Vena were waiting for him in the corridor outside. Vena offered her fingers to the newcomer; much more secure now, Astra sniffed them and purred. "She's lovely," Vena said in admiration. Dick had to agree; Astra was a velvety blue-gray from head to tail, and her slim, clean lines clearly showed her descent from Russian Blue ancestors.

:*She for Furrball,:* SKitty insisted, gently nipping at his neck.

Is this your idea or hers? Dick retorted.

:*Sees Furrball in head; likes Furrball.:* That seemed to finish it as far as SKitty was concerned. :*Good hunter, too.:* Dick gave in to the inevitable.

"Didn't we promise one of these new cats to the Lacu'teveras?" Dick asked. "This one seems very gentle; she'd probably do very well as a companion for Furrball." SKitty's kittens all had names as fancy as Astra's—or as SKitty's official name, for that matter. Furrball was "Andreas Widefarer of Lacu'un," Nuisance was "Misty Snowspirit of Lacu'un," Rags was "Lady Flamebringer of Lacu'un" and Trey was "Garrison Starshadow of Lacu'un." But they had, as cats always do, acquired their own nicknames that had nothing to do with the registered names. Astra would without a doubt do the same.

Each of the most prominent families of the Lacu'un had been granted one cat, but the Royal Family had three. Two of SKitty's original kittens, and one of the newcomers. Astra would bring that number up to four, a sacred number to the Lacu'un and very propitious.

"We did," Vena replied absently, scratching a pleased Astra beneath her chin. "And I agree with you; I think this one would please the Lacu'teveras very much." She laughed a little. "I'm beginning to think you're psychic or something, Dick; you haven't been wrong with your selections yet."

"Me?" he said ingenuously. "Psychic? Spirits of Space, Vena, the way these people are treating the cats, it doesn't matter anyway. Any 'match' I made would be a good one, so far as the cat is concerned. They couldn't be pampered more if they were Lacu'un girl-babies!"

"True," she agreed, and reluctantly took her hand away. "Well, four cats should be just about right to keep the Palace vermin-free. It's really kind of funny how they've divided the place up among them with no bickering. They almost act as if they were humans dividing up patrols!" Erica shot him an unreadable glance; did she remember how he had sat down with the original three and SKitty—and a floor-plan of the place—when he first brought them all to the Palace?

"They are bred for high intelligence," he reminded both of them hastily. "No one really knows how bright they are. They're bright enough to use their life-support pods in an emergency, and bright enough to learn how to use the human facilities in the ships. They seem to have ways of communicating with each other, or so the people at BioTech tell me, so maybe they did establish patrols."

"Well, maybe they did," Erica said after a long moment. He heaved a mental sigh of relief. The last thing he needed was to have someone suspect SKitty's telepathic link with him. BioTech was not breeding for telepathy, but if such a useful trait ever showed up in a *fertile* female, they would surely cancel *Brightwing's* lease and haul SKitty back to their nearest cattery to become a breeding queen. SKitty was his best friend; to lose her like that would be terrible.

:*No breeding,*: SKitty said firmly. :*Love Dick, love ship. No breeding; breeding dull, kittens a pain. Not leave ship ever.*:

Well, at least SKitty agreed.

For now, anyway, now that her kittens were weaned.

Whenever she came into season, she seemed to change her mind, at least about the part that resulted in breeding, if not the breeding itself.

The Lacu'teveras, the Ruling Consort of her people, accepted Astra into the household with soft cries of welcome and gladness. Erica was right, the Lacu'un could not possibly have pampered their cats more. Whenever a cat wanted a lap or a scratch, one was immediately provided, whether or not the object of feline affection was in the middle of negotiations or a session of Council or not. Whenever one wished to play—although with the number of kreshta about, there was very little energy left over for playing—everything else was set aside for that moment. And when one brought in a trophy kreshta, tail and ears held high with pride, the entire court applauded. Astra was introduced to Furrball at SKitty's insistence. Noses were sniffed, and the two rubbed cheeks. It appeared that Mama's matchmaking was going to work.

The three humans and the pleased feline headed back across the city to the spaceport and the Fence around it. The city of the Lacu'un was incredibly attractive, much more so than any other similar city Dick had ever visited. Because of the rapidity with which the kreshta multiplied given any food and shelter, the streets were kept absolutely spotless, and the buildings clean and in repair. Most had walls about them, giving the inhabitants little islands of privacy. The walls of the wealthy were of carved stone; those of the poor of cast concrete. In all cases, ornamentation was the rule, not the exception.

The Lacu'un themselves walked the streets of their city garbed in delicate, flowing robes, or shorter more practical versions of the same garments. Graceful and handsome, they resembled avians rather than reptiles; their skin varied in shade from a dark brown to a golden tan, and their heads bore a kind of frill like an iguana's, that ran from the base of the neck to a point just above and between the eyes.

Their faces were capable of something like a smile, and the expression meant the same for them as it did for humans. Most of them smiled when they saw Dick and SKitty; although the kreshta-destroying abilities of the cat were not something any of them would personally feel the impact of for many years, perhaps generations, they still appreciated what the cats Dick had introduced could do. The kreshta had been a plague upon them for as long as their history recorded, even being so bold as to steal the food from plates and injure unguarded infants. For as long as that history, it had seemed that there would never be a solution to the depredations of the little beasts. But now—the most pious claimed the advent of the cats was a sign of the gods' direct intervention and blessing, and even the skeptics were thrilled at the thought that an end to the plague was in sight. It was unlikely that, even with a cat in every household, the kreshta would ever be destroyed—but such things as setting a guard on sleeping babies and locking meals in metal containers set into the tables could probably be eliminated.

When they crossed the Fence into Terran territory, however, the surroundings dropped in quality by a magnitude or two. Dick felt obscurely ashamed of his world whenever he looked at the shabby, garish spaceport "facilities" that comprised most of the Terran spaceport area. At least the headquarters that Captain Singh and CatsEye had established were handsome; adaptations of the natives' own architecture, in cast concrete with walls decorated with stylized stars, spaceships, and suggestions of slit-pupiled eyes. SolarQuest and UVN, the other two Companies that had been given Trade permits, were following CatsEye's lead, and had hired the same local architects and contractors to build their own headquarters. It looked from the half-finished buildings as if SolarQuest was going with a motif taken from their own logo of a stylized sunburst; UVN was going for geometrics in their wall-decor.

There were four ships here at the moment rather than the authorized three; for some reason, the independent freighter that had brought in the twenty shipscats was still here on the landing field. Dick wondered about that for a moment, then shrugged mentally. Independents often ran on shoestring budgets; probably they had only loaded enough fuel to get them here, and refueling was taking more time than they had thought it would.

Suddenly, just as they passed through the doors of the building, SKitty howled, hissed, and leapt from Dick's shoulders, vanishing through the rapidly-closing door.

He uttered a muffled curse and turned to run after her. What had gotten into her, anyway?

He found himself looking into the muzzle of a weapon held by a large man in the nondescript coveralls favored by the crew of that independent freighter. The man was as nondescript as his clothing, with ash-blond hair cut short and his very ordinary face—with the exception of that weapon, and the cold, calculating look in his iron-gray eyes. Dick put up his hands, slowly. He had the feeling this was a very bad time to play hero.

"Where's the damn cat?" snapped the one Dick was coming to think of as "the Gray Man." One of his underlings shrugged.

"Gone," the man replied shortly. "She got away when we rounded up these three, and she just vanished somewhere. Forget the cat. How much damage could a cat do?"

The Gray Man shrugged. "The natives might get suspicious if they don't see her with our man."

"She probably wouldn't have cooperated with our man," the underling pointed out. "Not like she did with this one. It doesn't matter—White got the new cats installed, and we don't need an animal that was likely to be a handful anyway."

The Gray Man nodded after a while and went back to securing the latest of his prisoners. The offices in the new CatsEye building had been turned into impromptu cells; Dick had gotten a glimpse of Captain Singh in one of them as he had been frogmarched past. He didn't know what these people had done with the rest of the crew or with Vena and Erica, since Vena had been taken off somewhere separately and Erica had been stunned and dragged away without waiting for her surrender.

The Gray Man watched him with his weapon trained on him as two more underlings installed a tangle-field generator across the doorway. With no windows, these little offices made perfect holding-pens. Most of them didn't have furniture yet, those that did didn't really contain anything that could be used as a weapon. The desks were simple slabs of native wood on metal supports, the chairs molded plastile, and both were bolted to the floor. There was nothing in Dick's little cubicle that could even be thrown.

Dick was still trying to figure out who and what these people were, when something finally clicked. He looked up at the Gray Man. "You're from TriStar, aren't you?" he asked.

If the Gray Man was startled by this, he didn't show it. "Yes," the man replied, gun-muzzle never wavering. "How did you figure that out?"

"BioTech never ships with anyone other than TriStar if they can help it," Dick said flatly. "I wondered why they had hired a tramp-freighter to bring out their cats; it didn't seem like them, but then I thought maybe that was all they could get."

"You're clever, White," the Gray Man replied, expressionlessly. "Too clever for your own good, maybe. We might just have to make you disappear. You and the Makumba woman; she'll probably know some of us as soon as she wakes up, and we don't have the time or the equipment to brain-wipe you."

Dick felt a chill going down his back, as the men at the door finished installing the field and left, quickly. "BioTech is going to wonder if one of their designated handlers just vanishes. And without me, you're never going to get SKitty back; BioTech isn't going to care for that, either. They might start asking questions that you can't answer."

The Gray Man stared at him for a long moment; his expression did not vary in the least, but at least he didn't make any move to shoot. "I'll think about it," he said finally. He might have said more, but there was a shout from the corridor outside.

"The cat!" someone yelled, and the Gray Man was out of the door before Dick could blink. Unfortunately, he paused long enough to trigger the tangle-field before he ran off in pursuit of what could only have been SKitty.

Dick slumped down into the chair, and buried his face in his hands, but not in despair. He was thinking furiously.

TriStar didn't like getting cut out of the negotiations; what they can't get legally, they'll get any way they can. Probably they intend to use us as hostages against Vena's good behavior, getting her to put them up as the new negotiators. I solved the problem of getting the cats for them; now there's no reason they couldn't just step in. But that can't go on forever; sooner or later Vena is going to get to a com unit or send some kind of message offworld. So what would these people do then?

TriStar had a reputation as being ruthless, and he'd heard from Erica that it was justified. So how do you get rid of an entire crew of a spaceship *and* the Terran Consul? And maybe the crews of the other two ships into the bargain?

Well, there was always one answer to that, especially on a newly-opened world. Plague.

The chill threaded his backbone again as he realized just what a good answer that was. These TriStar goons could use sickness as the excuse for why the CatsEye people weren't in evidence. A rumor of plague might well drive the other two ships offworld before *they* came down with it. The TriStar people could even claim to be taking care of the *Brightwing*'s crew.

Then, after a couple of weeks, they all succumb to the disease, the Terran Consul with them. . . .

It was a story that would work, not only with the Terran authorities, but with the Lacu'un. The Fence was a very effective barrier to help from the natives; the Lacu'un would not cross it to find out the truth, even if they were suspicious.

I have to get to a com set, he thought desperately. His own usefulness would last only so long as it took them to trap SKitty and find some way of caging her. No one else, so far as he knew, could hear her thoughts. All they needed to do would be to catch her and ship her back to BioTech, with the message that the designated handler was dead of plague and the cat had become unmanageable. It wouldn't have been the first time.

A soft hiss made him look up, and he strangled a cry of mingled joy and apprehension. It was SKitty! She was right outside the door, and she seemed to be trying to do something with the tangle-field generator.

SKitty! he thought at her as hard as he could. *SKitty, you have to get away from here, they're trying to catch you*— There was no way SKitty was going to be able to deal with those controls; they were deliberately made difficult to handle, just precisely because shipscats were known to be curious. And how could she know what complicated series of things to do to take down the field anyway?

But SKitty ignored him, using her stubby raccoon-like hands on the controls of the generator and hissing in frustration when the controls would not cooperate.

Finally, with a muffled yowl of triumph, she managed to twist the dial into the "off" position and the field went down. Dick was out the door in a moment, but SKitty was uncharacteristically running off ahead of him instead of waiting for him. Not that he minded! She was safer on the ground in case someone spotted him and stunned him; she was small and quick, and if they caught him again, she would still have a chance to hide and get away. But there was something odd about her bounding run; as if her body was a little longer than usual. And her tail seemed to be a lot longer than he remembered—

Never mind that, get moving! he scolded himself, trying to recall where they'd set up all the coms and if any of them were translight. SKitty whisked ahead of him, around a corner; when he caught up with her, she was already at work on the tangle-field generator in front of another door.

Practice must have made perfect; she got the field down just before he reached the doorway, and shot down the hall like a streak of black lightning. Dick stopped; inside was someone lying down on a cot, arm over her dark mahogany head. Erica!

"Erica!" he hissed at her. She sat bolt upright, wincing as she did so, and he felt a twinge of sympathy. A stun-migraine was no picnic.

She saw who was at the door, saw at the same moment that there was no tangle-field shimmer between them, and was on her feet and out in a fraction of a second. "How?" she demanded, scanning the corridor and finding it as curiously empty as Dick had.

"SKitty took the generator offline," he said. "She got yours, too, and she headed off that way—" He pointed towards the heart of the building. "Do you remember where the translight coms are?"

"Eyeah," she said. "In the basement, if we can get there. That's the emergency unit and I don't think they know we've got it."

She cocked her head to one side, as if she had suddenly heard something. He strained his ears—and there was a clamor, off in the distance beyond the walls of the building. It sounded as if several people were chasing something. But it couldn't have been SKitty; she was still in the building.

"It sounds like they're busy," Erica said, and grinned. "Let's go while we have the chance!"

But before they reached the basement com room, they were joined by most of the crew of the *Brightwing*, some of whom had armed themselves with whatever might serve as a weapon. All of them told the same story, about how the shipscat had taken down their tangle-fields and fled. Once in the basement of the building—after scattering the multiple nests of kreshta that had moved right in—the Com Officer took over while the rest of them found whatever they could to make a barricade and Dick related what he had learned and what his surmises were. Power controls were all down here; there would be no way short of blowing the building up for the TriStar goons to cut power to the com. Now all they needed was time—time to get their message out, and wait for the Patrol to answer.

But time just might be in very short supply, Dick told himself as he grabbed a sheet of reflective insulation to use as a crude stun-shield. And as if in answer to that, just as the Com Officer got the link warmed up and began to send, Erica called out from the staircase.

"Front and center—here they come!"

Dick slumped down so that the tiny medic could reach his head to bandage it. He knew he looked like he'd been through a war, but either the feeling of elated triumph or the medic's drugs or both prevented him from really feeling any of his injuries. In the end, it had come down to the crudest of hand-to-hand combat on the staircase, as the Com Officer resent the message as many times as he could and the rest of them held off the TriStar bullies. He could only thank the Spirits of Space that they had no weapons stronger than stunners—or at least, they hadn't wanted to use them down in the basement where so many circuits lay bare. Eventually, of course, they had been overwhelmed, but by then it was too late. The Com Officer had gotten a reply from the Patrol. Help was on the way. Faced with the collapse of their plan, the TriStar people had done the only wise thing. They had retreated.

With them, they had taken all evidence that they *were* from TriStar; there was no way of proving who and what they were, unless the Patrol corvette now on the way in could intercept them and capture them. Contrary to what the Gray Man had thought, Erica had recognized none of her captors.

But right now, none of that mattered. What did matter was that *they* had come through this—and that SKitty had finally reappeared as soon as the TriStar ship blasted out, to take her accustomed place on Dick's shoulders, purring for all she was worth and interfering with the medic's work.

"Dick—" Vena called from the door to the medic's office, "I found your—"

Dick looked up. Vena was cradling SKitty in her arms.

But SKitty was already on his shoulders.

She must have looked just as stunned as he did, but he recovered first, doing a double-take. *His* SKitty was the one on her usual perch—Vena's SKitty was a little thinner, a little taller—

And most *definitely* had a lot longer tail!

:*Is Prrreet,*: SKitty said with satisfaction. :*Handsome, no? Is bred for being Patrol-cat, war-cat.*:

"Vena, what's the tattoo inside that cat's ear?" he asked, urgently. She checked.

"FX-003," she said, "and a serial number. But the X designation is for experimental, isn't it?"

"Uh—yeah." He got up, ignoring the medic, and came to look at the new cat. Vena's stranger also had much more human-like hands than his SKitty; suddenly the mystery of how the cat had managed to manipulate the tangle-field controls was solved.

Shoot, he might even have been trained to do that!

:Yes,: SKitty said simply. :*I go play catch-me-stupid, he open human-cages. He hear of me on station, come to see me, be mate. I think I keep him.*:

Dick closed his eyes for a moment. Somewhere, there was a frantic BioTech station trying to figure out where one of their experimentals had gone. He *should* turn the cat over to them!

:No,: SKitty said positively. :*No look. Is deaf one ear; is pet. Run away, find me.*:

"He uh—must have come in as an extra with that shipment," Dick improvised quickly. "I found an extra invoice, I just thought they'd made a mistake. He's deaf in one ear, that's why they washed him out. I uh—I suppose *Brightwing* could keep him."

"I was kind of hoping I could—" Vena began, and flushed, lowering her eyes. "I suppose I still could . . . after this, the embassy is going to have to have a full staff with Patrol guards and a real Consul. They won't need me anymore."

Dick began to grin, as he realized what Vena was saying. "Well, he will need a handler. And I have all I can do to take care of *this* SKitty."

:Courting?: SKitty asked slyly, reaching out to lick one of Prrreet's ears.

This time Dick did not bother to deny it.

SCat

"NoooOOOWOWOWOW!"

The metal walls of Dick's tiny cabin vibrated with the howl. Dick White ignored it, as he injected the last of the four contraception-beads into SKitty's left hind leg. The black-coated shipscat did not move, but she did continue her vocal and mental protest. :*Mean,*: she complained, as Dick held the scanner over the right spot to make certain that he *had* gotten the bead placed where it was supposed to go. :*Mean, mean Dick.*:

Indignation showing in every line of her, she sat up on his fold-down desk and licked the injection site. It hadn't hurt; he *knew* it hadn't hurt, for he'd tried it on himself with a neutral bead before he injected her.

Nice, nice Dick, you should be saying, he chided her. *One more unauthorized litter and BioTech would be coming to take you away for their breeding program. You're too fertile for your own good.*

SKitty's token whine turned into a real yowl of protest, and her mate, now dubbed "SCat," joined her in the wail from his seat on Dick's bunk. :*Not leave Dick!*: SKitty shrilled in his head. :*Not leave ship!*:

Then no more kittens—at least not for a while! he

responded. *No more kittens means SKitty and SCat stay with Dick.*

SKitty leapt to join her mate on the bunk, where both of them began washing each other to demonstrate their distress over the idea of leaving Dick. SKitty's real name was "Lady Sundancer of Greenfields," and she was the proud product of BioTech's masterful genesplicing. Shipscats, those sturdy, valiant hunters of vermin of every species, betrayed their differences from Terran felines in a number of ways. BioTech had given them the "hands" of a raccoon, the speed of a mongoose, the ability to adjust to rapid changes in gravity or no gravity at all, and greatly enhanced mental capacity. What they did not know was that "Lady Sundancer"—aka "Dick White's Kitty," or "SKitty" for short—had another, invisible enhancement. She was telepathic—at least with Dick.

Thanks to SKitty and to her last litter, the CatsEye Company trading ship *Brightwing* was one of the most prosperous in this end of the Galaxy. That was due entirely to SKitty's hunting ability; she had taken swift vengeance when a persistent pest native to the newly-opened world of Lacu'un had bitten the consort of the ruler, killing with a single blow a creature the natives had *never* been able to exterminate. That, and her own charming personality, had made her kittens-to-be *most* desirable acquisitions, so precious that not even the leaders of Lacu'un "owned" them; they were held in trust for the world. Thanks to the existence of that litter and the need to get them appropriately pedigreed BioTech mates, SKitty's own mate—called "Prrreet" by SKitty and unsurprisingly dubbed "SCat" by the crew, for his ability to vanish—had made his own way to SKitty, stowing aboard with the crates containing more BioTech kittens for Lacu'un.

Where *he* came from, only he knew, although he was definitely a shipscat. His tattoo didn't match anything in the BioTech register. Too dignified to be called a "kitty," this handsome male was "Dick White's Cat."

And thanks to SCat's timely arrival and intervention, an attempt to kill the entire crew of the *Brightwing* and the Terran Consul to Lacu'un in order to take over the trading concession had been unsuccessful. SCat had disabled critical equipment holding them all imprisoned, so that they were able to get to a com station to call for help from the Patrol, while SKitty had distracted the guards.

SCat had never demonstrated telepathic powers with Dick, for which Dick was grateful, but he certainly possessed something of the sort with SKitty, and he was odd in other ways. Dick would have been willing to take an oath that SCat's forepaws were even more handlike than SKitty's, and that his tail showed some signs of being prehensile. There were other secrets locked in that wide black-furred skull, and Dick only wished he had access to them.

Dick was worried, for the *Brightwing* was in space again and heading towards one of the major stations with the results of their year-long trading endeavor with the beings of Lacu'un in their hold. Shipscats simply did not come out of nowhere; BioTech kept very tight control over them, denying them to ships or captains with a record of even the slightest abuse or neglect, and keeping track of where every one of them was, from birth to death. They were expensive—traders running on the edge could not afford them, and had to rid themselves of vermin with periodic vacuum-purges. SKitty claimed that her mate had "heard about her" and had come specifically to find her—but she would not say from where. SCat had to come from *somewhere*, and wherever that was, someone from there was probably looking for him. They would very likely take a dim view of their four-legged Romeo heading off on his own in search of his Juliet.

Any attempt to question the tom through SKitty was

useless. SCat would simply stare at him with those luminous yellow eyes, then yawn, and SKitty would soon grow bored with the proceedings. After all, to her, the important thing was that SCat was *here*, not where he had come from.

Behind Dick, in the open door of the cabin, someone coughed. He turned to find Captain Singh regarding Dick and cats with a jaundiced eye. Dick saluted hastily.

"Sir—contraceptive devices in place and verified sir!" he affirmed, holding up the injector to prove it.

The Captain, a darkly handsome gentleman as popular with the females of his own species as SCat undoubtably was with felines, merely nodded. "We have a problem, White," he pointed out. "The *Brightwing*'s manifest shows *one* shipscat, not two. And we still don't know where number two came from. I know what will happen if we try to take SKitty's mate away from her, but I also know what will happen if anyone finds out we have a second cat, origin unknown. BioTech will take a dim view of this."

Dick had been thinking at least part of this through. "We *can* hide him, sir," he offered. "At least until I can find out where he came from."

"Oh?" Captain Singh's eyebrows rose. "Just how do you propose to hide him, and where?"

Dick grinned. "In plain sight, sir. Look at them—unless you have them side-by-side, you wouldn't be able to tell which one you had in front of you. They're both black with yellow eyes, and it's only when you can see the size difference and the longer tail on SCat that you can tell them apart."

"So we simply make sure they're never in the same compartment while strangers are aboard?" the Captain hazarded. "That actually has some merit; the Spirits of Space know that people are always claiming shipscats can teleport. No one will even notice the difference if we don't say anything, and they'll just think she's getting around by way of the access tubes. How do you intend to find out where this one came from without making people wonder why you're asking about a stray cat?"

Dick was rather pleased with himself, for he had actually thought of this solution first. "SKitty is fertile—unlike nine-tenths of the shipscats. That is why we had kittens to offer the Lacu'un in the first place, and was why we have the profit we do, even after buying the contracts of the other young cats for groundside duty as the kittens' mates."

The Captain made a faint grimace. "You're stating the obvious."

"Humor me, sir. Did you know that BioTech routinely offers their breeding cats free choice in mates? That otherwise, they don't breed well?" As the Captain shook his head, Dick pulled out his trump card. "I am—ostensibly—going to do the same for SKitty. As long as we 'find' her a BioTech mate that she approves of, BioTech will be happy. And we need more kittens for the Lacu'un; we have no reason to *buy* them when we have a potential breeder of our own."

"But we got mates for her kittens," the Captain protested. "Won't BioTech think there's something odd going on?"

Dick shook his head. "You're thinking of house-cats. Shipscats aren't fertile until they're four or five. At that rate, the kittens won't be old enough to breed for four years, and the Lacu'un are going to want more cats before then. So I'll be searching the BioTech breeding records for a tom of the right age and appearance. Solid black is recessive—there can't be *that* many black toms of the right age."

"And once you've found your group of candidates—?" Singh asked, both eyebrows arching. "You look for the one that's missing?" He did not ask how Dick was supposed to have found out that SKitty "preferred" a black tom; shipscats were more than intelligent enough to choose a color from a set of holos.

Dick shrugged. "The information may be in the

records. Once I know where SCat's from, we can open negotiations to add him to our manifest with BioTech's backing. *They* won't pass up a chance to make SKitty half of a breeding pair, and I don't think there's a captain willing to go on BioTech's record as opposing a shipscat's choice of mate."

"I won't ask how you intend to make that particular project work," Singh said hastily. "Just remember, no more kittens in freefall."

Dick held up the now-empty injector as a silent promise.

"I'll brief the crew to refer to both cats as 'SKitty'— most of the time they do anyway," the Captain said. "Carry on, White. You seem to have the situation well in hand."

Dick was nowhere near that certain, but he put on a confident expression for the Captain. He saluted Singh's retreating back, then sat down on the bunk beside the pair of purring cats. As usual, they were wound around each other in a knot of happiness.

I wish my love-life was going that well. He'd hit it off with the Terran Consul well enough, but she had elected to remain in her ground-bound position, and his life was with the ship. Once again, romance took a second place to careers. Which in his case, meant no romance. There wasn't a single female in this crew that had shown anything other than strictly platonic interest in him.

If he *wanted* a career in space, he had to be very careful about what he did and said. As most junior officer on the *Brightwing*, he was the one usually chosen for whatever unpleasant duty no one else wanted to handle. And although he could actually *retire*, thanks to the prosperity that the Lacu'un contract had brought the whole crew, he didn't want to. That would mean leaving space, leaving the ship—and leaving SKitty and SCat.

He could also transfer within the company, but why change from a crew full of people he liked and respected, with a good Captain like Singh, to one about which he knew nothing? That would be stupid. And he couldn't leave SKitty, no matter what. She was his best friend, even if she did get him into trouble sometimes.

He also didn't have the experience to be anything other than the most junior officer in any ship, so transferring wouldn't have any benefits.

Unless, of course, he parlayed his profit-share into a small fortune and bought his own ship. Then he could be Captain, and he might even be able to buy SKitty's contract—but he lacked the experience that made the difference between prosperity and bankruptcy in the shaky world of the Free Traders. He was wise enough to know this.

As for the breeding project—he had some ideas. The *Brightwing* would be visiting Lacu'un for a minimum of three weeks on every round of their trading-route. Surely something could be worked out. Things didn't get chancy until after the kittens were mobile and before SKitty potty-trained them to use crew facilities. Before they were able to leave the nest-box, SKitty took care of the unpleasant details. If they could arrange things so that the period of mobility-to-weaning took place while they were on Lacu'un. . . .

Well, he'd make that Jump when the coordinates came up. Right now, he had to keep outsiders from discovering that there was feline contraband on board, and find out where that contraband came from.

:*Dick smart,*: SKitty purred proudly. :*Dick fix everything.*:

Well, he thought wryly, *at least I have* her *confidence, if no-one else's!*

It had been a long time since the *Brightwing* had been docked at a major port, and predictably, everyone wanted shore leave. Everyone except Dick, that is. He had no intentions of leaving the console in Cargo where he was doing his "mate-hunting" unless and until he found his match. The fact that there was nothing but a skeleton crew aboard, once the inspectors left, only made it easier for Dick to run his searches through the BioTech database available through the station. This database was part of the public records kept on every station, and updated weekly by BioTech. Dick had a notion that he'd get his "hit" within a few hours of initiating his search.

He was pleasantly surprised to discover that there were portraits available for every entry. It might even be possible to identify SCat just from the portraits, once he had all of the black males of the appropriate age sorted out. That would give him even more rationale for the claim that SKitty had "chosen" her mate herself.

With an interested feline perching on each arm of the chair, he logged into the station's databases, identified himself and gave the station his billing information, then began his run.

There was nothing to do at that point but sit back and wait.

"I hope you realize all of the difficulties I'm going through for you," he told the tom, who was grooming his face thoughtfully. "I'm doing without shore-leave to help you here. I wouldn't do this for a fellow human!"

SCat paused in his grooming long enough to rasp Dick's hand with his damp-sandpaper tongue.

The computer *beeped* just at that moment to let him know it was done. He was running all this through the Cargo dumb-set; he could have used the *Brightwing*'s Expert-System AI, but he didn't want the AI to get curious, and he didn't want someone wondering why he was using a Mega-Brain to access feline family-trees. What he *did* want was the appearance that this was a brainstorm of his own, an attempt to boost his standing with his Captain by providing further negotiable items for the Lacu'un contract. There was something odd about all of this, something that he couldn't put his finger on, but something that just felt wrong and made him want to be extra-cautious. Why, he didn't know. He only knew that he didn't want to set off any tell-tales by acting as if this mate-search was a priority item.

The computer asked if he wanted to use the holo-table, a tiny square platform built into the upper right hand corner of the desk. He cleared off a stack of hard-copy manifests, and told it "yes." Then the first of his feline biographies came in.

He'd made a guess that SCat was between five and ten years old; shipscats lived to be fifty or more, but their useful lifespan was about twenty or thirty years. All too often their job was hazardous; alien vermin had poisonous fangs or stings, sharp claws and teeth. Cats suffered disabling injuries more often than their human crewmates, and would be retired with honors to the homes of retired spacers, or to the big "assisted living" stations holding the very aged and those with disabling injuries of their own. Shipscats were always welcome, anywhere in space.

And I can think of worse fates than spending my old age watching the stars with SKitty on my lap. He gazed down fondly at his furred friend, and rubbed her ears.

SKitty purred and butted her head into his hand. She paid very little attention to the holos as they passed slowly in review. SCat was right up on the desk, however, not only staring intently at the holos, but splitting his attention between the holos and the screen.

You don't suppose he can read . . . ?

Suddenly, SCat let out a yowl, and swatted the holoplate. Dick froze the image and the screen-biography that accompanied it.

He looked first at the holo—and it certainly looked more like SCat than any of the others had. But SCat's attention was on the screen, not the holo, and he stared fixedly at the modest insignia in the bottom right corner.

Patrol?

He looked down at SCat, dumbfounded. "You were with the Patrol?" He whispered it; you did not invoke the Patrol's name aloud unless you wanted a visit from them.

Yellow eyes met his for a moment, then the paw tapped the screen. He read further.

Type MF-025, designation Lightfoot of Sun Meadow. Patrol ID FX-003. Standard Military genotype, standard Military training. Well, that explained how he had known how to shut down the "pirate" equipment. Now Dick wondered how much else the cat had done, outside of his sight. And a military genotype? He hadn't even known there *was* such a thing.

Assigned to Patrol ship DIA-9502, out of Oklahoma Station, designated handler Major Logan Greene.

Oklahoma Station—that was *this* station. Drug Interdiction? He whistled softly.

Then a date, followed by the ominous words, *Ship missing, all aboard presumed dead.*

All aboard—except the shipscat.

The cat himself gave a mournful yowl, and SKitty jumped up on the desk to press herself against him comfortingly. He looked back down at SCat. "Did you jump ship before they went missing?"

He wasn't certain he would get an answer, but he had lived with SKitty for too long to underestimate shipscat intelligence. The cat shook his head, slowly and deliberately—in the negative.

His mouth went dry. "Are you saying—you got away?"

A definite nod.

"Your ship was boarded, and you got away?" He was astonished. "But how?"

For an answer, the cat jumped down off the desk and walked over to the little escape pod that neither he nor SKitty ever forgot to drag with them. He seized the tether in his teeth and dragged it over to an access tube. It barely fit; he wedged it down out of sight, then pawed open the door, and dropped down, hidden, and now completely protected from what must have happened.

He popped back out again, and walked to Dick's feet.

Dick was thinking furiously. There had been rumors that drug-smugglers were using captured Patrol ships; this more-or-less confirmed those rumors. *Disable the ship, take the exterior airlock and blow it. Whoever wasn't suited up would die. Then they board and finish off whoever was suited up. They patch the lock, restore the air, and weld enough junk to the outside of the ship to disguise it completely. Then they can bring it in to any port they care to—even the ship's home port.*

This station. Which is where SCat escaped.

"Can you identify the attackers?" he asked SCat. The cat slowly nodded.

:*They know he gone. He run, they chase. He try get home, they stop. He hear of me on dock, go hide in ship bringing mates. They kill he, get chance,*: SKitty put in helpfully.

He could picture it easily enough; SCat being pursued, cut off from the Patrol section of the station—hiding out on the docks—catching the scent of the mates being shipped for SKitty's kittens and deciding to seek safety offworld. Cats, even shipscats, did not tend to grasp the concept of "duty"; he knew from dealing with SKitty that she took her bonds of personal affection seriously, but little else. So once "his" people were dead, SCat's personal allegiance to the Patrol was nonexistent, and his primary drive would be self-preservation. *Wonderful. I wonder if they—whoever they are—figured out he got away on another ship.* Another, more alarming thought occurred to him. *I wonder if my fishing about in the BioTech database touched off any tell-tales!*

No matter. There was only one place to go now—straight to Erica Makumba, the Legal and Security Officer.

He dumped a copy of the pertinent datafile to a memory cube, then scooped up both cats and pried their life-support ball out of its hiding place. Then he *ran* for Erica's cabin, praying that she had not gone off on shore-leave.

The Spirits of Space were with him; the indicator outside her cabin door indicated that she was in there, but did not want to be disturbed. He pounded on the door anyway. Erica *might* kill him—but there were people after SCat who had murdered an entire Patrol DIA squad.

After a moment, the door cracked open a centimeter. "White." Erica's flat, expressionless voice boded extreme violence. "This had better be an emergency."

He said the one word that would guarantee her attention. "Hijackers."

The door snapped open; she grabbed him and pulled him inside, cats, support-ball and all, and slammed the door shut behind him. She was wearing a short robe, tying it hastily around herself, and she wasn't alone. But the man watching them both alertly from the disheveled bed wasn't one of the *Brightwing*'s crew, so Dick flushed, but tried to ignore him.

"I found out where SCat's from," he babbled, dropping one cat to hand the memory-cube to her. "Read that—quick!"

She punched up the console at her elbow and dropped the cube in the receiver. The BioTech file, minus the holo, scrolled up on the screen. The man in the bed leaned forward to read it too, and whistled.

Erica swiveled to glare at him. "You keep this to yourself, Jay!" she snapped. Then she turned back to Dick. "Spill it!" she ordered.

"SCat's ship was hijacked, probably by smugglers," he said quickly. "He hid his support-ball in an access tube, and he was in it when they blew the lock. They missed him in the sweep, and when they brought their prize in here, he got away. But they know he's gone, and they know he can ID them."

"And they'll be giving the hairy eyeball to every ship with a black cat on it." She bit her knuckle—and Jay added his own two credits' worth.

"I hate to say this, but they've probably got a telltale on the BioTech data files, so they know whenever anyone accesses them. It's not restricted data, so anyone could leave a tell-tale." The man's face was pale beneath his normally dusky skin-tone. "If they don't know you've gone looking by now, they will shortly."

They all looked at each other. "Who's still on board?" Dick asked, and gulped.

Erica's mouth formed a tight, thin line. "You, me, Jay and the cats. The cargo's offloaded, and regs say you don't need more than two crew on board in-station. *Theoretically* no one can get past the security at the lock."

Jay barked a laugh, and tossed long, dark hair out of his eyes. "Honey, I'm a comptech. Trust me, you can get past the security. You just hack into the system, tell it the ship in the bay is bigger than it really is, and upload whoever you want as additional personnel."

Erica swore—but Jay stood up, wrapping the sheet around himself like a toga, and pushed her gently aside. "What can be hacked can be unhacked—or at least I can make it a lot more difficult for them to get in and make those alterations stick. Give me your code to the AI."

Erica hesitated. He turned to stare into her eyes. "I need the AI's help. *You* two and the cats are going to get out of here—get over to the Patrol side of the station. I'm going to hold them off as long as I can, and play stupid when they do get in, but I need the speed of the AI to help me lay traps. You've known me for three years. You trusted me enough to bring me here, didn't you?"

She swore again, then reached past him to key in her code. He sat down, ignoring them and plunging straight into a trance of concentration.

"Come on!" Erica grabbed Dick's arm, and put the support-ball on the floor. SKitty and SCat must have been reading *her* mind, for they both squirmed into the ball, which was big enough for more than one cat. They'd upgraded the ball after SKitty had proved to be so—fertile. Erica shoved the ball at Dick, and kept hold of his arm, pulling him out into the corridor.

"Where are we going?" he asked.

"To get our suits, then to the emergency lock," she replied crisply. "If we try to go out the main lock into the station, they'll get us for certain. So we're going outside for a little walk."

A little walk? All the way around the station? Outside?

He could only hope that "they" hadn't thought of that as well. They reached the suiting-up room in seconds flat.

He averted his eyes and climbed into his own suit as Erica shed her robe and squirmed into hers. "How far is it to the Patrol section?" he asked.

"Not as far as you think," she told him. "And there's a maintenance lock just this side of it. What I want to know is how *you* got all this detailed information about the hijacking."

He turned, and saw that she was suited up, with her faceplate still open, staring at him with a calculating expression.

This is probably not the time to hold out on her.

He swallowed, and sealed his suit up, leaving his own faceplate open. Inside the ball, the cats were watching both of them, heads swiveling to look from one face to the other, as if they were watching a tennis-match.

"SKitty's telepathic with me," he admitted. "I think SCat's telepathic with her. She seems to be able to talk with him, anyway."

He waited for Erica to react, either with disbelief or with revulsion. Telepaths of any species were not always popular among humankind. . . .

But Erica just pursed her lips and nodded. "Eyeah. I thought she might be. And telepathy's one of the traits BioTech doesn't talk about, but security people have know for a while that the MF type cats are bred for it. Maybe SKitty's momma did a little wandering over on the miltech side of the cattery, hmm?"

SKitty made a "silent" meow, and he just shrugged, relieved that Erica wasn't phobic about it. And equally relieved to learn that telepathy was already a trait that BioTech had established in their shipscat lines. *So they won't be coming to take SKitty away from me when they find out that she's a 'path. . . .*

But right now, he'd better be worrying about making a successful escape. He pulled his faceplate down and sealed it, fastening the tether-line of the ball to a snaplink on his waistband. He warmed up his suit-radio, and she did the same. "I hope you know what you're getting us into," he said, as Erica sealed her own plate shut and led the way to the emergency lock.

She looked back over her shoulder at him.

"So do I," she replied soberly.

The trip was a nightmare.

Dick had never done a spacewalk on the exterior of a station before. It wasn't at all like going out on the hull of a ship. There were hundreds of obstacles to avoid—windows, antenna, instrument-packages, maintenance robots. Any time an inspection drone came along, they had to hide to avoid being picked up on camera. It was work, hard work, to inch their way along the station in this way, and Dick was sweating freely before a half an hour was up.

It seemed like longer. Every time he glanced up at the chronometer in his faceplate HUD, he was shocked to see how little time had passed. The suit-fans whined in his ears, as the life-support system alternately fought to warm him up when they hid in the shade, or cool him down when they paused in full sunlight. Stars burned down on them, silent points of light in a depth of darkness that made him dizzy whenever he glanced out at it. The knowledge that he could be lost forever out there if he just made one small mistake chilled his heart.

Finally, Erica pointed, and he saw the outline of a maintenance lock just ahead. The two of them pulled themselves hand-over-hand toward it, reaching it at the same instant. But it was Erica who opened it, while Dick reeled the cats in on their tether.

With all four of them inside, Erica sealed the lock from the inside and initiated pressurization. Within moments, they were both able to pop their faceplates and breathe station-air again.

Something prompted Dick to release the cats from their ball before Erica unsealed the inner hatch. He unsnapped the tether and was actually straightening up, empty ball in both hands, when Erica opened the door to a hallway—

—and dropped to the floor, as the shrill squeal of a stun-gun pierced the quiet of the lock.

"Erica!" Without thinking, he ran forward, and found himself facing the business-end of a powerful stunner, held by a nondescript man who held it as if he was quite used to employing it. He was *not* wearing a station-uniform.

The man looked startled to see him, and Dick did the only thing he could think of. He threw the support-ball at the man, as hard as he could.

It hit cleanly, knocking the man to the floor as it impacted with his chest. He clearly was not aware that the support-balls were as massy as they were. The two cats flashed past him, heading for freedom, and Dick tried to follow their example. But the man was quick to recover, and as Dick tried to jump over his prone body, the fellow grabbed his ankle and tripped him up.

Then it turned into a brawl, with Dick the definite underdog. Even in the suit, the stranger still outweighed him.

Within a few seconds, Dick was on his back on the floor, and the stranger held him down, easily. The stun-gun was no longer in his hands, but it didn't look to Dick as if he really needed it.

In fact, as the man's heavy fist pounded into Dick's face, he was quickly convinced that he didn't need it. Pain lanced through his jaw as the man's fist smashed into it; his vision filled with stars and red and white flashes of light. More agony burst into his skull as the blows continued. He flailed his arms and legs, but there was nothing he could do—he was trapped in the suit, and he couldn't even get enough leverage to defend himself. He tasted blood in his mouth—he couldn't see—

:*BAD MAN!*:

There was a terrible battle-screech from somewhere out in the corridor, and the blows stopped. Then the weight lifted from his body, as the man howled in pain.

Dick managed to roll to one side, and stagger blindly to his feet with the aid of the corridor bulkhead—he still couldn't see. He dashed blood out of his eyes with one hand, and shook his head to clear it, staring blindly in the direction of the unholy row.

"*Get it off! Get it off me!*" Human screams mixed with feline battle-cries, telling him that whichever of the cats had attacked, they were giving a good accounting of themselves.

But there were other sounds—the sounds of running feet approaching, and Dick tried frantically to get his vision to clear. A heavy body crashed into him, knocking him into the bulkhead with enough force to drive all the breath from his body, as the *zing* of an illegal neuro-gun went off somewhere near him.

SKitty!

But whoever was firing swore, and the cat-wail faded into the distance.

"It got away!" said one voice, over the sobbing of another.

A third swore, as Dick fought for air. "You. Go after it," the third man said, and there was the sound of running feet. Meanwhile, footsteps neared where Dick lay curled in a fetal bundle on the floor.

"What about this?" the second voice asked.

The third voice, cold and unemotional, wrote Dick's death warrant. "Get rid of it, and the woman, too."

And Dick could not even move. He heard someone breathing heavily just above him; sensed the man taking aim—

Then—

"Patrol! Freeze! Drop your weapons now!"

Something clattered to the deck beside him, as more running feet approached; and with a sob of relief, Dick finally drew a full breath. There was a scuffle just beside him, then someone helped him to stand, and he heard the hiss of a hypospray and felt the tell-tale sting against the side of his neck. A moment later, his eyes cleared—just in time for him to catch SKitty as she launched herself from the arms of a uniformed DIA officer into his embrace.

"So, the bottom line is, you'll let us take SCat's contract?" Captain Singh sat back in his chair while Dick rubbed SKitty's ears. She and SCat both burdened Dick's lap, as they had since SCat, the Captain, the DIA negotiator, and Erica had all walked into the sickbay where Dick was still recovering. Erica was clearly nursing a stun-headache; the Captain looked a little frazzled. The DIA man, as most of his ilk, looked as unemotional as an android. The DIA had spent many hours with a human-feline telepathic specialist debriefing SCat. Apparently SCat was naturally only a receptive telepath; it took a human who was also a telepath to "talk" to him.

"There's no reason why not," the DIA agent said. "You civilians have helped materially in this case; both you and he are entitled to certain compensation, and if that's what you all want, then he's yours with our blessing—the fact that he is only a receptive telepath makes him less than optimal for further Patrol duties." The agent shrugged. "We can always get other shipscats with full abilities. According to the records, the only reason we kept him was because Major Logan selected him."

SKitty bristled, and Dick sent soothing thoughts at her.

Then the agent smiled, making his face look more human. "Major Logan was a good agent, but he didn't particularly care for having a cat talking to him. I gather that Lightfoot and he got along all right, but there wasn't the strong bond between them that we would have preferred. It would have been just a matter of time before that squad and ship got a new cat-agent team. Besides, we aren't completely inhuman. If your SKitty and this boy here are happily mated, who and what in the Patrol can possibly want to separate them?"

"Judging by the furrows SKitty left in that 'jacker's face and scalp, it isn't a good idea to get between her and someone she loves," Captain Singh said dryly. "He's lucky she left him one eye."

The agent's gaze dropped briefly to the swath of black fur draped over Dick's lap. "Believe me," he said fervently. "That *is* a consideration we had taken into account. Your little lady there is a warrior for fair, and we have no intention of denying her anything her heart is set on. If she wants Lightfoot, and he wants her, then she's got him. We'll see his contract is transferred over to *Brightwing* within the hour." His eyes rose to meet Dick's. "You're a lucky man to have a friend like her, young man. She put herself between you and certain death. Don't you ever forget it."

SKitty's purr deepened, and SCat's joined with hers as Dick's hands dropped protectively on their backs. "I know that, sir," he replied, through swollen lips. "I knew it before any of this happened."

SKitty turned her head, and he gazed into amused yellow eyes. :*Smart Dick,*: she purred, then lowered her head to her paws. :*Smart man. Mate happy here, mate stay. Everything good. Love you.*:

And that, as far as SKitty was concerned, was the end of it. The rest were simply "minor human matters."

He chuckled, and turned his own attention to dealing with those "minor human matters," while his best friend and her mate drifted into well-earned sleep.

A Better Mousetrap

If there was one thing that Dick White had learned in all his time as SuperCargo of the CatsEye Company Free Trader *Brightwing*, it was that having a cat purring in your ear practically forced you to relax. The extremely comfortable form-molding chair he sat in made it impossible to feel anything but comfortable, and warm black fur muffled both of Dick White's ears, a steady vibration massaging his neck. "Build a better mousetrap, and the world will beat a path to your door," Dick said idly, as SCat poured himself like a second fluid, black rug over the blue-grey of his lap. It was SKitty who was curled up around his shoulders, vibrating contentedly in what Dick called her "subsonic purr-mode," while her mate took it as his responsibility to make sure there was plenty of shed hair on the legs of his grey shipsuit uniform.

"What?" asked Terran Ambassador Vena Ferducci, looking up from the list of Lacu'un nobles petitioning for one of SKitty's latest litter. The petite, dark-haired woman sat in a less comfortable, metal chair behind a stone desk, which stood next to a metal rack stuffed with archaic rolled paper documents. The Lacu'un had not yet devised the science of filing paperwork in multiples yet, which made them ultra-civilised in Vena's opinion. This, her office in the Palace of the Lacu'ara and Lacu'teveras, was not often used for that very reason. When she dealt with *Terran* bureaucracy, she needed every electronic helper she could get.

The list she perused was very long, and made rather cumbersome due to the Lacu'un custom of presenting all official court-documents in the form of a massively ornamented yellow-parchment scroll, with case and end caps of engraved bronze and illuminated capital-initials. Dick had a notion that somewhere in the universe there probably was a collector of handwritten documents who would pay a small fortune for it, but when every petitioner on the list had been satisfied, it would probably be sent to the under-clerks, scraped clean, and reused.

"It's an old Terran folk-saying," Dick elaborated, and gestured to the list by way of explanation. "One which certainly seems to be borne out by our present situation."

"Yes, well, given the length of this list we're doubly fortunate that SKitty and SCat are so—ah—*fertile*, and that BioTech is willing to send us their shipscat washouts." Vena stretched out her hand towards SCat's head, and the huge black tom cooperated by craning his neck towards her. Even before her fingers contacted his fur, SCat was purring loudly, giving Dick an uncannily similar sensation to being strapped in while the ship he served was under full power.

Dick White could well be one of the wealthiest supercargoes in the history of space-trade—his share of the profits from CatsEye Company's lucrative trade with the Lacu'un amounted to quite a tidy sum. It wasn't enough to buy and outfit his own ship—yet—but if trade progressed as it had begun, there was the promise that one day it would be.

Not that I want my own ship yet! he told himself. *Not until I know as much as Captain Singh. There are easier ways to commit suicide than pretending I know enough to command a starship when all I really know is how to run the cargo hold!*

Not that Captain Singh would *let* him take his profit-share and do something so stupid. Dick grinned to himself, imagining the Captain's face if he showed up in the office with *that* kind of harebrained proposal. Captain Singh's expression would be one to behold—following which, Dick would probably find himself stunned unconscious and wake under the solicitous attentions of a concerned head-shrinker!

The Captain *had* been willing, even more than willing, to let Dick stay on-planet for few Terran-months though, after SKitty and SCat announced the advent of a litter-to-be. One of her last litter was co-opted to serve as shipscat pro tem, while Dick and his two charges waited out the delivery, maturation, and weaning of eight little black furballs who were, if that was possible, even cuter than the last batch. It was a good thing that they all *were* on-planet, too, because the Octet managed to get themselves into a hundred times more mischief than the previous lot.

The trouble is, they have a lot of energy, absolutely no sense, and no fear at all at this age. Brainless kitten antics rapidly begin to pall when you've fished a wailing fuzz-mote out of the comconsole for the fifteenth time in a single shift.

But every Lacu'un in the palace, from the Lacu'teveras down to the lowliest scullery-lad, was thrilled to the toes—or rather, claws—to play with, rescue, and cuddle the Bratlings. If SKitty and SCat had not taken their duties as parents, palace-guardians, and role-models so seriously, they wouldn't have had to do anything but lie about and wait for the kittens to be carried in to them for feeding.

Fortunately for all concerned, their parents had powerful senses of responsibility towards their offspring. Both cats were born and bred—literally—for duty. Yes, they were cats, with a cat's sense of independence and contrariness, but they took duty very, very seriously. And their duty was Vermin Control.

This was a duty that went back centuries to the very beginnings of the association of man and cat, but until BioTech developed shipscats, never had a feline been better suited to or more cooperative in the execution of that duty. Furthermore, Dick now knew what few others did—that the shipscats so necessary to the safety of traders and their ships were actually a highly profitable byproduct of other research, secret research, designed to give the men and women of the Patrol uniquely clever comrades-in-arms.

These genetically altered cats were not just clever, it was not just that they had forepaws modeled after the forepaws of raccoons—oh no. That was not enough. Patrol cats were telepaths.

SCat had been a patrol cat—but although he could understand the thoughts of humans, he couldn't speak to them. This was a flaw, so far as the Patrol was concerned, though not an insurmountable flaw. However, when criminals took over the ship he served on and killed all of those aboard, SCat was the only survivor and the only witness—unable to call for help or relate what he had witnessed, he had sought for help from his own kind and found it in SKitty. When the same criminals learned SCat was still alive and tried to eliminate him and the crew of the Free Trader ship *Brightwing*, for good measure, it had been Dick's research and deductive reasoning that had learned the truth in time, and with SCat's and SKitty's help he had foiled the plot.

As for SKitty, she was something of an aberration herself—ordinary shipscats were not supposed to be telepathic *or* fertile; she was both.

As far as Dick could tell, she was telepathic only with him—though, given that she was all cat, with a cat's puckish sense of humor, she might well choose not to let him know she could "speak" to others. Everyone on the ship knew she was fertile, though—when they had first come to the world of the Lacu'un, she'd already had one litter and was pregnant with another. That first litter—born and raised in the ship—had shown just what kind of a nightmare two loose kittens could be within the close confines of a spaceship. Dick had not been looking forward to telling Captain Singh of the second litter, when SKitty had solved the problem for them.

The Lacu'un, a race of golden-skinned, vaguely reptilian anthropoids, suffered from the depredations of a particularly voracious, fast, and apparently indestructible pest called *kreshta*. The only way to keep them from taking over completely was to lock anything edible (and the creature could eat practically anything) in airtight containers of metal, glass, ceramic, or stone, and build only in materials the pest couldn't eat. The pests did keep the streets so clean that they sparkled and there was no such thing as a trash problem, but those were the only benefits to the plague.

The Lacu'un had just opened their planet to trade from outside, and the *Brightwing* was one of several ships that had arrived to represent either themselves or one of the large Companies. Only Captain Singh had the foresight to include SKitty in their delegation, however, for only he had bothered to research the Lacu'un thoroughly enough to learn that they placed great value on totemic animals and had virtually *nothing* in the way of domesticated predators themselves. He reckoned that a tame predator would be very impressive to them, and he was right.

SKitty had been on her best behavior, charming them all, and taking to this alien race immediately. The Lacu'teveras, the female co-ruler, had been particularly charmed, so much so that she had missed the presence of one of the little pests, which had bitten her. Enraged at this attack on someone she favored, SKitty had killed the creature.

For the Lacu'un, this was nothing short of a miracle, the end of a scourge that had been with them since the beginning of their civilization. After that moment, there was no question of anyone else getting most-favored trading status with the Lacu'un, ever.

CatsEye got the plum contract, SKitty's kittens-to-be got immediate homes, and Dick White's life became incredibly complicated.

Since then, he was no longer just an apprentice supercargo and Designated Shipscat Handler on a small Free Trader ship. He'd been imprisoned by Company goons, stalked and beaten within an inch of his life by cold-blooded murderous hijackers, and had to face the Patrol itself to bargain for SCat's freedom. He'd had enough adventure in two short Standard-years to last most people for the rest of their lives.

But all that was in the past. Or so he hoped.

For a while, anyway, it would be nice if the most difficult decision I had to make would be which of the Lacu'un nobles get SKitty-babies and which have to make do with shipscat washouts.

Those "washouts" were mature cats that for one reason or another couldn't adapt to ship life. Gengineering wasn't perfect, even now; there were cats that couldn't handle freefall, cats that were claustrophobes, cats that were shy or anti-social. Those had the opportunity to come here, to join the vermin-hunting crew. Thus far, thirty had made the trip, some to become mates for the first litter, others to take up solitary residence with a noble family. There were other washouts, who didn't pass the intelligence tests, but those were never offered to the Lacu'un—they already filled a steady need for companions in children's hospitals and retirement homes, where the high shipscat intelligence wasn't needed, just a loving friend smart enough to understand what not to do around someone sick or in pain.

There were still far more Lacu'un who urgently craved the boon of a cat than there were cats to fill the need. Thus far, none of SKitty's female offspring had carried that rare gene for fertility—when one did, that one would go back to BioTech, to be treated like the precious object she was, pampered and amused, asked to breed only so often as *she* chose. There was always a trade-off in any gengineering effort; lack of fertility was a small price to pay in a species as notoriously prolific as cats.

Meanwhile, the proud parents were in the last stages of educating their current offspring. There was a pile of the dead vermin just in front of Vena's desk; every so often, one of the half-grown kittens would bring another to add to the pile, then sit politely and wait for his parents to approve. Sometimes, when the pest was particularly large, SCat would descend from Dick's lap with immense dignity, inspect the kill, and bestow a rough lick by way of special reward.

Dick couldn't keep track of how many pests each of the kittens had destroyed, but from the size of the pile so far, the parents had reason to be proud of their offspring.

The kittens certainly inherited their parents' telepathic skills as well as their hunting skills, for just as it occurred to Dick that it was about time for them to be fed, they scampered in from all available doorways. In a moment, they were neatly lined up, eight identical pairs of yellow eyes staring avidly from eight little black faces beneath sixteen enormous ears. At this age, they seemed to consist mainly of eyes, ears, paws and tails.

The Lacu'un servant whose proud duty it was to feed the weanlings arrived with a bowl heaping with their imported food. She was clothed in the simple, silky draped tunic in the deep gold of the royal household. The frilled crest running from the back of her neck to just above her eye-ridge stood totally erect and was flushed to a deep salmon-color with pleasure and pride. She started to put the bowl on the floor, and the kittens leapt to their feet and ran for the food—

But suddenly SCat sprang from Dick's lap, every hair on end, spitting and yowling. He landed at the startled servant's feet and did a complete flip over, so that he faced his kittens. As they skidded on the slick stone, he growled and batted at them, sending them flying.

"*SCat!*" Vena shouted, as she jumped to her feet, horrified and angry. "What are you doing? Bad cat!"

"No he's not!" Dick replied, making a leap of his own for the food bowl and jerking it from the frightened servant's hands. He had already heard SKitty's frantic mental screech of :*Bad food!*: as she followed her mate off Dick's shoulders to keep the kittens from the deadly bowl.

"The food's poisoned," Dick added, sniffing the puffy brown nodules suspiciously, as the servant backed away, the slits in her golden-brown eyes so wide he could scarcely see the iris. "SCat must have scented it—that's probably one of the things Patrol cats are trained in. *I* can't tell the difference, but—" as SKitty held the kittens at bay, he held the bowl down to SCat, who took a delicate sniff and backed away, growling. "See?"

Vena's expression darkened, and she turned to the servant. "The food has been poisoned," she said flatly. "Who had access to it?" They both knew that Shivari, the servant, was trustworthy; she would sooner have thrown herself between the kittens and a ravening monster than see any hurt come to them. She proved that now by her behavior; her crest-frill flattened, she turned bright yellow—the Lacu'un equivalent of turning pale—and replied instantly.

"I do not know—I got the bowl from the kitchen—"

She grabbed Vena's hand and the two of them ran off, with Dick closely behind, still carrying the bowl. When they arrived at the kitchen, Vena and Shivari cornered all the staff while Dick blocked the exit. He had a fair grasp of Lacu'un by now, but Vena and Shivari were talking much too fast for him to get more than two words in four.

Soon enough, though, Vena turned away with anger and dissatisfaction on her face, while Shivari began a blistering harangue worthy of Captain Singh. "There was a new servant that no one recognized on staff this morning," Vena said in disgust. "Obviously they were smart enough to keep him away from the food meant for people, but no one thought anything of letting him open up the cat food into a bowl."

"Well, they know better now," Dick replied grimly. "I'll put the Embassy on alert—and give me that—" Vena took the bowl from him. "I'll have the Marines run it through an analyzer."

Embassy guards by long tradition were called "Marines," although they were merely another branch of the Patrol. Dick readily surrendered the poisoned food to Vena, knowing that if SCat could smell a poison, the forensic analyzer every Embassy possessed—just in case—would easily be able to find it. Relations with the Lacu'un were important enough that Vena had gone from being merely a trade advisor and titular Consul to a full-scale Ambassador, with the attendant staff and amenities. It was that promotion that had persuaded her to remain here instead of returning to her former position in the Scouts.

Dick himself went to the storage vault that held the imported cat-food, got a highly-compressed cube out, and opened it over a freshly washed bowl. The stuff puffed up to ten times its compressed size once it came into contact with air and humidity; it would be impossible to tamper with the packages without a resulting "explosion" of food. The entire feline family flowed into the kitchen as soon as his fingers touched the package; the kittens swarmed around his legs, mewling piteously, but he offered the bowl for SCat's inspection before allowing them to engulf it.

His mind buzzed with questions, but two were uppermost—who would have tried to poison the kittens, and why?

◆ ◆ ◆

SCat and SKitty herded their kittens along like a pair of attentive sheepdogs when they'd finished eating, following behind Dick as he left the palace, heading for the Embassy. The Marine at the entrance gave him a brisk nod of recognition, saving her grin for the moving black-furred flock behind him.

A second Marine at a desk just inside, skilled in the Lacu'un tongue, served double-duty as a receptionist. "The Ambassador is expecting you, sir," he said. "She left orders for you to go straight in."

Dick led his parade past the desk—a desk of cast marble reinforced with plastile, which would serve very nicely as a blast-and-projectile-proof bunker at need. The door to Vena's office (a cleverly concealed blast-door) was slightly ajar; it sensed his approach and opened fully for him after a retinal scan.

"Have you ever wondered why our peaceful hosts happen to field a battle-ready army?" Vena asked him, without even a preliminary greeting.

"Ah, no, I hadn't—but now that you mention it, it does seem odd." Dick took a seat, cats pooling around his ankles, as Vena tossed her compuslate aside.

"Our hosts aren't the sole representatives of their race on this dirtball," Vena replied, with no expression that Dick could see. "And *now* they finally get around to telling me this. It seems that there is another nation entirely on this continent—we thought that it was just another fief of the Lacu'ara, and they never disabused us of that impression."

"Let me guess—the other side doesn't like Terrans?" Dick hazarded.

"I wish it was that simple. Unfortunately, the other side worships the *kreshta* as children of their prime deity." Vena couldn't quite repress a snarl. "Kill one, and you've got a holy war on your hands—we've been slaughtering hundreds for better than two years. The attempt on the Octet was just the opening salvo for us heretics. The Chief Minister has been here, telling me all about it and falling all over himself in apology. Here—" She pulled a micro reader out of a drawer in her desk and tossed it to him. "My head of security advises that you commit this to memory."

"What is it?" Dick asked, thumbing it on, and seeing (with some puzzlement) the line drawing of a nude Lacu'un appear on the plate.

"How to kill or disable a Lacu'un in five easy lessons, as written by the Patrol Marines." Her face had gone back to that deadpan expression again. "Lieutenant Reynard thinks you might need it."

The prickling of claws set carefully into his clothing alerted him that one of the cats was swarming up to drape itself over his shoulders, but somewhat to his surprise, it wasn't SKitty, it was SCat. The tom peered at the screen in his hand with every evidence of fascinated concentration, too.

He was Patrol, after all. . . . was his second thought, after the initial surprise. And on the heels of that thought, he decided to hold the reader up so that SCat could use the touch screen too.

It was easier to disable a Lacu'un than to kill one, at least in hand to hand combat. Their throats were armored with bone plates, their heads with amazingly thick skulls. But there were vulnerable major nerve-points at all joints; concentrated pinpoint pressure would paralyze everything from the joint down when applied there. When Dick figured he had the scanty contents by heart, he tossed the reader back to Vena, though what he was supposed to do with the information was beyond him at the moment. He wasn't exactly trained in anything but the most basic of self-defense—that was more in Erica Makumba's line, and she was several light-years away at the moment.

"The Lacu'un Army has been alerted, the Palace has been put under tight security, and the caretakers of the other cats have been warned about the poisoning attempt. However, the mysterious kitchen-helper got clean away, so we can assume he'll make another attempt. My advisors and I would like to take him alive if we can—we've got some plans that may abort this mess before it gets worse than it already is."

SCat's deep-voiced growl showed what he thought of that idea, and Vena lowered her smoldering, dark eyes from Dick's to the tom's, and smiled grimly.

"I'd like to put a Marine guard on the cats—but I know that's hardly possible," Vena continued, as SCat and SKitty voiced identical snorts of disdain. "But let's walk back over to the Palace and talk about what we *can* do on the way."

SCat looked up at him and made an odd noise, easy enough to interpret. "SCat thinks he and SKitty can guard the kittens well enough," Dick replied, as Vena waved him through the door, a torrent of cats washing around his ankles.

"I'm sure he does," Vena retorted. "But let's remember that he's only a cat, however much his genes have been tweaked. I hardly think he's capable of understanding the danger of the current situation."

"He isn't just a cat, he was a *Patrol* cat," Dick pointed out, but Vena just shook her head at that.

"Dick, we don't even know exactly what we're into— all we know is that there was an attempt to poison the cats by an assassin that got away. We don't know if it was a lone fanatic, someone sent by our hosts' enemies, if there's only one or more than one—" She sighed as they reached the street. "We're doing all the intelligence gathering we can, but it's difficult to manage when you don't look anything like the dominant species on the planet."

The street was empty, which was fairly normal at this time of day when most Lacu'un were inside at their evening meal. The sky of this world seemed a bit greenish to him, but he'd gotten used to it—today, there were some clouds that might mean rain. Or might not, he didn't know very much about planet-side weather.

SCat's squall was all the warning Dick got to throw himself out of the way as something dark and fast whizzed through the place where he'd been standing. SKitty and the kittens fairly flew back to the safety of the Embassy, SCat whisked out of sight altogether; a larger, cloaked shape sprang from the shadows of a doorway, and before Dick managed to get halfway to his feet, the grey-cloaked, pale-skinned Lacu'un seized Vena and enveloped her, holding a knife to her throat.

"Be still, blasphemous she-demon!" it grated, holding both Vena's arms pinned behind her back in a way that had to be excruciatingly painful. She grimaced but said nothing. "And you, father of demons, be still also!" it snapped at Dick. "I am the righteous hand of Kresh'kali, the all-devouring, the purifier! I am the bringer of cleansing, the anointed of God! In His name, and by His mercy, I give you this choice—remove yourselves from our soil, take yourselves back into the sky forever, or you will die, first you and your she-demon and your god killing pests, then all of those who brought you." Its voice rose, taking on the tones of a hellfire-and-brimstone preacher. "Kresh'kali is the One, the true God, whose word is the only law, and whose minions cleanse the world in His image; His will shall not be flouted, and His servants not denied—"

It sounded like a well-rehearsed speech, and probably would have gone on for some time had it not been interrupted by the speaker's own scream of agony.

And small wonder, for SCat had crept up unseen even by Dick, until the instant he leapt for the assassin's knife-wielding wrist, and fastened his teeth unerringly into those sensitive nerves at the joining of hand and wrist.

The knife clattered to the street, Vena twisted away, and Dick charged, all at the same moment; his shoulder hit the assassin and they both went down on the hard stone paving. But not in a disorderly heap, no; by the time the Marines came piling out of the Embassy, alerted by the frantic herd of cats, Dick had the miscreant face-down on the ground with both arms paralyzed from the shoulders down. And, miracle of miracles, this time *he* wasn't the one battered and bruised—in fact, he was intact beyond a few scrapes!

He wasn't taking any chances though; he waited until the Marines had all four limbs of the assassin in stasis-cuffs before he got off his captive and surrendered him.

"Do we turn him over to the locals?" one of the Marines asked Vena diffidently.

"Not a chance," she growled. "Hustle him into the Embassy before anyone asks any questions."

"What are you going to do?" Dick asked *sotto voce*, following the Marines and their cursing burden.

"I told you, we've got some ideas—and a couple of experiments I'd rather try on this dirt-bag rather than any Lacu'un volunteers," was all she said, leaving him singularly unsatisfied. All he could be certain of was that she didn't plan to execute the assassin out-of-hand. "We caught him, and we've got a chance to try those ideas out."

He continued to follow, and was not prevented, as Vena led the way up the stairs to the Embassy med-lab. The entire entourage of cats followed, and Vena not only *let* them, she waved them all inside before shutting and locking the door. The prisoner was strapped into a dental chair and gagged, which at least put an end to the curses, though not to the glares he cast at them.

But Vena dropped down onto one knee and looked into SKitty's eyes. "I know you're a telepath, SKitty," she said, in Terran. "Can you project to anyone but Dick? Could you project into our prisoner's mind? Put your voice in his head?"

SKitty turned her head to look up at Dick. :*Walls,*: she complained. :*Dick has no walls for SKitty.*:

"She says he's got barriers," Dick interpreted. "I

understand that most nontelepathic people have and it's just an accident that the two of us are compatible."

"I may be able to change that," Vena replied, with a tight smile, as she got to her feet. "SKitty, I'm going to do some things to this prisoner, and I want you to tell me when the barriers are gone." She turned to a cabinet and unlocked it; inside were hypospray vials, and she selected one. "We've been cooperating with the Lacu'un Healers; putting together drugs we've been developing for the Lacu'un," she continued, "There are hypnotics that are proven to lower telepathic barriers in humans, and I have a few that may do the same for the Lacu'un. If they don't kill him, that is." She raised an eyebrow at Dick. "You can see why we didn't want to test them even on volunteers."

"But if the drugs kill him—" Dick gulped.

"Then we save the Lacu'ara the cost of an execution, and we apologize that the prisoner expired from fear," she replied smoothly. Dick gulped again; this was a ruthless side of Vena he'd had no notion existed!

She placed the first hypo against the side of the prisoner's neck; the device hissed as it discharged its contents, and the prisoner's eyes widened with fear.

An hour later, there were only two vials left in the cabinet; Vena had administered all the rest, and their antidotes, with sublime disregard for the strain this was probably putting on the prisoner's body. The effects of each had been duly noted, but none of them produced the desired effect of lowering the barriers nontelepaths had against telepathic intrusion.

Vena picked up the first of the last two, and sighed. "If one of these doesn't work, I'll have to make a decision about giving him to the locals," she said with what sounded like disappointment. "I'd really rather not do that."

Dick didn't ask why, but one of the two Marines in the room with them must have seen the question in his eyes. "If the Ambassador turns this fellow over to them, they'll execute him, and that might be enough to send cold war hostilities into a real blaze," the young lieutenant muttered as Vena administered the hypo. "And the word from the Palace is that the other side is as advanced in atomic physics as our lot is. In other words, these are religious fanatics with a nuclear arsenal."

Dick winced; the Terrans would be safe enough in a nuclear exchange, and so would the bulk of city-dwellers, for the Lacu'un had mastered force-shield technology. But in a nuclear exchange there were always accidents and as yet it wasn't possible to encase anything bigger than a city in a shield; he'd seen enough blasted lands never to wish a nuc-war on anyone, and *certainly* not on the decent folk here.

SKitty watched the prisoner as she would a mouse; his eyes unfocused when the drug took hold, and *this* time, she meowed with pleasure. It didn't take Dick's translation for Vena to know that the prisoner's telepathic barriers to SKitty's probing thoughts were gone.

"Excellent!" she exclaimed with relief. "All right, little one—we're going to leave the room until you send one of the kittens to come get us. Let him think we've lost interest in him for the moment, *then* get into his head and convince him that *he* is a very, very bad kitten and *you* are his mother and you're going to punish him unless he says he's sorry and he won't do it again. Make him think that you are so angry that you might kill him if he can't understand how bad he's been. In fact, any of you cats that can get into his head should do that. Then make him promise that he'll always obey everything you tell him to, and don't let up the pressure until he does."

SKitty looked at Vena as if she thought the human had gone crazy, then sighed. :*Stupid,*: she told Dick privately. :*But okay. I do.*:

Dick was as baffled as SKitty was, as he followed Vena out into the hall, leaving the cats with the prisoner. "Just what is that going to accomplish?" he demanded.

She chuckled. "I rather doubt he's ever heard anyone speak in his mind before," she pointed out. "Not even his god."

Now Dick saw exactly what she'd had in mind—and stifled his bark of laughter. "He's going to be certain SKitty's more powerful than *his* god if she can do that—and if she treats him like a naughty child rather than an enemy to be destroyed—"

"Exactly," Vena said with satisfaction. "This is what Lieutenant Reynard wanted me to try, though we thought we'd have to add halucinogens and a VR headset, rather than getting right directly into his head. My problem was finding a way to tell her to act like an all-powerful, rebuking god in a way she'd understand. In the drugged state he's in now, he'll accept whatever happens as the truth."

"So *he* won't threaten the cats anymore—but then what?" Dick asked.

"According to Reynard, the worst that will happen is that he'll be convinced that this new god of his enemies is a lot more powerful and real than his own, and that's the story he'll take back home."

"And the best?" Dick inquired.

She shrugged. "He converts."

"Just what will that accomplish?"

She paused, and licked her lips unconsciously. "We ran some simulations, based on what we've learned about Lacu'un psychology and projecting the rest from history. Historically, the most fanatic followers of a new religion are the converts who were just as fanatical in their former religion. In either case, imagine the reaction when he returns home, which he will, and miraculously, because we'll take a stealthed flitter and drop him over the border while he's drugged and unconscious. He'll probably figure out that we brought him, but there won't be any sign of how. Imagine what his superiors will think?"

The Marine lieutenant standing diffidently at her

elbow cleared his throat. "Actually, you don't have to guess," he said respectfully. "As the Ambassador mentioned, we've been running a psych-profiles for possible contingencies, and they agree with her educated assessment. No matter what, the fanatics will be too frightened of the power of this new 'god' to hazard either a war or another assassination attempt. And if we send back a convert—there's a seventy-four point three percent chance he'll end up starting his own crusade, or even a holy war *within* their culture. No matter what, they cease to be a problem."

"Now *that*," Dick replied with feeling, "Is really a better mousetrap!"

This is a very old story, dating back at least ten years. Published in a short-lived magazine called American Fantasy, *I doubt that many people had a chance to see it. It was old enough that I felt it needed a bit of rewriting, so although the general plot is the same, it's undergone a pretty extensive change.*

The Last of the Season

They said on TV that her name was Molly, but Jim already knew that. They also said that she was eight years old, but she didn't look eight, more like six; didn't look old enough to be in school, even. She didn't look anything like the picture they'd put up on the screen, either. The picture was at least a year old, and done by some cut-rate outfit for her school. Her hair was shorter, her face rounder, her expression so stiff she looked like a kid-dummy. There was nothing like the lively spark in her eyes, or the naughty smile she'd worn this afternoon. The kid in the picture was so clean she squeaked; where was the sticky popsicle residue on her face and hands, the dirt-smudges on her knees?

Jim lost interest as soon as the station cut away to the national news, and turned the set off.

The remote-controlled TV was the one luxury in his beige box of an apartment. His carpet was the cheapest possible brown industrial crap, the curtains on the picture-window a drab, stiff, cheap polyester stuff, backed with even cheaper vinyl that was seamed with cracks after less than a year. He had one chair (Salvation Army, brown corduroy), one lamp (imitation brass, from K-mart), one vinyl sofa (bright orange, St. Vincent de Paul) that was hard and uncomfortable, and one coffee-table (imitation Spanish, Goodwill) where the fancy color TV sat, like a king on a peasant's crude bench.

In the bedroom, just beyond the closed door, was his bedroom, no better furnished than the living-room. He stored his clothing in odd chests of folded cardboard, with a clamp-lamp attached to the cardboard table by the king-sized bed. Like the TV, the bed was top-of-the-line, with a satin bedspread. On that bed, sprawled over the royal blue satin, was Molly.

Jim rose, slowly and silently, and tiptoed across the carpet to the bedroom door, cracking it open just an inch or so, peering inside. She looked like a Norman Rockwell picture, lying on her side, so pale against the dark, vivid fabric, her red corduroy jumper rumpled across her stomach where she clutched her teddy bear with one arm. She was still out of it, sleeping off the little knock on the skull he'd given her. Either that, or she was still under the whiff of ether that had followed. When he was close to her, he could still smell the banana-scent of her popsicle, and see a sticky trace of syrup around her lips. The light from the door caught in the eyes of her teddy bear, and made them shine with a feral, red gleam.

She'd been easy, easy—so trusting, especially after all the contact he'd had with her for the past three weeks. He'd had his eye on two or three of the kids at Kennedy Grade School, but she'd been the one he'd really wanted; like the big TV, she was top-of-the-line, and any of the others would have been a disappointment. She was perfect, prime material, best of the season. Those big, chocolate-brown eyes, the golden-brown hair cut in a sweet page-boy, the round dolly-face—she couldn't have been any better.

He savored the moment, watching her at a distance, greedily studying her at his leisure, knowing that he had her all to himself and no one could interfere.

She'd been one of the last kids to leave the school on this warm, golden afternoon—the rest had scattered on down the streets, chasing the fallen leaves by the time she came out. He'd been loitering, waiting to see if he'd missed her, if someone had picked her up after school, or if she'd had a dentist appointment or something—but no one would ever give a second look at the ice-cream man loitering outside a grade school. He looked like what everybody expected, a man obviously trying to squeeze every last dime out of the rug-rats that he could.

The pattern while he'd had this area staked out was that Molly only had ice-cream money about a third of the time. He'd set her up so carefully—if she came out of the school alone, and started to pass the truck with a wistful look in her eyes, he'd made a big production out of looking around for other kids, then signalling her to come over. The first couple of times, she'd shaken her head and run off, but after she'd bought cones from him a time or two, *he* wasn't a stranger, and to her mind, was no longer in the catagory of people she shouldn't talk to. Then she responded, and he had given her a broken popsicle in her favorite flavor of banana. "Do me a favor and eat this, all right?" he'd said, in his kindest voice. "I can't sell a broken popsicle, and I'd hate for it to go to waste." Then he'd lowered his voice to a whisper and bent over her. "But don't tell the other kids, okay? Let's just keep it a secret."

She nodded, gleefully, and ran off. After that he had no trouble getting her to come over to the truck; after all, why should she be afraid of the friend who gave her ice cream for free, and only asked that she keep it a secret?

Today she'd had money, though, and from the sly gleam in her eyes he would bet she'd filched it from her momma's purse this morning. He'd laid out choices for her like a servant laying out feast-choices for a princess, and she'd sparkled at him, loving the attention as much as the treat.

She'd dawdled over her choice, her teddy bear clutched under one arm, a toy so much a part of her that it could have been another limb. That indecision bought time for the other kids to clear out of the way, and all the teachers to get to their cars and putt out of the parking-lot. His play-acting paid off handsomely, especially after he'd nodded at the truck and winked. She'd wolfed down her cone, and he gave her another broken popsicle; she lingered on, sucking on the yellow ice in a way that made his groin tighten with anticipation. He'd asked her ingenuous questions about her school and her teacher, and she chattered amiably with him between slurps.

Then she'd turned to go at the perfect moment, with not a child, a car, or a teacher in sight. He reached for the sock full of sand inside the freezer-door, and in one, smooth move, gave her a little tap in just the right place.

He caught her before she hit the ground. Then it was into the special side of the ice-cream truck with her; the side not hooked up to the freezer-unit, with ventilation holes bored through the walls in places where no one would find them. He gave her a whiff of ether on a rag, just in case, to make sure she stayed under, then he slid her limp body into the cardboard carton he kept on that side, just in case somebody wanted to look inside. He closed and latched the door, and was back in the driver's seat before two minutes were up, with still no sign of man nor beast. Luck, luck, all the way.

Luck, or pure genius. He couldn't lose; he was invulnerable.

Funny how she'd kept a grip on that toy, though. But that was luck, too; if she'd left it there—

Well, he might have forgotten she'd had it. Then somebody would have found it, and someone might have remembered her standing at the ice-cream truck with it beside her.

But it had all gone smoothly, perfectly planned, perfectly executed, ending with a drive through the warm September afternoon, bells tinkling slightly out-of-tune, no different from any other ice-cream man out for the last scores of the season. He'd felt supremely calm and in control of everything the moment he was in his seat; no one would ever suspect him, he'd been a fixture since the beginning of school. Who ever *sees* the ice-cream man? He was as much a part of the landscape as the fire-hydrant he generally stopped beside.

They'd ask the kids of course, now that Molly was officially missing—and they'd say the same stupid thing they always did. "Did you see any strangers?" they'd ask. "Any strange cars hanging around? Anyone you didn't recognize?"

Stupid; they were just stupid. *He* was the smart one. The kids would answer just like they always did, they'd say no, they hadn't seen any strangers.

No, *he* wasn't a stranger, he was the ice-cream man. The kids saw him today, and they'd see him tomorrow, he'd make sure of that. He'd be on his route for the next week at least, unless there was a cold snap. He knew how cops thought, and if he disappeared, they might look for him. No way was he going to break his pattern. Eventually the cops would question him—not tomorrow, but probably the day after that. He'd tell them he *had* seen the little girl, that she'd bought a cone from him. He'd cover his tracks there, since the other kids would probably remember that she'd been at the truck. But he'd shrug helplessly, and say that she hadn't been on the street when he drove off. He'd keep strictly to the truth, just not all the truth.

Now Molly was all his, and no one would take her away from him until he was done with her.

He drove home, stopping to sell cones when kids flagged him down, taking his time. It wouldn't do to break his pattern. He took out the box that held Molly and brought it upstairs, then made two more trips, for the leftover frozen treats, all in boxes just like the one that held Molly. The neighbors were used to this; it was another part of his routine. He was the invisible man; old Jim always brings in the leftovers and puts 'em in his freezer overnight, it's cheaper than running the truck-freezer overnight.

He knew what they said about him. That Jim was a good guy—kept to himself mostly, but when it was really hot or he had too much left over to fit in his freezer, he'd pass out freebies. A free ice-cream bar was appreciated in this neighborhood, where there wasn't a lot of money to spare for treats. Yeah, Jim was real quiet, but okay, never gave any trouble to anybody.

If the cops went so far as to look into his background, they wouldn't find anything. He ran a freelance ice-cream route in the summer and took odd jobs in the winter; there was no record of his ever getting into trouble.

Of course there was no record. He was smart. Nobody had ever caught him, not when he set fires as a kid, not when he prowled the back alleys looking for stray dogs and cats, and not later, when he went on to the targets he really wanted. He was careful. When he first started on kids, he picked the ones nobody would miss. And he kept up with the literature; he knew everything the cops would look for.

Jim's apartment was a corner-unit, under the roof. There was nobody above him, the old man under him was stone-deaf, the guy on one side was a stoner on the night-shift, and the couple on the other side kept their music blasting so loud it was a wonder that *they* weren't deaf. Nobody would ever hear a thing.

Meanwhile, Jim waited, as darkness fell outside, for Molly to sleep off her ether and her bump; it wasn't any fun for him when his trophies were out of it. Jim liked them awake; he liked to see their eyes when they realized that no one was coming to rescue them.

He changed into a pair of old jeans and a tee-shirt in the living-room, hanging his white uniform in the closet, then looked in on her again.

She still had a hold on that teddy bear. It was a really unusual toy; it was one of the many things that had marked her when he'd first looked for targets. Jim was really glad she'd kept such a tight grip on it; it was so different that there was little doubt it would have been spotted as hers if she'd dropped it. The plush was a thick, black fur, extremely realistic; in fact, he wasn't entirely certain that it *was* fake fur. There was no sign of the wear that kids usually put on that kind of beloved plaything. The mouth was half-open, lined with red felt, with white felt teeth and a red felt tongue. Instead of a ribbon bow, this bear had a real leather collar with an odd tag hanging from it; pottery or glass, maybe, or enameled metal, it certainly wasn't plastic. There was a faint, raised pattern on the back, and the word "Tedi" on the front in a childishly printed scrawl. The eyes were oddest of all—whoever had made this toy must have used the same eyes that taxidermists used; they looked real, alive.

It was going to prove a little bit of problem dealing with that bear, after. He was so careful not to leave any fiber or hair evidence; he always washed them when he was through with them, dressing them in fancy party clothing he took straight out of the packages, then wrapping them in plastic once they were dressed, to keep from contaminating them. Once he was through with her and dressed her in that frilly blue party-dress he'd bought, he'd cut up her old clothing into tiny pieces and flush them down the john, a few at a time, to keep from clogging the line. That could be fatal.

He'd do the part with the knife in the bathtub, of course, so there wouldn't be any bloodstains. He knew exactly how to get blood-evidence scrubbed out of the bathroom, what chemicals to use and everything. They'd have to swab out the pipes to find anything.

But the bear was a problem. He'd have to figure out a smart way to get rid of it, because it was bound to collect all kinds of evidence.

Maybe give it to a kid? Maybe not; there was a chance the kid would remember him. By now it had probably collected fibers. . . .

He had it; the Salvation Army box, the one on Colby, all the way across town. They'd let that thing get stuffed full before they ever emptied it, and by then the bear would have collected so much fiber and hair they'd never get it all sorted out. Then he could take her to MacArthur Park; it was far enough away from the collection box. He'd leave her there like he always did, propped up on a bench like an oversized doll, a bench off in an out-of-the-way spot. He'd used MacArthur Park before, but not recently, and at this time of year it might be days before anyone found her.

But the bear—better get it away from her now, before it collected something more than hair. For one thing, it would be harder to handle her if she kept clinging to it. Something about those eyes bothered him, too, and he wasn't in a mood to be bothered.

He cracked the door open, slipped inside, pried the bear out of her loose grip. He threw it into the bathroom, but Molly didn't stir; he was vaguely disappointed. He'd hoped she show *some* sign of coming around when he took the toy.

Well, he had all night, all weekend, as long as she lasted. He'd have to make the most of this one; she was the last of the season.

Might as well get the stuff out.

He went into the kitchenette and dragged out the plastic step-stool. Standing it in the closet in the livingroom, he opened up the hatch into the crawl-space. It wasn't tall enough for him to see what was up there, but what he wanted was right by the hatch anyway. He felt across the fiberglass battings; the paper over the insulation crackled under his fingers. He groped until his hand encountered the cardboard box he'd stored up there. Getting both hands around it, straining on tiptoe to do so, he lowered it carfully down through the hatch. He had to bring it through the opening catty-cornered to make it fit. It wasn't heavy, but it was an awkward shape.

He carried it to the center of the living-room and placed it on the carpet, kneeling beside it with his stomach tight with anticipation. Slowly, with movements ritualized over time, he undid the twine holding it closed, just so. He coiled up the twine and laid it to the side, exactly five inches from the side of the box. He reached for the lid.

But as he started to open it, he thought he heard a faint sound, as if something moved in the bedroom. Was Molly finally awake?

He got to his feet, and moved softly to the door. But when he applied his eye to the crack, he was disappointed to see that she hadn't moved at all. She lay exactly as he'd left her, head pillowed on one arm, hair scattered across his pillow, lips pursed, breathing softly but regularly. Her red corduroy jumper was still in the same folds it had been when he'd put her down on the bed, rucked up over her hip so that her little pink panties showed the tiniest bit.

Then he saw the bear.

It was back right where it had been before, sitting up in the curve of her stomach. Looking at him.

He shook his head, frowning. Of course it wasn't looking at him, it was his imagination; it was just a toy. He must have been so wrapped up in anticipation that he'd flaked—and *hadn't* thrown it in the bathroom as he'd intended, or else he'd absent-mindedly put it back on the bed.

Easily fixed. He took the few steps into the room,

grabbed the bear by one ear, and threw it into the bedroom closet, closing the door on it. Molly didn't stir, and he retired to the living room and his treasure chest.

On the top layer of the box lay a tangle of leather and rubber. He sorted out the straps carefully, laying out all the restraints in their proper order, with the rubber ball for her mouth and the gag to hold it in there first in line. That was one of the most important parts. Whatever sound got past the gag wouldn't get past the neighbors' various deficiencies.

Something was definitely moving in the next room. He heard the closet door opening, then the sounds of shuffling.

He sprinted to the door—

Only to see that Molly was lying in exactly the same position, and the bear was with her.

He shook his head. Damn! He couldn't be going crazy—

Then he chuckled at a sudden memory. The third kid he'd done had pulled something like this—the kid was a sleepwalker, with a knack for lying back down in precisely the same position as before, and it wasn't until he'd stayed in the bedroom instead of going through his collection that he'd proved it to himself. Molly had obviously missed her bear, gotten up, searched blindly for her toy, found it, then lay back down again. Yeah, come to think of it, her jumper was a bit higher on her hip, and she was more on her back than her side, now.

But that bear had to go.

He marched in, grabbed the bear again, and looked around. Now where?

The bathroom, the cabinet under the sink. There was nothing in there but a pair of dead roaches, and it had a child-proof latch on it.

The eyes flashed at him as he flipped on the bathroom light and whipped the cabinet open. For one moment he almost thought the eyes glared at him with a red light of their own before he closed the door on the thing and turned the lock with a satisfying click.

Back to the box.

The next layer was his pictures. They weren't of any of his kids; he wasn't that stupid. Nothing in this box would ever connect him with the guy they were calling the "Sunday-school killer" because he left them dressed in Sunday best, clean and shining, in places like parks and beaches, looking as if they'd just come from church.

But the pictures were the best the Internet had to offer, and a lot of these kids looked like the ones he'd had. Pretty kids, real pretty.

He took them out in the proper order, starting with the simple ones, letting the excitement build in his groin as he savored each one. First, the nudes—ten of them, he knew them all by heart. Then the nudes with the kids "playing" together, culled from the "My Little Fishie" newsletter of a nut-case religious cult that believed in kid-sex.

Then the good ones.

Halfway through, he slipped his hand into his pants without taking his eyes off the pictures.

This was going to be a good one. Molly looked just like the kid in the best of his pictures. She was going to be perfect; the last of the season, the best of the season.

He was pretty well occupied as he got to the last set, though he noted absently that it sounded as if Molly was up and moving around again. This was the bondage-and-snuff set, very hard to get, and the only reason he had them at all was because he'd stolen them from a storage-locker. He wouldn't have taken the risk of getting them personally, but they'd given him some of his best ideas.

Molly must be awake by now. But this wasn't to be hurried—there wouldn't be any Mollys or Jeffreys until next year, next spring, summer, and fall. He had to make this one last.

He savored the emotions in the pictured eyes as he would savor Molly's fear; savored their pleading expressions, their helplessness. Such pretty little things, like her, like all his kids.

They wanted it, anybody knew that. Freud said so—that had been in that psychology course he took by correspondence when he was trying to figure himself out. Look at the way kids played "doctor" the minute you turned your back on them. That religious cult had it right; kids wanted it, needed it, and the only thing getting in the way was the way a bunch of repressed old men felt about it.

He'd show her what it was she wanted, show her good. He'd make it last, take it slow. Then, once she was all his and would do anything he said, he'd make sure nobody else would ever have her again. He'd keep her his, forever. Not even her parents would have her the way he did.

Under the last layer of pictures was the knife, the beautiful, shining filleting knife, the best made. Absolutely stainless, rustproof, with a pristine black handle. He laid it reverently beside the leather straps, then zipped up his pants and rose to his feet.

No doubt, she was shuffling around on the other side of the door, moving uncertainly back and forth. She should be just dazed enough that he'd get her gagged before she knew enough to scream.

He paused a moment to order his thoughts and his face before putting his hand on the doorknob. Next to the moment when the kid lay trussed-up under him, this was the best moment.

He flung the door wide open. "*Hel*-lo, Mo—"

That was as far as he got.

The screams brought the neighbors to break down the door. There were two sets of screams; his, and those of a terrified little girl pounding on the closet door.

A dozen of them gathered in the hall before they got

up the courage to break in, and by then Jim wasn't screaming anymore. What they found in the living-room made the first inside run back out the way they had come.

One managed to get as far as the bedroom to release the child, a pale young woman who lived at the other end of the floor, whose maternal instincts over-rode her stomach long enough to rescue the weeping child.

Molly fell out of the closet into her arms, sobbing with terror. The young woman recognized her from news; how could she not? Her picture had been everywhere.

Meanwhile one of the others who had fled the whimpering thing on the living-room floor got to a phone and called the cops.

The young woman closed the bedroom door on the horror in the next room, took the hysterical, shivering child into her arms, and waited for help to arrive, absently wondering at her own, hitherto unsuspected courage.

While they were waiting, the thing on the floor mewled, gasped, and died.

Although the young woman hadn't known what to make of the tangle of leather she'd briefly glimpsed on the carpet, the homicide detective knew exactly what it meant. He owed a candle to Saint Jude for the solving of his most hopeless case and another to the Virgin for saving *this* child before anything had happened to her.

And a third to whatever saint had seen to it that there would be no need for a trial.

"You say there was no sign of anything or anyone else?" he asked the young woman. She'd already told him that she was a librarian—that was shortly after she'd taken advantage of their arrival to close herself into the bathroom and throw up. He almost took her to task for possibly destroying evidence, but what was the point? This was one murder he didn't really want to solve.

She was sitting in the only chair in the living-room, carefully not looking at the outline on the carpet, or the blood-spattered mess of pictures and leather straps a little distance from her feet. He'd asked the same question at least a dozen times already.

"Nothing, no one." She shook her head. "There's no back door, just the hatches to the crawl-space, in each closet."

He looked where she pointed, at the open closet door with the kitchen stool still inside it. He walked over to the closet and craned his head around sideways, peering upward.

"Not too big, but a skinny guy could get up there," he said, half to himself. "Is that attic divided at all?"

"No, it runs all along the top floor; I never put anything up there because anybody could get into it from any other apartment." She shivered. "And I put locks on all my hatches. Now I'm glad I did. Once a year they fumigate, so they need the hatches to get exhaust fans up there."

"A skinny guy, one real good with a knife—maybe a 'Nam Vet. A SEAL, a Green Beret—" he was talking mostly to himself. "It might not have been a knife; maybe claws, like in the karate rags. Ninja claws. That could be what he used—"

He paced back to the center of the living room. The librarian rubbed her hands along her arms, watching him out of sick blue eyes.

"Okay, he knows what this sicko is up to—maybe he *just* now found out, doesn't want to call the cops for whatever reason. He comes down into the bedroom, locks the kid in the closet to keep her safe—"

"She told me that a bear locked her into the closet," the woman interrupted.

The detective laughed. "Lady, that kid has a knot the size of a baseball on her skull; she could have seen Luke

Skywalker lock her in that closet!" He went back to his deductions. "Okay, he locks the kid in, then makes enough noise so joy-boy thinks she finally woke up. Then when the door opens—yeah. It'll fly." He nodded. "Then he gets back out by this hatch." He sighed, regretful that he wouldn't ever get a chance to thank this guy. "Won't be any fingerprints; guy like this would be too smart to leave any."

He stared at the outline on the blood-soaked carpet pensively. The librarian shuddered.

"Look, officer," she said, asserting herself, "If you don't need me anymore—"

"Hey, Pete—" the detective's partner poked his head in through the door. "The kid's parents are here. The kid wants her teddy—she's raising a real howl about it, and the docs at the hospital don't want to sedate her if they don't have to."

"Shit, the kid misses being a statistic by a couple of minutes, and all she can think about is her toy!" He shook his head, and refocused on the librarian. "Go ahead, miss. I don't think you can tell us anything more. You might want to check into the hospital yourself, get checked over for shock. Either that, or pour yourself a stiff one. Call in sick tomorrow."

He smiled, suddenly realizing that she was pretty, in a wilted sort of way—and after what she'd just been through, no wonder she was wilted.

"That was what I had in mind already, Detective," she replied, and made good her escape before he changed his mind.

"Pete, her folks say she won't be able to sleep without it," his partner persisted.

"Yeah, yeah, go ahead and take it," he responded absently. If things had gone differently—they'd be shaking out that toy for hair and fiber samples, if they found it at all.

He handed the bear to his partner.

"Oh—before you give it back—"

"What?"

"There's blood on the paws," he replied, already looking for trace evidence that would support his theories. "Wouldn't want to shake her up any further, so make sure you wash it off first."

Okay, so I don't always take Diana Tregarde very seriously. When this story appeared in Marion Zimmer Bradley's Fantasy Magazine, *however, there was a reader (a self-proclaimed romance writer) who took it seriously, and was quite irate at the rather unflattering picture I painted of romance writers. She wrote a long and angry letter about it to the editor.*

The editor, who like me has seen romance writers at a romance convention, declined to comment.

A note: The character of Robert Harrison and the concept of "whoopie witches" was taken from the excellent supernatural role-playing game, Stalking the Night Fantastic *by Richard Tucholka and used with the creator's permission. There is also a computer game version,* Bureau Thirteen. *Both are highly recommended!*

Satanic, Versus...

"Mrs. Peel," intoned a suave, urbane tenor voice from the hotel doorway behind Di Tregarde, "We're needed."

The accent was faintly French rather than English, but the inflection was dead-on.

Di didn't bother to look in the mirror, although she knew there *would* be a reflection there. Andre LeBrel might be a 200-year-old vampire, but he cast a perfectly good reflection. She was too busy trying to get her false eyelashes to stick.

"In a minute, lover. The glue won't hold. I can't understand it—I bought the stuff last year for that unicorn costume and it was fine then—"

"Allow me." A thin, graceful hand appeared over her shoulder, holding a tiny tube of surgical adhesive. "I had the sinking feeling that you would forget. This glue, *cherie*, it does not age well."

"Piffle. Figure a back-stage haunt would know that." She took the white plastic tube from Andre, and proceeded to attach the pesky lashes properly. This time they obliged by staying put. She finished her preparations with a quick application of liner, and spun around to face her partner. "Here," she said, posing, feeling more than a little smug about how well the black leather jumpsuit fit, "How do I look?"

Andre cocked his bowler to the side and leaned on his umbrella. "Ravishing. And I?" His dark eyes twinkled merrily. Although he looked a great deal more like Timothy Dalton than Patrick Macnee, anyone seeing the two of them together would have no doubt who he was supposed to be costumed as. Di was very glad they had a "pair" costume, and blessed Andre's infatuation with old TV shows.

And they're damned well going to see us together all the time, Di told herself firmly. *Why I ever agreed to this fiasco . . .*

"You look altogether too good to make me feel comfortable," she told him, snapping off the light over the mirror. "I hope you realize what you're letting yourself in for. You're going to think you're a drumstick in a pool of piranha."

Andre made a face as he followed her into the hotel room from the dressing alcove. "*Cherie*, these are only romance writers. They—"

"Are for the most part over-imaginative middle-aged *hausfraus*, married to guys that are going thin on top and thick on the bottom, and you're likely going to be one of a handful of males in the room. And the rest are going to be middle-aged copies of their husbands, agents, or gay." She raised an eyebrow at him. "So where do you think that leaves you?"

"Like Old Man Kangaroo, very much run after." He had the audacity to laugh at her. "Have no fear, *cherie*. I shall evade the sharp little piranha teeth."

"I just hope *I* can," she muttered under her breath. Under most circumstances she avoided the Romance Writers of the World functions like the plague, chucked the newsletter in the garbage without reading it, and paid her dues only because Morrie pointed out that it would look really strange if she didn't belong. The RWW, she had found, was a hotbed of infighting and jealousy, and "my advances are bigger than your advances, so I am writing Deathless Prose and you are writing tripe." The general attitude seemed to be, "the publishers are out to get you, the agents are out to get you and your fellow writers are out to get you." Since Di got along perfectly well with agent and publishers, and really didn't *care* how well or poorly other writers were doing, she didn't see the point.

But somehow Morrie had talked her into attending the RWW Halloween party. And for the life of her, she couldn't remember why or how.

"Why am I doing this?" she asked Andre, as she snatched up her purse from the beige-draped bed, transferred everything really necessary into a black-leather belt-pouch, and slung the latter around her hips, making very sure the belt didn't interfere with the holster on her other hip. "You were the one who talked to Morrie on the phone."

"Because M'sieur Morrie wishes you to give his client Robert Harrison someone to talk to," the vampire reminded her. "M'sieur Harrison agreed to escort Valentine Vervain to the party in a moment of weakness equal to yours."

"Why in Hades did he agree to *that*?" she exclaimed, giving the sable-haired vampire a look of profound astonishment.

"Because Miss Vervain—*cherie,* that is not her *real* name, is it?—is one of Morrie's best clients, is newly divorced and alone and Morrie claims most insecure, and M'sieur Harrison was kind to her," Andre replied.

Di took a quick look around the hotel room, to make sure she hadn't forgotten anything. One thing about combining her annual "make nice with the publishers" trip with Halloween, she had a chance to get together with all her old New York buddies for a *real* Samhain celebration and avoid the Christmas and Thanksgiving crowds and bad weather. "I remember. That was when she did that crossover thing, and the sci-fi people took her apart for trying to claim it was the best thing since Tolkien." She chuckled heartlessly. "The less said about that, the better. Her magic system had holes I could drive a Mack truck through. But Harrison was a gentleman and kept the bloodshed to a minimum. But Morrie doesn't know Valentine—and no, sexy, her name used to be Edith Bowman until she changed it legally—if he thinks she's as insecure as she's acting. Three quarters of what La Valentine does is an act. And everything is in Technicolor and Dolby enhanced sound. So what's Harrison doing in town?"

She snatched up the key from the desk, and stuffed it into the pouch, as Andre held the door open for her.

"I do not know," he replied, twirling the umbrella once and waving her past. "You should ask him."

"I hope Valentine doesn't eat him alive," she said, striding down the beige hall, and frankly enjoying the appreciative look a hotel room-service clerk gave her as she sauntered by. "I wonder if she's going to wear the outfit from the cover of her last book—if she does, Harrison may decide he wants to spend the rest of the party in the men's room." She reached the end of the hall a fraction of a second before Andre, and punched the button for the elevator.

"I gather that is what we are to save him from, *cherie*," Andre pointed out wryly, as the elevator arrived.

"Oh well," she sighed, stepping into the mirror-walled cubicle. "It's only five hours, and it can't be that bad. How much trouble can a bunch of romance writers get into, anyway?"

There was enough lace, chiffon, and satin to outfit an entire Busby Berkeley musical. Di counted fifteen Harem Girls, nine Vampire Victims, three Southern Belles (the South was Out this year), a round dozen Ravished Maidens of various time periods (none of them peasants), and assorted Frills and Furbelows, and one "witch" in a black chiffon outfit clearly purchased from the Frederick's catalog. Aside from the "witch," she and Andre were the only ones dressed in black—and they *were* the only ones covered from neck to toes—though in Di's case, that was problematical; the tight black leather jumpsuit really didn't leave anything to the imagination.

The Avengers outfits had been Andre's idea, when she realized she really *had* agreed to go to this party. She *had* suggested Dracula for him and a witch for her—but he had pointed out, logically, that there was no point in coming as what they really were.

Besides, I've always wanted a black leather jumpsuit, and this made a good excuse to get it. And since I'm doing this as a favor to Morrie, I might be able to deduct it. . . .

And even if I can't, the looks I'm getting are worth twice the price.

Most of the women here—and as she'd warned Andre, the suite at the Henley Palace that RWW had rented for this bash contained about eighty percent women—were in their forties at best. Most of them demonstrated amply the problems with having a sedentary job. And most of them were wearing outfits that might have been worn by their favorite heroines, though few of them went to the extent that Valentine Vervain did, and copied the exact dress from the front of the latest book. The problem was, their heroines were all no older than twenty-two, and as described, weighed *maybe* ninety-five pounds. Since a great many of the ladies in question weighed *at least* half again that, the results were not what the wearers intended.

The sour looks Di was getting were just as flattering as the wolf-whistle the bellboy had sent her way.

A quick sail through the five rooms of the suite with Andre at her side ascertained that Valentine and her escort had not yet arrived. A quick glance at Andre's face proved that he was having a very difficult time restraining his mirth. She decided then that discretion was definitely the better part of valor, and retired to the balcony with Andre in tow and a couple of glasses of Perrier.

It was a beautiful night; one of those rare, late-October nights that made Di regret—briefly—moving to Connecticut. Clear, cool and crisp, with just enough wind to sweep the effluvium of city life from the streets. Below them, hundreds of lights created a jewelbox effect. If you looked hard, you could even see a few stars beyond the light-haze.

The sliding glass door to the balcony had been opened to vent some of the heat and overwhelming perfume (Di's nose said, nothing under a hundred dollars a bottle), and Di left it that way. She parked her elbows on the balcony railing and looked down, Andre at her side, and sighed.

He chuckled. "You warned me, and I did not believe. I apologize, *cherie*. It is—most remarkable."

"Hmm. Exercise that vampiric hearing of yours, and you'll get an ear-full," she said, watching the car-lights crawl by, twenty stories below. "When they aren't slaughtering each other and playing little power-trip games, they're picking apart their agents and their editors. If you've ever wondered why I've never bothered going after the big money, it's because to get it I'd have to play by *those* rules."

"Then I devoutly urge you to remain with modest ambitions, *cherie*," he said, fervently. "I—"

"Excuse me?" said a masculine voice from the balcony door. It had a distinct note of desperation in it. "Are you Diana Tregarde?"

Di turned. Behind her, peering around the edge of the doorway, was a harried-looking fellow in a baggy, tweedy sweater and slacks—not a costume—with a shock of prematurely graying, sandy-brown hair, glasses and a moustache. And a look of absolute misery.

"Robert Harrison, I presume?" she said, archly. "Come, join us in the sanctuary. It's too cold out here for chiffon."

"Thank God." Harrison ducked onto the balcony with the agility of a man evading Iraqi border-guards, and threw himself down in an aluminum patio chair out of sight of the windows. "I think the password is, 'Morrie sent me.'"

"Recognized; pass, friend. Give the man credit; he gave you an ally and an escape-route," Di chuckled. "Don't tell me; she showed up as the Sacred Priestess Askenazy."

"In a nine-foot chiffon train and see-through harem pants, yes," Harrison groaned. "And let me know I was Out of the Royal Favor for *not* dressing as What's-His-Name."

"Watirion," Di said helpfully. "Do you realize you can pronounce that as 'what-tire-iron'? I encourage the notion."

"But that wasn't the worst of it!" Harrison shook his head, distractedly, as if he was somewhat in a daze. "The worst was the monologue in the cab on the way over here. Every other word was Crystal this and Vibration that, Past Life Regression, and Mystic Rituals. The woman's a whoopie witch!"

Di blinked. That was a new one on *her*. "A what?"

Harrison looked up, and for the first time, seemed to see her. "Uh—" he hesitated. "Uh, some of what Morrie said—uh, he seemed to think you—well, you've seen things—uh, he said you know things—"

She fished the pentagram out from under the neck of her jumpsuit and flashed it briefly. "My religion is non-traditional, yes, and there are more things in heaven and earth, etcetera. Now what in Tophet is a whoopie witch?"

"It's—uh—a term some friends of mine use. It's kind of hard to explain." Harrison's brow furrowed. "Look, let me give you examples. Real witches have grimorie, sometimes handed down through their families for centuries. Whoopie witches have books they picked up at the supermarket. Usually right at the check-out counter."

"Real witches have carefully researched spells—" Di prompted.

"Whoopie witches draw a baseball diamond in chalk on the living room floor and recite random passages from the *Satanic Bible*."

"When real witches make substitutions, they do so knowing the exact difference the substitute will make—"

"Whoopie witches slop taco sauce in their pentagram because it looks like blood."

"Real witches gather their ingredients by hand—" Di was beginning to enjoy this game.

"Whoopie witches have a credit card, and *lots* of catalogues." Harrison was grinning, and so was Andre.

"Real witches spend hours in meditation—"

"Whoopie witches sit under a pyramid they ordered from a catalogue and watch *Knot's Landing*."

"Real witches cast spells knowing that any change they make in someone's life will come back at them three-fold, for good or ill—"

"Whoopie witches call up the Hideous Slime from

Yosotha to eat their neighbor's poodle because the bitch got the last carton of Haagen-Daaz double-chocolate at the Seven-Eleven."

"I think I've got the picture. So dear Val decided to take the so-called research she did for the Great Fantasy Novel seriously?" Di leaned back into the railing and laughed. "Oh, Robert, I pity you! Did she try to tell you that the two of you just *must* have been priestly lovers in a past life in Atlantis?"

"Lemuria," Harrison said, gloomily. "My God, she must be supporting half the crystal miners in Arkansas."

"Don't feel too sorry for her, Robert," Di warned him. "With her advances, she can afford it. And I know some perfectly nice people in Arkansas who should only soak her for every penny they can get. Change the subject; you're safe with us—and if she decides to hit the punchbowl hard enough, you can send her back to her hotel in a cab and she'll never know the difference. What brings you to New York?"

"Morrie wants me to meet the new editors at Berkley; he thinks I've got a shot at selling them that near-space series I've been dying to do. And I had some people here in the City I really needed to see." He sighed. "And, I'll admit it, I'd been thinking about writing bodice-rippers under a pseudonym. When you know they're getting ten times what I am—"

Di shrugged. "I don't think you'd be happy doing it, unless you've written strictly to spec before. There's a lot of things you have to conform to that you might not feel comfortable doing. Listen, Harrison, you seem to know quite a bit about hot-and-cold-running esoterica— how did you—"

Someone in one of the other rooms screamed. Not the angry scream of a woman who has been insulted, but the soul-chilling shriek of pure terror that brands itself on the air and stops all conversation dead.

"What in—" Harrison was on his feet, staring in the direction of the scream. Di ignored him and launched herself at the patio door, pulling the Glock 19 from the holster on her hip, and thankful she'd loaded the silver-tipped bullets in the first clip.

Funny how everybody thought it couldn't be real because it was plastic....

"Andre—the next balcony!" she called over her shoulder, knowing the vampire could easily scramble over the concrete divider and come in through the next patio door, giving them a two-pronged angle of attack.

The scream hadn't been what alerted her—simultaneous with the scream had been the wrenching feeling in her gut that was the signal that someone had breached the fabric of the Otherworld in her presence. She didn't know who, or what—but from the stream of panicked chiffon billowing towards the door at supersonic speed, it probably wasn't nice, and it probably had a great deal to do with one of the party-goers.

Three amply-endowed females (one Belle, one Ravished and one Harem) had reached the door to the next room at the same moment, and jammed it, and rather than one of them pulling free, they all three kept shoving harder, shrieking at the tops of their lungs in tones their agents surely recognized.

You'd think their advances failed to pay out! Di kept the Glock in her hand, but sprinted for the door. She grabbed the nearest flailing arm (Harem), planted her foot in the midsection of her neighbor (Belle) and shoved and pulled at the same time. The clot of feminine hysteria came loose with a sound of ripping cloth; a crinoline parted company with its wearer. The three women tumbled through the door, giving Di a clear launching path into the next room. She took it, diving for the shelter of a huge wooden coffee table, rolling, and aiming for the door of the last room with the Glock. And her elbow hit someone.

"What are *you* doing here?" asked Harrison, and Di, simultaneously. Harrison cowered—no, *had taken cover*, there was a distinct difference—behind the sofa beside the coffee table, his own huge magnum aimed at the same doorway.

"My *job*," they said—also simultaneously.

"*What?*" (Again in chorus).

"This is all a very amusing study in synchronicity," said Andre, crouching just behind Harrison, bowler tipped and sword from his umbrella out and ready, "but I suggest you both pay attention to that most boorish party-crasher over there—"

Something very large occluded the light for a moment in the next room, then the lights went out, and Di distinctly heard the sound of the chandelier being torn from the ceiling and thrown against the wall. She winced.

There go my dues up again.

"I got a glimpse," Andre continued. "It was very large, perhaps ten feet tall, and—*cherie*, looked like nothing so much as a rubber creature from a very bad movie. Except that I do not think it was rubber."

At just that moment, there was a thrashing from the other room, and Valentine Vervain, long red hair liberally beslimed, minus nine-foot train and one of her sleeves, scrambled through the door and plastered herself against the wall, where she promptly passed out.

"Valentine?" Di murmured—and snapped her head towards Harrison when he moaned—"Oh *no*," in a way that made her *sure* he knew something.

"Harrison!" she snapped. "Cough it up!"

There was a sound of things breaking in the other room, as if something was fumbling around in the dark, picking up whatever it encountered, and smashing it in frustration.

"Valentine—she said something about getting some of her 'friends' together tonight and 'calling up her soulmate' so she could 'show that ex of hers.' I gather he appeared at the divorce hearing with a twenty-one-year-old blonde." Harrison gulped. "I figured she was just blowing it off—I never thought she had any power—"

"You'd be amazed what anger will do," Di replied grimly, keeping her eyes on the darkened doorway. "Sometimes it even transcends a total lack of talent. Put that together with the time of year—All Hallow's E'en—Samhain—is tomorrow. The Wall Between the Worlds is especially thin, and power flows are heavy right now. That's a recipe for disaster if I ever heard one."

"And here comes M'sieur Soul-Mate," said Andre, warningly.

What shambled in through the door was nothing that Di had ever heard of. It was, indeed, about ten feet tall. It was a very dark brown. It was covered with luxuriant brown hair—all over. Otherwise, it was nude. If there were any eyes, the hair hid them completely. It was built something along the lines of a powerful body-builder, taken to exaggerated lengths, and it drooled. It also stank, a combination of sulfur and musk so strong it would have brought tears to the eyes of a skunk.

"*Wah-wen-ine!*" it bawled, waving its arms around, as if it were blind. "*Wah-wen-ine!*"

"Oh goddess," Di groaned, putting two and two together and coming up with—*she called a soul-mate, and specified parameters. But she forgot to specify "human."* "Are you thinking what I'm thinking?"

The other writer nodded. "Tall, check. Dark, check. Long hair, check. Handsome—well, I suppose in some circles." Harrison stared at the thing in fascination.

"Some—thing—that will accept her completely as she is, and love her completely. Young, sure, he can't be more than five minutes old." Di watched the thing fumble for the doorframe and cling to it. "Look at that, he can't see. So love *is* blind. Strong and as masculine as you can get. And not too bright, which I bet she also specified. Oh, my ears and whiskers."

Valentine came to, saw the thing, and screamed.

"*Wah-wen-ine!*" it howled, and lunged for her. Reflexively, Di and Harrison both shot. He emptied his cylinder, and one speed-loader; Di gave up after four shots, when it was obvious they *were* hitting the thing, to no effect.

Valentine scrambled on hands and knees over the carpet, still screaming—but crawling in the wrong direction, towards the balcony, not the door.

"*Merde!*" Andre flung himself between the creature's clutching hands and its summoner, before Di could do anything.

And before Di could react to *that*, the thing backhanded Andre into a wall hard enough to put him through the plasterboard.

Valentine passed out again. Andre was already out for the count. There are some things even a vampire has a little trouble recovering from.

"Jesus!" Harrison was on his feet, fumbling for something in his pocket. Di joined him, holstering the Glock, and grabbed his arm.

"Harrison, distract it, make a noise, anything!" She pulled the atheme from her boot sheath and began cutting Sigils in the air with it, getting the Words of Dismissal out as fast as she could without slurring the syllables.

Harrison didn't even hesitate; he grabbed a couple of tin serving trays from the coffee table, shook off their contents, and banged them together.

The thing turned its head toward him, its hands just inches away from its goal. "Wah-wen-ine?" it said.

Harrison banged the trays again. It lunged toward the sound. It was a lot faster than Di had thought it was.

Evidently Harrison made the same error in judgment. It missed him by inches, and he scrambled out of the way by the width of a hair, just as Di concluded the Ritual of Dismissal.

To no effect.

"Hurry *up*, will you?" Harrison yelped, as the thing threw the couch into the wall and lunged again.

"I'm *trying!*" she replied through clenched teeth—

though not loud enough to distract the thing, which had concluded either (a) Harrison was Valentine or (b) Harrison was keeping it from Valentine. Whichever, it had gone from wailing Valentine's name to simply wailing, and lunging after Harrison, who was dodging with commendable agility in a man of middle age.

Of course, he has a lot of incentive.

She tried three more dismissals, still with no effect, the room was trashed, and Harrison was getting winded, and running out of heavy, expensive things to throw. . . .

And the only thing she could think of was the "incantation" she used—as a joke—to make the stoplights change in her favor.

Oh hell—a cockamamie incantation pulled it up—

"By the Seven Rings of Zsa Zsa Gabor and the Rock of Elizabeth Taylor I command thee!" she shouted, stepping between the thing and Harrison (who was beginning to stumble). "By the Six Wives of Eddie Fisher and the Words of Karnak the Great I compel thee! *Freeze, buddy!*"

Power rose, through her, crested over her—and hit the thing. And the thing—stopped. It whimpered, and struggled a little against invisible bonds, but seemed unable to move.

Harrison dropped to the carpet, right on top of a spill of guacamole and ground-in tortilla chips, whimpering a little himself.

I have to get rid of this thing, quick, before it breaks the compulsion— She closed her eyes and trusted to instinct, and shouted the first thing that came into her mind. The Parking Ritual, with one change. . . .

"Great Squat, send him *to* a spot, and I'll send you three nuns—"

Mage-energies raged through the room, whirling about her, invisible, intangible to eyes and ears, but she felt them. She was the heart of the whirlwind, she and the other—

There was a *pop* of displaced air; she opened her eyes to see that the creature was gone—but the mage-energies continued to whirl—faster—

"Je-*sus*," said Harrison, "How did you—"

She waved him frantically to silence as the energies sensed his presence and began to circle in on him.

"Great Squat, thanks for the spot!" she yelled desperately, trying to complete the incantation before Harrison could be pulled in. *"Your nuns are in the mail!"*

The energies swirled up and away, satisfied. Andre groaned, stirred, and began extracting himself from the powdered sheetrock wall. Harrison stumbled over to give him a hand.

Just as someone pounded on the outer door of the suite.

"Police!" came a muffled voice. "Open the door!"

"It's open!" Di yelled back, unzipping her belt-pouch and pulling out her wallet.

Three people, two uniformed NYPD and one fellow in a suit with an impressive .357 Magnum in his hand, peered cautiously around the doorframe.

"Jee-zus Christ," one said in awe.

"Who?" the dazed Valentine murmured, hand hanging limply over her forehead. "Wha' hap . . ."

Andre appeared beside Di, bowler in hand, umbrella spotless and innocent-looking again.

Di fished her Hartford PD Special OPs ID out of her wallet and handed it to the man in the suit. "This lady," she said angrily, pointing to Valentine, "played a little Halloween joke that got out of hand. Her accomplices went out the back door, then down the fire escape. If you hurry you might be able to catch them."

The two NYCPD officers looked around at the destruction, and didn't seem any too inclined to chase after whoever was responsible. Di checked out of the corner of her eye; Harrison's own .44 had vanished as mysteriously as it had appeared.

"Are you certain this woman is responsible?" asked

the hard-faced, suited individual with a frown, as he holstered his .357. He wasn't paying much attention to the plastic handgrip in the holster at Di's hip, for which she was grateful.

House detective, I bet. With any luck, he's never seen a Glock.

Di nodded. "These two gentlemen will back me up as witnesses," she said. "I suspect some of the ladies from the party will be able to do so as well, once you explain that Ms. Vervain was playing a not-very-nice joke on them. Personally, I think she ought to be held accountable for the damages."

And keep my RWW dues from going through the roof.

"Well, I think so too, miss." The detective hauled Valentine ungently to her feet. The writer was still confused, and it wasn't an act this time. "Ma'am," he said sternly to the dazed redhead, "I think you'd better come with me. I think we have a few questions to ask you."

Di projected outraged innocence and harmlessness at them as hard as she could. The camouflage trick worked, which after this evening, was more than she expected. The two uniformed officers didn't even look at her weapon; they just followed the detective out without a single backwards glance.

Harrison cleared his throat, audibly. She turned and raised an eyebrow at him.

"You—I thought you were just a writer—"

"And I thought *you* were just a writer," she countered. "So we're even."

"But—" He took a good look at her face, and evidently thought better of prying. "What did you do with that—thing? That was the strangest incantation I've ever heard!"

She shrugged, and began picking her way through the mess of smashed furniture, spilled drinks, and crushed and ground-in refreshments. "I have *no* idea. Valentine brought it in with something screwy, I got rid of it the same way. And that critter has no idea how lucky he was."

"Why?" asked Harrison, as she and Andre reached the door.

"Why?" She turned and smiled sweetly. "Do you have any idea how hard it is to get a parking place in Manhattan at this time of night?"

This is the very first attempted professional appearance of Diana Tregarde, my occult detective. I've always enjoyed occult detectives, but there is a major problem with them—what are they supposed to do for a living? Ghosts don't pay very well! So Di writes romances for a living and saves the world on the side. This story was originally rejected by the anthology I submitted it to; it became the basis for Children of the Night *by Another Company, and was then published in this form by* Marion Zimmer Bradley's Fantasy Magazine.

Nightside

It was early spring, but the wind held no hint of verdancy, not even the promise of it—it was chill and odorless, and there were ghosts of dead leaves skittering before it. A few of them jittered into the pool of weak yellow light cast by the aging streetlamp—a converted gaslight that was a relic of the previous century. It was old and tired, its pea-green paint flaking away; as weary as this neighborhood, which was older still. Across the street loomed an ancient church, its congregation dwindled over the years to a handful of little old women and men who appeared like scrawny blackbirds every Sunday, and then scattered back to the shabby houses that stood to either side of it until Sunday should come again. On the side of the street that the lamp tried (and failed) to illuminate, was the cemetery.

Like the neighborhood, it was very old—in this case, fifty years shy of being classified as "Colonial." There were few empty gravesites now, and most of those belonged to the same little old ladies and men that had lived and would die here. It was protected from vandals by a thorny hedge as well as a ten-foot wrought-iron fence. Within its confines, as seen through the leafless branches of the hedge, granite cenotaphs and enormous Victorian monuments bulked shapelessly against the bare sliver of a waning moon.

The church across the street was dark and silent; the houses up and down the block showed few lights, if any. There was no reason for anyone of this neighborhood to be out in the night.

So the young woman waiting beneath the lamp-post seemed that much more out-of-place.

Nor could she be considered a typical resident of this neighborhood by any stretch of the imagination—for one thing, she was young; perhaps in her mid-twenties, but no more. Her clothing was neat but casual, too casual for someone visiting an elderly relative. She wore dark, knee-high boots, old, soft jeans tucked into their tops, and a thin windbreaker open at the front to show a leotard beneath. Her attire was far too light to be any real protection against the bite of the wind, yet she seemed unaware of the cold. Her hair was long, down to her waist, and straight—in the uncertain light of the lamp it was an indeterminate shadow, and it fell down her back like a waterfall. Her eyes were large and oddly slanted, but not Oriental; catlike, rather. Even the way she held herself was feline; poised, expectant—a graceful tension like a dancer's or a hunting predator's. She was not watching for something—no, her eyes were unfocused with concentration. She was *listening*.

A soft whistle, barely audible, carried down the street

on the chill wind. The tune was of a piece with the neighborhood—old and timeworn.

Many of the residents would have smiled in recollection to hear "Lili Marlene" again.

The tension left the girl as she swung around the lamp-post by one hand to face the direction of the whistle. She waved, and a welcoming smile warmed her eyes.

The whistler stepped into the edge of the circle of light. He, too, was dusky of eye and hair—and heartbreakingly handsome. He wore only dark jeans and a black turtleneck, no coat at all—but like the young woman, he didn't seem to notice the cold. There was an impish glint in his eyes as he finished the tune with a flourish.

"A flair for the dramatic, Diana, *mon cherie*?" he said mockingly. "Would that you were here for the same purpose as the lovely Lili! Alas, I fear my luck cannot be so good. . . ."

She laughed. His eyes warmed at the throaty chuckle. "Andre," she chided, "don't you ever think of anything else?"

"Am I not a son of the City of Light? I must uphold her reputation, *mais non*?" The young woman raised an ironic brow. He shrugged. "Ah well—since it is you who seek me, I fear I must be all business. A pity. Well, what lures you to my side this unseasonable night? What horror has *mademoiselle* Tregarde unearthed this time?"

Diana Tregarde sobered instantly, the laughter fleeing her eyes. "I'm afraid you picked the right word this time, Andre. It *is* a horror. The trouble is, I don't know what kind."

"Say on. I wait in breathless anticipation." His expression was mocking as he leaned against the lamppost, and he feigned a yawn.

Diana scowled at him and her eyes darkened with anger. He raised an eyebrow of his own. "If this weren't so serious," she threatened, "I'd be tempted to pop you one—Andre, people are dying out there. There's a 'Ripper' loose in New York."

He shrugged, and shifted restlessly from one foot to the other. "So? This is new? Tell me when there is *not*! That sort of criminal is as common to the city as a rat. Let your police earn their salaries and capture him."

Her expression hardened. She folded her arms tightly across the thin nylon of her windbreaker; her lips tightened a little. "Use your head, Andre! If this was an ordinary slasher-killer, would *I* be involved?"

He examined his fingernails with care. "And what is it that makes it *extraordinaire*, eh?"

"The victims had no souls."

"I was not aware," he replied wryly, "that the dead possessed such things anymore."

She growled under her breath, and tossed her head impatiently, and the wind caught her hair and whipped it around her throat. "You are *deliberately* being difficult! I have half a mind—"

It finally seemed to penetrate the young man's mind that she was truly angry—and truly frightened, though she was doing her best to conceal the fact; his expression became contrite. "Forgive me, *cherie*. I *am* being recalcitrant."

"You're being a pain in the ass," she replied acidly. "Would I have come to you if I wasn't already out of my depth?"

"Well—" he admitted. "No. But—this business of souls, *cherie*, how can you determine such a thing? I find it most difficult to believe."

She shivered, and her eyes went brooding. "So did I. Trust me, my friend, I know what I'm talking about. There isn't a shred of doubt in my mind. There are at least six victims who no longer exist in *any* fashion anymore."

The young man finally evidenced alarm. "But—how?" he said, bewildered. "How is such a thing possible?"

She shook her head violently, clenching her hands

on the arms of her jacket as if by doing so she could protect herself from an unseen—but not unfelt—danger. "I don't know, I don't know! It seems incredible even now—I keep thinking it's a nightmare, but—Andre, it's real, it's not my imagination—" Her voice rose a little with each word, and Andre's sharp eyes rested for a moment on her trembling hands.

"*Eh bien,*" he sighed, "I believe you. So there is something about that devours souls—and mutilates bodies as well, since you mentioned a 'Ripper' persona?"

She nodded.

"Was the devouring before or after the mutilation?"

"Before, I think—it's not easy to judge." She shivered in a way that had nothing to do with the cold.

"And you came into this how?"

"Whatever it is, it took the friend of a friend; I—happened to be there to see the body afterwards, and I knew immediately there was something wrong. When I unshielded and used the Sight—"

"Bad." He made it a statement.

"Worse. I—I can't describe what it felt like. There were still residual emotions, things left behind when—" Her jaw clenched. "Then when I started checking further I found out about the other five victims—that what I had discovered was no fluke. Andre, whatever it is, it has to be stopped." She laughed again, but this time there was no humor in it. "After all, you could say stopping it is in my job description."

He nodded soberly. "And so you become involved. Well enough, if you must hunt this thing, so must I." He became all business. "Tell me of the history. When, and where, and who does it take?"

She bit her lip. "'Where'—there's no pattern. 'Who' seems to be mostly a matter of opportunity; the only clue is that the victims were always out on the street and entirely alone, there were no witnesses whatsoever, so the thing needs total privacy and apparently can't strike where it will. And 'when'—is moon-dark."

"Bad." He shook his head. "I have no clue at the moment. The *loup-garou* I know, and others, but I know nothing that hunts beneath the dark moon."

She grimaced. "You think I do? That's why I need your help; you're sensitive enough to feel something out of the ordinary, and you can watch and hunt undetected. I can't. And I'm not sure I *want* to go trolling for this thing alone—without knowing what it is, I could end up as a late-night snack for it. But if that's what I have to do, I will."

Anger blazed up in his face like a cold fire. "You go hunting alone for this creature over my dead body!"

"That's a little redundant, isn't it?" Her smile was weak, but genuine again.

"Pah!" he dismissed her attempt at humor with a wave of his hand. "Tomorrow is the first night of moon-dark; *I* shall go a-hunting. Do *you* remain at home, else I shall be most wroth with you. I know where to find you, should I learn anything of note."

"You ought to—" Diana began, but she spoke to the empty air.

The next night was warmer, and Diana had gone to bed with her windows open to drive out some of the stale odors the long winter had left in her apartment. Not that the air of New York City was exactly fresh—but it was better than what the heating system kept recycling through the building. She didn't particularly like leaving her defenses open while she slept, but the lingering memory of Katy Rourk's fish wafting through the halls as she came in from shopping had decided her. Better exhaust fumes than burned haddock.

She hadn't had an easy time falling asleep, and when she finally managed to do so, tossed restlessly, her dreams uneasy and readily broken—

—as by the sound of someone in the room.

Before the intruder crossed even half the distance between the window and her bed, she was wide awake, and moving. She threw herself out of bed, somersaulted across her bedroom, and wound up crouched beside the door, one hand on the lightswitch, the other holding a polished dagger she'd taken from beneath her pillow.

As the lights came on, she saw Andre standing in the center of the bedroom, blinking in surprise, wearing a sheepish grin.

Relief made her knees go weak. "Andre, you *idiot!*" She tried to control her tone, but her voice was shrill and cracked a little. "You could have been *killed!*"

He spread his hands wide in a placating gesture. "Now, Diana—"

"'Now Diana' my eye!" she growled. "Even *you* would have a hard time getting around a severed spine!" She stood up slowly, shaking from head to toe with released tension.

"I didn't wish to wake you," he said, crestfallen.

She closed her eyes and took several long, deep, calming breaths; focusing on a mantra, moving herself back into stillness until she knew she would be able to reply without screaming at him.

"Don't," she said carefully, "Ever. Do. That. Again." She punctuated the last word by driving the dagger she held into the doorframe.

"*Certainement, mon petite,*" he replied, his eyes widening a little as he began to calculate how fast she'd moved. "The next time I come in your window when you sleep, I shall blow a trumpet first."

"You'd be a *lot* safer. *I'd* be a lot happier," she said crossly, pulling the dagger loose with a snap of her wrist. She palmed the light-switch and dimmed the lamps down to where they would be comfortable to his light-sensitive eyes, then crossed the room, the plush brown carpet warm and soft under her bare feet. She bent slightly, and put the silver-plated dagger back under her pillow. Then with a sigh she folded her long legs beneath her to sit on her rumpled bed. This was the first time Andre had ever caught her asleep, and she was irritated far beyond what her disturbed dreams warranted. She was somewhat obsessed with her privacy and with keeping her night-boundaries unbreached—she and Andre were off-and-on lovers, but she'd never let him stay any length of time.

He approached the antique wooden bed slowly. "*Cherie*, this was no idle visit—"

"I should bloody well hope not!" she interrupted, trying to soothe her jangled nerves by combing the tangles out of her hair with her fingers.

"—I have seen your killer."

She froze.

"It is nothing I have ever seen or heard of before."

She clenched her hands on the strand of hair they held, ignoring the pull. "Go on—"

"It—no, *he*—I could not detect until he made his first kill tonight. I found him then, found him just before he took his hunting-shape, or I never would have discovered him at all; for when he is in that shape there is nothing about him that *I* could sense that marked him as different. So ordinary—a man, an Oriental; Japanese, I think, and like many others—not young, not old; not fat, not thin. So unremarkable as to be invisible. I followed him—he was so normal I found it difficult to believe what my own eyes had seen a moment before; then, not ten minutes later, he found yet another victim and—fed again."

He closed his eyes, his face thoughtful. "As I said, I have never seen or heard of his like, yet—yet there was something familiar about him. I cannot even tell you what it was, and yet it was familiar."

"You said you saw him attack—*how*, Andre?" she leaned forward, her face tight with urgency as the bed creaked a little beneath her.

"The second quarry was—the—is it 'bag lady' you say?" At her nod he continued. "He smiled at her—just smiled, that was all. She froze like the frightened rabbit. Then he—changed—into dark, dark smoke; only smoke, nothing more. The smoke enveloped the old woman until I could see her no longer. Then—he fed. I—I can understand your feelings now, *cherie*. It was—nothing to the eye, but—what I felt *within*—"

"Now you see," she said gravely.

"*Mais oui*, and you have no more argument from me. This thing is abomination, and must be ended."

"The question is—" She grimaced.

"How? I have given some thought to this. One cannot fight smoke. But in his hunting form—I think perhaps he is vulnerable to physical measures. As you say, even *I* would have difficulty in dealing with a severed spine or crushed brain. I think maybe it would be the same for him. Have you the courage to play the wounded bird, *mon petite*?" He sat beside her on the edge of the bed and regarded her with solemn and worried eyes.

She considered that for a moment. "Play bait while you wait for him to move in? It sounds like the best plan to me—it wouldn't be the first time I've done that, and I'm not exactly helpless, you know," she replied, twisting a strand of hair around her fingers.

"I think you have finally proved that to me tonight!" There was a hint of laughter in his eyes again, as well as chagrin. "I shall never again make the mistake of thinking you to be a fragile flower. *Bien*. Is tomorrow night too soon for you?"

"Tonight wouldn't be too soon," she stated flatly.

"Except that he has already gone to lair, having fed twice." He took one of her hands, freeing it from the lock of hair she had twisted about it. "No, we rest—I know where he is to be found, and tomorrow night we face him at full strength." Abruptly he grinned. "*Cherie*, I have read one of your books—"

She winced, and closed her eyes in a grimace. "Oh Lord—I was afraid you'd ferret out one of my pseudonyms. You're as bad as the Elephant's Child when it comes to 'satiable curiosity."

"It was hardly difficult to guess the author when she

used one of my favorite expressions for the title—and then described me so very intimately not three pages from the beginning."

Her expression was woeful. "Oh *no*! Not *that* one!"

He shook an admonishing finger at her. "I do not think it kind, to make me the villain, and all because I told you I spent a good deal of the Regency in London."

"But—but—Andre, these things follow *formulas*, I didn't really have a choice—anybody French in a Regency romance *has* to be either an expatriate aristocrat or a villain—" She bit her lip and looked pleadingly at him. "—I needed a villain and I didn't have a clue—I was in the middle of that phony medium thing *and* I had a deadline—and—" Her words thinned down to a whisper, "—to tell you the truth, I didn't think you'd ever find out. You—you aren't angry, are you?"

He lifted the hair away from her shoulder, cupped his hand beneath her chin and moved close beside her. "I *think* I may possibly be induced to forgive you—"

The near-chuckle in his voice told her she hadn't offended him. Reassured by that, she looked up at him, slyly. "Oh?"

"You could—" He slid her gown off her shoulder a little, and ran an inquisitive finger from the tip of her shoulderblade to just behind her ear "—write another, and let me play the hero—"

"Have you any—suggestions?" she replied, finding it difficult to reply when his mouth followed where his finger had been.

"In that 'Burning Passions' series, perhaps?"

She pushed him away, laughing. "The soft-core porn for housewives? Andre, you can't be serious!"

"Never more." He pulled her back. "Think of how much enjoyable the research would be—"

She grabbed his hand again before it could resume its explorations. "Aren't we supposed to be resting?"

He stopped for a moment, and his face and eyes were

deadly serious. "*Cherie*, we must face this thing at strength. You need sleep—and to relax. Can you think of any better way to relax body and spirit than—"

"No," she admitted. "I always sleep like a rock when you get done with me."

"Well then. And I—I have needs; I have not tended to those needs for too long, if I am to have full strength, and I should not care to meet this creature at less than that."

"Excuses, excuses—" She briefly contemplated getting up long enough to take care of the lights—then decided a little waste of energy was worth it, and extinguished them with a thought. "C'mere, you—let's do some research."

He laughed deep in his throat as they reached for one another with the same eager hunger.

She woke late the next morning—so late that in a half hour it would have been "afternoon"—and lay quietly for a long, contented moment before wriggling out of the tumble of bedclothes and Andre. No fear of waking him—he wouldn't rouse until the sun went down. She arranged him a bit more comfortably and tucked him in, thinking that he looked absurdly young with his hair all rumpled and those long, dark lashes of his lying against his cheek—he looked much better this morning, now that she was in a position to pay attention. Last night he'd been pretty pale and hungry-thin. She shook her head over him. Someday his gallantry was going to get him into trouble. "Idiot—" she whispered, touching his forehead, "—all you ever have to do is *ask*—"

But there were other things to take care of—and to think of. A fight to get ready for; and she had a premonition it wasn't going to be an easy one.

So she showered and changed into a leotard, and took herself into her barren studio at the back of the apartment to run through her *katas* three times—once slow, twice at full speed—and then into some *Tai Chi* exercises to rebalance everything. She followed that with a half hour of meditation, then cast a circle and charged herself with all of the Power she thought she could safely carry.

Without knowing what it was she was to face, that was all she could do, really—that, and have a really good dinner—

She showered and changed again into a bright red sweatsuit and was just finishing that dinner when the sun set and Andre strolled into the white-painted kitchen, shirtless, and blinking sleepily.

She gulped the last bite of her liver and waggled her fingers at him. "If you want a shower, you'd better get a fast one—I want to get in place before he comes out for the night."

He sighed happily over the prospect of a hot shower. "The perfect way to start one's—day. *Petite*, you may have difficulty in dislodging me now that you have let me stay overnight—"

She showed her teeth. "Don't count your chickens, kiddo. I can be very nasty!"

"*Mon petite—I—*" He suddenly sobered, and looked at her with haunted eyes.

She saw his expression and abruptly stopped teasing. "Andre—please don't say it—I can't give you any better answer now than I could when you first asked—if I— cared for you as more than a friend."

He sighed again, less happily. "Then I will say no more, because you wish it—but—what of this notion— would you permit me to stay with you? No more than that. I could be of some use to you, I think, and I would take nothing from you that you did not offer first. I do not like it that you are so much alone. It did not matter when we first met, but you are collecting powerful enemies, *cherie*."

"I—" She wouldn't look at him, but only at her hands, clenched white-knuckled on the table.

"Unless there are others—" he prompted, hesitantly.

"No—no, there isn't anyone but you." She sat in silence for a moment, then glanced back up at him with one eyebrow lifted sardonically. "You *do* rather spoil a girl for anyone else's attentions."

He was genuinely startled. *"Mille pardons, cherie,"* he stuttered, "I—I did not know—"

She managed a feeble chuckle. "Oh Andre, you idiot—I *like* being spoiled! I don't get many things that are just for me—" she sighed, then gave in to his pleading eyes. "All right then, move in if you want—"

"It is what *you* want that concerns me."

"I want," she said, very softly. "Just—the commitment—don't ask for it. I've got responsibilities as well as Power, you know that; I—can't see how to balance them with what you offered before—"

"Enough," he silenced her with a wave of his hand. "The words are unsaid, we will speak of this no more unless you wish it. I seek the embrace of warm water—"

She turned her mind to the dangers ahead, resolutely pushing the dangers *he* represented into the back of her mind. "And I will go bail the car out of the garage."

He waited until he was belted in on the passenger's side of the car to comment on her outfit. "I did not know you planned to race him, Diana," he said with a quirk of one corner of his mouth.

"Urban camouflage," she replied, dodging two taxis and a kamikaze panel truck. "Joggers are everywhere, and they run at night a lot in deserted neighborhoods. Cops won't wonder about me or try to stop me, and our boy won't be surprised to see me alone. One of his other victims was out running. His boyfriend thought he'd had a heart attack. Poor thing. He wasn't one of us, so I didn't enlighten him. There are some things it's better the survivors don't know."

"Oui. Left here, *cherie."*

The traffic thinned down to a trickle, then to nothing. There are odd little islands in New York at night; places as deserted as the loneliest country road. The area where Andre directed her was one such; by day it was small warehouses, one floor factories, an odd store or two. None of them had enough business to warrant running second or third shifts, and the neighborhood had not been gentrified yet, so no one actually lived here. There were a handful of night-watchmen, perhaps, but most of these places depended on locks, burglar-alarms, and dogs that were released at night to keep out intruders.

"There—" Andre pointed at a building that appeared to be home to several small manufactories. "He took the smoke-form and went to roost in the elevator control house at the top. That is why I did not advise going against him by day."

"Is he there now?" Diana peered up through the glare of sodium-vapor lights, but couldn't make out the top of the building.

Andre closed his eyes, a frown of concentration creasing his forehead. "No," he said after a moment. "I think he has gone hunting."

She repressed a shiver. "Then it's time to play bait."

Diana found a parking space marked dimly with the legend "President"—she thought it unlikely it would be wanted within the next few hours. It was deep in the shadow of the building Andre had pointed out, and her car was dead-black; with any luck, cops coming by wouldn't even notice it was there and start to wonder.

She hopped out, locking her door behind her, looking now exactly like the lone jogger she was pretending to be, and set off at an easy pace. She did not look back.

If absolutely necessary, she knew she'd be able to keep this up for hours. She decided to take all the north-south streets first, then weave back along the east-west. Before the first hour was up she was wishing she'd dared bring a "walk-thing"—every street was like every other street; blank brick walls broken by dusty, barred windows and metal doors, alleys with only the occasional dumpster visible, refuse blowing along the gutters. She was bored; her nervousness had worn off, and she was lonely. She ran from light to darkness, from darkness to light, and saw and heard nothing but the occasional rat.

Then he struck, just when she was beginning to get a little careless. Careless enough not to see him arrive.

One moment there was nothing, the next, he was before her, waiting halfway down the block. She knew it was him—he was exactly as Andre had described him, a nondescript Oriental man in a dark windbreaker and slacks. He was tall for an Oriental—taller than she by several inches. His appearance nearly startled her into stopping—then she remembered that she was supposed to be an innocent jogger, and resumed her steady trot.

She knew he meant her to see him, he was standing directly beneath the streetlight and right in the middle of the sidewalk. She would have to swerve out of her path to avoid him.

She started to do just that, ignoring him as any real jogger would have—when he raised his head and smiled at her.

She was stopped dead in her tracks by the purest terror she had ever felt in her life. She froze, as all of his other victims must have—unable to think, unable to cry out, unable to run. Her legs had gone numb, and nothing existed for her but that terrible smile and those hard, black eyes that had no bottom—

Then the smile vanished, and the eyes flinched away. Diana could move again, and staggered back against the brick wall of the building behind her, her breath coming in harsh pants, the brick rough and comforting in its reality beneath her hands.

"Diana?" It was Andre's voice behind her.

"I'm—all right—" she said, not at all sure that she really was.

Andre strode silently past her, face grim and

purposeful. The man seemed to sense his purpose, and smiled again—

But Andre never faltered for even the barest moment.

The smile wavered and faded; the man fell back a step or two, surprised that his weapon had failed him—

Then he scowled, and pulled something out of the sleeve of his windbreaker; and to Diana's surprise, charged straight for Andre, his sneakered feet scuffing on the cement—

And something suddenly blurring about his right hand. As it connected with Andre's upraised left arm, Diana realized what it was—almost too late.

"Andre—he has nunchuks—they're *wood*," she cried out urgently as Andre grunted in unexpected pain. "He can *kill* you with them! Get the *hell* out of here!"

Andre needed no second warning. In the blink of an eye, he was gone.

Leaving Diana to face the creature alone.

She dropped into guard-stance as he regarded her thoughtfully, still making no sound, not even of heavy breathing. In a moment he seemed to make up his mind, and came for her.

At least he didn't smile again in that terrible way—perhaps the weapon was only effective once.

She hoped fervently he wouldn't try again—as an empath, she was doubly-vulnerable to a weapon forged of fear.

They circled each other warily, like two cats preparing to fight—then Diana thought she saw an opening—and took it.

And quickly came to the conclusion that she was overmatched, as he sent her tumbling with a badly bruised shin. The next few moments reinforced that conclusion—as he continued scatheless while she picked up injury after painful injury.

She was a brown-belt in karate—but he was a black-belt in kung-fu, and the contest was a pathetically uneven match. She knew before very long that he was toying with her—and while he still swung the wooden nunchuks, Andre did not dare move in close enough to help.

She realized, (as fear dried her mouth, she grew more and more winded, and she searched frantically for a means of escape) that she was as good as dead.

If only she could get those damn 'chucks away from him!

And as she ducked and stumbled against the curb, narrowly avoiding the strike he made at her, an idea came to her. He knew from her moves—as she knew from his—that she was no amateur. He would never expect an amateur's move from her—something truly stupid and suicidal—

So the next time he swung at her, she stood her ground. As the 'chuk came at her she took one step forward, smashing his nose with the heel of her right hand and lifting her left to intercept the flying baton.

As it connected with her left hand with a sickening crunch, she whirled and folded her entire body around hand and weapon, and went limp, carrying it away from him.

She collapsed in a heap at his feet, hand afire with pain, eyes blurring with it, and waited for either death or salvation.

And salvation in the form of Andre rose behind her attacker. With one *savate* kick he broke the man's back; Diana could hear it cracking like green wood—and before her assailant could collapse, a second double-handed blow sent him crashing into the brick wall, head crushed like an eggshell.

Diana struggled to her feet, and waited for some arcane transformation.

Nothing.

She staggered to the corpse, face flat and expressionless—a sign she was suppressing pain and shock with utterly implacable iron will. Andre began to move forward as if to stop her, then backed off again at the look in her eyes.

She bent slightly, just enough to touch the shoulder of the body with her good hand—and released the Power.

Andre pulled her back to safety as the corpse exploded into flame, burning as if it had been soaked in oil. She watched the flames for one moment, wooden-faced; then abruptly collapsed.

Andre caught her easily before she could hurt herself further, lifting her in his arms as if she weighed no more than a kitten. "*Mon pauvre petite*," he murmured, heading back towards the car at a swift but silent run, "It is the hospital for you, I think—"

"Saint—Francis—" she gasped, every step jarring her hand and bringing tears of pain to her eyes, "One of us—is on the night-staff—Dr. Crane—"

"*Bien*," he replied. "Now be silent—"

"But—how are you—"

"In your car, foolish one. I have the keys you left in it."

"But—"

"I can drive."

"But—"

"*And* I have a license. Will you be silent?"

"How?" she said, disobeying him.

"Night school," he replied succinctly, reaching the car, putting her briefly on her feet to unlock the passenger-side door, then lifting her into it. "You are not the only one who knows of urban camouflage."

This time she did not reply—mostly because she had fainted from pain.

The emergency room was empty—for which Andre was very grateful. His invocation of Dr. Crane brought a thin, bearded young man around to the tiny examining cubicle in record time.

"Good godalmighty! What did you tangle with, a

bus?" he exclaimed, when stripping the sweatsuit jacket and pants revealed that there was little of Diana that was not battered and black-and-blue.

Andre wrinkled his nose at the acrid antiseptic odors around them, and replied shortly. "No. Your 'Ripper.'"

The startled gaze the doctor fastened on him revealed that Andre had scored. "Who—won?" he asked at last.

"We did. I do not think he will prey upon anyone again."

The doctor's eyes closed briefly; Andre read prayerful thankfulness on his face as he sighed with relief. Then he returned to business. "You must be Andre, right? Anything I can supply?"

Andre laughed at the hesitation in his voice. "Fear not, your blood supply is quite safe, and I am unharmed. It is Diana who needs you."

The relief on the doctor's face made Andre laugh again.

Dr. Crane ignored him. "Right," he said, turning to the work *he* knew best.

She was lightheaded and groggy with the Demerol Dr. Crane had given her as Andre deftly stripped her and tucked her into her bed; she'd dozed all the way home in the car.

"I just wish I knew *what* that thing was—" she said inconsequentially, as he arranged her arm in its light Fiberglas cast a little more comfortably. "—I won't be happy until I *know*—"

"Then you are about to be happy, *cherie*, for I have had the brainstorm—" Andre ducked into the livingroom and emerged with a dusty leather-bound book. "Remember I said there was something familiar about it? Now I think I know what it was." He consulted the index, and turned pages rapidly—found the place he sought, and read for a few moments. "As I thought—listen. 'The *gaki*—also known as the Japanese vampire—also takes its nourishment only from the living. There are many kinds of *gaki*, extracting their sustenance from a wide variety of sources. The most harmless are the "perfume" and "music" *gaki*—and they are by far the most common. Far deadlier are those that require blood, flesh—or souls.' "

"Souls?"

"Just so. 'To feed, or when at rest, they take their normal form of a dense cloud of dark smoke. At other times, like the *kitsune*, they take on the form of a human being. Unlike the *kitsune*, however, there is no way to distinguish them in this form from any other human. In the smoke form, they are invulnerable—in the human form, however, they can be killed; but to permanently destroy them, the body must be burned—preferably in conjunction with or solely by Power.' I said there was something familiar about it—it seems to have been a kind of distant cousin." Andre's mouth smiled, but his eyes reflected only a long-abiding bitterness.

"There is *no way* you have any relationship with that—thing!" she said forcefully. "It had no more honor, heart or soul than a rabid beast!"

"I—I thank you, *cherie*," he said, slowly, the warmth returning to his eyes. "There are not many who would think as you do."

"Their own closed-minded stupidity."

"To change the subject—what was it made you burn it as you did? I would have abandoned it. It seemed dead enough."

"I don't know—it just seemed the thing to do," she yawned. "Sometimes my instincts just work . . . right. . . ."

Suddenly her eyes seemed too leaden to keep open.

"Like they did with you. . . ." She fought against exhaustion and the drug, trying to keep both at bay.

But without success. Sleep claimed her for its own.

He watched her for the rest of the night, until the leaden lethargy of his own limbs told him dawn was near. He had already decided not to share her bed, lest any movement on his part cause her pain—instead, he made up a pallet on the floor beside her.

He stood over her broodingly while he in his turn fought slumber, and touched her face gently. "Well—" he whispered, holding off torpor far deeper and heavier than hers could ever be—while she was mortal. "You are not aware to hear, so I may say what I will and you cannot forbid. Dream; sleep and dream—I shall see you safe— my only love."

And he took his place beside her, to lie motionless until night should come again.

This was originally for a Susan Shwartz anthology, Sisters of Fantasy 2.

Wet Wings

Katherine watched avidly, chin cradled in her old, arthritic hands, as the chrysalis heaved, and writhed, and finally split up the back. The crinkled, sodden wings of the butterfly emerged first, followed by the bloated body. She breathed a sigh of wonder, as she always did, and the butterfly tried to flap its useless wings in alarm as it caught her movement.

"Silly thing," she chided it affectionately. "You know you can't fly with wet wings!" Then she exerted a little of her magic; just a little, brushing the butterfly with a spark of calm that jumped from her trembling index finger to its quivering antenna.

The butterfly, soothed, went back to its real job, pumping the fluid from its body into the veins of its wings, unfurling them into their full glory. It was not a particularly rare butterfly, certainly not an endangered one; nothing but a common Buckeye, a butterfly so ordinary that no one even commented on seeing them when she was a child. But Katherine had always found the markings exquisite, and she had used this species and the Sulfurs more often than any other to carry her magic.

Magic. That was a word hard to find written anymore. No one approved of magic these days. Strange that in a country that gave the Church of Gaia equal rights with the Catholic Church, that no one believed in magic.

But magic was not "correct." It was not given equally to all, nor could it be given equally to all. And that which could not be made equal, must be destroyed. . . .

"We always knew that there would be repression and a burning time again," she told the butterfly, as its wings unfolded a little more. "But we never thought that the ones behind the repression would come from our own ranks."

Perhaps she should have realized it would happen. So many people had come to her over the years, drawn by the magic in her books, demanding to be taught. Some had the talent and the will; most had only delusions. How they had cursed her when she told them the truth! They had wanted to be like the heroes and heroines of her stories; *special, powerful.*

She remembered them all; the boy she had told, regretfully, that his "telepathy" was only observation and the ability to read body-language. The girl whose "psychic attacks" had been caused by potassium imbalances. The would-be "bardic mage" who had nothing other than a facility to delude himself. And the many who could not tell a tale, because they would not let themselves see the tales all around them. They were neither powerful nor special, at least not in terms either of the power of magic, nor the magic of storytelling. More often than not, they would go to someone else, demanding to be taught, unwilling to hear the truth.

Eventually, they found someone; in one of the many movements that sprouted on the fringes like parasitic mushrooms. She, like the other mages of her time, had simply shaken her head and sighed for them. But what she had not reckoned on, nor had anyone else, was that these movements had gained strength and a life of their own—and had gone political.

Somehow, although the process had been so gradual she had never noticed when it had become unstoppable, those who cherished their delusions began to legislate some of those delusions. "Politically correct" they called it—and *some* of the things they had done she had welcomed, seeing them as the harbingers of more freedom, not less.

But they had gone from the reasonable to the unreasoning; from demanding and getting a removal of sexism to a denial of sexuality and the differences that should have been celebrated. From legislating the humane treatment of animals to making the possession of any animal or animal product without licenses and yearly inspections a crime. Fewer people bothered with owning a pet these days—no, not a pet, an "Animal Companion," and one did not "own" it, one "nurtured" it. Not when inspectors had the right to come into your home day or night, make certain that you were giving your Animal Companion all the rights to which it was entitled. And the rarer the animal, the more onerous the conditions. . . .

"That wouldn't suit you, would it, Horace?" she asked the young crow perched over the window. Horace was completely illegal; there was no way she could have gotten a license for him. She lived in an apartment, not on a farm; she could never give him the four-acre "hunting preserve" he required. Never mind that he had come to her, lured by her magic, and that he was free to come and go through her window, hunting and exercising at will. He also came and went with her little spell-packets, providing her with eyes on the world where she could not go, and bringing back the cocoons and chrysalises that she used for her butterfly-magics.

She shook her head, and sighed. They had sucked all the juice of life out of the world, that was what they had done. Outside, the gray overcast day mirrored the gray sameness of the world they had created. There were no bright colors anymore to draw the eye, only pastels. No passion, no fire, nothing to arouse any kind of emotions. They had decreed that everyone *must* be equal, and no one must be offended, ever. And they had begun the burning and the banning. . . .

She had become alarmed when the burning and banning started; she knew that her own world was doomed when it reached things like "Hansel and Gretel"—banned, not because there was a witch in it, but because the witch was evil, and that might offend witches. She had known that her own work was doomed when a book that had been lauded for its portrayal of a young gay hero was banned because the young gay hero was unhappy and suicidal. She had not even bothered to argue. She simply announced her retirement, and went into seclusion, pouring all her energies into the magic of her butterflies.

From the first moment of spring to the last of autumn, Horace brought her caterpillars and cocoons. When the young butterflies emerged, she gave them each a special burden and sent them out into the world again.

Wonder. Imagination. Joy. Diversity. Some she sent out to wake the gifts of magic in others. Some she sent to wake simple stubborn will.

Discontent. Rebellion. She sowed her seeds, here in this tiny apartment, of what she hoped would be the next revolution. She would not be here to see it—but the day would come, she hoped, when those who *were* different and special would no longer be willing or content with sameness and equality at the expense of diversity.

Her door-buzzer sounded, jarring her out of her reverie.

She got up, stiffly, and went to the intercom. But the face there was that of her old friend Piet, the "Environmental Engineer" of the apartment building, and he wore an expression of despair.

"Kathy, the Psi-cops are coming for you," he said, quickly, casting a look over his shoulder to see if there was anyone listening. "They made me let them in—"

The screen darkened abruptly.

Oh Gods— She had been so careful! But—in a way, she had expected it. She had been a world-renowned fantasy writer; she had made no secret of her knowledge of real-world magics. The Psi-cops had not made any spectacular arrests lately. Possibly they were running out of victims; she should have known they would start looking at peoples' pasts.

She glanced around at the apartment reflexively—

No. There was no hope. There were too many thing she had that were contraband. The shelves full of books, the feathers and bones she used in her magics, the freezer full of meat that she shared with Horace and his predecessors, the wool blankets—

For that matter, they could arrest her on the basis of her jewelry alone, the fetish-necklaces she carved and made, the medicine-wheels and shields, and the prayer-feathers. She was not Native American; she had no right to make these things even for private use.

And she knew what would happen to her. The Psi-cops would take her away, confiscate all her property, and "re-educate" her.

Drugged, brainwashed, wired and probed. There would be nothing left of her when they finished. They had "re-educated" Jim three years ago, and when he came out, everything, even his magic and his ability to tell a story, was gone. He had not even had the opportunity to gift it to someone else; they had simply crushed it. He had committed suicide less than a week after his release.

She had a few more minutes at most, before they zapped the lock on her door and broke in. She had to save something, anything!

Then her eyes lighted on the butterfly, his wings fully unfurled and waving gently, and she knew what she would do.

First, she freed Horace. He flew off, squawking indignantly at being sent out into the overcast. But there was no other choice; if they found him, they would probably cage him up and send him to a forest preserve somewhere. He did not know how to find food in a wilderness—let him at least stay here in the city, where he knew how to steal food from birdfeeders, and where the best dumpsters were.

Then she cupped her hands around the butterfly, and gathered all of her magic. *All* of it this time; a great burden for one tiny insect, but there was no choice.

Songs and tales, magic and wonder; power, vision, will, strength— She breathed them into the butterfly's wings, and he trembled as the magic swirled around him, in a vortex of sparkling mist.

Pride. Poetry. Determination. Love. Hope—

She heard them at the door, banging on it, ordering her to open in the name of the Equal State. She ignored them. There was at least a minute or so left.

The gift of words. The gift of difference—

Finally she took her hands away, spent and exhausted, and feeling as empty as an old paper sack. The butterfly waved his wings, and though she could no longer see it, she knew that a drift of sparkling power followed the movements.

There was a whine behind her as the Psi-cops zapped the lock.

She opened the window, coaxed the butterfly onto her hand, and put him outside. An errant ray of sunshine broke through the overcast, gilding him with a glory that mirrored the magic he carried.

"Go," she breathed. "Find someone worthy."

He spread his wings, tested the breeze, and lifted off her hand, to be carried away.

And she turned, full of dignity and empty of all else, to face her enemies.

Here is the only Valdemar short story I have ever done, largely because I hate to waste a good story idea on something as small as a short story! This first appeared in the anthology, Horse Fantastic.

Stolen Silver

Silver stamped restively as another horse on the picket-line shifted and blundered into his hindquarters. Alberich clucked to quiet him and patted the stallion's neck; the beast swung his head about to blow softly into the young Captain's hair. Alberich smiled a little, thinking wistfully that the stallion was perhaps the only creature in the entire camp that felt anything like friendship for him.

And possibly the only creature that isn't waiting for me to fail.

Amazingly gentle, for a stallion, Silver had caused no problems either in combat or here, on the picket-line. Which was just as well, for if he had, Alberich would have had him gelded or traded off for a more tractable mount, gift of the Voice of Vkandis Sunlord or no. Alberich had enough troubles without worrying about the behavior of his beast.

He wasn't sure where the graceful creature had come

from; *Shin'a'in-bred,* they'd told him. Chosen for him out of a string of animals "liberated from the enemy." Which meant war-booty, from one of the constant conflicts along the borders. Silver hadn't come from one of the bandit-nests, that was sure—the only beasts the bandits owned were as disreputable as their owners. Horses "liberated" from the bandits usually weren't worth keeping. Silver probably came from Menmellith via Rethwellan; the King was rumored to have some kind of connection with the horse-breeding, blood-thirsty Shin'a'in nomads.

Whatever; when Alberich lost his faithful old Smoke a few weeks ago he hadn't expected to get anything better than the obstinate, intractable gelding he'd taken from its bandit-owner.

But fate ruled otherwise; the Voice chose to "honor" him with a superior replacement along with his commission, the letter that accompanied the paper pointing out that Silver was the perfect mount for a Captain of light cavalry. It was also another evidence of favoritism from above, with the implication that he had earned that favoritism outside of performance in the field. Not a gift that was likely to increase his popularity with some of the men under his command, and a beast that was going to make him pretty damned conspicuous in any encounter with the enemy.

Plus one that's an unlucky color. Those witchy-Heralds of Valdemar ride white horses, and the blue-eyed beasts may be witches too, for all I know.

The horse nuzzled him again, showing as sweet a temper as any lady's mare. He scratched its nose, and it sighed with content; he wished *he* could be as contented. Things had been bad enough before getting this commission. Now—

There was an uneasy, prickly sensation between his shoulder-blades as he went back to brushing his new mount down. He glanced over his shoulder, to intercept the glare of Leftenant Herdahl; the man dropped his gaze and brushed his horse's flank vigorously, but not quickly enough to prevent Alberich from seeing the hate and anger in the hot blue eyes.

The Voice had done Alberich no favors in rewarding him with the Captaincy and this prize mount, passing over Herdahl and Klaus, both his seniors in years of service, if not in experience. Neither of them had expected that *he* would be promoted over their heads; during the week's wait for word to come from Headquarters, they had saved their rivalry for each other.

Too bad they didn't murder each other, he thought resentfully, then suppressed the rest of the thought. It was said that some of the priests of Vkandis could pluck the thoughts from a man's head. It could have been thoughts like that one that had led to Herdahl's being passed over for promotion. But it could also be that this was a test, a way of flinging the ambitious young Leftenant Alberich into deep water, to see if he would survive the experience. If he did, well and good; he was of suitable material to continue to advance, perhaps even to the rank of Commander. If he did not—well, that was too bad. If his ambition undid him, then he wasn't fit enough for the post.

That was the way of things, in the armies of Karse. You rose by watching your back, and (if the occasion arose) sticking careful knives into the backs of your less-cautious fellows, and insuring other enemies took the punishment. All the while, the priests of the Sunlord, who were the ones who were truly in charge, watched and smiled and dispensed favors and punishments with the same dispassionate aloofness displayed by the One God.

But Alberich had given a good account of himself along the border, at the corner where Karse met Menmellith and the witch-nation Valdemar, in the campaign against the bandits there. He'd *earned* his rank, he told himself once again, as Silver stamped and shifted his weight beneath the strokes of Alberich's brush. The spring sun burned down on his head, hotter than he expected without the breeze to cool him.

There was no reason to feel as if he'd cheated to get where he was. He'd led more successful sorties against the bandits in his first year in the field than the other two had achieved in their entire careers together. He'd cleared more territory than anyone of Leftenant rank ever had in that space of time—and when Captain Anberg had met with one too many arrows, the men had seemed willing that the Voice chose him over the other two candidates.

It had been the policy of late to permit the brigands to flourish, provided they confined their attentions to Valdemar and the Menmellith peasantry and left the inhabitants of Karse unmolested. A stupid policy, in Alberich's opinion; you couldn't trust bandits, that was the whole reason why they became bandits in the first place. If they could be trusted, they'd be in the army themselves, or in the Temple Guard, or even have turned mercenary. He'd seen the danger back when he was a youngster in the Academy, in his first tactics classes. He'd even said as much to one of his teachers—phrased as a question, of course—and had been ignored.

But as Alberich had predicted, there had been trouble from the brigands, once they began to multiply; problems that escalated past the point where they were useful. With complete disregard for the unwritten agreements between them and Karse, they struck everyone, and when they finally began attacking villages, the authorities deemed it time they were disposed of.

Alberich had just finished cavalry training as an officer when the troubles broke out; he'd spent most of his young life in the Karsite military schools. The ultimate authority was in the hands of the Voices, of course; the highest anyone not of the priesthood could expect to rise was to Commander. But officers were never taken from the ranks; many of the rank-and-file were conscripts, and although it was never openly stated, the

Voices did not trust their continued loyalty if they were given power.

Alberich, and many others like him, had been selected at the age of thirteen by a Voice sent every year to search out young male-children, strong of body and quick of mind, to school into officers.

Alberich had both those qualities, developing expertise in many weapons with an ease that was the envy of his classmates, picking up his lessons in academic subjects with what seemed to be equal ease.

It wasn't ease; it was the fact that Alberich studied long and hard, knowing that there was no way for the bastard son of a tavern whore to advance in Karse except in the army. There was no place for him to go, no way to get into a trade, no hope for any but the most menial of jobs. The Voices didn't care about a man's parentage once he was chosen as an officer, they cared only about his abilities and whether or not he would use them in service to his God and country. It was a lonely life, though—his mother had loved and cared for him to the best of her abilities, and he'd had friends among the other children of similar circumstances. When he came to the Academy, he had no friends, and his mother was not permitted to contact him, lest she "distract him," or "contaminate his purity of purpose." Alberich had never seen her again, but both of them had known this was the only way for him to live a better life than she had.

Alberich had no illusions about the purity of the One God's priesthood. There were as many corrupt and venal priests as there were upright, and more fanatic than there were forgiving. He had seen plenty of the venal kind in the tavern; had hidden from one or two that had come seeking pleasures strictly forbidden by the One God's edicts. He had known they were coming, looking for him, and had managed to make himself scarce long before they arrived. Just as, somehow, he had known when the Voice was coming to look for young male children for the Academy, and had made certain he was noticed and questioned—

And that he had known which customers it was safe to cadge for a penny in return for running errands—

Or that he had known that drunk was going to try to set the stable afire.

Somehow. That was Alberich's secret. He knew things were going to happen. That was a witch-power, and forbidden by the Voices of the One God. If anyone knew he had it—

But he had also known, as surely as he had known all the rest, that he had to conceal the fact that he had this power, even before he knew the law against it.

He'd succeeded fairly well over the years, though it was getting harder and harder all the time. The power struggled inside him, wanting to break free, once or twice overwhelming him with visions so intense that for a moment he was blind and deaf to everything else. It was getting harder to concoct reasons for knowing things he had no business knowing, like the hiding places of the bandits they were chasing, the bolt-holes and escape routes. But it was harder still to ignore them, especially when subsequent visions showed him innocent people suffering because he didn't act on what he knew.

He brushed Silver's neck vigorously, the dust tickling his nose and making him want to sneeze—

—and between one brush-stroke and the next, he lost his sense of balance, went light-headed, and the dazzle that heralded a vision-to-come sparkled between his eyes and Silver's neck.

Not here! he thought desperately, clinging to Silver's mane and trying to pretend there was nothing wrong. *Not now, not with Herdahl watching—*

But the witch-power would not obey him, not this time.

A flash of blue light, blinding him. *The bandits he'd thought were south had slipped behind him, into the north, joining with two more packs of the curs, becoming a group large enough to take on his troops and give them an even fight. But first, they wanted a secure base. They were going to make Alberich meet them on ground of their choosing. Fortified ground.*

That this ground was already occupied was only a minor inconvenience . . . one that would soon be dealt with.

He fought free of the vision for a moment, clinging to Silver's shoulder like a drowning man, both hands full of the beast's silky mane, while the horse curved his head back and looked at him curiously. The big brown eyes flickered blue, briefly, like a half-hidden flash of lightning, reflecting—

—another burst of sapphire. *The bandits' target was a fortified village, a small one, built on the top of a hill, above the farm-fields. Ordinarily, these people would have no difficulty in holding off a score of bandits. But there were three times that number ranged against them, and a recent edict from the High Temple decreed that no one but the Temple Guard and the Army could possess anything but the simplest of weapons. Not three weeks ago, a detachment of priests and a Voice had come through here, divesting them of everything but knives, farm-implements, and such simple bows and arrows as were suitable for waterfowl and small game. And while they were at it, a third of the able-bodied men had been conscripted for the regular Army.*

These people didn't have a chance.

The bandits drew closer, under the cover of a brush-filled ravine.

Alberich found himself on Silver's back, without knowing how he'd gotten there, without remembering that he'd flung saddle and bridle back on the beast—

No, not bridle; Silver still wore the hackamore he'd had on the picket-line. Alberich's bugle was in his hand; presumably he'd blown the muster, for his men were running towards him, buckling on swords and slinging quivers over their shoulders.

Blinding flash of cerulean—

The bandits attacked the village walls, overpowering the poor man who was trying to bar the gate against them, and swarming inside.

It hadn't happened yet, he knew that with the surety with which he knew his own name. It wasn't even going to happen in the next few moments. But it was going to happen *soon*—

They poured inside, cutting down anyone who resisted them, then throwing off what little restraint they had shown and launching into an orgy of looting and rapine. Alberich gagged as one of them grabbed a pregnant woman and with a single slash of his sword, murdered the child that ran to try and protect her, followed through to her—

The vision released him, and he found himself surrounded by dust and thunder, still on Silver's back—

—but leaning over the stallion's neck as now he led his troops up the road to the village of Sunsdale at full gallop. Hooves pounded the packed-earth of the road, making it impossible to hear or speak; the vibration thrummed into his bones as he shifted his weight with the stallion's turns. Silver ran easily, with no sign of distress, though all around him and behind him the other horses streamed saliva from the corners of their mouths, and their flanks ran with sweat and foam, as they strained to keep up.

The lack of a bit didn't seem to make any difference to the stallion; he answered to neck-rein and knee so readily he might have been anticipating Alberich's thoughts.

Alberich dismissed the uneasy feelings *that* prompted. Better not to think that he might have a second witch-power along with the first. He'd never shown any ability to control beasts by thought before. There was no reason to think he could now. The stallion was just superbly trained, that was all. And he had more important things to worry about.

They topped the crest of a hill; Sunsdale lay atop the next one, just as he had seen in his vision, and the brush-filled ravine beyond it.

There was no sign of trouble.

This time it's been a wild hare, he thought, disgusted at himself for allowing blind panic to overcome him. And for what? A daytime-nightmare? *Next time I'll probably see trolls under my bed,* he thought, just about to pull Silver up and bring the rest of his men to a halt—

When a flash of sunlight on metal betrayed the bandits' location.

He grabbed for the bugle dangling from his left wrist instead, and pulled his blade with the right; sounded the charge, and led the entire troop down the hill, an unstoppable torrent of hooves and steel, hitting the brigands' hidden line like an avalanche.

Sword in hand, Alberich limped wearily to another body sprawled amid the rocks and trampled weeds of the ravine, and thrust it through to make death certain. His sword felt heavy and unwieldy, his stomach churned, and there was a sour taste in his mouth. He didn't think he was going to lose control of himself, but he was glad he was almost at the end of the battle-line. He hated this part of the fighting—which wasn't fighting at all; it was nothing more than butchery.

But it was necessary. This scum was just as likely to be feigning death as to actually be dead. Other officers hadn't been that thorough—and hadn't lived long enough to regret it.

Silver was being fed and watered along with the rest of the mounts by the youngsters of Sunsdale; the finest fodder and clearest spring water, and a round dozen young boys to brush and curry them clean. And the men were being fed and made much of by the older villagers. Gratitude had made them forgetful of the loss of their weapons and many of their men. Suddenly the army that had conscripted their relatives was no longer their adversary. Or else, since the troops had arrived out of nowhere like Vengeance of the Sunlord Himself, they assumed the One God had a hand in it, and it would be prudent to resign themselves to the sacrifice. And meanwhile, the instrument of their rescue probably ought to be well treated. . . .

Except for the Captain, who was doing a dirty job he refused to assign to anyone else.

Alberich made certain of two more corpses and looked dully around for more.

There weren't any, and he saw to his surprise that the sun was hardly more than a finger-breadth from the horizon. Shadows already filled the ravine, the evening breeze had picked up, and it was getting chilly. Last year's weeds tossed in the freshening wind as he gazed around at the long shadows cast by the scrubby trees. More time had passed than he thought—and if he didn't hurry, he was going to be late for SunDescending.

He scrambled over the slippery rocks of the ravine, cursing under his breath as his boots (meant for riding) skidded on the smooth, rounded boulders. The last thing he needed now was to be late for a Holy Service, especially this one. The priest here was bound to ask him for a Thanks-Prayer for the victory. If he was late, it would look as if he was arrogantly attributing the victory to his own abilities, and not the Hand of the Sunlord. And with an accusation like that hanging over his head, he'd be in danger not only of being deprived of his current rank, but of being demoted into the ranks, with no chance of promotion, a step up from stable-hand, but not a big one.

He fought his way over the edge, and half-ran, half-limped to the village gates, reaching them just as the sun touched the horizon. He put a little more speed into his weary, aching legs, and got to the edge of the crowd in the village square a scant breath before the priest began the First Chant.

He bowed his head with the others, and not until he raised his head at the end of it did he realize that the robes the priest wore were not black, but red. This was no mere village priest—this was a Voice!

He suppressed his start of surprise, and the shiver of fear that followed it. He didn't know what this village meant, or what had happened to require posting a Voice here, but there was little wonder now why they had submitted so tamely to the taking of their men and the confiscation of their weapons. No one sane would contradict a Voice.

The Voice held up his hand, and got instant silence; a silence so profound that the sounds of the horses on the picket-line came clearly over the walls. Horses stamped and whickered a little, and in the distance, a few lonely birds called, and the breeze rustled through the new leaves of the trees in the ravine. Alberich longed suddenly to be able to mount Silver and ride away from here, far away from the machinations of Voices and the omnipresent smell of death and blood. He yearned for somewhere clean, somewhere that he wouldn't have to guard his back from those he should be able to trust. . . .

"Today this village was saved from certain destruction," the Voice said, his words ringing out, but without passion, without any inflection whatsoever. "And for that, we offer Thanks-giving to Vkandis Sunlord, Most High, One God, to whom all things are known. The instrument of that salvation was Captain Alberich, who mustered his men in time to catch our attackers in the very act. It seems a miracle—"

During the speech, some of the men had been moving closer to Alberich, grouping themselves around him to bask in the admiration of the villagers.

Or so he thought. Until the Voice's tone hardened, and his next words proved their real intent.

"It *seems* a miracle—but it was not!" he thundered. "You were saved by the power of the One God, whose wrath destroyed the bandits, but Alberich betrayed the Sunlord by using the unholy powers of witchcraft! *Seize him!*"

The men grabbed him as he turned to run, throwing him to the ground and pinning him with superior numbers. He fought them anyway, struggling furiously, until someone brought the hilt of a knife down on the back of his head.

He didn't black out altogether, but he couldn't move or see; his eyes wouldn't focus, and a gray film obscured everything. He felt himself being dragged off by the arms—heaved into darkness—felt himself hitting a hard surface—heard the slamming of a door.

Then heard only confused murmurs as he lay in shadows, trying to regain his senses and his strength. Gradually his sight cleared, and he made out walls on all sides of him, close enough to touch. He raised his aching head cautiously, and made out the dim outline of an ill-fitting door. The floor, clearly, was dirt. And smelled unmistakably of birds.

They must have thrown him into some kind of shed, something that had once held chickens or pigeons. He was under no illusions that this meant his prison would be easy to escape; out here, the chicken-sheds were frequently built better than the houses, for chickens were more valuable than children.

Still, once darkness descended, it might be possible to get away. If he could overpower whatever guards that the Voice had placed around him. If he could find a way out of the shed. . . .

If he could get past the Voice himself. There were stories that the Voices had other powers than plucking the thoughts from a man's head—stories that they commanded the services of demons tamed by the Sunlord—

While he lay there gathering his wits, another smell invaded the shed, overpowering even the stench of old bird-droppings. A sharp, thick smell . . . it took a moment for him to recognize it.

But when he did, he clawed his way up the wall he'd been thrown against, to stand wide-eyed in the darkness, nails digging into the wood behind him, heart pounding with stark terror.

Oil. They had poured oil around the foundations, splashed it up against the sides of the shed. And now he heard them out there, bringing piles of dry brush and wood to stack against the walls. The punishment for witchery was burning, and they were taking no chances; they were going to burn him now.

The noises outside stopped; the murmur of voices faded as his captors moved away—

Then the Voice called out, once—a set of three sharp, angry words—

And every crack and crevice in the building was outlined in yellow and red, as the entire shed was engulfed in flames from outside.

Alberich cried out, and staggered away from the wall he'd been leaning against. The shed was bigger than he'd thought—but not big enough to protect him. The oil they'd spread so profligately made the flames burn hotter, and the wood of the shed was old, weathered, probably dry. Within moments, the very air scorched him; he hid his mouth in a fold of his shirt, but his lungs burned with every breath. His eyes streamed tears of pain as he turned, staggering, searching for an escape that didn't exist.

One of the walls burned through, showing the flames leaping from the wood and brush piled beyond it. He couldn't hear anything but the roar of the flames. At any moment now, the roof would cave in, burying him in burning debris—

:*Look out!*:

How he heard the warning—or how he knew to stagger back as far as he could without being incinerated on the spot—he did not know. But a heartbeat after that warning shout in his mind, a huge, silver-white shadow lofted through the hole in the burning wall, and landed beside him. It was still wearing his saddle and hackamore—

And it turned huge, impossibly *blue* eyes on him as he stood there gaping at it. It? No. *Him.*

:*On!*: the stallion snapped at him. :*The roof's about to go!*:

Whatever fear he had of the beast, he was more afraid of a death by burning. With hands that screamed with pain, he grabbed the saddle-bow and threw himself onto it. He hadn't even found the stirrups when the stallion turned on his hind feet.

There was a crack of collapsing wood, as fire engulfed them. Burning thatch fell before and behind them, sparks showering as the air was sucked into the blaze, hotter. . . .

But, amazingly, no fire licked at his flesh once he had mounted. . . .

Alberich sobbed with relief as the cool air surged into his lungs—the stallion's hooves hit the ground beyond the flames, and he gasped with pain as he was flung forward against the saddle-bow.

Then the real pain began, the torture of half-scorched skin, and the broken bones of his capture, jarred into agony by the stallion's headlong gallop into the night. The beast thundered towards the villagers, and they screamed and parted before it; soldiers and Voice alike were caught unawares, and not one of them raised a weapon in time to stop the flight.

:*Stay on,*: the stallion said grimly, into his mind, as the darkness was shattered by the red lightning of his own pain. :*Stay on, stay with me; we have a long way to go before we're safe. Stay with me. . . .*:

Safe where? he wanted to ask—but there was no way to ask around the pain. All he could do was to hang on, and hope he could do what the horse wanted.

An eternity later—as dawn rose as red as the flames that had nearly killed him—the stallion had slowed to a walk. Dawn was on their right, which meant that the stallion was heading north, across the border, into the witch-kingdom of Valdemar. Which only made sense, since what he'd thought was a horse had turned out to be one of the blue-eyed witch-beasts. . . .

None of it mattered. Now that the stallion had slowed to a walk, his pain had dulled, but he was exhausted and out of any energy to think or even feel with. What could the witches do to him, after all? Kill him? At the moment, that would be a kindness. . . .

The stallion stopped, and he looked up, trying to see through the film that had come over his vision. At first he thought he was seeing double; two white witch-beasts and two white-clad riders blocked the road. But then he realized that there *were* two of them, hastily dismounting, reaching for him.

He let himself slide down into their hands, hearing nothing he could understand, only a babble of strange syllables.

Then, in his mind—

:*Can you hear me?*:

:*I—what?*: he replied, without thinking.

:*Taver says his name's Alberich,*: came a second voice in his head. :*Alberich? Can you stay with us a little longer? We need to get you to a Healer. You're going into shock; fight it for us. Your Companion will help you, if you let him.*:

His what? He shook his head; not in negation, in puzzlement. Where was he? All his life he'd heard that the witches of Valdemar were evil—but—

:*And all our lives we've heard that nothing comes out of Karse but brigands and bad weather,*: said the first voice, full of concern, but with an edge of humor to it. He shook his head again and peered up at the person supporting him on his right. A woman, with many laugh-lines etched around her generous mouth. She seemed to fit that first voice in his head, somehow. . . .

:*So, which are you, Alberich?*: she asked, as he fought to stay awake, feeling the presence of the stallion *(his*

Companion?) like a steady shoulder to lean against, deep inside his soul. :*Brigand, or bad weather?*:

:*Neither . . . I hope . . .*: he replied, absently, as he clung to consciousness as she'd asked.

:*Good. I'd hate to think of a Companion Choosing a brigand to be a Herald,*: she said, with her mouth twitching a little, as if she was holding back a grin, :*And a thunderstorm in human guise would make uncomfortable company.*:

:*Choosing?*: he asked. :*What—what do you mean?*:

:*I mean that you're a Herald, my friend,*: she told him. :*Somehow your Companion managed to insinuate himself across the Border to get you, too. That's how Heralds of Valdemar are made; Companions Choose them—*: She looked up and away from him, and relief and satisfaction spread over her face at whatever it was she saw. :—*and the rest of it can wait. Aren's brought the Healer. Go ahead and let go, we'll take over from here.*:

He took her at her word, and let the darkness take him. But her last words followed him down into the shadows, and instead of bringing the fear they *should* have given him, they brought him comfort, and a peace he never expected.

:*It's a hell of a greeting, Herald Alberich, and a hell of a way to get here—but welcome to Valdemar, brother. Welcome . . .*:

This odd little story was first published in Marion Zimmer Bradley's Fantasy Magazine. *It's the one I always use as an example when people ask me where I get my ideas. This one literally came as I was driving to work, saw a piece of cardboard skitter across the road in front of me as if it was alive, and thought, "Now what if it* was *alive?"*

Roadkill

A gust of wind hit the side of George Randal's van and nearly tore the steering wheel out of his hands. He cursed as the vehicle lurched sideways, and wrestled it back into his own lane.

It was a good thing there weren't too many people on the road. It was just a damned good thing that Mingo Road *was* a four-lane at this point, or he'd have been in the ditch. A mile away, it wasn't, but all the shift traffic from the airline maintenance base, the Rockwell plant and the McDonald-Douglas plant where he worked would have put an intolerable strain on a two-lane road.

The stoplight at Mingo and 163rd turned yellow, and rather than push his luck, he obeyed it, instead of doing an "Okie caution" ("Step on the gas, Fred, she's fixin' to turn red"). This was going to be another typical late spring Oklahoma day. Wind gusting up to 60 per, and rain off and on. Used to be, when he was a kid, it'd be dry as old bones by this late in the season, but not anymore. All the flood-control projects and water-management dams had changed the micro-climate, and it was unlikely this part of Oklahoma would ever see another Dust-Bowl.

Although with winds like this, he could certainly extrapolate what it had been like, back then during the thirties.

The habit of working a mental simulation was so ingrained it was close to a reflex; once the thought occurred, his mind took over, calculating wind-speed, type of dust, carrying capacity of the air. He was so intent on the internal calculations that he hardly noticed when the light turned green, and only the impatient honk of the car behind him jolted him out of his reverie. He pulled the van out into the intersection, and the red sports-car behind him roared around him, driver giving him the finger as he passed.

"You son of a—" he noted with satisfaction the MacDac parking permit in the corner of the rear window: the vanity plate was an easy one to remember, "HOTONE." He'd tell a little fib to the guard at the guard shack, and have the jerk cited for reckless driving in the parking-lot. That would go on his work-record, and serve him right, too.

If it hadn't been for the combination of the wind gust and the fool in the red IROC, he would never have noticed the strange behavior of that piece of cardboard in the median strip.

But because of the gust, he *knew* which direction the wind was coming from. When the IROC screamed right over the center-line, heading straight toward a piece of flattened box, and the box skittered just barely out of the way as if the wind had picked it up and moved it in time, something went off in his brain.

As he came up even to where the box had been, he

saw what the thing had been covering; roadkill, a dead 'possum. At that exact moment he knew what had been wrong with the scene a second before, when the box had moved. Because it had moved *against* the wind.

He cast a startled glance in his rear-view mirror just in time to see the box skitter back, with the wind this time, and stop just covering the dead animal.

That brought all the little calculations going on in his head to a screeching halt. George was an orderly man, a career engineer, whose one fervent belief was that everything could be explained in terms of physics if you had enough data.

Except that this little incident was completely outside his ordered universe.

He was so preoccupied with trying to think of an explanation for the box's anomalous behavior that he didn't remember to report the kid in the sports-car at the guard-shack. He couldn't even get his mind on the new canard specs he'd been so excited about yesterday. Instead he sat at his desk, playing with the CAD/CAM computer, trying to find *some* way for that box to have done what it did.

And coming up dry. It should not, *could* not, have moved that way, and the odds against it moving back to exactly the same place where it had left were unbelievable.

He finally grabbed his gym-bag, left his cubicle, and headed for the tiny locker-room MacDac kept for those employees who had taken up running or jogging on their lunch-breaks. Obviously he was not going to get anything done until he checked the site out, and he might just as well combine that with his lunch-time exercise. Today he'd run out on Mingo instead of around the base.

A couple of Air National Guard A-4s cruised by overhead, momentarily distracting him. He'd forgotten exactly where the roadkill had been, and before he was quite ready for it, he was practically on top of it. Suddenly he was no longer quite sure that he wanted to do this. It seemed silly, a fantasy born of too many late-night movies. But as long as he was out here . . .

The box was nowhere in sight. Feeling slightly foolish, he crossed to the median and took a good look at the body.

It was half-eaten, which wasn't particularly amazing. Any roadkill that was relatively fresh was bound to get chewed on.

Except that the last time he'd seen roadkill on the median, it had stayed there until it bloated, untouched. Animals didn't like the traffic; they wouldn't go after carrion in the middle of the road if they could help it.

And there was something wrong with the way the bite-marks looked too. Old Boy Scout memories came back, tracking and identifying animals by signs. . . .

The flesh hadn't been bitten off so much as carved off—as if the carcass had been chewed by something with enormous buck teeth, like some kind of carnivorous horse, or beaver. Nothing in his limited experience made marks like that.

As a cold trickle ran down his spine, a rustle in the weeds at the side of the road made him jump. He looked up.

The box was there, in the weeds. He hadn't seen it, half-hidden there, until it had moved. It almost seemed as if the thing was watching him; the way it had a corner poked out of the weeds like a head. . . .

His reaction was stupid and irrational, and he didn't care. He bolted, ran all the way back to the guard-shack with a chill in his stomach that all his running couldn't warm.

He didn't stop until he reached the guard-shack and the safety of the fenced-in MacDac compound, the sanity and rational universe of steel and measurement where nothing existed that could not be simulated on a computer screen.

He slowed to a gentle jog as he passed the shack; he'd have liked to stop, because his heart was pounding so hard he couldn't hear anything, but if he did, the guards would ask him what was wrong. . . .

He waited until he was just out of sight, and then dropped to a walk. He remembered from somewhere, maybe one of his jogging tapes, that it was a bad idea just to stop, that his muscles would stiffen. Actually he had the feeling if he went to his knees on the verge like he wanted to, he'd never get up again.

He reached the sanctuary of his air-conditioned office and slumped down into his chair, still panting. He waited with his eyes closed for his heart to stop pounding, while the sweat cooled and dried in the gust of metallic-flavored air from the vent over his chair. He tried to summon up laughter at himself, a grown man, for finding a flattened piece of cardboard so frightening, but the laughter wouldn't come.

Instead other memories of those days as a Boy Scout returned, of the year he'd spent at camp where he'd learned those meager tracking skills. One of the counselors had a grandfather who was—or so the boy claimed—a full Cherokee medicine man. He'd persuaded the old man to make a visit to the camp. George had found himself impressed against his will, as had the rest of the Scouts; the old man still wore his hair in two long, iron-gray braids and a bone necklace under his plain work-shirt. He had a dignity and self-possession that kept all of the rowdy adolescents in awe of him and silent when he spoke.

He'd condescended to tell stories at their campfire several times. Most of them were tales of what his life had been like as a boy on the reservation at the turn of the century—but once or twice he'd told them bits of odd Indian lore, not all of it Cherokee.

Like the shape-changers. George didn't remember what he'd called them, but he did recall what had started the story. One of the boys had seen *I Was A Teen-age Werewolf* before he'd come to camp, and he was regaling all of them with a vivid description of

Michael Landon's transformation into the monster. The old man had listened, and scoffed. That was no kind of shape-changer, he'd told them scornfully. Then he had launched into a new story.

George no longer recalled the words, but he remembered the gist of it. How the shape-changers would prey upon the Indians in a peculiar fashion; stealing what they wanted by deception. If one wanted meat, for instance, he would transform himself into a hunter's game-bag and wait for the Indian to stuff the "bag" full, then shift back and carry the game off while the hunter's back was turned. If one wanted a new buffalo-robe, he would transform himself into a stretching-frame—or if very ambitious, into a tipi, and make off with all of the inhabitant's worldly goods.

"Why didn't they just turn into horses and carry everything off?" he'd wanted to know. The old man had shaken his head. "Because they cannot take a living form," he'd said, "only a dead one. And you do not want to catch them, either. Better for you to pretend it never happened."

But he wouldn't say what would happen if someone *did* catch the thief at work. He only looked, for a brief instant, very frightened, as if he had not intended to say that much.

George felt suddenly sick. What if these things, these shape-changers, *weren't* just legend. What could they be living on now? They wouldn't be able to sneak into someone's house and counterfeit a refrigerator.

But there was all that roadkill, enough dead animals along Mingo alone each year to keep someone going, if that someone wasn't too fastidious.

And what would be easier to mimic than an old, flattened box?

He wanted to laugh at himself, but the laughter wouldn't come. This was such a stupid fantasy, built out of nothing but a boy's imagination and a box that didn't behave the way it ought to.

Instead, he only felt sicker, and more frightened. Now he could recall the one thing the old man had said about the creatures and their fear of discovery.

"They do not permit it," he'd said, as his eyes widened in that strange flicker of fear. *"They do not permit it."*

Finally he just couldn't sit there anymore. He picked up the phone and mumbled something to his manager about feeling sick, grabbed his car keys and headed for the parking lot. Several of the others on the engineering staff looked at him oddly as he passed their desks; the secretary even stopped him and asked him if he felt all right. He mumbled something at her that didn't change her look of concern, and assured her that he was going straight home.

He told himself that he was going to do just that. He even had his turn-signal on for a right-hand turn, fully intending to take the on-ramp at Pine and take the freeway home.

But instead he found himself turning left, where the roadkill was still lying.

He saw it as he came up over the rise; and the box was lying on top of it once again.

Suddenly desperate to prove to himself that this entire fantasy he'd created around a dead 'possum and a piece of cardboard was nothing more than that, he jerked the wheel over and straddled the median, gunning the engine and heading straight for the dingy brown splotch of the flattened box.

There was no wind now; if the thing moved, it would have to do so under its own power.

He floored the accelerator, determined that the thing wasn't going to escape his tires.

It didn't move; he felt a sudden surge of joy—

Then the thing struck.

It leapt up at the last possible second, landing with a *splat*, splayed across his windshield. He had a brief, horrifying impression of some kind of face, flattened and distorted, red eyes and huge, beaver-like teeth as long as his hand—

Then it was gone, and the car was out of control, tires screaming, wheel wrenching under his hands.

He pumped his brakes—once, twice—then the pedal went flat to the floor.

And as the car heeled over on two wheels, beginning a high-speed roll that could have only one ending, that analytical part of his mind that was not screaming in terror was calculating just how easy it would be for a pair of huge, chisel-like teeth to shear through a brake-line.

Larry and I wrote this for the Keith Laumer "Bolo" anthology, but it stands pretty well alone. All you have to know is that Bolos are fairly unstoppable, self-aware, intelligent tanks.

Operation Desert Fox

Mercedes Lackey & Larry Dixon

Siegfried O'Harrigan's name had sometimes caused confusion, although the Service tended to be color-blind. He was black, slight of build and descended from a woman whose African tribal name had been long since lost to her descendants.

He wore both Caucasian names—Siegfried and O'Harrigan—as badges of high honor, however, as had all of that lady's descendants. Many times, although it might have been politically correct to do so, Siegfried's ancestors had resisted changing their name to something more ethnic. Their name was a gift—and not a badge of servitude to anyone. One did not return a gift, especially not one steeped in the love of ancestors. . . .

Siegfried had heard the story many times as a child,

and had never tired of it. The tale was the modern equivalent of a fairy-tale, it had been so very unlikely. *O'Harrigan* had been the name of an Irish-born engineer, fresh off the boat himself, who had seen Siegfried's many-times-great grandmother and her infant son being herded down the gangplank and straight to the Richmond Virginia slave market. She had been, perhaps, thirteen years old when the Arab slave-traders had stolen her. That she had survived the journey at all was a miracle. And she was the very first thing that O'Harrigan set eyes on as he stepped onto the dock in this new land of freedom.

The irony had not been lost on him. Sick and frightened, the woman had locked eyes with Sean O'Harrigan for a single instant, but that instant had been enough.

They had shared neither language nor race, but perhaps Sean had seen in her eyes the antithesis of everything he had come to America to find. *His* people had suffered virtual slavery at the hands of the English landlords; he knew what slavery felt like. He was outraged, and felt that he had to do *something*. He could not save all the slaves offloaded this day—but he could help these two.

He had followed the traders to the market and bought the woman and her child "off the coffle," paying for them before they could be put up on the auction-block, before they could even be warehoused. He fed them, cared for them until they were strong, and then put them on *another* boat, this time as passengers, before the woman could learn much more than his name. The rest the O'Harrigans learned later, from Sean's letters, long after.

The boat was headed back to Africa, to the newly-founded nation of Liberia, a place of hope for freed slaves, whose very name meant "land of liberty." Life there would not be easy for them, but it would not be a life spent in chains, suffering at the whims of men who called themselves "Master."

Thereafter, the woman and her children wore the name of O'Harrigan proudly, in memory of the stranger's kindness—as many other citizens of the newly-formed nation would wear the names of those who had freed them.

No, the O'Harrigans would not change their name for any turn of politics. Respect earned was infinitely more powerful than any messages beaten into someone by whips or media.

And as for the name "Siegfried"—that was also in memory of a stranger's kindness; this time a member of Rommel's Afrika Korps. Another random act of kindness, this time from a first lieutenant who had seen to it that a captured black man with the name O'Harrigan was correctly identified as Liberian and not as American. He had then seen to it that John O'Harrigan was treated well and released.

John had named his first-born son for that German, because the young lieutenant had no children of his own. The tradition and the story that went with it had continued down the generations, joining that of Sean O'Harrigan. Siegfried's people remembered their debts of honor.

Siegfried O'Harrigan's name was at violent odds with his appearance. He was neither blond and tall, nor short and red-haired—and in fact, he was not Caucasian at all.

In this much, he matched the colonists of Bachman's World, most of whom were of East Indian and Pakistani descent. In every other way, he was totally unlike them.

He had been in the military for most of his life, and had planned to stay in. He was happy in uniform, and for many of the colonists here, that was a totally foreign concept.

Both of those stories of his ancestors were in his mind as he stood, travel-weary and yet excited, before a massive piece of the machinery of war, a glorious hulk of purpose-built design. It was larger than a good many of the buildings of this far-off colony at the edges of human space.

Bachman's World. A poor colony known only for its single export of a medicinal desert plant, it was not a place likely to attract a tourist trade. Those who came here left because life was even harder in the slums of Calcutta, or the perpetually typhoon-swept mud-flats of Bangladesh. They were farmers, who grew vast acreages of the "saje" for export, and irrigated just enough land to feed themselves. A hot, dry wind blew sand into the tight curls of his hair and stirred the short sleeves of his desert-khaki uniform. It occurred to him that he could not have chosen a more appropriate setting for what was likely to prove a life-long exile, considering his hobby—his obsession. And yet, it was an exile he had chosen willingly, even eagerly.

This behemoth, this juggernaut, this mountain of gleaming metal, was a Bolo. Now, it was *his* Bolo, his partner. A partner whose workings he knew intimately . . . and whose thought processes suited his so uniquely that there might not be a similar match in all the Galaxy.

RML-1138. Outmoded now, and facing retirement—which, for a Bolo, meant *deactivation.*

Extinction, in other words. Bolos were more than "super-tanks," more than war machines, for they were inhabited by some of the finest AIs in human space. When a Bolo was "retired," so was the AI. Permanently.

There were those, even now, who were lobbying for AI rights, who equated deactivation with murder. They were opposed by any number of special-interest groups, beginning with religionists, who objected to the notion than anything housed in a "body" of electronic circuitry could be considered "human" enough to "murder." No matter which side won, nothing would occur soon enough to save this particular Bolo.

Siegfried had also faced retirement, for the same reason. *Outmoded.* He had specialized in weapons'- systems repair, the specific, delicate tracking and targeting systems.

Which were now outmoded, out-of-date; *he* had been

deemed too old to retrain. He had been facing an uncertain future, relegated to some dead-end job with no chance for promotion, or more likely, given an "early-out" option. He had applied for a transfer, listing, in desperation, everything that might give him an edge somewhere. On the advice of his superiors, he had included his background and his hobby of military strategy of the pre-Atomic period.

And to his utter amazement, it had been that background and hobby that had attracted the attention of someone in the Reserves, someone who had been looking to make a most particular match. . . .

The wind died; no one with any sense moved outside during the heat of midday. The port might have been deserted, but for a lone motor running somewhere in the distance.

The Bolo was utterly silent, but Siegfried knew that he—*he*, not *it*—was watching him, examining him with a myriad of sophisticated instruments. By now, he probably even knew how many fillings were in his mouth, how many grommets in his desert-boots. He had already passed judgment on Siegfried's service record, but there was this final confrontation to face, before the partnership could be declared a reality.

He cleared his throat, delicately. Now came the moment of truth. It was time to find out if what one administrator in the Reserves—and one human facing early-out and a future of desperate scrabbling for employment—thought was the perfect match really *would* prove to be the salvation of that human and this huge marvel of machinery and circuits.

Siegfried's hobby was the key—desert warfare, tactics, and most of all, the history and thought of one particular desert commander.

Erwin Rommel. The "Desert Fox," the man his greatest rival had termed "the last chivalrous knight." Siegfried knew everything there was to know about the great tank-commander. He had fought and refought every campaign Rommel had ever commanded, and his admiration for the man whose life had briefly touched on that of his own ancestor's had never faded, nor had his fascination with the man and his genius.

And there was at least one other being in the universe whose fascination with the Desert Fox matched Siegfried's. This being; the intelligence resident in this particular Bolo, the Bolo that called *himself* "Rommel." Most, if not all, Bolos acquired a name or nickname based on their designations—LNE became "Lenny," or "KKR" became "Kicker." Whether this Bolo had been fascinated by the Desert Fox because of his designation, or had noticed the resemblance of "RML" to "Rommel" because of his fascination, it didn't much matter. Rommel was as much an expert on his namesake as Siegfried was.

Like Siegfried, RML-1138 was scheduled for "earlyout," but like Siegfried, the Reserves offered him a reprieve. The Reserves didn't usually take or need Bolos; for one thing, they were dreadfully expensive. A Reserve unit could requisition a great deal of equipment for the "cost" of one Bolo. For another, the close partnership required between Bolo and operator precluded use of Bolos in situations where the "partnerships" would not last past the exercise of the moment. Nor were Bolo partners often "retired" to the Reserves.

And not too many Bolos were available to the Reserves. Retirement for both Bolo and operator was usually permanent, and as often as not, was in the front lines.

But luck (good or ill, it remained to be seen) was with Rommel; he had lost his partner to a deadly virus, he had not seen much in the way of combat, and he was in near-new condition.

And Bachman's World wanted a Reserve battalion. They could not field their own—every able-bodied human here was a farmer or engaged in the export trade. A substantial percentage of the population was of some form of pacifistic religion that precluded bearing arms—Janist, Buddhist, some forms of Hindu.

Bachman's World was *entitled* to a Reserve force; it was their right under the law to have an on-planet defense force supplied by the regular military. Just because Bachman's World was back-of-beyond of nowhere, and even the most conservative of military planners thought their insistence on having such a force in place to be paranoid in the extreme, that did not negate their right to have it. Their charter was clear. The law was on their side.

Sending them a Reserve battalion would be expensive in the extreme, in terms of maintaining that battalion. The soldiers would be full-timers, on full pay. There was no base—it would have to be built. There was no equipment—that would all have to be imported.

That was when one solitary bean-counting accountant at High Command came up with the answer that would satisfy the letter of the law, yet save the military considerable expense.

The law had been written stipulating, not numbers of personnel and equipment, but a monetary amount. That unknown accountant had determined that the amount so stipulated, meant to be the equivalent value of an infantry battalion, exactly equaled the worth of one Bolo and its operator.

The records-search was on.

Enter one Reserve officer, searching for a Bolo in good condition, about to be "retired," with no current operator-partner—

—and someone to match him, familiar with at least the rudiments of mech-warfare, the insides of a Bolo, and willing to be exiled for the rest of his life.

Finding RML-1138, called "Rommel," and Siegfried O'Harrigan, hobbyist military historian.

The government of Bachman's World was less than pleased with the response to their demand, but there was little they could do besides protest. Rommel was shipped to Bachman's World first; Siegfried was given a crash-course in Bolo operation. He followed on the first regularly-scheduled freighter as soon as his training was over. If, for whatever reason, the pairing did not work, he would leave on the same freighter that brought him.

Now, came the moment of truth.

"*Guten tag, Herr Rommel,*" he said, in careful German, the antique German he had learned in order to be able to read first-hand chronicles in the original language. "*Ich bin Siegfried O'Harrigan.*"

A moment of silence—and then, surprisingly, a sound much like a dry chuckle.

"*Wie geht's, Herr O'Harrigan.* I've been expecting you. Aren't you a little dark to be a Storm Trooper?"

The voice was deep, pleasant, and came from a point somewhere above Siegfried's head. And Siegfried knew the question was a trap, of sorts. Or a test, to see just how much he really *did* know, as opposed to what he claimed to know. A good many pre-Atomic historians could be caught by that question themselves.

"Hardly a Storm Trooper," he countered. "Field-Marshall Erwin Rommel would not have had one of *those* under his command. And no Nazis, either. Don't think to trap *me* that easily."

The Bolo uttered that same dry chuckle. "Good for you, Siegfried O'Harrigan. *Willkommen.*"

The hatch opened, silently; a ladder descended just as silently, inviting Siegfried to come out of the hot, desert sun and into Rommel's controlled interior. Rommel had replied to Siegfried's response, but had done so with nothing unnecessary in the way of words, in the tradition of his namesake.

Siegfried had passed the test.

Once again, Siegfried stood in the blindingly hot sun, this time at strict attention, watching the departing back of the mayor of Port City. The interview had not been pleasant, although both parties had been strictly polite; the mayor's back was stiff with anger. He had not cared for what Siegfried had told him.

"They do not much care for us, do they, Siegfried?" Rommel sounded resigned, and Siegfried sighed. It was impossible to hide anything from the Bolo; Rommel had already proven himself to be an adept reader of human body-language, and of course, anything that was broadcast over the airwaves, scrambled or not, Rommel could access and read. Rommel was right; he and his partner were not the most popular of residents at the moment.

What amazed Siegfried, and continued to amaze him, was how *human* the Bolo was. He was used to AIs of course, but Rommel was something special. Rommel cared about what people did and thought; most AIs really didn't take a great interest in the doings and opinions of mere humans.

"No, Rommel, they don't," he replied. "You really can't blame them; they thought they were going to get a battalion of conventional troops, not one very expensive piece of equipment and one single human."

"But we are easily the equivalent of a battalion of conventional troops," Rommel objected, logically. He lowered his ladder, and now that the mayor was well out of sight, Siegfried felt free to climb back into the cool interior of the Bolo.

He waited until he was settled in his customary seat, now worn to the contours of his own figure after a year, before he answered the AI he now consciously considered to be his best friend as well as his assigned partner. Inside the cabin of the Bolo, everything was clean, if a little worn—cool—the light dimmed the way Siegfried liked it. This was, in fact, the most comfortable quarters Siegfried had ever enjoyed. Granted, things were a bit cramped, but he had everything he needed in here, from shower and cooking facilities to multiple kinds of entertainment. And the Bolo did not need to worry about "wasting" energy; his power-plant was geared to supply full-combat needs in any and all climates; what Siegfried needed to keep cool and comfortable was miniscule. Outside, the ever-present desert sand blew everywhere, the heat was enough to drive even the most patient person mad, and the sun bleached everything to a bone-white. Inside was a compact world of Siegfried's own.

Bachman's World had little to recommend it. That was the problem.

"It's a complicated issue, Rommel," he said. "If a battalion of conventional troops had been sent here, there would have been more than the initial expenditure—there would have been an ongoing expenditure to support them."

"Yes—that support money would come into the community. I understand their distress." Rommel would understand, of course; Field Marshal Erwin Rommel had understood the problems of supply only too well, and his namesake could hardly do less. "Could it be they demanded the troops in the first place in order to gain that money?"

Siegfried grimaced, and toyed with the controls on the panel in front of him. "That's what High Command thinks, actually. There never was any real reason to think Bachman's World was under any sort of threat, and after a year, there's even less reason than there was when they made the request. They expected something to bring in money from outside; you and I are hardly bringing in big revenue for them."

Indeed, they weren't bringing in any income at all. Rommel, of course, required no support, since he was not expending anything. His power-plant would supply all his needs for the next hundred years before it needed refueling. If there had been a battalion of men here, it would have been less expensive for High Command to set up a standard mess hall, buying their supplies from the local farmers, rather than shipping in food and other supplies. Further, the men would have been spending their pay locally. In fact, local suppliers would have been found for nearly everything except weaponry.

But with only one man here, it was far less expensive for High Command to arrange for his supplies to come in at regular intervals on scheduled freight-runs. The Bolo ate nothing. They didn't even use "local" water; the Bolo recycled nearly every drop, and distilled the rest from occasional rainfall and dew. Siegfried was not the usual soldier-on-leave; when he spent his pay, it was generally off-planet, ordering things to be shipped in, and not patronizing local merchants. He bought books, not beer; he didn't gamble, his interest in food was minimal and satisfied by the R.E.M.s (Ready-to-Eat-Meals) that were standard field issue and shipped to him by the crateful. And he was far more interested in that four-letter word for "intercourse" that began with a "t" than in intercourse of any other kind. He was an ascetic scholar; such men were not the sort who brought any amount of money into a community. He and his partner, parked as they were at the edge of the spaceport, were a continual reminder of how Bachman's World had been "cheated."

And for that reason, the mayor of Port City had suggested—stiffly, but politely—that his and Rommel's continuing presence so near the main settlement was somewhat disconcerting. He had hinted that the peace-loving citizens found the Bolo frightening (and never mind that they had requested some sort of defense from the military). And if they could not find a way to make themselves useful, perhaps they ought to at least *earn* their pay by pretending to go on maneuvers. It didn't matter that Siegfried and Rommel were perfectly capable of conducting such exercises without moving. That was hardly the point.

"You heard him, my friend," Siegfried sighed. "They'd like us to go away. Not that they have any authority to order us to do so—as I reminded the mayor. But I suspect seeing us constantly is something of an embarrassment to whoever it was that promised a battalion of troops to bring in cash and got us instead."

"In that case, Siegfried," Rommel said gently, "we probably should take the mayor's suggestion. How long do you think we should stay away?"

"When's the next ship due in?" Siegfried replied. "There's no real reason for us to be here until it arrives, and then we only need to stay long enough to pick up my supplies."

"True." With a barely-audible rumble, Rommel started his banks of motive engines. "Have you any destination in mind?"

Without prompting, Rommel projected the map of the immediate area on one of Siegfried's control-room screens. Siegfried studied it for a moment, trying to work out the possible repercussions of vanishing into the hills altogether. "I'll tell you what, old man," he said slowly, "we've just been playing at doing our job. Really, that's hardly honorable, when it comes down to it. Even if they don't need us and never did, the fact is that they asked for on-planet protection, and we haven't even planned how to give it to them. How about if we actually go out there in the bush and *do* that planning?"

There was interest in the AI's voice; he did not imagine it. "What do you mean by that?" Rommel asked.

"I mean, let's go out there and scout the territory ourselves; plan defenses and offenses, as if this dustball *was* likely to be invaded. The topographical surveys stink for military purposes; let's get a real war plan in place. What the hell—it can't hurt, right? And if the locals see us actually doing some work, they might not think so badly of us."

Rommel was silent for a moment. "They will still blame High Command, Siegfried. They did not receive what they wanted, even though they received what they were entitled to."

"But they won't blame *us*." He put a little coaxing

into his voice. "Look, Rommel, we're going to be here for the rest of our lives, and we really can't afford to have the entire population angry with us forever. I know our standing orders are to stay at Port City, but the mayor just countermanded those orders. So let's have some fun, and show'em we know our duty at the same time! Let's use Erwin's strategies around here, and see how they work! We can run all kinds of scenarios—let's assume in the event of a real invasion we could get some of these farmers to pick up a weapon; that'll give us additional scenarios to run. Figure troops against you, mechs against you, troops and mechs against you, plus untrained men against troops, men against mechs, you against another Bolo-type AI—"

"It would be entertaining." Rommel sounded very interested. "And as long as we keep our defensive surveillance up, and an eye on Port City, we would not technically be violating orders. . . ."

"Then let's do it," Siegfried said decisively. "Like I said, the maps they gave us stink; let's go make our own, then plot strategy. Let's find every wadi and overhang big enough to hide you. Let's act as if there really *was* going to be an invasion. Let's give them some options, log the plans with the mayor's office. We can plan for evacuations, we can check resources, there's a lot of things we can do. And let's start right now!"

They mapped every dry stream-bed, every dusty hill, every animal-trail. For months, the two of them rumbled across the arid landscape, with Siegfried emerging now and again to carry surveying instruments to the tops of hills too fragile to bear Rommel's weight. And when every inch of territory within a week of Port City had been surveyed and accurately mapped, they began playing a game of "hide and seek" with the locals.

It was surprisingly gratifying. At first, after they had vanished for a while, the local news-channel seemed to reflect an attitude of "and good riddance." But then, when *no one* spotted them, there was a certain amount of concern—followed by a certain amount of annoyance. After all, Rommel was "their" Bolo—what was Siegfried doing, taking him out for some kind of vacation? As if Bachman's World offered any kind of amusement. . . .

That was when Rommel and Siegfried began stalking farmers.

They would find a good hiding place and get into it well in advance of a farmer's arrival. When he would show up, Rommel would rise up, seemingly from out of the ground, draped in camouflage-net, his weaponry trained on the farmer's vehicle. Then Siegfried would pop up out of the hatch, wave cheerfully, retract the camouflage, and he and Rommel would rumble away.

Talk of "vacations" ceased entirely after that.

They extended their range, once they were certain that the locals were no longer assuming the two of them were "gold-bricking." Rommel tested all of his abilities to the limit, making certain everything was still up to spec. And on the few occasions that it wasn't, Siegfried put in a requisition for parts and spent many long hours making certain that the repairs and replacements *were* bringing Rommel up to like-new condition.

Together they plotted defensive and offensive strategies; Siegfried studied Rommel's manuals as if a time would come when he would have to rebuild Rommel from spare parts. They ran every kind of simulation in the book—and not just on Rommel's computers, but with Rommel himself actually running and dry-firing against plotted enemies. Occasionally one of the news-people would become curious about their whereabouts, and lie in wait for them when the scheduled supplies arrived. Siegfried would give a formal interview, reporting in general what they had been doing—and then, he would carefully file another set of emergency plans with the mayor's office. Sometimes it even made the evening news. Once, it was even accompanied by a clip someone had shot of Rommel roaring at top speed across a ridge.

Nor was that all they did. As Rommel pointed out, the presumptive "battalion" would have been available in emergencies—there was no reason why *they* shouldn't respond when local emergencies came up.

So—when a flash-flood trapped a young woman and three children on the roof of her vehicle, it was Rommel and Siegfried who not only rescued them, but towed the vehicle to safety as well. When a snowfall in the mountains stranded a dozen truckers, Siegfried and Rommel got them out. When a small child was lost while playing in the hills, Rommel found her by having all searchers clear out as soon as the sun went down, and using his heat-sensors to locate every source of approximately her size. They put out runaway brushfires by rolling over them; they responded to Maydays from remote locations when they were nearer than any other agency. They even joined in a manhunt for an escaped rapist—who turned himself in, practically soiling himself with fear, when he learned that Rommel was part of the search-party.

It didn't hurt. They were of no help for men trapped in a mine collapse; or rather, of no *more* help than Siegfried's two hands could make them. They couldn't rebuild bridges that were washed away, nor construct roads. But what they could do, they did, often before anyone thought to ask them for help.

By the end of their second year on Bachman's World, they were at least no longer the target of resentment. Those few citizens they had aided actually looked on them with gratitude. The local politicians whose careers had suffered because of their presence had found other causes to espouse, other schemes to pursue. Siegfried and Rommel were a dead issue.

But by then, the two of them had established a routine of monitoring emergency channels, running their private war-games, updating their maps, and adding changes in the colony to their defense and offense plans. There was no reason to go back to simply sitting beside the spaceport. Neither of them cared for sitting idle, and what they were doing was the nearest either of them would ever get to actually refighting the battles their idol had lost and won.

When High Command got their reports and sent recommendations for further "readiness" preparations, and *commendations* for their "community service"— Siegfried, now wiser in the ways of manipulating public opinion, issued a statement to the press about both.

After that, there were no more rumblings of discontent, and things might have gone on as they were until Siegfried was too old to climb Rommel's ladder.

But the fates had another plan in store for them.

Alarms woke Siegfried out of a sound and dreamless sleep. Not the synthesized pseudo-alarms Rommel used when surprising him for a drill, either, but the real thing—

He launched himself out of his bunk before his eyes were focused, grabbing the back of the com-chair to steady himself before he flung himself into it and strapped himself down. As soon as he moved, Rommel turned off all the alarms but one; the proximity alert from the single defense-satellite in orbit above them.

Interior lighting had gone to full-emergency red. He scrubbed at his eyes with the back of his hand, impatiently; finally they focused on the screens of his console, and he could read what was there. And he swore, fervently and creatively.

One unknown ship sat in geosynch orbit above Port City; a big one, answering no hails from the port, and seeding the skies with what appeared to his sleep-fogged eyes as hundreds of smaller drop-ships.

"The mother-ship has already neutralized the port air-to-ground defenses, Siegfried," Rommel reported grimly. "I don't know what kind of stealthing devices they have, or if they've got some new kind of drive, but they don't match anything in my records. They just appeared out of nowhere and started dumping drop-ships. I think we can assume they're hostiles."

They had a match for just this in their hundreds of plans; unknown ship, unknown attackers, dropping a pattern of offensive troops of some kind—

"What are they landing?" he asked, playing the console board. "You're stealthed, right?"

"To the max," Rommel told him. "I don't detect anything like life-forms on those incoming vessels, but my sensors aren't as sophisticated as they could be. The vessels themselves aren't all that big. My guess is that they're dropping either live troops or clusters of very small mechs, mobile armor, maybe the size of a Panzer."

"Landing pattern?" he asked. He brought up all of Rommel's weaponry; AIs weren't allowed to activate their own weapons. And they weren't allowed to fire on living troops without permission from a human, either. That was the only real reason for a Bolo needing an operator.

"Surrounding Port City, but starting from about where the first farms are." Rommel ran swift readiness-tests on the systems as Siegfried brought them up; the screens scrolled too fast for Siegfried to read them.

They had a name for that particular scenario. It was one of the first possibilities they had run when they began plotting invasion and counter-invasion plans.

"Operation Cattle Drive. Right." If the invaders followed the same scheme he and Rommel had anticipated, they planned to drive the populace into Port City, and either capture the civilians, or destroy them at leisure. He checked their current location; it was out beyond the drop-zone. "Is there anything landing close to us?"

"Not yet—but the odds are that something will soon." Rommel sounded confident, as well he should be—his ability to project landing-patterns was far better than any human's. "I'd say within the next fifteen minutes."

Siegfried suddenly shivered in a breath of cool air

from the ventilators, and was painfully aware suddenly that he was dressed in nothing more than a pair of fatigue-shorts. Oh well; some of the Desert Fox's battles had taken place with the men wearing little else. What they could put up with, he could. There certainly wasn't anyone here to complain.

"As soon as you think we can move without detection, close on the nearest craft," he ordered. "I want to see what we're up against. And start scanning the local freqs; if there's anything in the way of organized defense from the civvies, I want to know about it."

A pause, while the ventilators hummed softly, and glowing dots descended on several screens. "They don't seem to have anything, Siegfried," Rommel reported quietly. "Once the ground-to-space defenses were fried, they just collapsed. Right now, they seem to be in a complete state of panic. They don't even seem to remember that *we're* out here—no one's tried to hail us on any of our regular channels."

"Either that—or they think we're out of commission," he muttered absently. "Or just maybe they are giving us credit for knowing what we're doing and are trying *not* to give us away. I hope so. The longer we can go without detection, the better chance we have to pull something out of a hat."

An increase in vibration warned him that Rommel was about to move. A new screen lit up, this one tracking a single vessel. "Got one," the Bolo said shortly. "I'm coming in behind his sensor sweep."

Four more screens lit up; enhanced front, back, top, and side views of the terrain. Only the changing views on the screens showed that Rommel was moving; other than that, there was no way to tell from inside the cabin what was happening. It would be different if Rommel had to execute evasive maneuvers of course, but right now, he might have still been parked. The control cabin and living quarters were heavily shielded and cushioned against the shocks of ordinary movement. Only if

Rommel took a direct hit by something impressive would Siegfried feel it. . . .

And if he takes a direct hit by something more than impressive—we're slag. Bolos are the best, but they can't take everything.

"The craft is down."

He pushed the thought away from his mind. This was what Rommel had been built to do—this moment justified Rommel's very existence. And *he* had known from the very beginning that the possibility, however remote, had existed that he too would be in combat one day. That was what being in the military was all about. There was no use in pretending otherwise.

Get on with the job. That's what they've sent me here to do. Wasn't there an ancient royal family whose motto was "God, and my Duty?" Then let that be his.

"Have you detected any sensor scans from the mothership?" he asked, his voice a harsh whisper. "Or anything other than a forward scan from the landing craft?" He didn't know why he was whispering—

"Not as yet, Siegfried," Rommel replied, sounding a little surprised. "Apparently, these invaders are confident that there is no one out here at all. Even that forward scan seemed mainly to be a landing-aid."

"Nobody here but us chickens," Siegfried muttered. "Are they offloading yet?"

"Wait—yes. The ramp is down. We will be within visual range ourselves in a moment—there—"

More screens came alive; Siegfried read them rapidly—

Then read them again, incredulously.

"Mechs?" he said, astonished. *"Remotely controlled mechs?"*

"So it appears." Rommel sounded just as mystified. "This does not match any known configuration. There is one limited AI in that ship. Data indicates it is hardened against any attack conventional forces at the port could mount. The ship seems to be digging in—

look at the seismic reading on 4-B. The limited AI is in control of the mechs it is deploying. I believe that we can assume this will be the case for the other invading ships, at least the ones coming down at the moment, since they all appear to be of the same model."

Siegfried studied the screens; as they had assumed, the mechs were about the size of pre-Atomic Panzers, and seemed to be built along similar lines. "Armored mechs. Good against anything a civilian has. Is that ship hardened against anything *you* can throw?" he asked finally.

There was a certain amount of glee in Rommel's voice. "I think not. Shall we try?"

Siegfried's mouth dried. There was no telling what weaponry that ship packed—or the mother-ship held. The mother-ship might be monitoring the drop-ships, watching for attack. *God and my Duty*, he thought.

"You may fire when ready, Herr Rommel."

They had taken the drop-ship by complete surprise; destroying it before it had a chance to transmit distress or tactical data to the mother-ship. The mechs had stopped in their tracks the moment the AI's direction ceased.

But rather than roll on to the next target, Siegfried had ordered Rommel to stealth again, while he examined the remains of the mechs and the controlling craft. He'd had an idea—the question was, would it work?

He knew weapons systems; knew computer-driven control. There were only a limited number of ways such controls could work. And if he recognized any of those here—

He told himself, as he scrambled into clothing and climbed the ladder out of the cabin, that he would give himself an hour. The situation would not change much in an hour; there was very little that he and Rommel could accomplish in that time in the way of mounting a campaign. As it happened, it took him fifteen minutes more than that to learn all he needed to know. At the end of that time, though, he scrambled back into Rommel's guts with mingled feelings of elation and anger.

The ship and mechs were clearly of human origin, and some of the vanes and protrusions that made them look so unfamiliar had been tacked on purely to make both the drop-ships and armored mechs look alien in nature. Someone, somewhere, had discovered something about Bachman's World that suddenly made it valuable. From the hardware interlocks and the programming modes he had found in what was left of the controlling ship, he suspected that the "someone" was not a government, but a corporation.

And a multiplanet corporation could afford to mount an invasion force fairly easily. The best force for the job would, of course, be something precisely like this—completely mechanized. There would be no troops to "hush up" afterwards; no leaks to the interstellar press. Only a nice clean invasion—and, in all probability, a nice, clean extermination at the end of it, with no humans to protest the slaughter of helpless civilians.

And afterwards, there would be no evidence anywhere to contradict the claim that the civilians had slaughtered each other in some kind of local conflict.

The mechs and the AI itself were from systems he had studied when he first started in this specialty—outmoded even by his standards, but reliable, and when set against farmers with hand-weapons, perfectly adequate.

There was one problem with this kind of setup . . . from the enemy's standpoint. It was a problem they didn't know they had.

Yet.

He filled Rommel in on what he had discovered as he raced up the ladder, then slid down the handrails into the command cabin. "Now, here's the thing—I got the access code to command those mechs with a little fiddling in the AI's memory. Nice of them to leave in so many manual overrides for me. I reset the command interface freq to one you have, and hardwired it so they shouldn't be able to change it—"

He jumped into the command chair and strapped in; his hands danced across the keypad, keying in the frequency and the code. Then he saluted the console jauntily. "Congratulations, Herr Rommel," he said, unable to keep the glee out of his voice. "You are now a Field Marshal."

"*Siegfried!*" Yes, there was astonishment in Rommel's synthesized voice. "You just gave me command of an armored mobile strike force!"

"I certainly did. And I freed your command circuits so that you can run them without waiting for my orders to do something." Siegfried couldn't help grinning. "After all, you're not going against living troops, you're going to be attacking AIs and mechs. The next AI might not be so easy to take over, but if you're running in the middle of a swarm of 'friendlies,' you might not be suspected. And when we knock out *that* one, we'll take over again. I'll even put the next bunch on a different command freq so you can command them separately. Sooner or later they'll figure out what we're doing, but by then I hope we'll have at least an equal force under our command."

"This is good, Siegfried!"

"You bet it's good, *mein Freund*," he retorted. "What's more, we've studied the best—they can't possibly have that advantage. All right—let's show these amateurs how one of the old masters handles armor!"

The second and third takeovers were as easy as the first. By the fourth, however, matters had changed. It might have dawned on either the AIs on the ground or whoever was in command of the overall operation in the mother-ship above that the triple loss of AIs and mechs was not due to simple malfunction, but to an unknown and unsuspected enemy.

In that, the hostiles were following in the mental footsteps of another pre-Atomic commander, who had once stated, "Once is happenstance, twice is circumstance, but three times is enemy action."

So the fourth time their forces advanced on a ship, they met with fierce resistance.

They lost about a dozen mechs, and Siegfried had suffered a bit of a shakeup and a fair amount of bruising, but they managed to destroy the fourth AI without much damage to Rommel's exterior. Despite the danger from unexploded shells and some residual radiation, Siegfried doggedly went out into the wreckage to get that precious access code.

He returned to bad news. "They know we're here, Siegfried," Rommel announced. "That last barrage gave them a silhouette upstairs; they know I'm a Bolo, so now they know what they're up against."

Siegfried swore quietly, as he gave Rommel his fourth contingent of mechs. "Well, have they figured out exactly what we're doing yet? Or can you tell?" Siegfried asked while typing in the fourth unit's access codes.

"I can't—I—can't—Siegfried—" the Bolo replied, suddenly without any inflection at all. "Siegfried. There is a problem. Another. I am stretching my—resources—"

This time Siegfried swore with a lot less creativity. That was something he had not even considered! The AIs they were eliminating were much less sophisticated than Rommel—

"Drop the last batch!" he snapped. To his relief, Rommel sounded like himself again as he released control of the last contingent of mechs.

"That was not a pleasurable experience," Rommel said mildly.

"What happened?" he demanded.

"As I needed to devote more resources to controlling the mechs, I began losing higher functions," the Bolo replied simply. "We should have expected that; so far

I am doing the work of three lesser AIs and all the functions you require, *and* maneuvering of the various groups we have captured. As I pick up more groups, I will inevitably lose processing functions."

Siegfried thought, frantically. There were about twenty of these invading ships; their plan absolutely required that Rommel control at least eight of the groups to successfully hold the invasion off Port City. There was no way they'd be anything worse than an annoyance with only three; the other groups could outflank them. "What if you shut down things in here?" he asked. "Run basic life-support, but nothing fancy. And I could drive—run your weapons' systems."

"You could. That would help." Rommel pondered for a moment. "My calculations are that we can take the required eight of the groups if you also issue battle orders and I simply carry them out. But there is a further problem."

"Which is?" he asked—although he had the sinking feeling that he knew what the problem was going to be.

"Higher functions. One of the functions I will lose at about the seventh takeover is what you refer to as my personality. A great deal of my ability to maintain a personality is dependent on devoting a substantial percentage of my central processor to that personality. And if it disappears—"

The Bolo paused. Siegfried's hands clenched on the arms of his chair.

"—it may not return. There is a possibility that the records and algorithms which make up my personality will be written over by comparison files during strategic control calculations." Again Rommel paused. "Siegfried, this is our duty. I am willing to take that chance."

Siegfried swallowed, only to find a lump in his throat and his guts in knots. "Are you sure?" he asked gently. "Are you very sure? What you're talking about is—is a kind of deactivation."

"I am sure," Rommel replied firmly. "The Field Marshal would have made the same choice."

Rommel's manuals were all on a handheld reader. He had studied them from front to back—wasn't there something in there? "Hold on a minute—"

He ran through the index, frantically keyword searching. This was a memory function, right? Or at least it was software. The designers didn't encourage operators to go mucking around in the AI functions . . . what would a computer jock call what he was looking for?

Finally he found it; a tiny section in programmerese, not even listed in the index. He scanned it, quickly, and found the warning that had been the thing that had caught his eye in the first place.

This system has been simulation proven in expected scenarios, but has never been fully field-tested.

What the hell did that mean? He had a guess; this was essentially a full-copy backup of the AI's processor. He suspected that they had never tested the backup function on an AI with a full personality. There was no way of knowing if the restoration function would actually "restore" a lost personality.

But the backup memory-module in question had its own power-supply, and was protected in the most hardened areas of Rommel's interior. Nothing was going to destroy it that didn't slag him and Rommel together, and if "personality" was largely a matter of memory—

It might work. It might not. It was worth trying, even if the backup procedure was fiendishly hard to initiate. They really *didn't* want operators mucking around with the AIs.

Twenty command-strings later, a single memory-mod began its simple task; Rommel was back in charge of the fourth group of mechs, and Siegfried had taken over the driving.

He was not as good as Rommel was, but he was better than he had thought.

They took groups five, and six, and it was horrible—

listening to Rommel fade away, lose the vitality behind the synthesized voice. If Siegfried hadn't had his hands full already, literally, it would have been worse.

But with group seven—

That was when he just about lost it, because in reply to one of his voice-commands, instead of a "Got it, Siegfried," what came over the speakers was the metallic "Affirmative" of a simple voice-activated computer.

All of Rommel's resources were now devoted to self-defense and control of the armored mechs.

God and my Duty. Siegfried took a deep breath, and began keying in the commands for mass armor deployment.

The ancient commanders were right; from the ground, there was no way of knowing when the moment of truth came. Siegfried only realized they had won when the mother-ship suddenly vanished from orbit, and the remaining AIs went dead. Cutting their losses; there was nothing in any of the equipment that would betray *where* it came from. Whoever was in charge of the invasion force must have decided that there was no way they would finish the mission before *someone,* a regularly scheduled freighter or a surprise patrol, discovered what was going on and reported it.

By that time, he had been awake for fifty hours straight; he had put squeeze-bulbs of electrolytic drink near at hand, but he was starving and still thirsty. With the air-conditioning cut out, he must have sweated out every ounce of fluid he drank. His hands were shaking and every muscle in his neck and shoulders were cramped from hunching over the boards.

Rommel was battered and had lost several external sensors and one of his guns. But the moment that the mother-ship vanished, he had only one thought.

He manually dropped control of every mech from Rommel's systems, and waited, praying, for his old friend to "come back."

But nothing happened—other than the obvious things that any AI would do, restoring all the comfort-support and life-support functions, and beginning damage checks and some self-repair.

Rommel was gone.

His throat closed; his stomach knotted. But—

It wasn't tested. That doesn't mean it won't work.

Once more, his hands moved over the keyboard, with another twenty command-strings, telling that little memory-module in the heart of his Bolo to initiate full restoration. He hadn't thought he had water to spare for tears—yet there they were, burning their way down his cheeks. Two of them.

He ignored them, fiercely, shaking his head to clear his eyes, and continuing the command-sequence.

Damage checks and self-repair aborted. Life-support went on automatic.

And Siegfried put his head down on the console to rest his burning eyes for a moment. Just for a moment—

Just—

"Ahem."

Siegfried jolted out of sleep, cracking his elbow on the console, staring around the cabin with his heart racing wildly.

"I believe we have visitors, Siegfried," said that wonderful, familiar voice. "They seem most impatient."

Screens lit up, showing a small army of civilians approaching, riding in everything from outmoded sandrails to tractors, all of them cheering, all of them heading straight for the Bolo.

"We seem to have their approval at least," Rommel continued.

His heart had stopped racing, but he still trembled. And once again, he seemed to have come up with the moisture for tears. He nodded, knowing Rommel would see it, unable for the moment to get any words out.

"Siegfried—before we become immersed in grateful

civilians—how *did* you bring me back?" Rommel asked. "I'm rather curious—I actually seem to remember fading out. An unpleasant experience."

"How did I get you back?" he managed to choke out—and then began laughing.

He held up the manual, laughing, and cried out the famous quote of George Patton—

"'Rommel, you magnificent bastard, *I read your book!*'"

Sometimes we write for odd markets; I wrote this piece for a magazine called Pet Bird Report, *which is bird behaviorist Sally Blanchard's outlet for continuing information on parrot behavior and psychology. It's a terrific magazine, and if you have a bird but haven't subscribed, I suggest you would find it worth your while. With twelve birds, I need all the help I can get! At any rate, Sally asked me for some fiction, and I came up with this.*

Grey

For nine years, Sarah Jane Lyon-White lived happily with her parents in the heart of Africa. Her father was a physician, her mother, a nurse, and they worked at a Protestant mission in the Congo. She was happy there, not the least because her mother and father were far more enlightened than many another mission worker in the days when Victoria was Queen; taking the cause of healing as more sacred than that of conversion, they undertook to work *with* the natives, and made friends instead of enemies among the shamans and medicine-people. Because of this, Sarah was a cherished and protected child, although she was no stranger to the many dangers of life in the Congo.

When she was six, and far older in responsibility than most of her peers, one of the shaman brought her a parrot-chick still in quills; he taught her how to feed and care for it, and told her that while *it* was a child, she was to protect it, but when it was grown, it would protect and guide *her*. She called the parrot "Grey," and it became her best friend—and indeed, although she never told her parents, it became her protector as well.

But when she was nine, her parents sent her to live in England for the sake of her health. And because her mother feared that the climate of England would not be good for Grey's health, she had to leave her beloved friend behind.

Now, this was quite the usual thing in the days when Victoria was Queen and the great British Empire was so vast that there was never an hour when some part of it was not in sunlight. It was thought that English children were more delicate than their parents, and that the inhospitable humors of hot climes would make them sicken and die. Not that their *parents* didn't sicken and die quite as readily as the children, who were, in fact, far sturdier than they were given credit for—but it was thought, by anxious mothers, that the climate of England would be far kinder to them. So off they were shipped, some as young as two and three, torn away from their anxious mamas and native nurses and sent to live with relatives or even total strangers.

Now, as Mr. Kipling and Mrs. Hope-Hodgson have shown us, many of these total strangers—and no few of the relatives—were bad, wicked people, interested only in the round gold sovereigns that the childrens' parents sent to them for their care. There were many schools where the poor lonely things were neglected or even abused; where their health suffered far more than if they had stayed safely at the sides of their mamas.

But there were good schools too, and kindly people, and Sarah Jane's mama had been both wise and careful in her selection. In fact, Sarah Jane's mama had made a choice that was far wiser than even she had guessed. . . .

Nan—that was her only name, for no one had told her of any other—lurked anxiously about the back gate of the Big House. She was new to this neighborhood, for her slatternly mother had lost yet another job in a gin-mill and they had been forced to move all the way across Whitechapel, and this part of London was as foreign to Nan as the wilds of Australia. She had been told by more than one of the children hereabouts that if she hung about the back gate after tea, a strange man with a towel wrapped about his head would come out with a basket of food and give it out to any child who happened to be there. Now, there were not as many children willing to accept this offering as might have been expected, even in this poor neighborhood. They were afraid of the man, afraid of his piercing, black eyes, his swarthy skin, and his way of walking like a great hunting-cat. Some suspected poison in the food, others murmured that he and the woman of the house were foreigners, and intended to kill English children with terrible curses on the food they offered. But Nan was faint with hunger; she hadn't eaten in two days, and was willing to dare poison, curses, and anything else for a bit of bread.

Furthermore, Nan had a secret defense; under duress, she could often sense the intent and even dimly hear the thoughts of others. That was how she avoided her mother when it was most dangerous to approach her, as well as avoiding other dangers in the streets themselves. Nan was certain that if this man had any ill intentions, she would know it.

Still, as tea-time and twilight both approached, she hung back a little from the wrought-iron gate, beginning to wonder if it wouldn't be better to see what, if anything, her mother brought home. If she'd found a job—or a "gen'lmun"—there might be a farthing or two to spare for food before Aggie spent the rest on gin. Behind the high, grimy wall, the Big House loomed dark and ominous against the smoky, lowering sky, and the strange, carved creatures sitting atop every pillar in the wall and every corner of the House fair gave Nan the shivers whenever she looked at them. There were no two alike, and most of them were beasts out of a rummy's worst deliriums. The only one that Nan could see that looked at all normal was a big, grey bird with a fat body and a hooked beak that sat on top of the right-hand gatepost of the back gate.

Nan had no way to tell time, but as she waited, growing colder and hungrier—and more nervous—with each passing moment, she began to think for certain that the other children had been having her on. Teatime was surely long over; the tale they'd told her was nothing more than that, something to gull the newcomer with. It was getting dark, there were no other children waiting, and after dark it was dangerous even for a child like Nan, wise in the ways of the evil streets, to be abroad. Disappointed, and with her stomach a knot of pain, Nan began to turn away from the gate.

"I think that there is no one here, Missy S'ab," said a low, deep voice, heavily accented, sounding disappointed. Nan hastily turned back, and peering through the gloom, she barely made out a tall, dark form with a smaller one beside it.

"No, Karamjit—look there!" replied the voice of a young girl, and the smaller form pointed at Nan. A little girl ran up to the gate, and waved through the bars. "Hello! I'm Sarah—what's your name? Would you like some tea-bread? We've plenty!"

The girl's voice, also strangely accented, had none of the imperiousness that Nan would have expected coming from the child of a "toff." She sounded only friendly and helpful, and that, more than anything, was what drew Nan back to the wrought-iron gate.

"Indeed, Missy Sarah speaks the truth," the man said; and as Nan drew nearer, she saw that the other children had not exaggerated when they described him. His head was wrapped around in a cloth; he wore a long, high-collared coat of some bright stuff, and white trousers that were tucked into glossy boots. He was as fiercely erect as the iron gate itself; lean and angular as a hunting tiger, with skin so dark she could scarcely make out his features, and eyes that glittered at her like beads of black glass.

But strangest, and perhaps most ominous of all, Nan could sense nothing from the dark man. He might not even have been there; there was a blank wall where his thoughts should have been.

The little girl beside him was perfectly ordinary by comparison; a bright little wren of a thing, not pretty, but sweet, with a trusting smile that went straight to Nan's heart. Nan had a motherly side to her; the younger children of whatever neighborhood she lived in tended to flock to her, look up to her, and follow her lead. She in her turn tried to keep them out of trouble, and whenever there was extra to go around, she fed them out of her own scant stocks.

But the tall fellow frightened her, and made her nervous, especially when further moments revealed no more of his intentions than Nan had sensed before; the girl's bright eyes noted that, and she whispered something to the dark man as Nan withdrew a little. He nodded, and handed her a basket that looked promisingly heavy.

Then he withdrew out of sight, leaving the little girl alone at the gate. The child pushed the gate open enough to hand the basket through. "Please, won't you come and take this? It's awfully heavy."

In spite of the clear and open brightness of the little girl's thoughts, ten years of hard living had made Nan suspicious. The child might know nothing of what the dark man wanted. "Woi're yer givin' food away?" she asked, edging forward a little, but not yet quite willing to take the basket.

The little girl put the basket down on the ground and clasped her hands behind her back. "Well, Mem'sab says that she won't tell Maya and Selim to make less food for tea, because she won't have us going hungry while we're growing. And she says that old, stale toast is fit only for starlings, so people ought to have the good of it before it goes stale. And she says that there's no reason why children outside our gate have to go to bed hungry when we have enough to share, and my Mum and Da say that sharing is charity and Charity is one of the cardinal virtues, so Mem'sab is being virtuous, which is a good thing, because she'll go to heaven and she would make a good angel."

Most of that came out in a rush that quite bewildered Nan, especially the last, about cardinal virtues and heaven and angels. But she did understand that "Mem'sab," whoever that was, must be one of those daft religious creatures that gave away food free for the taking, and Nan's own Mum had told her that there was no point in letting other people take what you could get from people like that. So Nan edged forward and made a snatch at the basket-handle.

She tried, that is; it proved a great deal heavier than she'd thought, and she gave an involuntary grunt at the weight of it.

"Be careful," the little girl admonished mischievously. "It's heavy."

"Yer moight'o warned me!" Nan said, a bit indignant, and more than a bit excited. If this wasn't a trick—if there wasn't a brick in the basket—oh, she'd eat well tonight, and tomorrow, too!

"Come back tomorrow!" the little thing called, as she shut the gate and turned and skipped towards the house. "Remember me! I'm Sarah Jane, and I'll bring the basket tomorrow!"

"Thenkee, Sarah Jane," Nan called back, belatedly;

then, just in case these strange creatures would think better of their generosity, she made the basket and herself vanish into the night.

She came earlier the next day, bringing back the now-empty basket, and found Sarah Jane waiting at the gate. To her disappointment, there was no basket waiting beside the child, and Nan almost turned back, but Sarah saw her and called to her before she could fade back into the shadows of the streets.

"Karamjit is bringing the basket in a bit," the child said, "There's things Mem'sab wants you to have. And—what am I to call you? It's rude to call you 'girl,' but I don't know your name."

"Nan," Nan replied, feeling as if a cart had run over her. This child, though younger than Nan herself, had a way of taking over a situation that was all out of keeping with Nan's notion of how things were. "Wot kind'o place is this, anyway?"

"It's a school, a boarding-school," Sarah said promptly. "Mem'sab and her husband have it for the children of people who live in India, mostly. Mem'sab can't have children herself, which is very sad, but she says that means she can be a mother to us. Mem'sab came from India, and that's where Karamjit and Selim and Maya and the others are from, too; they came with her."

"Yer mean the black feller?" Nan asked, bewildered. "Yer from In'ju too?"

"No," Sarah said, shaking her head. "Africa. I wish I was back there." Her face paled and her eyes misted, and Nan, moved by an impulse she did not understand, tried to distract her with questions.

"Wot's it loik, then? Izit loik Lunnun?"

"Like London! Oh, no, it couldn't be less like London!" Nan's ploy worked; the child giggled at the idea of comparing the Congo with a metropolis, and she painted a vivid word-picture of the green jungles, teeming with birds and animals of all sorts; of the natives who came to her father and mother for medicines. "Mum and Da don't do what some of the others do—they went and talked to the magic men and showed them they weren't going to interfere in the magic work, and now whenever Mum and Da have a patient who thinks he's cursed, they call the magic man in to help, and when a magic man has someone that his magic can't help right away, he takes the patient to Mum and Da and they all put on feathers and Mum and Da give him White Medicine while the magic man burns his herbs and feathers and makes his chants, and everyone is happy. There haven't been any uprisings at our station for *ever* so long, and our magic men won't let anyone put black chickens at our door. One of them gave me Grey, and I wanted to bring her with me, but Mum said I shouldn't." Now the child sighed, and looked woeful again.

"Wot's a Grey?" Nan asked.

"She's a Polly, a grey parrot with the beautifullest red tail; the medicine man gave her to me when she was all prickles, he showed me how to feed her with mashed-up yams and things. She's *so* smart, she follows me about, and she can say, oh, hundreds of things. The medicine man said that she was to be my guardian and keep me from harm. But Mum was afraid the smoke in London would hurt her, and I couldn't bring her with me." Sarah looked up at the fat, stone bird on the gatepost above her. "That's why Mem'sab gave me *that* gargoyle, to be my guardian instead. We all have them, each child has her own, and that one's mine." She looked down again at Nan, and lowered her voice to a whisper. "Sometimes when I get lonesome, I come here and talk to her, and it's like talking to Grey."

Nan nodded her head, understanding. "Oi useta go an' talk t' a stachew in one'a the yards, 'til we 'adta move. It looked loik me grammum. Felt loik I was talkin' to 'er, I fair did."

A footstep on the gravel path made Nan look up, and

she jumped to see the tall man with the head-wrap standing there, as if he had come out of the thin air. She had not sensed his presence, and once again, even though he stood materially before her she *could not*. He took no notice of Nan, which she was grateful for; instead, he handed the basket he was carrying to Sarah Jane, and walked off without a word.

Sarah passed the basket to Nan; it was heavier this time, and Nan *thought* she smelled something like roasted meat. Oh, if *only* they'd given her the drippings from their beef! Her mouth watered at the thought.

"I hope you like these," Sarah said shyly, as Nan passed her the much-lighter empty. "Mem'sab says that if you'll keep coming back, I'm to talk to you and ask you about London; she says that's the best way to learn about things. She says otherwise, when I go out, I might get into trouble I don't understand."

Nan's eyes widened at the thought that the head of a school had said anything of the sort—but Sarah Jane hardly seemed like the type of child to lie. "All roit, I s'pose," she said dubiously. "If you'll be 'ere, so'll Oi."

The next day, faithful as the rising sun, Sarah was waiting with her basket, and Nan was invited to come inside the gate. She wouldn't venture any farther in than a bench in the garden, but as Sarah asked questions, she answered them as bluntly and plainly as she would any similar question asked by a child in her own neighborhood. Sarah learned about the dangers of the dark side of London first-hand—and oddly, although she nodded wisely and with clear understanding, they didn't seem to *frighten* her.

"Garn!" Nan said once, when Sarah absorbed the interesting fact that the opium den a few doors from where Nan and her mother had a room had pitched three dead men out into the street the night before. "Yer ain't never seen nothin' loik that!"

"You forget, Mum and Da have a hospital, and it's very dangerous where they are," Sarah replied matter-of-factly. "I've seen dead men, and dead women and even babies. When Nkumba came in clawed up by a lion, I helped bring water and bandages, while Mum and Da sewed him up. When there was a black-water fever, I saw lots of people die. It was horrid and sad, but I didn't fuss, because Nkumba and Da and Mum were worked nearly to bones and needed me to be good."

Nan's eyes widened again. "Wot else y'see?" she whispered, impressed in spite of herself.

After that, the two children traded stories of two very different sorts of jungles. Despite its dangers, Nan thought that Sarah's was the better of the two.

She learned other things as well; that "Mem'sab" was a completely remarkable woman, for she had a Sikh, a Gurkha, two Moslems, two Buddhists, and assorted Hindus working in peace and harmony together—"and Mum said in her letter that it's easier to get leopards to herd sheep than that!" Mem'sab was by no means a fool; the Sikh and the Gurkha shared guard duty, patrolling the walls by day and night. One of the Hindu women was the "ayah," who took care of the smallest children; the rest of the motley assortment were servants and even teachers.

She heard many stories about the remarkable Grey, who really *did* act as Sarah's guardian, if Sarah was to be believed. Sarah described times when she had inadvertently gotten lost; she had called frantically for Grey, who was allowed to fly free, and the bird had come to her, leading her back to familiar paths. Grey had kept her from eating some pretty but poisonous berries by flying at her and nipping her fingers until she dropped them. Grey alerted the servants to the presence of snakes in the nursery, always making a patrol before she allowed Sarah to enter. And once, according to Sarah, when she had encountered a lion on the path, Grey had flown off and made sounds like a young gazelle in distress, attracting the lion's attention before it could scent Sarah. "She led it away, and didn't come back to me until it was too far away to bother coming back," the little girl claimed solemnly, "Grey is *very* clever." Nan didn't know whether to gape at her or laugh; she couldn't imagine how a mere bird could be intelligent enough to talk, much less act with purpose.

Nan had breath to laugh with, nowadays, thanks to baskets that held more than bread. The food she found in there, though distinctly odd, was always good, and she no longer felt out of breath and tired all the time. She had stopped wondering and worrying about why "Mem'sab" took such an interest in her, and simply accepted the gifts without question. They might stop at any moment; she accepted that without question, too.

The only thing she couldn't accept so easily was the manservant's eerie mental silence.

"How is your mother?" Sarah asked, since yesterday Nan had confessed that Aggie been "on a tear" and had consumed, or so Nan feared, something stronger and more dangerous than gin.

Nan shook her head. "I dunno," she replied reluctantly. "Aggie didn' wake up when I went out. Tha's not roight, she us'lly at least waked up t'foind out wha' I got. She don' half loik them baskets, 'cause it means I don' go beggin' as much."

"And if you don't beg money, she can't drink," Sarah observed shrewdly. "You hate begging, don't you?"

"Mostly I don' like gettin' kicked an' cursed at," Nan temporized. "It ain't loik I'm gettin' underfoot . . ."

But Sarah's questions were coming too near the bone, tonight, and Nan didn't want to have to deal with them. She got to her feet and picked up her basket. "I gotter go," she said abruptly.

Sarah rose from her seat on the bench and gave Nan a penetrating look. Nan had the peculiar feeling that the child was looking at *her* thoughts, and deciding whether or not to press her further. "All right," Sarah said. "It *is* getting dark."

It wasn't, but Nan wasn't about to pass up the offer of a graceful exit. "'Tis, that," she said promptly, and squeezed through the narrow opening Karamjit had left in the gate.

But she had not gone four paces when two rough-looking men in shabby tweed jackets blocked her path. "You Nan Killian?" said one hoarsely. Then when Nan stared at him blankly, added, "Aggie Killian's girl?"

The answer was surprised out of her; she hadn't been expecting such a confrontation, and she hadn't yet managed to sort herself out. "Ye—es," she said slowly.

"Good," the first man grunted. "Yer Ma sent us; she's gone t' a new place, an' she wants us t'show y' the way."

Now, several thoughts flew through Nan's mind at that moment. The first was, that as they were paid up on the rent through the end of the week, she could not imagine Aggie ever vacating before the time was up. The second was, that even if Aggie *had* set up somewhere else, she would never have sent a pair of strangers to find Nan.

And third was that Aggie had turned to a more potent intoxicant than gin—which meant she would need a deal more money. And Aggie had only one thing left to sell.

Nan.

Their minds were such a roil that she couldn't "hear" any distinct thoughts, but it was obvious that they meant her no good.

"Wait a minnit—" Nan said, her voice trembling a little as she backed away from the two men, edging around them to get to the street. "Did'jer say Aggie *Killian's* gel? Me Ma ain't called Killian, yer got th' wrong gel—"

It was at that moment that one of the men lunged for her with a curse. He had his hands nearly on her, and would have gotten her, too, except for one bit of interference.

Sarah came shooting out of the gate like a little bullet. She body-slammed the fellow, going into the back of his knees and knocking him right off his feet. She danced out of the way as he fell in the nick of time, ran to Nan, and caught her hand, tugging her towards the street. "Run!" she commanded imperiously, and Nan ran.

The two of them scrabbled through the dark alleys and twisted streets without any idea where they were, only that they had to shake off their pursuers. Unfortunately, the time that Nan would have put into learning her new neighborhood like the back of her grimy little hand had been put into talking with Sarah, and before too long, even Nan was lost in the maze of dark, fetid streets. Then their luck ran out altogether, and they found themselves staring at the blank wall of a building, in a dead-end cul-de-sac.

They whirled around, hoping to escape before they were trapped, but it was already too late. The bulky silhouettes of the two men loomed against the fading light at the end of the street.

"Oo's yer friend, ducky?" the first man purred. "Think she'd loik t'come with?"

To Nan's astonishment, Sarah stood straight and tall, and even stepped forward a pace. "I think you ought to go away and leave us alone," she said clearly. "You're going to find yourselves in a lot of trouble."

The talkative man laughed. "Them's big words from such a little gel," he mocked. "We ain't leavin' wi'out we collect what's ours, an' a bit more fer th' trouble yer caused."

Nan was petrified with fear, shaking in every limb, as Sarah stepped back, putting her back to the damp wall. As the first man touched Sarah's arm, she shrieked out a single word.

"Grey!"

As Sarah cried out the name of her pet, Nan let loose a wordless prayer for something, *anything*, to come to their rescue.

Something screamed behind the man; startled and distracted for a moment, he turned. For a moment, a fluttering shape obscured his face, and *he* screamed in pain. He shook his head, violently.

"Get it off!" he screamed at his partner. "*Get it off!*"

"Get what off?" the man said, bewildered. "There ain't nothin' there!"

The man clawed frantically at the front of his face, but whatever had attacked him had vanished without a trace. But not before leading more substantial help to the rescue.

Out of the dusk and the first wisps of fog, Karamjit and another swarthy man ran on noiseless feet. In their hands were cudgels which they used to good purpose on the two who opposed them. Nor did they waste any effort, clubbing the two senseless with a remarkable economy of motion.

Then, without a single word, each of the men scooped up a girl in his arms, and bore them back to the school. At that point, finding herself safe in the arms of an unlooked-for rescuer, Nan felt secure enough to break down into hysterical tears.

Nor was that the end of it; she found herself bundled up into the sacred precincts of the school itself, plunged into the first hot bath of her life, wrapped in a clean flannel gown, and put into a real bed. Sarah was in a similar bed beside her. As she sat there, numb, a plain-looking woman with beautiful eyes came and sat down on the foot of Sarah's bed, and looked from one to the other of them.

"Well," the lady said at last, "what have you two to say for yourselves?"

Nan couldn't manage anything, but that was all right, since Sarah wasn't about to let her get in a word anyway. The child jabbered like a monkey, a confused speech about Nan's mother, the men she'd sold Nan to, the virtue of Charity, the timely appearance of Grey, and a great deal more besides. The lady listened and nodded, and when Sarah ran down at last, she turned to Nan.

"I believe Sarah is right in one thing," she said

gravely. "I believe we will have to keep you. Now, both of you—sleep."

And to Nan's surprise, she fell asleep immediately.

But that was not the end to the story. A month later, Sarah's mother arrived, with Grey in a cage. Nan had, by then, found a place where she could listen to what went on in the best parlor without being found, and she glued her ear to the crack in the pantry to listen when Sarah was taken into that hallowed room.

"—found Grey senseless beside her perch," Sarah's mother was saying. "I thought it was a fit, but the Shaman swore that Sarah was in trouble and the bird had gone to help. Grey awoke none the worse, and I would have thought nothing more of the incident, until your message arrived."

"And so you came, very wisely, bringing this remarkable bird." Mem'sab made chirping noises at the bird, and an odd little voice said, "Hello, bright eyes!"

Mem'sab chuckled. "How much of strangeness are you prepared to believe in, my dear?" she asked gently. "Would you believe me if I told you that I have seen this bird once before——fluttering and pecking at my window, then leading my men to rescue your child?"

"I can only answer with Hamlet," Sarah's mother said after a pause. "That there are more things in heaven and earth than I suspected."

"Good," Mem'sab replied decidedly. "Then I take it you are not here to remove Sarah from our midst."

"No," came the soft reply. "I came only to see that Sarah was well, and to ask if you would permit her pet to be with her."

"Gladly," Mem'sab said. "Though I might question which of the two was the pet!"

"Clever bird!" said Grey.

I enjoyed the characters in "Grey" so much that I decided to write another novella for this anthology using the same characters. You might think of Mem'sab Harton as the Victorian version of Diana Tregarde, sans vampire boyfriend. I'm toying with the idea of doing an entire book about the Harton School, Nan, Sarah, and Grey, and I'd be interested to hear if anyone besides parrot-lovers would want to read it.

Grey's Ghost

When Victoria was the Queen of England, there was a small, unprepossessing school for the children of expatriate Englishmen that had quite an interesting reputation in the shoddy Whitechapel neighborhood on which it bordered, a reputation that kept the students safer than all the bobbies in London.

Once, a young, impoverished beggar-girl named Nan Killian had obtained leftovers at the back gate, and most of the other waifs and gutter-rats of the neighborhood shunned the place, though they gladly shared in Nan's bounty when she dared the gate and its guardian.

But now another child picked up food at the back gate of the Harton School For Boys and Girls on the edge of Whitechapel in London, not Nan Killian. Children no longer shunned the back gate of the school, although they treated its inhabitants with extreme caution. Adults—particularly the criminal, disreputable criminals who preyed on children—treated the place and its inhabitants with a great deal more than mere caution. Word had gotten around that two child-pimps had tried to take one of the pupils, and had been found with arms and legs broken, beaten senseless. Word had followed that anyone who threatened another child protected by the school would be found dead—*if* he was found at all.

The two tall, swarthy "blackfellas" who served as the school's guards were rumored to have strange powers, or be members of the *thugee* cult, or worse. It was safer just to pretend the school didn't exist and go about one's unsavory business elsewhere.

Nan Killian was no longer a child of the streets; she was now a pupil at the school herself, a transmutation that astonished her every morning when she awoke. To find herself in a neat little dormitory room, papered with roses, curtained in gingham, made her often feel as if she was dreaming. To then rise with the other girls, dress in clean, fresh clothing, and go off to lessons in the hitherto unreachable realms of reading and writing was more than she had ever dared dream of.

Her best friend was still Sarah, the little girl from Africa who had brought her that first basket of leftovers. But now she slept in the next bed over from Sarah's, and they shared many late-night giggles and confidences, instead of leftover tea-bread.

Nan also had a job; she had discovered, somewhat to her own bemusement, that the littlest children instinctively trusted her and would obey her when they obeyed no-one else. So Nan "paid" for her tutoring and keep by helping Nadra, the babies' nurse, or "ayah," as they all called her. Nadra was from India, as were most of the servants, from the formidable guards, the Sikh Karamjit and the Gurkha Selim, to the cook, Maya. Mrs. Helen Harton—or Mem'sab, as everyone called her—

and her husband had once been expatriates in India themselves. Master Harton—called, with ultimate respect, Sahib Harton—now worked as an advisor to an import firm; his service in India had left him with a small pension, and a permanent limp. When he and his wife had returned and had learned quite by accident of the terrible conditions children returned to England often lived in, they had resolved that the children of their friends back in the Punjab, at least, would not have that terrible knowledge thrust upon them.

Here the children sent away in bewilderment by anxious parents fearing that they would sicken in the hot foreign lands found, not a cold and alien place with nothing they recognized, but the familiar sounds of Hindustani, the comfort and coddling of a native nanny, and the familiar curries and rice to eat. Their new home, if a little shabby, held furniture made familiar from their years in the bungalows. But most of all, they were not told coldly to "be a man" or "stop being a crybaby"— for here they found friendly shoulders to weep out their homesickness on. If there were no French Masters here, there *was* a great deal of love and care; if the furniture was unfashionable and shabby, the children were well-fed and rosy.

It never ceased to amaze Nan that more parents didn't send their children to the Harton School, but some folks mistakenly trusted relatives to take better care of their precious ones than strangers, and some thought that a school owned and operated by someone with a lofty reputation or a title was a wiser choice for a boy-child who would likely join the Civil Service when he came of age. And as for the girls, there would always be those who felt that lessons by French dancing-masters and language teachers, lessons on the harp and in water-color painting, were more valuable than a sound education in the same basics given to a boy.

Sometimes these parents learned their lessons the hard way.

◆ ◆ ◆

"Ready for m'lesson, Mem'sab," Nan called into the second-best parlor, which was Mem'sab's private domain. It was commonly understood that sometimes Mem'sab had to do odd things—"Important things that we don't need to know about," Sarah said wisely—and she might have to do them at a moment's notice. So it was better to announce oneself at the door before venturing over the threshold.

But today Mem'sab was only reading a book, and looked up at Nan with a smile that transformed her plain face and made her eyes bright and beautiful.

By now Nan had seen plenty of ladies who dressed in finer stuffs than Mem'sab's simple Artistic gown of common stuffs, made bright with embroidery courtesy of Maya. Nan had seen ladies who were acknowledged Beauties like Mrs. Lillie Langtry, ladies who obviously spent many hours in the hands of their dressers and hairdressers rather than pulling their hair up into a simple chignon from which little curling strands of brown-gold were always escaping. Mem'sab's jewelry was not of diamonds and gold, but odd, heavy pieces in silver and semi-precious gems. But in Nan's eyes, not one of those ladies was worth wasting a single glance upon.

Then again, Nan *was* a little prejudiced.

"Come in, Nan," the Headmistress said, patting the flowered sofa beside her invitingly. "You're doing much better already, you know. You have a quick ear."

"Thenkee, Mem'sab," Nan replied, flushing with pleasure. She, like any of the servants, would gladly have laid down her life for Mem'sab Harton; they all worshipped her blatantly, and a word of praise from their idol was worth more than a pocketful of sovereigns. Nan sat gingerly down on the chintz-covered sofa and smoothed her clean pinafore with an unconscious gesture of pride.

Mem'sab took a book of etiquette from the table beside her, and opened it, looking at Nan expectantly. "Go ahead, dear."

"Good morning, ma'am. How do you do? I am quite well. I trust your family is fine," Nan began, and waited for Mem'sab's response, which would be her cue for the next polite phrase. The point here was not that Nan needed to learn manners and mannerly speech, but that she needed to *lose* the dreadful cadence of the streets which would doom her to poverty forever, quite literally. Nan spoke the commonplace phrases slowly and with great care, as much care as Sarah took over her French. An accurate analogy, since the King's English, as spoken by the middle and upper classes, was nearly as much a foreign language to Nan as French and Latin were to Sarah.

She had gotten the knack of it by thinking of it exactly as a foreign language, once Mem'sab had proven to her how much better others would treat her if she didn't speak like a guttersnipe. She was still fluent in the language of the streets, and often went out with Karamjit as a translator when he went on errands that took him into the slums or Chinatown. But gradually her tongue became accustomed to the new cadences, and her habitual speech marked her less as "untouchable."

"Beautifully done," Mem'sab said warmly, when Nan finished her recitation. "Your new assignment will be to pick a poem and recite it to me, properly spoken, and memorized."

"I think I'd loike—*like*—to do one uv Mr. Kipling's, Mem'sab," Nan said shyly.

Mem'sab laughed. "I hope you aren't thinking of 'Gunga Din,' you naughty girl!" the woman mock-chided. "It had better be one from the *Jungle Book*, or *Puck of Pook's Hill*, not something written in Cockney dialect!"

"Yes, Mem'sab, I mean, no, Mem'sab," Nan replied quickly. "I'll pick a right'un. Mebbe the lullaby for the White Seal?" Ever since discovering Rudyard Kipling's stories, Nan had been completely enthralled; Mem'sab often read them to the children as a go-to-bed treat, for the stories often evoked memories of India for the children sent away.

"That will do very well. Are you ready for the other lesson?" Mem'sab asked, so casually that no one but Nan would have known that the "other lesson" was one not taught in any other school in this part of the world.

"I—think so." Nan got up and closed the parlor door, signaling to all the world that she and Mem'sab were not to be disturbed unless someone was dying or the house was burning down.

For the next half hour, Mem'sab turned over cards, and Nan called out the next card before she turned it over. When the last of the fifty-two lay in the face-up pile before her, Nan waited expectantly for the results.

"Not at all bad; you had almost half of them, and all the colors right," Mem'sab said with content. Nan was disappointed; she knew that Mem'sab could call out all fifty-two without an error, though Sarah could only get the colors correctly.

"Sahib brought me some things from the warehouse for you to try your 'feeling' on," Mem'sab continued. "I truly think that is where you true Gifts lie, dear."

Nan sighed mournfully. "But knowin' the cards would be a lot more *useful*," she complained.

"What, so you can grow up to cheat foolish young men out of their inheritances?" Now Mem'sab actually laughed out loud. "Try it, dear, and the Gift will desert you at the time you need it most! No, be content with what you have and learn to use it wisely, to help yourself and others."

"But card-sharpin' *would* help me, an' I could use takin's to help others," Nan couldn't resist protesting, but she held out her hand for the first object anyway.

It was a carved beetle; very interesting, Nan thought, as she waited to "feel" what it would tell her. It felt like pottery or stone, and it was of a turquoise-blue, shaded with pale brown. "It's old," she said finally. Then, "*Really* old. Old as—Methusalum! It was made for an important man, but not a king or anything."

She tried for more, but couldn't sense anything else. "That's all," she said, and handed it back to Mem'sab.

"Now this." The carved beetle that Mem'sab gave her was, for all intents and purposes, identical to the one she'd just held, but immediately Nan sensed the difference.

"Piff! That 'un's new!" She also felt something else, something of *intent*, a sensation she readily identified since it was one of the driving forces behind commerce in Whitechapel. "Feller as made it figgers he's put one over on somebody."

"Excellent, dear!" Mem'sab nodded. "They are both *scarabs*, a kind of good-luck carving found with mummies—which are, indeed, often as old as Methuselah. The first one I knew was real, as I helped unwrap the mummy myself. The second, however, was from a shipment that Sahib suspected were fakes."

Nan nodded, interested to learn that this Gift of hers had some practical application after all. "So could be I could tell people when they been gammoned?"

"Very likely, and quite likely that they would pay you for the knowledge, as long as they don't think that *you* are trying to fool them as well. Here, try this." The next object placed in Nan's hand was a bit of jewelry, a simple silver brooch with "gems" of cut iron. Nan dropped it as soon as it touched her hand, overwhelmed by fear and horror.

"Lummy!" she cried, without thinking. "He *killed* her!"

Who "they" were, she had no sense of; that would require more contact, which she did *not* want to have. But Mem'sab didn't seem at all surprised; she just shook her head very sadly and put the brooch back in a little box which she closed without a word.

She held out a child's locket on a worn ribbon. "Don't be afraid, Nan," she coaxed, when Nan was reluctant to accept it, "This one isn't bad, I promise you."

Nan took the locket gingerly, but broke out into a smile when she got a feeling of warmth, contentment, and happiness. She waited for other images to come, and sensed a tired, but exceedingly happy woman, a proud man, and one—no, *two* strong and lively mites with the woman.

Slyly, Nan glanced up at her mentor. "She's 'ad twins, 'asn't she?" Nan asked. "When was it?"

"I just got the letter and the locket today, but it was about two months ago," Mem'sab replied. "The lady is my best friend's daughter, who was given that locket by her mother for luck just before the birth of her children. She sent it to me to have it duplicated, as she would like to present one to each little girl."

"I'd 'ave it taken apart, an' put half of th' old 'un with half of the new 'un," Nan suggested, and Mem'sab brightened at the idea.

"An excellent idea, and I will do just that. Now, dear, are you feeling tired? Have you a headache? We've gone on longer than we did at your last lesson."

Nan nodded, quite ready to admit to both.

Mem'sab gave her still-thin shoulders a little hug, and sent her off to her afternoon lessons.

Figuring came harder to Nan than reading; she'd already had some letters before she had arrived, enough to spell out the signs on shops and stalls and the like and make out a word here and there on a discarded broadsheet. When the full mystery of letters had been disclosed to her, mastery had come as naturally as breathing, and she was already able to read her beloved Kipling stories with minimal prompting. But numbers were a mystery arcane, and she struggled with the youngest of the children to comprehend what they meant. Anything past one hundred baffled her for the moment, and Sarah did her best to help her friend.

After arithmetic came geography, but for a child to whom Kensington Palace was the end of the universe, it was harder to believe in the existence of Arabia than of Fairyland, and Heaven was quite as real and solid as South America, for she reckoned that she had an equal chance of seeing either. As for how all those odd names and shapes fit together . . . well!

History came easier, although she didn't yet grasp that it was as real as yesterday, for to Nan it was just a chain of linking stories. Perhaps that was why she loved the Kipling stories so much, for she often felt as out-of-place as Mowgli when the human-tribe tried to reclaim him.

At the end of lessons Nan usually went to help Nadra in the nursery; the children there, ranging in age from two to five, were a handful when it came to getting them bathed and put to bed. They tried to put off bedtime as long as possible; there were a half-dozen of them, which was just enough that when Nadra had finally gotten two of them into a bathtub, the other four had escaped, and were running about the nursery like dripping, naked apes, screaming joyfully at their escape.

But tonight, Karamjit came for Nan and Sarah as soon as the history lesson was over, summoning them with a look and a gesture. As always, the African parrot Grey sat on Sarah's shoulder; she was so well-behaved, even to the point of being housebroken, that he was allowed to be with her from morning to night. The handsome grey parrot with the bright red tail had adapted very well to this new sort of jungle when Sarah's mother brought her to her daughter; Sarah was very careful to keep her warm and out of drafts, and she ate virtually the same food that she did. Mem'sab seemed to understand the kind of diet that let her thrive; she allowed her only a little of the chicken and beef, and made certain that she filled up on carrots and other vegetables before she got any of the curried rice she loved so much. In fact, she often pointed to Grey as an example to the other children who would rather have had sweets than green stuffs, telling them that Grey was smarter than they were, for *she* knew what would make her grow big and strong. Being unfavorably compared to a bird often made the difference with the little boys in particular, who were behaving better at table since the parrot came to live at the school.

So Grey came along when Karamjit brought them to the door of Mem'sab's parlor, cautioning them to wait quietly until Mem'sab called them.

"What do you suppose can be going on?" Sarah asked curiously, while Grey turned her head to look at Nan with her penetrating pale-yellow eyes.

Nan shushed her, pressing her ear to the keyhole to see what she could hear. "There's another lady in there with Mem'sab, and she sounds sad," Nan said at last.

Grey cocked her head to one side, then turned his head upside down as she sometimes did when something puzzled her. "Hurt," she said quietly, and made a little sound like someone crying.

Nan had long since gotten used to the fact that Grey noticed everything that went on around her and occasionally commented on it like a human person. If the wolves in the *Jungle Book* could think and talk, she reasoned, why not a parrot? She accepted Grey's abilities as casually as Sarah, who had raised her herself and had no doubt of the intelligence of her feathered friend.

Had either of them acquired the "wisdom" of their elders, they might have been surprised that Mem'sab accepted those abilities too.

Nan jumped back as footsteps warned her that the visitor had risen and was coming towards the door; she and Sarah pressed themselves back against the wall as the strange woman passed them, her face hidden behind a veil. She took no notice of the children, but turned back to Mem'sab.

"Katherine, I believe going to this woman is a grave mistake on your part," Mem'sab told her quietly. "You and I have been friends since we were in school together; you know that I would never advise you against anything you felt so strongly about unless I thought you might be harmed by it. This woman does you no good."

The woman shook her head. "How could I be harmed by it?" she replied, her voice trembling. "What *possible* ill could come of this?"

"A very great deal, I fear," Mem'sab, her expression some combination of concern and other emotions that Nan couldn't read.

Impulsively, the woman reached out for Mem'sab's hand. "Then come *with* me!" she cried. "If this woman cannot convince *you* that she is genuine, and that she provides me with what I need more than breath, then I will not see her again."

Mem'sab's eyes looked keenly into her friend's, easily defeating the concealment of the veil about her features. "You are willing to risk her unmasking as a fraud, and the pain for you that will follow?"

"I am certain enough of her that I know that you will be convinced, even against your will," the woman replied with certainty.

Mem'sab nodded. "Very well, then. You and I—and these two girls—will see her together."

Only now did the woman notice Sarah and Nan, and her brief glance dismissed them as unimportant. "I see no reason why you wish to have children along, but if you can guarantee they will behave, and that is what it takes you to be convinced to see Madame Varonsky, then so be it. I will have an invitation sent to you for the next seance."

Mem'sab smiled, and patted her friend's hand. "Sometimes children see things more clearly than we adults do," was all she replied. "I will be waiting for that invitation."

The woman squeezed Mem'sab's hand, then turned and left, ushered out by one of the native servants. Mem'sab gestured to the two girls to precede her into the parlor, and shut the door behind them.

"What did you think of the lady, Nan?" asked their

teacher, as the two children took their places side-by-side, on the loveseat they generally shared when they were in the parlor together.

Nan assessed the woman as would any street-child; economics came first. "She's in mournin' an' she's gentry," Nan replied automatically. "Silk gowns fer mournin' is somethin' only gentry kin afford. I 'spect she's easy t' gammon, too; paid no attention t'us, an' I was near enough t' get me hand into 'er purse an' her never knowin' till she was home. An' she didn' ask fer a cab t' be brung, so's I reckon she keeps 'er carriage. That's not jest gentry, tha's *quality*."

"Right on all counts, my dear," Mem'sab said, a bit grimly. "Katherine has no more sense than one of the babies, and never had. Her parents didn't spoil her, but they never saw any reason to educate her in practical matters. They counted on her finding a husband who would do all her thinking for her, and as a consequence, she is pliant to any hand that offers mastery. She married into money; her husband has a very high position in the Colonial Government. Nothing but the best school would do for her boy, and a spoiled little lad he was, too."

Grey suddenly began coughing, most realistically, a series of terrible, racking coughs, and Sarah turned her head to look into her eyes. Then she turned back to Mem'sab. "He's dead, isn't he?" the child said, quite matter-of-factly. "He got sick, and died. That's who she's in mourning for."

"Quite right, and as Grey showed us, he caught pneumonia." Mem'sab looked grim. "Poor food, icy rooms, and barbaric treatment—" She threw up her hands, and shook her head. "There's no reason to go on; at least Katherine has decided to trust her twins to us instead of the school her husband wanted. She'll bring them to Nadra tomorrow, Nan, and they'll probably be terrified, so I'm counting on you to help Nadra soothe them."

Nan could well imagine that they would be terrified; not only were they being left with strangers, but they would know, at least dimly, that their brother had come away to school and died. They would be certain that the same was about to happen to them.

"That, however, is not why I sent for you," Mem'sab continued. "Katherine is seeing a medium; do either of you know what that is?"

Sarah and Nan shook their heads, but Grey made a rude noise. Sarah looked shocked, but Nan giggled and Mem'sab laughed.

"I am afraid that Grey is correct in her opinions, for the most part," the woman told them. "A *medium* is a person who claims to speak with the dead, and help the souls of the dead speak to the living." Her mouth compressed, and Nan sensed her carefully controlled anger. "All this is accomplished for a very fine fee, I might add."

"Ho! Like them gypsy palm-readers, an' the conjure-men!" Nan exclaimed in recognition. "Aye, there's a mort'a gammon there, and that's sure. You reckon this lady's been gammoned, then?"

"Yes I do, and I would like you two—*three*—" she amended, with a penetrating look at Grey, "—to help me prove it. Nan, if there is trickery afoot, do you think you could catch it?"

Nan had no doubt. "I bet I could," she said. "Can't be harder'n keepin' a hand out uv yer pocket—or grabbin' the wrist once it's in."

"Good girl—you *must* remember to speak properly, and only when you're spoken to, though," Mem'sab warned her. "If this so-called medium thinks you are anything but a gently-reared child, she might find an excuse to dismiss the seance." She turned to Sarah. "Now, if by some incredible chance this woman *is* genuine, could you and Grey tell?"

Sarah's head bobbed so hard her curls tumbled into her eyes. "Yes, Mem'sab," she said, with as much confidence as Nan. "M'luko, the Medicine Man that gave me Grey, said that Grey could tell when the spirits were there, and someday I might, too."

"Did he, now?" Mem'sab gave her a curious look. "How interesting! Well, if Grey can tell us if there are spirits or not, that will be quite useful enough for our purposes. Are either of you afraid to go with me? I expect the invitation will come quite soon." Again, Mem'sab had that grim look. "Katherine is too choice a fish to be allowed to swim free for long; the Madame will want to keep her under her control by 'consulting' with her as often as possible."

Sarah looked to Nan for guidance, and Nan thought that her friend might be a little fearful, despite her brave words. But Nan herself only laughed. "I ain't afraid of nobody's sham ghost," she said, curling her lip scornfully. "An' I ain't sure I'd be afraid uv a *real* one."

"Wisely said, Nan; spirits can only harm us as much as we permit them to." Nan thought that Mem'sab looked relieved, like maybe she hadn't wanted to count on their help until she actually got it. "Thank you, both of you." She reached out and took their hands, giving them a squeeze that said a great deal without words. "Now, both of you get back to whatever it was that I took you from. I will let you know in plenty of time when our excursion will be."

It was past the babies' bed-time, so Sarah and Nan went together to beg Maya for their delayed tea, and carried the tray themselves up to the now-deserted nursery. They set out the tea-things on one of the little tables, feeling a mutual need to discuss Mem'sab's strange proposition.

Grey had her tea, too; a little bowl of curried rice, carrots, and beans. They set it down on the table and Grey climbed carefully down from Sarah's shoulder to the table-top, where she selected a bean and ate it neatly, holding in on one claw while she took small bites, watching them both.

"Do you think there might be real ghosts?" Sarah asked immediately, shivering a little. "I mean, what if this lady can bring real ghosts up?"

Grey and Nan made the same rude noise at the same time; it was easy to tell where Grey had learned it. "Garn!" Nan said scornfully. "Reckon that Mem'sab only ast if you could tell as an outside bet. *But* the livin' people might be the ones as is dangerous." She ate a bite of bread-and-butter thoughtfully. "I dunno as Mem'sab's thought that far, but that Missus Katherine's a right easy mark, an' a fat 'un, too. People as is willin' t' gammon the gentry *might* not be real happy about bein' found out."

Sarah nodded. "Should we tell Karamjit?" she asked, showing a great deal more common sense than she would have before Nan came into her life. "Mem'sab's thinking hard about her friend, but she might not think a bit about herself."

"Aye, an' Selim an' mebbe Sahib, too." Nan was a little dubious about that, having only seen the lordly Sahib from a distance.

"I'll ask Selim to tell Sahib, if you'll talk to Karamjit," Sarah said, knowing the surest route to the Master from her knowledge of the School and its inhabitants. "But tell me what to look for! Three sets of eyes are better than two."

"Fust thing, whatever they *want* you t' look at is gonna be what makes a fuss—noises or voices or whatever," Nan said after a moment of thought. "I dunno how this *medium* stuff is gonna work, but that's what happens when a purse gets nicked. You gotta get the mark's attention, so he won't be thinkin' of his pocket. So whatever they *want* us to look at, we look away from. That's the main thing. Mebbe Mem'sab can tell us what these things is s'pposed to be like—if I know what's t' happen, I kin guess what tricks they're like t' pull." She finished her bread and butter, and began her own curry; she'd quickly acquired a taste for the spicy Indian dishes that the other children loved. "If there ain't ghosts, I bet they got somebody dressed up t' *look* like one." She grinned slyly at Grey. "An' I betcha a good pinch or a bite would make 'im yell proper!"

"And you couldn't hurt a real ghost with a pinch." Sarah nodded. "I suppose we're just going to have to watch and wait, and see what we can do."

Nan, as always, ate as a street-child would, although her manners had improved considerably since coming to the School; she inhaled her food rapidly, so that no one would have a chance to take it from her. She was already finished, although Sarah hadn't eaten more than half of her tea. She put her plates aside on the tray, and propped her head up on her hands with her elbows on the table. "We got to talk to Karamjit an' Selim, that's the main thing," she said, thinking out loud. "They might know what we should do."

"Selim will come home with Sahib," Sarah answered, "But Karamjit is probably leaving the basket at the back gate right now, and if you run, you can catch him alone."

Taking that as her hint, for Sarah had a way of knowing where most people were at any given time, Nan jumped to her feet and ran out of the nursery and down the back stairs, flying through the kitchen, much to the amusement of the cook, Maya. She burst through the kitchen door, and ran down the path to the back gate, so quickly she hardly felt the cold at all, though she had run outside without a coat. Mustafa swept the garden paths free of snow every day, but so soon after Boxing Day there were mounds of the stuff on either side of the path, snow with a faint tinge of gray from the soot that plagued London in almost every weather.

Nan saw the Sikh, Karamjit, soon enough to avoid bouncing off his legs. The tall, dark, immensely dignified man was bundled up to the eyes in a heavy quilted coat and two mufflers, his head wrapped in a dark brown turban. Nan no longer feared him, though she respected him as only a street child who has seen a superior fighter in action could. "Karamjit!" she called, as she slowed her headlong pace. "I need t' talk wi' ye!"

There was an amused glint in the Sikh's dark eyes, though only much association with him allowed Nan to see it. "And what does Missy Nan wish to speak of that she comes racing out into the cold like the wind from the mountains?"

"Mem'sab ast us t' help her with somethin'—there's this lady as is a *meedeeyum* that she thinks is gammonin' her friend. We—tha's Sarah an' Grey an' me—we says a'course, but—" Here Nan stopped, because she wasn't entirely certain how to tell an adult that she thought another adult didn't know what she was getting herself into. "I just got a bad feelin'," she ended, lamely.

But Karamjit did not belittle her concerns, nor did he chide her. Instead, his eyes grew even darker, and he nodded. "Come inside, where it is warm," he said, "I wish you to tell me more."

He sat her down at the kitchen table, and gravely and respectfully asked Maya to serve them both tea. He took his with neither sugar nor cream, but saw to it that Nan's was heavily sweetened and at least half milk. "Now," he said, after she had warmed herself with the first sip, "Tell me all."

Nan related everything that had happened from the time he came to take both of them to the parlor to when she had left Sarah to find him. He nodded from time to time, as he drank tea and unwound himself from his mufflers and coat.

"I believe this," he said when she had finished. "I believe that Mem'sab is a wise, good, and brave woman. I also believe that *she* does not think that helping her friend will mean any real danger. But the wise, the good, and the brave often do not think as the mean, the bad, and the cowardly do—the jackals that feed on the pain of others will turn to devour those who threaten their meal. And a man can die from the bite of a jackal as easily as that of a tiger."

"So you think my bad feelin' was right?" Nan's relief was total; not that she didn't trust Mem'sab, but—Mem'sab didn't know the kind of creatures that Nan did.

"Indeed I do—but I believe that it would do no good to try to persuade Mem'sab that she should not try to help her friend." Karamjit smiled slightly, the barest lifting of the corners of his mouth. "Nevertheless, Sahib will know how best to protect her without insulting her great courage." He placed one of his long, brown hands on Nan's shoulder. "You may leave it in our hands, Missy Nan—though we may ask a thing or two of you, that we can do our duty with no harm to Mem'sab's own plans. For now, though, you may simply rely upon us."

"Thenkee, Karamjit," Nan sighed. He patted her shoulder, then unfolded his long legs and rose from his chair with a slight bow to Maya. Then he left the kitchen, allowing Nan to finish her tea and run back up to the nursery, to give Sarah and Grey the welcome news that they would not be the only ones concerned with the protection of Mem'sab from the consequences of her own generous nature.

Sahib took both Nan and Sarah aside just before bedtime, after Karamjit and Selim had been closeted with him for half an hour. "Can I ask you two to come to my study with me for a bit?" he asked quietly. He was often thought to be older than Mem'sab, by those who were deceived by the streaks of grey at each temple, the stiff way that he walked, and the odd expression in his eyes, which seemed to Nan to be the eyes of a man who had seen so much that nothing surprised him anymore. Nan had trusted him the moment that she set eyes on him, although she couldn't have said why.

"So long as Nadra don't fuss," Nan replied for both of them. Sahib smiled, his eyes crinkling at the corners.

"I have already made it right with Nadra," he promised. "Karamjit, Selim, and Mem'sab are waiting for us."

Nan felt better immediately, for she really hadn't wanted to go sneaking around behind Mem'sab's back. From the look that Sarah gave her, Nan reckoned that she felt the same.

"Thank you, sir," Sarah said politely. "We will do just as you say."

Very few of the children had ever been inside the sacred precincts of Sahib's office; the first thing that struck Nan was that it did *not* smell of tobacco, but of sandalwood and cinnamon. That surprised her; most of the men she knew smoked although their womenfolk disapproved of the habit, but evidently Sahib did not, not even in his own private space.

There was a tiger-skin on the carpet in front of the fire, the glass eyes in its head glinting cruelly in a manner unnerving and lifelike. Nan shuddered, and thought of Shere Khan, with his taste for man-cub. Had this been another terrible killer of the jungle? Did tigers leave vengeful ghosts?

Heavy, dark drapes of some indeterminate color shut out the cold night. Hanging on the walls, which had been papered with faded gold arabesque upon a ground of light brown, was a jumble of mementos from Sahib's life in India: crossed spears, curious daggers and swords, embroidered tapestries of strange characters twined with exotic flowers and birds, carved plaques of some heavy, dark wood inlaid with brass, bizarre masks that resembled nothing less than brightly painted demons. On the desk and adorning the shelves between the books were statues of half- and fully-naked gods and goddesses, more bits of carving in wood, stone, and ivory. Bookshelves built floor-to-ceiling held more books than Nan had known existed. Sahib took his place behind his desk, while Mem'sab perched boldly on the edge of it. Selim and Karamjit stood beside the fire like a pair of guardian statues themselves, and Sahib gestured to the children to take their places on the over-stuffed chairs on either side of the fireplace. Nan waited tensely, wondering if

Mem'sab was going to be angry because they went to others with their concerns. Although it had not fallen out so here, she was far more used to being in trouble over something she had done than in being encouraged for it, and the reflexes were still in place.

"Karamjit tells me that you four share some concern over my planned excursion to the medium, Nan," Mem'sab said, with a smile that told Nan she was *not* in trouble for her meddling, as she had feared. "They went first to Sahib, but as we never keep secrets from one another, he came to me. And I commend all four of you for your concern and caution, for after some discussion, I was forced to agree with it."

"And I would like to commend both of you, Nan, Sarah, for having the wisdom to go to an adult with your concerns," added Sahib, with a kindly nod to both of them that Nan had not expected in the least. "That shows great good sense, and please, continue to do so in the future."

"I thought—I was afeared—" Nan began, then blurted out all that she'd held in check. "Mem'sab is 'bout the smartest, goodest lady there is, but she don't *know* bad people! Me, I know! I seed 'em, an' I figgered that they weren't gonna lay down an' lose their fat mark without a fight!"

"And very wise you were to remind us of that," Sahib said gravely. "I pointed out to Mem'sab that we have no way of knowing *where* this medium is from, and she is just as likely to be a criminal as a lady—more so, in fact. Just because she speaks, acts, and dresses like a lady, and seeks her clients from among the gentry, means nothing; she could easily have a crew of thugs as her accomplices."

"As you say, Sahib," Karamjit said gravely. "For, as it is said, it is a short step from a deception to a lie, from a lie to a cheat, from a cheat to a theft, and from a theft to a murder."

Mem'sab blushed. "I will admit that I was very angry

with you at first, but when my anger cooled, it was clear that your reasoning was sound. And after all, am I some Gothic heroine to go wide-eyed into the villains' lair, never suspecting trouble? So, we are here to plan what we *all* shall do to free Katherine of her dangerous obsession."

"Me, I needta know what this see-ants is gonna be like, Mem'sab," Nan put in, sitting on the edge of the chair tensely. "What sorta things happens?"

"Generally, the participants are brought into a room that has a round table with chairs circling it." Mem'sab spoke directly to Nan as if to an adult, which gave Nan a rather pleasant, if shivery, feeling. "The table often has objects upon it that the spirits will supposedly move; often a bell, a tambourine and a megaphone are among them, though why spirits would feel the need to play upon a tambourine when they never had that urge in life is quite beyond me!"

She laughed, as did Sahib; the girls giggled nervously.

"At any rate, the participants are asked to sit down and hold hands. Often the medium is tied to the chair; her hands are secured to the arms, and her feet to the legs." Nan noticed that Mem'sab used the word "legs" rather than the mannerly "limbs," and thought the better of her for that. "The lights are brought down, and the seance begins. Most often objects are moved, including the table, the tambourine is played, the bell is rung, all as a sign that the spirits have arrived. The spirits most often speak by means of raps on the table, but Katherine tells me that the spirit of her little boy spoke directly, through the floating megaphone. Sometimes a spirit will actually appear; in this case, it was just a glowing face of Katherine's son."

Nan thought that over for a moment. "Be simple 'nuff t' tilt the chair an' get yer legs free by slippin the rope down over the chair-feet," she observed, "An' all ye hev t' do is have chair-arms as isn't glued t' *their* pegs, an' ye got yer arms free too. Be easy enough to make all kind uv things dance about when ye got arms free. Be easy 'nuff t' make th' table lift if's light enough, an' rap on it, too."

Sahib stared at her in astonishment. "I do believe that you are the most valuable addition to our household in a long time, young lady!" he said with delight that made Nan blush. "I would never have thought of any of that."

"I dunno how ye'd make summat glow, though," Nan admitted.

"Oh, *I* know that," Sarah said casually. "There's stuff that grows in rotten wood that makes a glow; some of the magic-men use it to frighten people at night. It grows in swamps, so it probably grows in England, too."

Karamjit grinned, his teeth very white in his dark face, and Selim nodded with pride. "What is it that the Black Robe's Book says, Sahib? Out of the mouths of babes comes wisdom?"

Mem'sab nodded. "I should have told you more, earlier," she said ruefully. "Well, that's mended in time. Now we all know what to look for."

Grey clicked her beak several times, then exclaimed, "Ouch!"

"Grey is going to try to bite whatever comes near her," Sarah explained.

"I don't want her venturing off your arm," Mem'sab cautioned. "I won't chance her getting hurt." She turned to Sahib. "The chances are, the room we will be in will have very heavy curtains to prevent light from entering or escaping, so if you and our warriors are outside, you won't know what room we are in."

"Then I'd like one of you girls to exercise childish curiosity and go *immediately* to a window and look out," Sahib told them. "At least one of us will be where we can see both the front and the back of the house. Then if there is trouble, one of you signal us and we'll come to the rescue."

"Just like the shining knights you are, all three of you," Mem'sab said warmly, laying her hand over the one Sahib had on the desk. "I think that is as much of a plan as we can lay, since we really don't know what we will find in that house."

"It's enough, I suspect," Sahib replied. "It allows two of us to break into the house if necessary, while one goes for the police." He stroked his chin thoughtfully with his free hand. "Or better yet, I'll take a whistle; that will summon help in no time." He glanced up at Mem'sab. "What time did you say the invitation specified?"

"Seven," she replied promptly. "Well after dark, although Katherine tells me that *her* sessions are usually later, nearer midnight."

"The medium may anticipate some trouble from sleepy children," Sahib speculated. "But that's just a guess." He stood up, still holding his wife's hand, and she slid off her perch on the desk and turned to face them. "Ladies, gentlemen, I think we are as prepared as we can be for trouble. So let us get a good night's sleep, and hope that we will not find any."

Then Sahib did a surprising thing; he came around his desk, limping stiffly, and bent over Nan and took her hand. "Perhaps only I of all of us can realize how brave you were to confide your worry to an adult you have only just come to trust, Nan," he said, very softly, then grinned at her so impishly that she saw the little boy he must have been in the eyes of the mature man. "Ain't no doubt 'uv thet, missy. Yer a cunnin' moit, an' 'ad more blows then pats, Oi reckon," he continued in street cant, shocking the breath out of her. "I came up the same way you are now, dear, thanks to a very kind man with no son of his own. I want you to remember that to us here at this school, there is no such thing as a stupid question, nor will we dismiss *any* worry you have as trivial. Never fear to bring either to an adult."

He straightened up, as Mem'sab came to his side, nodding. "Now both of you try and get some sleep, for every warrior knows that sleep is more important than anything else before a battle."

Ha, Nan thought, as she and Sarah followed Karamjit out of the study. *There's gonna be trouble; I kin feel it, an' so can he. He didn' get that tiger by not havin' a nose fer trouble. But—I reckon the trouble's gonna have its hands full with him.*

The medium lived in a modest house just off one of the squares in the part of London that housed those clerks and the like with pretensions to a loftier address than their purses would allow, an area totally unfamiliar to Nan. The house itself had seen better days, though, as had most of the other homes on that dead-end street, and Nan suspected that it was rented. The houses had that peculiarly faded look that came when the owners of a house did not actually live there, and those who did had no reason to care for the property themselves, assuming that was the duty of the landlord.

Mem'sab had chosen her gown carefully, after discarding a walking-suit, a mourning-gown and veil, and a peculiar draped garment she called a *sari,* a souvenir of her time in India. The first, she thought, made her look untrusting, sharp, and suspicious, the second would not be believed had the medium done any research on the backgrounds of these new sitters, and the third smacked of mockery. She chose instead one of the plain, simple gowns she preferred, in the mode called "Artistic Reform"; not particularly stylish, but Nan thought it was a good choice. For one thing, she could move in it; it was looser than the highest mode, and did not require tight corseting. If Mem'sab needed to run, kick, or dodge, she could.

The girls followed her quietly, dressed in their starched pinafores and dark dresses, showing the best possible manners, with Grey tucked under Sarah's coat to stay warm until they got within doors.

It was quite dark as they mounted the steps to the

house and rang the bell. It was answered by a sour-faced woman in a plain black dress, who ushered them into a sitting room and took their coats, with a startled glance at Grey as he popped her head out of the front of Sarah's jacket. She said nothing, however, and neither did Grey as she climbed to Sarah's shoulder.

The woman returned a moment later, but not before Nan had heard the faint sounds of surreptitious steps on the floor above them. She knew it had not been the sour woman, for she had clearly heard *those* steps going off to a closet and returning. If the seance-room was on this floor, then, there was someone else above.

The sitting-room had been decorated in a very odd style. The paintings on the wall were all either religious in nature, or extremely morbid, at least so far as Nan was concerned. There were pictures of women weeping over graves, of angels lifting away the soul of a dead child, of a woman throwing herself to her death over a cliff, of the spirits of three children hovering about a man and woman mourning over pictures held in their listless hands. There was even a picture of a girl crying over a dead bird lying in her hand.

Crystal globes on stands decorated the tables, along with bouquets of funereal lilies whose heavy, sweet scent dominated the chill room. The tables were all draped in fringed cloths of a deep scarlet. The hard, severe furniture was either of wood or upholstered in prickly horsehair. The two lamps had been lit before they entered the room, but their light, hampered as it was by heavy brocade lamp shades, cast more shadows than illumination.

They didn't have to wait long in that uncomfortable room, for the sour servant departed for a moment, then returned, and conducted them into the next room.

This, evidently, was only an antechamber to the room of mysteries; heavy draperies swathed all the walls, and there were straight-backed chairs set against them on all four walls. The lily-scent pervaded this room as well, mixed with another, that Nan recognized as the Hindu incense that Nadra often burned in her own devotions.

There was a single picture in this room, on the wall opposite the door, with a candle placed on a small table beneath it so as to illuminate it properly. This was a portrait in oils of a plump woman swathed in pale draperies, her hands clasped melodramatically before her breast, her eyes cast upwards. Smoke, presumably that of incense, swirled around her, with the suggestion of faces in it. Nan was no judge of art, but Mem'sab walked up to it and examined it with a critical eye.

"Neither good nor bad," she said, measuringly. "I would say it is either the work of an unknown professional or a talented amateur."

"A talented amateur," said the lady that Mem'sab had called "Katherine," as she too was ushered into the chamber. "My dear friend Lady Harrington painted it; it was she who introduced me to Madame Varonsky." Mem'sab turned to meet her, and Katherine glided across the floor to take her hand in greeting. "It is said to be a very speaking likeness," she continued. "I certainly find it so."

Nan studied the woman further, but saw nothing to change her original estimation. Katherine wore yet another mourning gown of expensive silk and mohair, embellished with jet beadwork and fringes that shivered with the slightest movement. A black hat with a full veil perched on her carefully coiffed curls, fair hair too dark to be called golden, but not precisely brown either. Her full lips trembled, even as they uttered words of polite conversation, her eyes threatened to fill at every moment, and Nan thought that her weak chin reflected an overly sentimental and vapid personality. It was an assessment that was confirmed by her conversation with Mem'sab, conversation that Nan ignored in favor of listening for other sounds. Over their heads, the floor creaked softly as someone moved to and fro, trying very hard to be quiet. There were also some odd scratching sounds that didn't sound like mice, and once, a dull thud, as of something heavy being set down a little too hard.

Something was going on up there, and the person doing it didn't want them to notice.

At length the incense-smell grew stronger, and the drapery on the wall to the right of the portrait parted, revealing a door, which opened as if by itself.

Taking that as their invitation, Katherine broke off her small talk to hurry eagerly into the sacred precincts; Mem'sab gestured to the girls to precede her, and followed on their heels. By previous arrangement, Nan and Sarah, rather than moving towards the circular table at which Madame Varonsky waited, went to the two walls likeliest to hold windows behind their heavy draperies before anyone could stop them.

It was Nan's luck to find a corner window overlooking the street, and she made sure that some light from the room within flashed to the watcher on the opposite side before she dropped the drapery.

"Come away from the windows, children," Mem'sab said in a voice that gently chided. Nan and Sarah immediately turned back to the room, and Nan assessed the foe.

Madame Varonsky's portraitist had flattered her; she was decidedly paler than she had been painted, with a complexion unpleasantly like wax. She wore similar draperies, garments which could have concealed anything. The smile on her thin lips did not reach her eyes, and she regarded the parrot on Sarah's shoulder with distinct unease.

"You did not warn me about the bird, Katherine," the woman said, her voice rather reedy.

"The bird will be no trouble, Madame Varonsky," Mem'sab soothed. "It is better behaved than a good many of my pupils."

"Your pupils—I am not altogether clear on why they were brought," Madame Varonsky replied, turning her sharp black eyes on Nan and Sarah.

"Nan is an orphan, and wants to learn what she can of her parents, since she never knew them," Mem'sab said smoothly. "And Sarah lost a little brother to an African fever."

"Ah." Madame Varonsky's suspicions diminished, and she gestured to the chairs around the table. "Please, all of you, do take your seats, and we can begin at once."

As with the antechamber, this room had walls swathed in draperies, which Nan decided could conceal an entire army if Madame Varonsky were so inclined. The only furnishings besides the seance table and chairs were a sinuous statue of a female completely enveloped in draperies on a draped table, with incense burning before it in a small charcoal brazier of brass and cast iron.

The table at which Nan took her place was very much as Mem'sab had described. A surreptitious bump as Nan took her seat on Mem'sab's left hand proved that it was quite light and easy to move; it would be possible to lift it with one hand with no difficulty at all. On the draped surface were some of the objects Mem'sab had described; a tambourine, a megaphone, a little handbell. There were three lit candles in a brass candlestick in the middle of the table, and some objects Nan had not expected—a fiddle and bow, a rattle, and a pair of handkerchiefs.

This is where we're supposed to look, Nan realized, as Sarah took her place on Mem'sab's right, next to Madame Varonsky, and Katherine on Nan's left, flanking the medium on the other side. She wished she could look *up*, as Grey was unashamedly doing, her head over to one side as one eye peered upwards at the ceiling above them.

"If you would follow dear Katherine's example, child," said Madame, as Katherine took one of the handkerchiefs and used it to tie the medium's wrist to the arm of her chair. She smiled crookedly. "This is to assure you that I am not employing any trickery." Sarah, behaving with absolute docility, did the same on the other side, but cast Nan a knowing look as she finished. Nan knew what that meant; Sarah had tried the arm of the chair and found it loose.

"Now, if you all will hold hands, we will beseech the spirits to attend on us." The medium turned her attention to Mem'sab as Katherine and Sarah stretched their arms across the table to touch hands, and the rest reached for the hands of their partners. "Pray do not be alarmed when the candles are extinguished; the spirits are shy of light, for they are so delicate that it can destroy them. They will put out the candles themselves."

For several long moments they sat in complete silence, as the incense smoke thickened and curled around. Then although there wasn't a single breath of moving air in the room, the candle-flames began to dim, one by one, and go out!

Nan felt the hair on the back of her neck rising, for this was a phenomena she could not account for—to distract herself, she looked up quickly at the ceiling just in time to see a faint line of light in the form of a square vanish.

She felt better immediately. However the medium had extinguished the candles, it had to be a trick. If she had any real powers, she wouldn't need a trapdoor in the ceiling of her seance-room. As she looked back down, she realized that the objects on the table were all glowing with a dim, greenish light.

"Spirits, are you with us?" Madame Varonsky called. Nan immediately felt the table begin to lift.

Katherine gasped; Mem'sab gave Nan's hand a squeeze; understanding immediately what she wanted, Nan let go of it. Now Mem'sab was free to act as she needed.

"The spirits are strong tonight," Madame murmured, as the table settled again. "Perhaps they will give us a further demonstration of their powers."

Exactly on cue, the tambourine rose into the air, shaking uncertainly; first the megaphone joined it, then the rattle, then the hand-bell, all floating in mid-air, or seeming to. But Nan was looking *up*, not at the objects, and saw a very dim square, too dim to be called *light*, above the table. A deeper shadow moved back and forth over that area, and Nan's lip curled with contempt. She had no difficulty in imagining how the objects were "levitating"; one by one, they'd been pulled up by wires or black strings, probably hooked by means of a fishing-rod from the room above.

Now rapping began on the table, to further distract their attention. Madame began to ask questions.

"Is there a spirit here for Helen Harton?" she asked. One rap—that was a *no*; not surprising, since the medium probably wouldn't want to chance making a mistake with an adult. "Is there a spirit here for Katherine Boughmont?" Two raps—yes. "Is this the spirit of a child?" Two raps, and already Katherine had begun to weep softly. "Is it the spirit of her son, Edward?" Two raps plus the bell rang and the rattle and tambourine played, and Nan found herself feeling very sorry for the poor, silly woman.

"Are there other spirits here tonight?" Two raps. "Is there a spirit for the child Nan?" Two raps. "Is it her father?" One rap. "Her mother?" Two raps, and Nan had to control her temper, which flared at that moment. She knew very well that her mother was still alive, though at the rate she was going, she probably wouldn't be for long, what with the gin and the opium and the rest of her miserable life. But if she had been a young orphan, her parents dead in some foreign land like one or two of the other pupils, what would she not have given for the barest word from them, however illusory? Would she not have been willing to believe anything that sounded warm and kind?

There appeared to be no spirit for Sarah, which was just as well. Madame Varonsky was ready to pull out the next of her tricks, for the floating objects settled to the table again.

"My spirit-guide was known in life as the great Paganini, the master violinist," Madame Varonsky announced. "As music is the food of the soul, he will employ the same sweet music he made in life to bridge the gap between our world and the next. Listen, and he will play this instrument before us!"

Fiddle music appeared to come from the instrument on the table, although the bow did not actually move across the strings. Katherine gasped.

"Release the child's hand a moment and touch the violin, dear Katherine," the medium said, in a kind, but distant voice. Katherine evidently let go of Sarah's hand, since she still had hold of Nan's, and the shadow of her fingers rested for a moment on the neck of the fiddle.

"The strings!" she cried. "Helen, the strings are vibrating as they are played!"

If this was supposed to be some great, long-dead music-master, Nan didn't think much of his ability. If she wasn't mistaken, the tune he was playing was the child's chant of "London Bridge Is Falling Down," but played very, very slowly, turning it into a solemn dirge.

"Touch the strings, Helen!" Katherine urged. "See for yourself!"

Nan felt Mem'sab lean forward, and another hand-shadow fell over the strings. "They are vibrating. . . ." she said, her voice suddenly uncertain.

The music ground to a halt before she took her hand away—and until this moment, Grey had been as silent as a stuffed bird on a lady's hat. Now she did something.

She began to sing. It was a very clever imitation of a fiddle, playing a jig-tune that a street-musician often played at the gate of the School, for the pennies the pupils would throw to him.

She quit almost immediately, but not before Mem'sab took her hand away from the strings, and Nan sensed that somehow Grey had given her the clue she needed to solve that particular trick.

But the medium must have thought that her special spirit was responsible for that scrap of jig-tune, for she didn't say or do anything.

Nan sensed that all of this was building to the main turn, and so it was.

Remembering belatedly that she should be keeping an eye on that suspicious square above. She glanced up just in time to see it disappear. As the medium began to moan and sigh, calling on Paganini, Nan kept her eye on the ceiling. Sure enough, the dim line of light appeared again, forming a greyish square. Then the lines of the square thickened, and Nan guessed that a square platform was being lowered from above.

Pungent incense smoke thickened about them, filling Nan's nose and stinging her eyes so that they watered, and she smothered a sneeze. It was hard to breathe, and there was something strangely, disquietingly familiar about the scent.

The medium's words, spoken in a harsh, accented voice, cut through the smoke. "I, the great Paganini, am here among you!"

Once again, Katherine gasped.

"Harken and be still! Lo, the spirits gather!"

Nan's eyes burned, and for a moment, she felt very dizzy; she thought that the soft glow in front of her was due to nothing more than eyestrain, but the glow strengthened, and she blinked in shock as two vague shapes took form amid the writhing smoke.

For a new brazier, belching forth such thick smoke that the coals were invisible, had "appeared" in the center of the table, just behind the candlestick. It was above this brazier that the glowing shapes hovered, and slowly took on an identifiable form. Nan felt dizzier, sick; the room seemed to turn slowly around her.

The faces of a young woman and a little boy looked vaguely out over Nan's head from the cloud of smoke. Katherine began to weep—presumably she thought she recognized the child as her own. But the fact that the young woman looked *nothing* like Nan's mother (and in fact, looked quite a bit like the sketch in an advertisement for Bovril in the *Times*) woke Nan out of her mental haze.

And so did Grey.

She heard the flapping of wings as Grey plummeted to the floor. She sneezed urgently, and shouted aloud, "Bad air! Bad air!"

And *that* was the moment when she knew what it was that was so familiar in the incense smoke, and why she felt as tipsy as a sailor on shore leave.

"*Hashish!*" she choked, trying to shout, and not managing very well. She knew this scent; on the rare occasions when her mother could afford it—and before she'd turned to opium—she'd smoked it in preference to drinking. Nan could only think of one thing; that she *must* get fresh air in here before they all passed out!

She shoved her chair back and staggered up and out of it; it fell behind her with a clatter that seemed muffled in the smoke. She groped for the brazier as the two faces continued to stare, unmoved and unmoving, from the thick billows. Her hands felt like a pair of lead-filled mittens; she had to fight to stay upright as she swayed like a drunk. She didn't find it, but her hands closed on the cool, smooth surface of the crystal ball.

That was good enough; before the medium could stop her, she heaved up the heavy ball with a grunt of effort, and staggered to the window. She half-spun and flung the ball at the draperies hiding the unseen window; it hit the drapes and carried them into the glass, crashing through it, taking the drapery with it.

A gush of cold air, as fresh as air in London ever got, streamed in through the broken panes, as bedlam erupted in the room behind Nan.

She dropped to the floor, ignoring everything around her for the moment, as she breathed in the air tainted only with smog, waiting for her head to clear. Grey ran to her and huddled with her rather than joining her beloved mistress in the poisonous smoke.

Katherine shrieked in hysteria, there was a man as well as the medium shouting, and Mem'sab cursed all of them in some strange language. Grey gave a terrible shriek and half-ran, half flew away. Nan fought her dizziness and disorientation; looked up to see that Mem'sab was struggling in the grip of a stringy fellow she didn't recognize. Katherine had been backed up into one corner by the medium, and Sarah and Grey were pummeling the medium with small fists and wings. Mem'sab kicked at her captor's shins and stamped on his feet with great effect, as his grunts of pain demonstrated.

Nan struggled to her feet, guessing that *she* must have been the one worst affected by the hashish fumes. She wanted to run to Mem'sab's rescue, but she couldn't get her legs to work. In a moment the sour-faced woman would surely break into the room, turning the balance in favor of the enemy—

The door *did* crash open behind her just as she thought that, and she tried to turn to face the new foe—

But it was not the foe.

Sahib charged through the broken door, pushing past Nan to belabor the man holding Mem'sab with his cane; within three blows the man was on the floor, moaning. Before Nan fell, Karamjit caught her and steadied her. More men flooded into the room, and Nan let Karamjit steer her out of the way, concentrating on those steadying breaths of air. She thought perhaps that she passed out of consciousness for a while, for when she next noticed anything, she was sitting bent over in a chair, with Karamjit hovering over her, frowning. At some point the brazier had been extinguished, and a policeman was collecting the ashes and the remains of the drug-laced incense.

Finally her head cleared; by then, the struggle was over. The medium and her fellow tricksters were in the custody of the police, who had come with Sahib when Nan threw the crystal ball through the window. Sahib was talking to a policeman with a sergeant's badge, and Nan guessed that he was explaining what Mem'sab and Katherine were doing here. Katherine wept in a corner, comforted by Mem'sab. The police had brought lamps into the seance-room from the sitting-room, showing all too clearly how the medium had achieved her work; a hatch in the ceiling to the room above, through which things could be lowered; a magic-lantern behind the drapes, which had cast its image of a woman and boy onto the thick brazier smoke. That, and the disorienting effect of the hashish had made it easy to trick the clients.

Finally the bobbies took their captives away, and Katherine stopped crying. Nan and Sarah sat on the chairs Karamjit had set up, watching the adults, Grey on her usual perch on Sarah's shoulder. A cushion stuffed in the broken window cut off most of the cold air from outside.

"I can't believe I was so foolish!" Katherine moaned. "But—I wanted to see Edward so very much—"

"I hardly think that falling for a clever deception backed by drugs makes you foolish, ma'am," Sahib said gravely. "But you are to count yourself fortunate in the loyalty of your friends, who were willing to place themselves in danger for you. I do not think that these people would have been willing to stop at mere fraud, and neither do the police."

His last words made no impression on Katherine, at least none that Nan saw—but she did turn to Mem'sab and clasp her hand fervently. "I thought so ill of you, that you would not believe in Madame," she said tearfully. "Can you forgive me?"

Mem'sab smiled. "Always, my dear," she said, in the voice she used to soothe a frightened child. "Since your motive was to enlighten me, not to harm me—and your motive in seeking your poor child's spirit—"

A chill passed over Nan at that moment that had

nothing to do with the outside air. She looked sharply at Sarah, and saw a very curious thing.

There was a very vague and shimmery shape standing in front of Sarah's chair; Sarah looked at it with an intense and thoughtful gaze, as if she was listening to it. More than that, Grey was doing the same. Nan got the distinct impression that it was asking her friend for a favor.

Grey and Sarah exchanged a glance, and the parrot nodded once, as grave and sober as a parson, then spread her wings as if sheltering Sarah like a chick.

The shimmering form melted into Sarah; her features took on a mischievous expression that Nan had never seen her wear before, and she got up and went directly to Katherine.

The woman looked up at her, startled at the intrusion of a child into an adult discussion, then paled at something she saw in Sarah's face.

"Oh, Mummy, you don't have to be so sad," Sarah said in a curiously hollow, piping soprano. "I'm all right, really, and it wasn't your fault anyway, it was that horrid Lord Babbington that made you and Papa send me to Overton. But you *must* stop crying, please! Laurie is already scared of being left, and you're scaring her more."

Now, Nan knew very well that Mem'sab had not said anything about a Lord Babbington, nor did she and Sarah know what school the poor little boy had been sent to. Yet, she wasn't frightened; in fact, the protective but calm look in Grey's eye made her feel rather good, as if something inside her told her that everything was going wonderfully well.

The effect on Katherine was not what Nan had expected, either.

She reached out tentatively, as if to touch Sarah's face, but stopped short. "This *is* you, isn't it, darling?" she asked in a whisper.

Sarah nodded—or was it Edward who nodded? "Now,

I've *got* to go, Mummy, and I can't come back. So don't look for me, and don't cry anymore."

The shimmering withdrew, forming into a brilliant ball of light at about Sarah's heart, then shot off, so fast that Nan couldn't follow it. Grey pulled in her wings, and Sarah shook her head a little, then regarded Katherine with a particularly measuring expression before coming back to her chair and sitting down.

"Out of the mouths of babes, Katherine," Mem'sab said quietly, then looked up at Karamjit. "I think you and Selim should take the girls home now; they've had more than enough excitement for one night."

Karamjit bowed silently, and Grey added her own vote. "Wan' go back," she said in a decidedly firm tone. When Selim brought their coats and helped them to put them on, Grey climbed right back inside Sarah's, and didn't even put her head back out again.

They didn't have to go home in a cab, either; Katherine sent them back to the school in her own carriage, which was quite a treat for Nan, who'd had no notion that a private carriage would come equipped with such comforts as heated bricks for the feet and fur robes to bundle in. Nan didn't say anything to Sarah about the aftermath of the seance until they were alone together in their shared dormitory room.

Only then, as Grey took her accustomed perch on the headboard of Sarah's bed, did Nan look at her friend and ask—

"That last—was that—?"

Sarah nodded. "I could see him, clear as clear, too." She smiled a little. "He must've been a horrid brat at times, but he really wasn't bad, just spoiled enough to be a bit selfish, and he's been—learning better manners, since."

All that Nan could think of to say was—"Ah."

"Still; I think it was a *bit* rude of him to have been so impatient with his Mother," she continued, a little irritated.

"I 'spose that magic-man friend of yours is right," Nan replied, finally. "About what you c'n do, I mean."

"Oh! You're right!" Sarah exclaimed. "But you know, I don't think I could have done it if Grey hadn't been there. I thought if I ever saw a spirit I'd be too scared to do anything, but I wasn't afraid, since she wasn't."

The parrot took a little piece of Sarah's hair in her beak and preened it.

"*Wise* bird," replied Grey.

MERCEDES LACKEY
Hot! Hot! Hot!

Whether it's elves at the racetrack, bards battling evil mages or brainships fighting planet pirates, Mercedes Lackey is always compelling, always fun, always a great read. Complete your collection today!

The Bardic Voices series:

The Lark and the Wren, 72099-6 ♦ $6.99 ☐

The Robin & The Kestrel, 87628-7 ♦ $5.99 ☐

The Eagle & The Nightingales, 87706-2 ♦ $5.99 ☐

Four & Twenty Blackbirds, 57778-6 ♦ $6.99 ☐

The SERRAted Edge series:

Born to Run (with Larry Dixon), 72110-0 ♦ $5.99 ☐

Wheels of Fire (with Mark Shepherd), 72138-0 ♦ $5.99 ☐

When the Bough Breaks (with Holly Lisle), 72154-1 ♦ $5.99 ☐

Chrome Circle (with Larry Dixon), 87615-5 ♦ $5.99 ☐

Bard's Tale novels:

Castle of Deception (with Josepha Sherman), 72125-9 ♦ $5.99 ☐

Fortress of Frost & Fire (with Ru Emerson), 72162-3 ♦ $5.99 ☐

Prison of Souls (with Mark Shepherd), 72193-3 ♦ $5.99 ☐

Bedlam's Bard (with Ellen Guon), 87863-8 ♦ $6.99 ☐

The Fire Rose, 87750-X ♦ $6.99 ☐

Fiddler Fair, 87866-2 ♦ $5.99 ☐

Available at your local bookstore. If not, fill out this coupon and send a check or money order for the cover price + $1.50 s/h to Baen Books, Dept. BA, P.O. Box 1403, Riverdale, NY 10471.

Name: _____

Address: _____

_____

I have enclosed a check or money order in the amount of $ _____

PRAISE FOR LOIS MCMASTER BUJOLD

What the critics say:

The Warrior's Apprentice: "Now here's a fun romp through the spaceways—not so much a space opera as space ballet.... it has all the 'right stuff.' A lot of thought and thoughtfulness stand behind the all-too-human characters. Enjoy this one, and look forward to the next." —Dean Lambe, *SF Reviews*

"The pace is breathless, the characterization thoughtful and emotionally powerful, and the author's narrative technique and command of language compelling. Highly recommended." —*Booklist*

Brothers in Arms: "... she gives it a geniune depth of character, while reveling in the wild turnings of her tale.... Bujold is as audacious as her favorite hero, and as brilliantly (if sneakily) successful." —*Locus*

"Miles Vorkosigan is such a great character that I'll read anything Lois wants to write about him.... a book to re-read on cold rainy days." —Robert Coulson, *Comics Buyer's Guide*

Borders of Infinity: "Bujold's series hero Miles Vorkosigan may be a lord by birth and an admiral by rank, but a bone disease that has left him hobbled and in frequent pain has sensitized him to the suffering of outcasts in his very hierarchical era.... Playing off Miles's reserve and cleverness, Bujold draws outrageous and outlandish foils to color her high-minded adventures." —*Publishers Weekly*

Falling Free: "In *Falling Free* Lois McMaster Bujold has written her fourth straight superb novel.... How to break down a talent like Bujold's into analyzable components? Best not to try. Best to say 'Read, or you will be missing something extraordinary.'" —Roland Green, *Chicago Sun-Times*

The Vor Game: "The chronicles of Miles Vorkosigan are far too witty to be literary junk food, but they rouse the kind of craving that makes popcorn magically vanish during a double feature." —Faren Miller, *Locus*

MORE PRAISE FOR LOIS MCMASTER BUJOLD

What the readers say:

"My copy of *Shards of Honor* is falling apart I've reread it so often.... I'll read whatever you write. You've certainly proved yourself a grand storyteller."
—Liesl Kolbe, Colorado Springs, CO

"I experience the stories of Miles Vorkosigan as almost viscerally uplifting.... But certainly, even the weightiest theme would have less impact than a cinder on snow were it not for a rousing good story, and good storytelling with it. This is the second thing I want to thank you for.... I suppose if you boiled down all I've said to its simplest expression, it would be that I immensely enjoy and admire your work. I submit that, as literature, your work raises the overall level of the science fiction genre, and spiritually, your work cannot avoid positively influencing all who read it."
—Glen Stonebraker, Gaithersburg, MD

" 'The Mountains of Mourning' [in *Borders of Infinity*] was one of the best-crafted, and simply best, works I'd ever read. When I finished it, I immediately turned back to the beginning and read it again, and I can't remember the last time I did that." —Betsy Bizot, Lisle, IL

"I can only hope that you will continue to write, so that I can continue to read (and of course buy) your books, for they make me laugh and cry and think ... rare indeed." —Steven Knott, Major, USAF

What Do You Say?

Send me these books!

Shards of Honor	72087-2	$5.99 ☐
Barrayar	72083-X	$5.99 ☐
Cordelia's Honor (trade)	87749-6	$15.00 ☐
The Warrior's Apprentice	72066-X	$5.99 ☐
The Vor Game	72014-7	$5.99 ☐
Young Miles (trade)	87782-8	$15.00 ☐
Cetaganda (hardcover)	87701-1	$21.00 ☐
Cetaganda (paperback)	87744-5	$5.99 ☐
Ethan of Athos	65604-X	$5.99 ☐
Borders of Infinity	72093-7	$5.99 ☐
Brothers in Arms	69799-4	$5.99 ☐
Mirror Dance (paperback)	87646-5	$6.99 ☐
Memory (paperback)	87845-X	$6.99 ☐
The Spirit Ring (paperback)	72188-7	$5.99 ☐

LOIS MCMASTER BUJOLD
Only from Baen Books
visit our website at www.baen.com

If not available at your local bookstore, send this coupon and a check or money order for the cover price(s) + $1.50 s/h to Baen Books, Dept. BA, P.O. Box 1403, Riverdale, NY 10471. Delivery can take up to 8 weeks.

NAME: _____

ADDRESS: _____

_____

I have enclosed a check or money order in the amount of $ _____

THE SHIP WHO SANG IS NOT ALONE!

Anne McCaffrey, with Margaret Ball, Mercedes Lackey, S.M. Stirling, and Jody Lynn Nye, explores the universe she created with her ground-breaking novel, The Ship Who Sang.

PARTNERSHIP
by Anne McCaffrey & Margaret Ball

"[PartnerShip] captures the spirit of *The Ship Who Sang*...a single, solid plot full of creative nastiness and the sort of egocentric villains you love to hate."
—Carolyn Cushman, **Locus**

THE SHIP WHO SEARCHED
by Anne McCaffrey & Mercedes Lackey

Tia, a bright and spunky seven-year-old accompanying her exo-archaeologist parents on a dig, is afflicted by a paralyzing alien virus. Tia won't be satisfied to glide through life like a ghost in a machine. Like her predecessor Helva, *The Ship Who Sang*, she would rather strap on a spaceship!

THE CITY WHO FOUGHT
by Anne McCaffrey & S.M. Stirling

Simeon was the "brain" running a peaceful space station—but when the invaders arrived, his only hope of protecting his crew and himself was to become *The City Who Fought*.

THE SHIP WHO WON
by Anne McCaffrey & Jody Lynn Nye

"Oodles of fun." —*Locus*
"Fast, furious and fun." —*Chicago Sun-Times*

ANNE McCAFFREY: QUEEN OF THE SPACEWAYS

"Readers will find themselves riveted by the nonstop action adventure that constantly surpasses even the most jaded reader's expectations, and by a relationship as beautiful as it is indestructible."
—*Affaire de Coeur*

PARTNERSHIP ☐
by Anne McCaffrey & Margaret Ball
0-671-72109-7 ♦ 336 pages ♦ $5.99

THE SHIP WHO SEARCHED ☐
by Anne McCaffrey & Mercedes Lackey
0-671-72129-1 ♦ 320 pages ♦ $5.99

THE CITY WHO FOUGHT ☐
by Anne McCaffrey & S.M. Stirling
0-671-72166-6 ♦ 432 pages ♦ HC $19.00 ♦ PB $5.99 ♦ 87599-X

THE SHIP WHO WON ☐
by Anne McCaffrey & Jody Lynn Nye
0-671-87595-7 ♦ HC $21.00 ♦ PB $5.99 ♦ 87657-0

And don't miss:

THE PLANET PIRATES ☐
by Anne McCaffrey,
with Elizabeth Moon & Jody Lynn Nye
3-in-1 trade paperback edition
0-671-72187-9 ♦ 864 pages ♦ $12.00

If not available through your local bookstore send this coupon and a check or money order for the cover price(s) to Baen Books, Dept. BA, P.O. Box 1403, Riverdale, NY 10471. Delivery can take up to ten weeks.

NAME: _____

ADDRESS: _____

_____

I have enclosed a check or money order in the amount of $ _____

EXPLORE OUR WEB SITE

BAEN.COM

VISIT THE BAEN BOOKS WEB SITE AT:

http://www.baen.com
or just search for baen.com

Get information on the latest releases,
sample chapters of upcoming novels,
read about your favorite authors,
enter contests, and much more! ;)

Consequently, after three decades and over thirty research studies we are still waiting for the one type of study that would confirm or refute whether there are any structural or functional differences between the brains of children diagnosed with ADHD and otherwise normal children. However, even if such a study was to be done and show a definite difference, this still does not mean that an abnormality in the brain has been proven as the cause of ADHD type behaviours.

It is well known that the brain, particularly the developing brain, is very sensitive during its growth to the environment it finds itself in. For example, we know that a person under stress is likely to produce higher levels of the hormone cortisone than a person who is not. Furthermore, there is evidence to suggest that high levels of cortisone occurring over many months and years can have a significant effect on brain growth and development, particularly in infancy when the brain is growing at its fastest. We also know that everyone develops at different rates and so what we might be seeing (if a statistically significant difference in the size of particular brain structures were indeed proven) is simply those who are developing slower, or later, than their age group or the effects on the developing brain of living in a stressful environment[9].

The belief that ADHD is a genetic condition is another of those ideas that has developed as a result of supporters of the diagnosis, ignoring matters of context. If we take as our starting assumption that behaviour such as motor activity, attention and impulsivity are temperamental characteristics (in other words part of normal variation, like personality characteristics), then the evidence fits much better. Viewing these behaviours as temperamental characteristics as opposed to signs of a medical condition, allows more attention to other factors. Research on children's temperament has shown that problems result from a mismatch between the child's temperament and their environment. Even children who are highly difficult temperamentally can become well adjusted behaviourally if their family and other social circumstances are supportive[10]. Indeed a difficult temperament (such as high levels of activity and low attention span) is a poor predictor of future problems at school, the best predictors being parents' and then schools' ability to cope. What the genetic studies may have been discovering is that the behaviours we call ADHD are inherited in much the same way as other personality traits, whether these behaviours come to be perceived as a problem is 'shaped' by social factors. In their international consensus statement on ADHD, Russell Barkley and other prominent ADHD researchers[11] virtually admit this, when, they compare the genetics of ADHD to the genetics of height. Since when has height been considered a medical disorder? It is simply a biological characteristic that varies from one person and one family to another.

Genetic studies on children diagnosed with ADHD suffer from many other problems. The main source of the evidence said to support the idea that genes are responsible for ADHD, come from the finding that identical twins have higher rates of ADHD than non-identical twins. Because identical twins share 100% of their genes whilst non-identical twins share about 50% of their genes, it is (falsely) concluded that the higher percentage of identical twins both having ADHD compared to non-identical twins, is the result of genetics. Concluding that the higher rates of diagnosis in the twin of identical as opposed to non-identical twins, is evidence of genetic transmission, ignores the substantial psychological difference involved in being an identical as opposed to non-identical twin. For example substantially more identical as opposed to non-identical twins report identity confusion and are more likely to be reared 'as a unit'. Similar methodological problems have been shown to occur in the two other main methods used to try and establish a genetic link- familial studies and studies of adopted children with ADHD. None of the methods used are able to disentangle environmental and psychological effects from biological/genetic ones. Thus, just as we cannot conclude that genetics has no role, we do not yet have the evidence to conclude genetics has any role to play whatsoever. Indeed, we now have a growing number of molecular genetic studies that have set out to search for ADHD genes but have yet to reliably find any. This would seem to be leading us to the conclusion that genetics have a minor (if any) role to play in ADHD[12].

So thus far in ADHD research no unique causes in the person's biology have been identified, very much the reverse in fact as the evidence above demonstrates.

Myth 3: Stimulants such as Ritalin are a first line treatment of choice for ADHD. Stimulants are safe and effective. Drug treatment may need to be given for the rest of that person's life.

Fact and discussion: The most common medications used in the treatment of ADHD are central nervous system stimulants such as Ritalin. These stimulants are from the same chemical family as the street drugs speed and cocaine; hence all stimulants are potential drugs of abuse and categorized as 'controlled drugs' (like heroine and methadone). Stimulants' effects are not limited to those children who are diagnosed with ADHD. Stimulants have the same cognitive and behavioural effects on otherwise normal children and children with other psychiatric diagnoses.

A beneficial effect beyond four weeks of treatment in children diagnosed with ADHD has not been demonstrated yet in what is considered 'the gold standard' for drug trials- A placebo controlled double blind trial (This means comparing the active pill with an inactive sugar pill, where those participating in the study and those studying them don't know whether they are taking the active or inactive pill). There is no evidence that stimulants result in any long-term improvement in either behaviour or academic achievement, with articles reviewing the literature on treatment with stimulants concluding that a beneficial effect on ADHD symptoms beyond 4 weeks of treatment has not been demonstrated[13].

Stimulants have the potential to cause many side effects, including serious ones. Common side effects include poor appetite, weight loss, growth suppression, disturbed sleep, unhappiness, irritability, mood swings, confusion, obsessive-compulsive behaviours, stomachaches, headaches and dizziness. Less common, but serious, side effects include, explosive violent behaviour, a flattening of emotions and psychosis. Established side effects of long-term administration of stimulants include heart disease, lowered self-esteem, suppression of creativity, learning difficulties, excessive repetition, deterioration in performance on complex tasks and, occasionally, death due to the toxic effects of stimulants on the heart. In the past couple of years hardly a month goes by without new concerns emerging regarding the safety and efficacy of prescribing psychiatric drugs to the young, forcing the regulatory body the Food and Drug Administration (FDA) in the USA to issue new labelling in 2006 that warns about the danger of stimulants (and the new non-stimulant drug 'Strattera') due to concerns about them causing suicidal ideation, heart attacks, strokes, sudden death and psychosis.

Animal studies have found that giving stimulants to rats can cause a long-lasting change in the brain chemistry. There has been a dramatic increase in the number of children who are receiving stimulants in Western society. The majority of children who are prescribed stimulants will remain on them for many years and increasing numbers are continuing to take stimulants into their adulthood. We do not know the effects on the developing brain, and the long-term effects on the heart, of giving children stimulants for many years due to a lack of long term follow up studies.

We often forget that stimulants are powerful amphetamine like drugs with potentially addictive properties. Children become tolerant to its effect resulting in gradually increasing doses being given to children as years on a stimulant clock up. The potential for tolerance and addiction is further demonstrated by withdrawal states (known as the rebound effect, which presents as increased excitability, activity, talkativeness, irritability and insomnia) seen when the last dose of the day is wearing off or when the drug is withdrawn suddenly. Stories of adults becoming addicted to prescribed stimulants are becoming more common.

Research has focused almost exclusively on short-term outcomes. Why so little long-term studies from the manufacturers? Outcome research in stimulant treatment has been shown to have serious problems in methodology (the way the study was conducted). The few long-term studies that have been completed (usually by looking at what is now happening in the lives of adults who were prescribed stimulants when they were young) have shown that stimulants do not result in any long-term improvement in behaviour, relationships, or academic achievement. Despite the complete lack of evidence for any long -term effectiveness, stimulants are usually prescribed continuously for seven, eight or more years, with children as young as two being prescribed the drug in increasing numbers despite the manufacturer's licence stating that it should not be prescribed to children under six.

A big fuss has been made about a large multi-centre trial in the United States, which was testing the effectiveness of one stimulant- Ritalin- in the treatment of ADHD[14]. I have heard an eminent professor of child psychiatry in this country (the UK) state, at a large conference attended by child psychiatrists and paediatricians that the implication of the results of this study is that we should be treating children diagnosed with ADHD with medication as the first line treatment and possibly only treatment. This extraordinarily narrow interpretation of the results, shows how some clinicians are hell bent on ignoring wider factors and controversies to bolster their own beliefs (and probably their pockets too) and without regard for the enormous impact such statements have on clinical practice and ultimately on children's lives.

The study in question compared four groups of children who were given; medication only (Ritalin), intensive behavioural treatment only, combined behavioural treatment and medication, and standard community care. The study lasted 14 months. The study concluded that the medication only and combined behavioural and medication groups had the best outcome, with the combined group having an only slightly better outcome than the medication only group. A closer look inevitably brings up important questions about the study and how to interpret their results. Firstly this study was not the 'gold standard' for drug trials that I mentioned above, in other words it was not a placebo controlled double blind trial. This meant that those taking part in the study (children, their parents and the doctors/psychologists treating them) all knew they who was taking active medication, and as nobody was taking a placebo (a non-active sugar pill), it is impossible to know how much any positive response was due to the expectation for a positive response. All the principle investigators in this study were well known staunch supporters of medication with long established financial ties to the pharmaceutical industry- a conflict of interest that could seriously compromise their judgments. The parents and teachers who participated in the study were all exposed to pro-drug propaganda at the start of the study, putting them in a mindset of positive expectation for change in those children receiving medication. Interestingly there was one group who rated symptoms through observing children in the classroom, and who were 'blind' to the treatment status of the children they were observing (in other words they didn't know which children were taking medication). These researchers found no difference between any of the treatment groups on the behavioural measures they were using. Not surprisingly this important finding was given no importance in the study conclusions. There are also many question marks with regard the selection and recruiting process, the behavioural interventions used and the lack of attention to the number of children experiencing side effects (up to two thirds experienced some side effects) and the dismissing of some reported side effects as probably being due to 'non medication' factors.

Even if we accept the conclusions at face value, the findings are not particularly remarkable and only confirm what we already know, namely that this powerful medication has the potential to bring about some changes in behaviour in the short term (This study was for 14 months, a long way off the many years Ritalin is usually given for). The comparison psychological treatment of behaviour therapy is another based on a medicalised idea (of a specific treatment for children with a medical condition of ADHD) and therefore of questionable quality. Presumably all those taking part in the study are assuming there is such a 'biological' thing as ADHD and so are already being cultured into a way of thinking where the belief is that it's mainly the children who need to change.

Then there's the small print, the bits that you don't notice if you only advertise the particular bias of the researchers in their conclusion. All four groups in the treatment program showed sizable reductions in symptoms. The conclusion could have read 'Children not on medication made significant improvements'. In none of the treatment groups was there a significant improvement in academic performance and there was little effect on social skills. Two thirds of the community treated group were also receiving the same stimulant medication (Ritalin) during the period of the study, and yet were placed in the poorest outcome category. The conclusion of the study that medication only is the most efficient and cost effective treatment for ADHD would seem to reflect the interests and agenda of the researchers and their paymasters, rather than pure scientific ones.

A follow up study was conducted where the children in this study were assessed again after a further 10 months (in other words after a total of 24 months in the study)[15]. These results are no longer looking so impressive. While the percentages of children with normalized symptom levels (in other words those who in the opinion of the researchers were no longer displaying any ADHD symptoms) were essentially unchanged for the behaviour therapy only and community care groups, they had declined substantially for the combined (from 68% to 47%) and medication only (from 56% to 37%) groups. The medication only group now had a similar percentage to the behaviour therapy only group. Furthermore those who had taken medication in this study were now significantly shorter (by about an inch on average) than those who had not taken medication. By chance I also ended up speaking to a psychologist I met at a conference I attended in 2001. He was involved in the California wing of the above study. He told me that they had completed an analysis of their group after 36 months in the trial. He claimed that in their results only those who had received behaviour therapy had maintained a better outcome than the community care group (the group with the poorest outcome) adding *"our child psychiatrist has said he will never prescribe stimulants again as a result of this"*. I have been waiting to see the 36-month follow up results published. So far there is no sign of them.

Thus the only scientific conclusion that we can come to from analysing the evidence on treatment of ADHD with stimulants is that despite many studies, there is no reliable evidence to support the idea that treatment with stimulants produces long-lasting benefits. Indeed, according to Dr William Pelham, who was on the steering committee for the above studies, and who recently 'broke ranks' and spoke about the negative effects of drug company influence: *"No drug company in its literature mentions the fact that 40 years of research says there is no long-term benefit of medications [for ADHD]. That is something parents need to know."*[16]

More difficult to assess is the possible social and cultural affects such widespread use of stimulants in children may have. Doctors may be unwittingly convincing children to control and manage themselves using medication, a pattern that may carry on into adulthood as the preferred or only way to cope with life's stresses. Clinically I often come across children on stimulants that have admitted that they were secretly self-medicating at times of stress. Parents, teachers and others may lose interest in understanding the meaning behind an ADHD labelled child's behaviour beyond that of an illness internal to the child that needs medication.

In North America concern has been voiced about ADHD being diagnosed more frequently amongst children from working class families leading some authors to conclude that Ritalin is being misused as a drug for social control of children from disadvantaged communities. The dynamics of Ritalin prescription in North America have changed in recent years however, with the majority of those who get the prescription coming from white middle class families. Here the dynamic seems to be middle class parents' fears about their children's education. The worry is that if their children don't get into college or university, they are 'sunk'. Thus parents and the middle class teachers of their children are converting this anxiety into requests for the perceived performance enhancing properties of stimulants and with more children in classrooms taking stimulants many parents end up feeling their child is at a disadvantage if they don't. This dynamic is reflected in the trend where stimulants are being prescribed to children without making a diagnosis. This trend has now become so established that in many areas of the United States, less than half the children prescribed stimulants reach even the broad criteria for making a diagnosis of ADHD.

This social dynamic in the USA has been confirmed by a recent study that showed an interesting 'gender' issue. The gender gap in the child population diagnosed with ADHD is matched by a significant and opposite gap among adults initiating the labelling process. While young males form the majority of those labelled with ADHD, it is overwhelmingly adult females, their mothers and teachers, who make the first determination that a child's behaviour falls outside the normal range of what little boys are expected to do. Although this reflects the fact that adult females are more involved in the day-to-day care of children, mothers and fathers frequently disagree on the 'pathological' nature of their sons' behaviour. The research also showed that prescriptions of stimulants is highest in prosperous white communities where education is a high priority, where the educational achievement of both sexes is above the national average and, most importantly, where the gender gap in educational achievement favouring females is at its highest[17].

Stimulants like Ritalin are also drugs of abuse as they can be crushed and snorted to produce a high. Surveys have shown that a significant proportion of adolescents in the United States self report using Ritalin for non-medical purposes. Accounts of abuse of Ritalin and other stimulants are increasingly being reported in the press. Surveys have shown that between 3 and 16% of college students in the US admit to the use of non-prescribed stimulants, as well as a significant proportion of those prescribed stimulants for ADHD have also been found to be either taking other stimulants in addition to their own, or were misusing their prescribed medication[18]. The chemical effects of Ritalin on the brain are very similar to that of Cocaine, which is one of the most addictive drugs and Cocaine users report that the effect of injected Ritalin is almost indistinguishable from that of Cocaine.

Studies on the likelihood of substance misuse amongst those with a diagnosis of ADHD treated with a stimulant often conclude that those treated with a stimulant are less likely to abuse substances when compared to those with ADHD who were not treated with stimulants. Whilst it is thankfully rare for children prescribed a stimulant which they are taking by mouth, to becoming physically 'addicted', an unanswered question remains as to whether taking stimulants as a child sensitises the brain toward future substance abuse. The largest, community based study examining this issue, followed up nearly 500 children since the 1970s and right into their late twenties. They found a significant increase in amphetamine, cocaine and tobacco dependence amongst ADHD subjects who had taken stimulants when compared to 'untreated' controls. Furthermore they discovered a linear relationship between the amount of stimulant treatment and the likelihood of either tobacco or cocaine dependence (in other words the more stimulant these young people had received over the years, the greater the likelihood of their becoming addicted to tobacco, speed or cocaine by their late twenties)[19].

Use of stimulants in children therefore remains a controversial issue for reasons that go well beyond simply its side effects. Yet these important issues that should be important information for all parents trying to make the difficult decision as to whether or not to agree for their children to take a stimulant is information that is rarely given by prescribers.

Despite these contradictions and concerns, the availability of a drug that is believed to treat a childhood biomedical illness has proved so attractive that prescription levels, certainly in North America and more recently in the United Kingdom, have spiralled to reach what can be considered epidemic proportions. General practitioners and paediatricians as well as child psychiatrists routinely prescribe stimulants to children in North America. National surveys of paediatricians and family practitioners in the United States have found that over 80% of children they diagnosed as having ADHD were treated with a stimulant like Ritalin. National consumption of Ritalin in the United States more than doubled between 1981 and 1992. Prescriptions of Ritalin have continued to increase in the nineties, with over 11 million prescriptions of Ritalin written in 1996 in The United States. The amount of psychiatric medication prescribed to children in the United States increased nearly three fold between 1987 and 1996, with over 6% of boys between the ages of six to fourteen taking stimulants by 1996, which had risen to an estimated 10% of school boys by 2005. One study in Virginia in 1999, found that in two school districts, 17% of white boys at primary school were diagnosed with ADHD and taking stimulants. There has also been a large increase in prescriptions of stimulants to preschoolers (children aged 2 to 4 years). We are also catching up here in the UK, with recent figures suggesting about 5% of school age boys in England and Wales have been or are now prescribed a stimulant. Despite this alarming evidence, high profile professionals who believe in ADHD and use of stimulants in children, still claim that the majority of children who warrant this diagnosis are not getting it or the (drug) treatment they need.

This phenomenal rise has led to the suggestion that ADHD has been conceived and promoted by the pharmaceutical industry in order for there to be an entity for which stimulants could be prescribed, after all the pharmaceutical industry knows that the way to sell psychiatric drugs is to sell psychiatric diagnoses. The ADHD drugs market is now a multi million dollar industry, with the National Institute of Mental Health and the Food and Drug Administration in the United States, all having been involved in funding and promoting treatment which calls for medicating children with behavioural problems. Drug company tactics includes funding parent support groups, pro-medication research and payments to professionals to act as spokespeople for their companies or products. The situation with drug companies controlling the agenda of scientific debate has become so bad in many areas of medicine in recent years, that it is virtually impossible to climb up the career ladder without promotional support (e.g. to fund research, to speak at conferences, to write papers for journals) from drug companies. This is a situation that the medical profession have begun to debate in the knowledge that the ties that have developed between doctors and drug companies are causing conflicts of interest on a colossal scale leading to the public questioning the credibility of much of the 'science' being undertaken.

The one area in child and adolescent psychiatry where drug company involvement is most obvious is in ADHD research. Thus we have reached the situation were many senior academics have long standing financial links with drug companies, that inevitably compromises the impartiality of their opinions. Similarly the impartiality of patient support organizations has to be questioned. In recent years it has become apparent that drug companies are using such consumer lobbying groups to their advantage not only by (often secretly) generous donations, but also by sometimes setting up patient groups themselves. The main pro-medication pro-ADHD consumer support group in North America is CHADD- Children and Adults with Attention Deficit Hyperactivity Disorder. CHADD has long received substantial amounts from drug companies. Critics point out that CHADD's basic function has become that of promoting stimulant medications manufactured by its corporate donors. Pharmaceutical companies donated a total of $674,000 in the fiscal year 2002-2003. CHADD also produce a monthly magazine called *Attention!* Which drug companies buy in the tens of thousands and then place them in doctors' offices. In the UK, the main parent support ADDISS- Attention Deficit Disorder Information and Support Service- is also receiving significant funding from the pharmaceutical industry. For example a recent educational campaign 'launched to support parents of children with ADHD' includes a glossy booklet on ADHD called 'Family Stress Points' produced using an educational grant from a drug company. There are other support groups, for example in the United Kingdom the parent support group 'Overload', have been campaigning for prescribing doctors to provide more information to parents about the cardiovascular and psychiatric side effects of stimulants, believing that many more parents would be likely to reject such medication if they were being properly informed about it by the medical profession. However, without the financial support of the multinational giants, their message rarely gets heard.

Myth 4: Treatment for ADHD with medication improves public health with minimum risks.

Facts and discussion: There is no evidence to support the idea that children and young people's behaviour has improved as a result of a large percentage of children and young people being treated with stimulant medication. Problems with antisocial behaviour and violence amongst the young have been increasing in most Western countries. Short-acting stimulants such as Ritalin can be crushed and snorted or injected to produce a 'high'. As a result, selling of Ritalin for recreational drug use is a widespread problem in many Western countries, as are other illicit uses of it (such as an examination revising aid, increasingly common amongst university students). Stimulants such as Ritalin and Dexedrine can be highly addictive and there are many personal accounts of addiction to prescribed stimulants.

The claim that prescribing stimulants for ADHD reduces the likelihood of drug abuse later in life has the support of a number of studies. However, doubt has been cast on that conclusion by the largest study (involving nearly 500 young people) which followed up the young people for the longest number of years (into their late twenties- unlike the other studies which usually went up to about 18 to 21 years) and which found that the higher the dosage of a stimulant that was prescribed during childhood and adolescence the higher the likelihood of developing an addiction to tobacco, amphetamine and cocaine in later life (see above page 24). This should serve as a warning that, in addition to the side effects the individual suffers as a result of stimulants, there maybe some very real public health dangers.

Myth 5: Any treatment for ADHD type behaviours that does not include medication is unlikely to be successful.

Facts and discussion: Successful treatment with medication of ADHD type behaviours beyond four weeks of using the drug has not yet been established (see above, page 16). Thus, the evidence to confirm the effectiveness of stimulants in treating ADHD type behaviours has yet to be established, and as mentioned above, currently the evidence is strongly suggesting that medication does not produce any long-lasting improvements. Furthermore, concerns about stimulants safety and public health effects means that demonstrating that the advantages outweigh the disadvantages of using stimulant medication has not yet been established. The responsibility from both a scientific and ethical point of view, to provide such evidence to justify the risks associated with prescribing stimulants for many years rests squarely on the shoulders of those who promote such practice. Without such evidence supporters of prescribing stimulants and the prescribers themselves risk breaking the most basic responsibility that medical practitioners are taught in their ethical code, which is that first and foremost that our practice must "not cause any harm".

There is a large scientific literature supporting the usefulness (more of that later in the book) of non-medication based treatments for ADHD type behaviours in children and young people, including changes in lifestyle, diet, parenting, behaviour management, family therapy and individual therapy. However, as with the effectiveness of Ritalin none of these interventions can claim to have proven beyond doubt their long-term effectiveness. However, all the non-psychiatric medication approaches have demonstrated a much more favourable safety profile than treatment with stimulants, thus from a scientific and ethical point of view, it surely stands to reason that at the very least non-medication alternatives should be made available to those who use our services and should be tried and thoroughly exhausted before considering medication as an option.

CHAPTER 2

Making sense of the scientific evidence

In the last chapter I explained the current state of the scientific evidence with regards to understanding ADHD. Thus, at present the scientific evidence does not allow us to conclude that ADHD is the result of an abnormality in the development of the brain that is genetically inherited and that can be successfully treated with stimulants like Ritalin. This does not mean that such a view will never prove to be justified. It does mean that with the current state of evidence, such a view remains a theory not a fact. Indeed, I wish to go further and state that the evidence available makes a strong case that there is no such thing as a condition called ADHD that is the result of an abnormality in the development of the brain. It is up to those who believe that there exists a condition caused by a biological abnormality of the brain to prove it, not up to those (like myself) who don't believe it to prove that it doesn't exist.

This is a very basic idea from science (it's sometimes called the 'Null hypothesis', meaning that you assume your theory is untrue until you have proven it to be true). ADHD is the most thoroughly biologically researched child psychiatric condition, and yet that has produced no good evidence to support the idea. The true scientist has to maintain scepticism, and that means keeping an open mind to the possibility that in time we may discover a definite physical abnormality in the brains of at least some of those currently diagnosed with ADHD, *and* to the possibility that, as a biological condition, it simply doesn't exist.

Even if the science did eventually produce some firm evidence to back the view that ADHD is best understood as a medical disorder effecting the brain, we currently have no way of knowing how many of those children who are being diagnosed as having ADHD will prove to have that particular abnormality in the development of their brains. Furthermore, we will not be able to answer this question until we have some reliable way of testing for a known physical abnormality.

Let me give you an example. Let's suppose that we eventually manage to produce a reliable method of testing for a deficiency in one of the chemical transmitters in the brain called dopamine (although first of all we would have to establish what 'normal' levels of dopamine are, which is likely to be fraught with difficulties). One of the most popular, biological theories about ADHD at present is that ADHD is caused by abnormally low levels of dopamine in the brain (and it is believed that stimulants such as Ritalin work by elevating these abnormally low levels of dopamine up to normal levels). What we do not know is how many of the children currently diagnosed as having ADHD would be discovered to have a low level of dopamine and therefore an apparently clear biological basis to their symptoms. However, what we also don't know is how many children who have other mental health problems or psychiatric diagnoses (for example, Autism, Tourettes syndrome and so on) would also test positive for dopamine deficiency. Finally, we don't know how many children regarded as normal and healthy would also test positive for dopamine deficiency. Therefore, once we have a reliable way of testing for dopamine deficiency (as in this example) we would now have a solid scientific basis on which to start building an objective factual knowledge base. Until that happens (and there is certainly no sign of that happening in the near future) *any* conclusion that a child has a chemical imbalance of dopamine in their brain, is false and unscientific.

If we ever do get to the point of understanding and being able to measure what a chemical balance in the brain looks like, then our current diagnostic system in psychiatry is likely to disappear and be replaced with a more robust system based around the abnormality that has been discovered. In the above example, the problem may be labelled something like 'dopamine deficiency syndrome'. It may be discovered that many young people with this dopamine deficiency syndrome simply outgrow this given enough time. It may be discovered that there is a large crossover between children who develop symptoms as a result of this dopamine deficiency syndrome and those who have dopamine deficiency syndrome but do not develop mental ill health symptoms. Thus, rational and logical research could then take place to try and identify what factors differentiate those children who develop symptoms as a result of dopamine deficiency and those who don't. Such research will form the foundations for developing safe interventions to help those who develop symptoms. Some of the interventions may be environmental, if it is discovered that one of the main reasons behind some children developing symptoms as opposed to others who don't, are to do with factors in a child's environment that cause this dopamine deficiency to result in the symptoms. For others natural approaches to boosting dopamine, such as dietary interventions and exercise may be seen to be the way forward and for others still who may have more severe deficiencies, psychoactive medication may end up being used.

Even if we do get to the point of having a clear scientific and objective basis for understanding the biological component of young people's mental health problems debates and controversies would still continue and be relevant. For example, many people now believe that Western medicine's strengths tend to be in early intervention of urgent problems (for example, dealing with trauma, severe infection, survival rates form heart attacks, etc) but it is not so good at dealing with managing long-term illnesses (such as asthma, celiac disease, chronic fatigue syndrome, unexplained symptoms and so on).

A large and increasing number of the population are turning to complimentary medicine practitioners for help with these long-term health problems. Many systems of medicine used in complimentary medicine derive from more ancient systems of medicine (particularly of Eastern origin such as 'Ayurvedic' medicine from India and South Asia and traditional Chinese medicine). These more ancient systems of medicine tend to use a more holistic approach and focus on reinvigorating the overall health of a person and developing a balance between different parts of the body that are felt to have got out of balance with each other or between the person and their environment (as opposed to Western medicine which focuses on getting rid of a disease in a particular organ of the body). Thus, even though a more rational, scientific understanding of the biological component of the problems that children currently diagnosed with ADHD have, should also lead to more rational, scientific interventions to treat this, it will not eliminate the need to consider alternative models of intervention.

The Role Of Meaning:

I hope what I have said so far makes some sort of sense in an area which can feel very confusing and bewildering, not to mention frustrating for any parent trying to make sense of their child's problems and how to help them. What I have so far tried to explain is that in reality the many claims made about ADHD simply do not stand up to proper scientific scrutiny and that much of what is presented as fact is actually a number of professionals' pet theories and opinions. I realise that such a reality takes us into a place where it might feel that the solid ground, which we thought was under our feet, is shifting. It is easier for all of us to cope with the moral certainties in an argument presented as being as factual as night and day, as black and white, and less easy for us to cope with the ambiguity of the shades of grey that I am arguing as the real state of science as regards ADHD. However, if parents are to make informed choices I believe they need to be aware of this and fully informed about, not only the controversies that exist, but also the alternatives available should they decide (as I am advocating) against using psychiatric drugs for their children.

Now that we have considered fact and opinion it is time to explore in a little more depth the current state of the evidence. What this means is that we have to now consider what sense we make of the evidence. It is the different meanings we give to the facts that we have, which has caused many of the controversies and confusion that exist with regard to ADHD and its treatment. Thus, it is now time to depart from the language of pure science and objective facts into the territory of the humanities (which includes areas such as philosophy, cultural studies, anthropology, sociology and many aspects of psychology). A humanities perspective will help us to try and understand some of the human, social, cultural and political processes that are involved when we come to make sense out of the world around us and when we come to decide on the relevance of the facts that are given to us and the situations we find ourselves in. This means looking at complexity from a 'subjective' rather than a purely 'objective' point of view.

Let me give you a simple example from everyday life. I recently picked up a lovely ripe Pomegranate in the supermarket. My 8-year-old daughter was later persuaded to try a bit when I was eating it. Now there are many objective things I could say about this pomegranate. For example, I could weigh it, measure its volume, the thickness of its skin, the chemical constituents held within it, the types of sugars, vitamins and minerals and relative amounts of each and so on. I could carry out a scientific study of the life cycle of a pomegranate from seed to tree to flowering to pollination to the growth of the fruit and so on. All of this is of course useful information, enlarging my understanding of the natural world as well as informing me about how healthy (or otherwise) it is for me and my children to eat this fruit.

How far, however, can this objective, scientific approach capture the different experience that my daughter and I had when we then ate this pomegranate? For my daughter the pomegranate was not a fruit she was familiar with and so she approached it tentatively, perhaps with her already imagining that she was not going to like it. My daughter tried a couple of pieces from the pomegranate and indeed decided she did not like the texture or the taste. For me the pomegranate had an altogether different significance that weaves into the different personal history that I carry. Pomegranate was a favourite fruit of mine when I was growing up in Iraq. When pomegranate was in season I would eat copious amounts. Sometimes just the very act of peeling away the thin, rubbery lining that divides the seeds in the fruit into compartments brings back memories of my childhood, long summer days during the school holidays spent with one of my cousins who also loved the pomegranate. We both used to like picking out the seeds, putting them in a bowl and sprinkling a bit of sugar on them. Just remembering this brings a smile to my face.

So if we simply stick with studying the objective we will miss a huge and important part of, arguably, the very thing that makes us human, our subjective life. It is that unique context of our personal history and how this interacts with our wider, social and cultural contexts, that is very the thing that structures our sense of meaning, values and what it is we consider important to us throughout our lives. Just as the pomegranate has a particular meaning for me, which often makes me seek a pomegranate out when I see one in a shop, so it is likely that for my daughter pomegranates will have a very different meaning in her life- one which will probably make her behave rather differently to me when she sees a pomegranate amongst the fruits at the grocers. This is not to say that objective knowledge about pomegranate becomes redundant or loses its usefulness or relevance when it comes to deciding whether to eat a pomegranate or not. However, it is to say that it is only by incorporating sensitivity to understanding the subjective that we have a hope in hell of beginning to make sense of human behaviour, emotions and experience.

One of the problems with the type of thinking that has taken place within academic circles that have been and continue to promote the idea that some children suffer from a biological condition called ADHD which causes behaviours such as poor concentration, hyperactivity and impulsivity, is that it comes from a particular, philosophical approach to the study of science that does exactly what I have described above- that is it attempts to find only 'objective' knowledge and marginalises the importance of understanding the subjective. This has a long tradition in Western culture over the past few decades.

Positivism:

In Western culture since the age of 'enlightenment' and the industrial revolution, a particular philosophical outlook known as 'positivism' has shaped our understanding of the world. Positivism was first developed by the French philosopher August Comte (1798-1857), who emphasized the importance of reason and logic, suggesting that we can uncover 'scientific laws' which order the world. This 'positivist' approach to knowledge brought great progress for many technologies, but 'blanket' application of this approach (which suggests that natural laws are out there waiting to be discovered) to the study of human life and its problems has not been so fruitful. More recent philosophy has questioned whether and how much 'positivism' can tell us about the inner and inter-personal life. What these philosophers (such as Michel Foucault, Martin Heidegger and Medard Boss) note is that the frameworks we choose to interpret the meaning of any finding can radically change our conclusions. The frameworks that we choose are in turn influenced by many complex interacting things such as our personal histories, cultural background, gender, political climate, professional outlook and so on.

As we begin to appreciate the limits of what the positivist approach can tell us, so more recently a mixture of professional groups such as sociologists, philosophers (particularly post-modernist philosophers) and indeed psychiatrists have been writing about the relative failure that purely objective methods of knowledge gathering has had with regards to uncovering the objective, particularly biological, basis for human behaviour, emotions and experience[21]. Indeed, many have gone much further than this pointing out that the practice of professional groups, including that of scientists, is heavily dependent on more subjective things, like meaning and values. A good example here is the debate about global warming where there is a continuing complex interplay between the belief that the future warming of the planet will cause irreparable damage to the planet and subsequently us, the human race, and the implication that we will have to get used to curtailing our lifestyles and consuming less. Politically there is a conflict between economically developed countries urging the economically developing ones (such as China and India) to opt for more (expensive) sustainable developments as against these countries wishes to catch up and compete with the economically developed world.

We can see here that there is a whirlpool of different meanings and values that come into play which will continue to have an influence on the shape of the science behind understanding the influence of carbon emissions on our global environment. The politics will shape which scientists are going to get funded, whose voice will be listened to, what types of research will be viewed as legitimate and so on. Thus, the idea of a value neutral science with the scientist's task being that of gathering knowledge to uncover the natural laws that shape the world, as much as that may appear desirable, is simply naïve. Science is a human endeavour like any other and therefore it takes place within a certain political context and is supported (or not) by certain interests.

So, I hope you are beginning to see how our broader context (such as political, cultural and economic) interacts with our personal history to create our subjective beliefs and values which in turn shape how we behave and perceive the world and these themselves interact with the practice of science, both in terms of what we choose to investigate and in terms of how we then interpret the results of what we have investigated. This continuous interaction we sometimes refer to as a 'dynamic'. When we talk about the dynamics of a situation we are referring to interacting processes that form certain patterns. So, for example, to return to my global warming example, the current dynamic is shaped by America being the biggest contributor to carbon emissions in the world. In signing up to a requirement to reduce their carbon emissions they fear they will seriously affect their economy. This in turn interacts with the dynamics of their political system, built as it is on the ideal of modern democracy, and their economy, built as it is on a value of aggressive consumerism on which their economic growth relies and so on.

I have given you an example of how far even areas of more clear-cut physical science, is influenced (and influences) by some of the broader contexts of meaning, values, politics and economy. The problem of teasing out the pure science from these broader factors becomes even harder if we are going to use purely objective methods in our attempt to understand subjective life. After all, although we don't know for sure as of yet whether and to what degree global warming is happening and what the environmental consequences of this will be, as this is a feature of the physical world an objective approach, studying and accumulating factual data should answer many of these questions. However, when the very essence of the thing that you are trying to study (the human experience) is subjective I hope you can appreciate why I believe that an understanding of the broader context that shapes and exists in a dynamic with our subjective life is also of fundamental importance.

Culture And Social Construction:

This is where the concept of culture is useful even though different people mean different things when they use the word "culture". Here is one definition of culture that I have found useful, "The peculiar and distinctive way of life of a group, the meanings, values and ideas embodied in institutions, in social relations, in systems of belief, in customs, in the uses of objects and material life… the 'maps of meaning' that make things intelligible to its members"[22]. In other words, a set of beliefs and a 'way of doing things' that a group of people have in common.

This means that we can examine and talk about 'culture' at many different levels as we can draw an imaginary boundary around groups of people that have something in common in many different ways from small groups right up sets of nations and whole regions. So for example we can talk about the culture of a particular family, a particular profession, a particular city, a particular country, a particular religion, a particular continent even. Each of these groupings will contain 'something' in common to mark them out from other similar groupings (like a different family, a different profession, a different religion and so on). This of course also means we have to be very careful when we talk about 'the culture' of a particular group, as each group is made of individuals who are going to posses significant differences between them and will simultaneously belong to several different possible cultural groupings (for example if we were to take a city as our starting cultural grouping, people within this city will also belong to different families, professional groups, religions, speak different languages and so on). This means we always must be careful not to 'tar everyone with the same brush'; not to stereotype.

The process by which different cultures develop a set of beliefs and values that guide the way they subsequently behave in the world and in relation to each other is often summarised by the term 'social construction'. In other words, groups of people who share a common cultural set of values and beliefs are said to socially construct their understanding of the world around them.

Let me give you a simple example in relation to a child who is perceived to be displaying persistent poor behaviour. As a generalisation (remembering my warning about stereotyping) we can see that different cultures will interpret the reasons for this differently and go about the task of trying to modify this differently. In the West today, it may lead to a concern that the child has a medical condition and so a visit to the doctor may be organised that may eventually result in a diagnosis of ADHD or something similar and possibly the prescription of medication. In many other parts of the world and amongst some religious groups, because they have a different set of beliefs about children and about how the world works, a concern might be that the child is possessed by some supernatural entity. This belief will lead to a different strategy, for example a traditional healer or religious leader may be consulted and certain rituals may then be prescribed. I am not making any value judgement about which of the above two is 'better', just illustrating that if we 'socially construct' our world differently then how we understand a problem and what we do about it will also be different.

Of course social construction is nothing more than a useful idea and real life is much more complicated than can be summarised with ideas or phrases like 'social construction'. A person's view of the world is going to be influenced by many things, not just the beliefs and values that they have absorbed from whatever cultural groups they have been a part of. Thus, individuals' perception of the world is likely to be shaped by a complex and continuing interaction between their biology (for example, inherited personality traits), their own personal history (for example, trauma and abuse during childhood is thought to have many long term consequences on the way a person then perceives and behaves in relationships during the rest of their lives) as well as the different cultural groups whose values and beliefs a person has absorbed.

Using these ideas of culture and social construction, I will summarise two contrasting versions of the ADHD story in the next two chapters. Firstly, in Chapter 3 I will explore the social construction of the current dominant story about ADHD (that it is a biological, brain based disorder requiring treatment with psychiatric drugs). Secondly, in Chapter 4 I will provide alternative ways of interpreting the current evidence. Naturally, as I write I cannot avoid my own personal perception and my own meaning that I make of the world around me and of the story of ADHD.

I think it is important for any of these arguments (mine or others) not to be viewed as some sort of final, definitive 'truth' about ADHD and the story of ADHD. This to me, however, is the whole point of writing chapters like these. It is to illustrate that there are different ways of making sense of the modern phenomena of ADHD and perhaps the only 'truth' that can be claimed about this is that the ADHD story, in our current state of knowledge, is socially constructed and therefore open to challenge and open to debate and dialogue that, hopefully, will bring new ideas and new ways forward, not only for individual children but also for us as a culture in the West.

Meaning And Values:

Before going on to discuss the different stories that exist about ADHD, I would like to pause briefly and consider further the importance of how we interpret the meaning and significance of whatever version of the ADHD story we choose. This is because different meanings lead you to act in different ways (as in the example of the poorly behaved child above, page 42). If I, as a doctor, decide that the young person I am seeing is experiencing problems because she/he is suffering from a disorder of his brain called 'ADHD' then it may well result in me deciding to prescribe medication for this young person. If on the other hand I interpret their problems as being due to nutritional imbalances then I might prescribe supplements instead. However, I may choose to interpret the child's behaviour as being within the normal spectrum that I expect for children of their age, in which case this might lead me to work with the child's parents and/or school to try and influence their perception of that child. As all three are perfectly plausible alternatives from the current literature, which route I choose to go down says a lot about me as a practitioner and the value system I have that guides my choices and influences my interpretation of the evidence. I believe that this is true for all clinicians who work in this area (and many other areas where there are controversies and disputed ideas), with those who claim that they know the 'truth' about ADHD (from whichever side of the argument they come) simply being unaware of how much their personal values and external influences (such as drug company propaganda) has influenced their choices.

To help understand the potential consequences of the value judgements we make, let me cite one area of dispute. In this particular dispute (most noted in an on-going dispute with a series of articles criticising each other, between two heavy weights in the field- Russell Barkley and Thom Hartmann) both sides accept the idea that ADHD-type behaviours are primarily the result of biological processes. However one side (the Russell Barkley camp) sees this biological process as something that causes an undesirable deficit and disability and thus believes that these behaviours should be viewed as a medical disease, called ADHD, and which thus needs medical treatment. The other side (the Thom Hartmann camp) views ADHD-type behaviours as being down to a 'difference' in biological make up that can also bring several advantages and desirable qualities to the individual and thus it should not be classified as a medical disease.

So what are the potential implications of these two views? Lets look at the arguments from the Thom Hartmann camp (to which my views are more closely aligned, hence my analysis is necessarily going to be bias in favour of this view). What this camp point out is that studies on children believed to have ADHD are more interested in areas where these children perform poorly compared to non-ADHD children and that they rarely look at those areas of ability where 'ADHD' children may actually outperform non-ADHD children such as for example, in their ability to outscore their peers in one of the new, high-stimulation video games or on a skateboard. In other words the idea that ADHD is a medical disease shapes how the research is then conducted in such a way that it is already primed to discover that ADHD children are 'losers'[23].

This then takes us to a related question of whether there is any evidence to suggest that viewing ADHD-type behaviours as being the product of a biological difference that is sometimes advantageous to that individual, is available. One answer comes in the peculiar form of claims that are made that many famous and successful people had (or have) ADHD. I say peculiar as this can be interpreted as evidence that they were (or are) living proof that their biology was not (or is not) causing a disabling disease state in their brain, as it is their mental talents that have caused them to excel[24]. Indeed, multi-millionaire entrepreneur Wilson Harrell (former publisher of Inc. Magazine and founder of the Formula 409 Company) claims in his book *For Entrepreneurs Only*, that ADHD is 'essential' for the success of an entrepreneur and devotes two chapters to his own 'ADHD'[25].

There are also several studies that support the idea that in certain contexts ADHD-type behaviours are useful. For example a study at Washington University in which 'ADHD' persons were tested against non-ADHD controls for their ability to handle emergencies, concluded that those with 'ADHD' did considerably better. Taking this line of thinking further some authors have noted a striking similarity between descriptions of ADHD and descriptions of 'creative' children. For example University of Georgia's Bonnie Cramond asks the question *"There are so many similarities in the behavioural descriptions of creativity and ADHD that one is left to wonder, could these be overlapping phenomena?"* After a thorough search of the literature in both fields she concludes that the answer to that question is yes[26]. Her idea seems to be that both 'creative' and/or 'ADHD' children are individuals who have trouble with verbal learning but have a very imaginative, visual manner of thinking. Whilst this can cause great problems in the school environment where verbal learning is highly valued but visual/imaginative (as well as physical) learning isn't; it can prove to be an advantage once the 'ADHD child' leaves school and embarks on their career, in a way that pushes many of these 'ADHD sufferers' to end up at the forefront of innovation in our society.

One implication of this line of thinking is that if we were to provide education that acknowledges the differences in the way people learn, we might soon be tapping a source of creativity that could be useful to our entire society. At the individual level it could help us think more positively about the attributes and strengths of young people with problems that can be called ADHD, rather than start on the path of focussing on their inadequacies. It would also require that we open ourselves up to the possibility that the kinds of skills we reward (particularly in schools) today may not be the only worthwhile skills. At the collective level this can lead us to ask some taxing political questions about whether the way we organize our society and education system is part of the problem that must first change (rather than what could be seen as re-victimising the victim- in other words some children, particularly boys are being failed by the education system, but instead of reforming our education we victimise boys further by labelling them as 'ill' and the cause of the problems at school).

When such questions are on the agenda, the rapid rise in our labelling of children as having a disability called 'ADHD' begins to look more like a symptom of a 'dysfunctional' society, than a growing realisation about a previously unrecognised disease.

For those who believe that ADHD is a medical disease that is genetically inherited (the Barkley camp), the implication is that such individuals are genetically dysfunctional and less evolved than the rest of us, and thus they are placed in a position of dependence upon experts. In a caring society, the experts who then do the 'diagnosing' and 'treating' of ADHD become the group endowed with the positive attributes of health, knowledge, intelligence and kindness, for it is these professionals whom we then need to rely on to come and 'save' ADHD children from themselves, and who can also bring peace and happiness to families and schools. As for the person diagnosed with ADHD, they are then effectively seen as largely unable (due to their disability) to make a positive contribution to culture and society- particularly if they are not 'treated' so that they can get 'rid' of their ADHD.

But what if society wasn't caring? What are the implications then? Would there be a call for adults diagnosed with ADHD not have children, for fear that this 'defect' will continue to spread? Even if society claims to be caring, does this extend to all sections of the population? Does the reality of living in a culture based around economic need for profit which places money before people, mean that despite our claims of being caring, we are (as a culture) intolerant of children who will be a financial burden? Does this mean that the social control of children has become more important to our culture than nurturing and caring for them? Of course this needs to be balanced up against the claim that we live in a caring society and claims made by many that the diagnosis and subsequent medication made a positive influence on their lives. However, for the sake of exploring this question of values further, a bit of history may be helpful, so that you can understand what concerns me about the focus on deficit and disability within the individual.

The Spectre Of Eugenics:

Towards the end of the nineteenth century and the beginning of the twentieth century a new sinister movement appeared in Western psychiatry. A belief was emerging, claimed to be based on science, that the 'mentally ill' were carriers of bad genes, and that they posed a serious threat to the future health of Western societies. Many scientific articles, newspaper editorials and popular books were written about this at that time. In these articles and books, the mentally ill were described as a degenerate strain of humanity that bred at alarming rates and burdened the 'normal' population with the great expense of paying for their upkeep. In North America this led to a wholesale societal assault on those deemed mentally ill. They were prohibited from marrying in many states, forcibly committed to state hospitals in great numbers, and many were sterilised against their will[27].

This movement first started with studies conducted by Sir Francis Galton, (cousin of Charles Darwin). In 1869, Galton published a scientific work, *Hereditary Genius*, in which he concluded that it was nature, rather than nurture (genes rather than up-bringing) that made the 'superior' man. Galton studied the family trees of nearly one thousand prominent English leaders and found that this top class came from a small, select group of people. Although this was probably stating the obvious- that in a class conscious England privilege led to success- to Galton his research provided proof that intelligence was inherited and that a small group of successful English families enjoyed the benefits of being born with 'superior' genes. In 1883, Galton invented the term 'eugenics' derived from the Greek word 'well-born' as a name for the science that he believed would improve human beings by giving the more intelligent and superior races a better chance of reproducing.

Galton was trying to apply in a crude and simplistic way the concept, discovered by his cousin Charles Darwin, of natural selection to the complexities of human society. It was to be a science devoted to dividing the human race into two classes, the eugenic (or well-born) and the cacogenic (or poorly-born). The cacogenic group would be seen as having inherited bad or inferior genes and therefore, as a group, they should, at the very least, not be allowed to breed. In this new eugenic view of humankind the mentally ill were seen as among the most unfit, with insanity seen as the final stage of a progressive deterioration of a family's gene pool.

The eugenic ideology found a receptive audience in the United States where many prominent authors and scientists began arguing that the mentally unfit should not be allowed to breed. At the turn of the last century private funding to Harvard educated biologist, Charles Davenport, began the trend into the 'scientific' study of the genetics of human inheritance with the underlying agenda of proving that eugenics was based on good science. Davenport applied a genetic model to studying complex behaviours in humans, proposing that a single gene controlled each behavioural trait. After a few years Davenport was suggesting that immigrants, the mentally ill and all sorts of societal misfits were genetically inferior and confidently writing that people could inherit genes for 'shiftlessness', thieving, prostitution and insincerity.

The selling of the eugenic ideals to the public began in earnest in 1921 in North America, when the American museum of natural history hosted the second international congress on eugenics, a meeting financed in a large part by the Carnegie institution and the Rockefeller foundation. At this conference papers on the financial cost incurred to society by caring for 'defectives', the inheritability of insanity and other disorders, and the low birth rates of the 'elite' in America were presented. Talks were given on topics such as the Jewish problem, the dangers of Negro and white intermixture and the families of 'paupers' (the poor). At the close of the conference a national eugenics society was established, sending out a message that warned that society was seeing a 'racial deterioration' and that societal leaders needed to resist what they saw as the forthcoming complete destruction of the white race, if their message was ignored. The congress was covered in the leading national newspapers that reported on the eugenic ideals in a sympathetic manner.

At the close of this international conference Davenport together with other prominent eugenicists formed a committee, which led to the establishment of a national eugenics society. The American Eugenics Society (AES) focused on promoting eugenics to the American public through textbooks, pamphlets and information campaigns, aimed at building support for sterilisation laws. By the 1930's eugenic ideas had become popular among the public. Franz Kallman, Chief of research at the New York State Psychiatric Institute, claimed that even lovers of individual liberty had to agree that mankind would be much happier if societies could get rid of their 'mentally ill' individuals who were, in his belief, not biologically satisfactory. Earnest Hooton, Harvard professor of anthropology, in his 1937 book *Apes, men and morons*, compared the insane to cancers in society whose genes should be considered poisonous, suggesting that the situation in America was so critical that it demanded an urgent 'surgical' operation.

From the late nineteenth century, American eugenicists had been arguing that the mentally ill should be prevented from having children. This propaganda began to influence state legislators in the United States from 1896 when Connecticut became the first state to prohibit the 'insane' from the right to marry. By 1914, more than twenty states had passed such laws and by 1933 all states in US had passed laws effectively prohibiting marriage for those deemed to be mentally ill. Yet few eugenicists believed such laws did much good, most considering this to be an inadequate response to the problem. Eugenicists were instead arguing that the insane should firstly be segregated in asylums and then sterilised to prevent their 'bad' genes from reproducing.

In 1907, Indiana became the first state in the United States to pass a compulsory sterilisation law. It did so in the name of science, the bill stating that hereditary research had been shown to play a dominant role in the transmission of crime, 'idiocy' and 'imbecility'. Over the next two decades thirty state legislatures approved sterilisation bills and repeatedly they did so based on an argument that science had proven that 'defectives' bred 'defectives'. Opponents, who included Catholics and non-English immigrant groups, argued that these laws violated constitutional safeguards against cruel and unusual punishments, leading some states to be challenged on their sterilisation laws. However, in 1927 the United States Supreme Court, by an eight to one majority, in the case of Buck V. Bell, ruled that sterilization laws were constitutional adding that scientific experience had shown that heredity played an important part in the transmission of 'insanity' and 'imbecility'. Soon institutions such as the California department of mental hygiene began listing sterilisation as a medical 'treatment' that could be provided to 'mentally ill' patients in its state hospitals.

Before the existence of Hitler's death camps became common knowledge in the United States, eugenics had become a popular topic among psychiatrists and psychologists there. As in Germany, the debate had by then expanded from the wisdom of breeding better humans to include the topic of preventing and even doing away altogether, with those who considered genetically inferior.

Two years after the United States Supreme Court, deemed it constitutional, Denmark passed a sterilisation law. Over the next few years Norway, Sweden, Finland and Iceland did too. America's influence on Nazi Germany was particularly pronounced and it was, of course, in that country that eugenics ran its full course. In the 1920s America was the world centre of eugenic activity: between 1907 and 1940 more than 100,000 Americans were involuntarily sterilized in more than thirty states. State bureaucracies determined who would be sterilized and who could breed; the banner of building national racial superiority was picked up in England, Finland, Sweden, and a dozen other countries by 1930.

Much as United States eugenicists had done, German eugenicists sought to develop scientific evidence that 'mental illnesses' were inherited and that these 'genetic diseases' were spreading through its population and causing deterioration in the population's gene pool. In 1925, the American 'Rockefeller foundation' gave two and a half million dollars to the psychiatric institute in Munich, which quickly became Germany's leading centre for eugenic research. The 'Rockefeller foundation' also gave money to the institute for anthropology, human genetics and eugenics in Berlin, which used this money to pay for a national survey of 'degenerative traits' in the German population.

After Hitler came to power in 1933, Germany passed a comprehensive sterilisation bill. The German eugenicists who drew up that legislation had learned from the United States experience, which many American eugenicists noted with some pride. Many in Germany and in the United States saw the Nazi bill as morally superior to any United States state law, praising Germany's sterilisation programme as an example of a desirable modern health programme. Praise for German eugenics found particular favour amongst American psychiatrists. For example, the American Neurological Association published an official report on eugenic sterilisation, praising Hitler's sterilisation programme. A year before war broke out with Germany, American psychiatrist Aaron Rosanhoff, in his textbook *Manual of psychiatry and mental hygiene* favourably compared the German to the American sterilisation programme, concluding that eugenics is a scientific rather than political exercise.

With eugenic ideology talking about the 'mentally ill' as social wastage, malignant cancerous growths and so on, it was only a short step to move from sterilisation to getting rid of such people all together. In 1935, Alexis Carrel, a Nobel Prize winning physician at the Rockefeller institute for medical research in New York, made this point in his book *Man, the unknown*. In this book Carrel wondered why societies preserve useless and potentially harmful human beings by suggesting that society should dispose of criminals and the insane in a humane and economical manner in small euthanasia institutions supplied with 'proper gasses'.

Learning from these American ideas, Nazi Germany began killing their mentally ill with these 'proper gasses, in January 1940. Over the course of the next 18 months the Nazi's gassed more than 70,000 mental patients. Euthanasia forms were filled in on thousands of patients by hospital doctors throughout Germany and these forms were then sent to Berlin for the final life and death determination by a team of fifty psychiatrists, including ten professors of psychiatry. Unlike the subsequent mass enslavement and murder of the Jews, the killing of mental patients drew heated criticism from the public and some religious leaders and in August 1941, Hitler withdrew his approval. However, acting without official sanction doctors continued killing on their own in local mental hospitals, a practice that spread to occupied countries, for example in France where without an official order, psychiatrists killed an estimated 40,000 of their patients. A path that had begun seventy five years earlier with Galton's study of the English ruling classes had wound its way through the corridors of American science finally reaching its stated goal in the hands of German psychiatry who took the lead in developing Germany's murderous euthanasia programme.

To help us understand how doctors in general, and psychiatrists in particular, have played such a leading role in developing, first the ideology and then the technology, that led initially to the extermination of thousands of psychiatric patients and then to millions of Jews we need to examine the dynamics of medicalization. Human experience examined through the prism of apparent scientific objectivity lends itself perfectly to be used by the political system of the day. With the idea that bad genes possess these 'deviants', it is a short step to proposing eugenic solutions for this perceived 'medical' problem. Medical practitioners can then excuse their actions by believing that they are participating in a 'treatment' that is for the good of the future medical wellbeing of society (a kind of public health/prevention programme). Thus psychiatrists involved in exterminating inpatients did not merely supervise, but it was often the duty of a psychiatrist to open the valve of the cylinder containing the carbon monoxide as if they were supervising a treatment. If doctors can legitimize and even carry out murders (under the guise of 'treatment') then others can more easily rationalize their own participation in this endeavour.

Following the euthanasia programme on psychiatric inpatients, the equipment used in these euthanasia centres was dismantled and then used to construct the holocaust extermination camps. Not only was the equipment that psychiatrists had helped develop used, but also, psychiatrists went to the camps and conducted the first official, systematic murders of Jews. These teams diagnosed and then selected victims using the euthanasia forms and then had the inmates sent to their deaths at the psychiatric extermination centres during the early stages of the holocaust. Furthermore, historians agree that the psychiatrists were in no way forced indeed they often did this task without protest and often on their own initiative.

With this grizzly episode in the history of medicine and psychiatry behind us you would have thought that the eugenic ideals would be firmly confined to the pages of history. Not so, this is because of what I have been arguing above- that the central idea that made eugenics seem desirable and then turned it into a reality is still with us – that of medicalizing the social complexities of the human experience. This is where I have concerns about the possible unintended consequences of the Russell Barkley camp's point of view. Doctors and other senior professionals have a huge influence and power to turn our social and cultural expectations for children's behaviour into medical definitions of physical health. Those who don't conform to our social and cultural expectations can then be labelled as being medically unwell or disabled. We must now ask the question- can or indeed is eugenics slipping in through the back door?

After World War II exposed the horrors of the extermination camps, proponents of eugenics became, not surprisingly, rather quiet. The only high-profile American scientist in the 1950's who was willing to publicly suggest that we should continue eugenics programs was Nobel Laureate William Shockley (1910-1989), a physicist at Stanford University. After winning his Nobel Prize in Physics (not in genetics), he openly suggested people with IQs lower than 100 should submit to voluntary sterilization. His widely-published views gave encouragement to the quiet but ongoing eugenics programs in the United States which were only stopped in the 1960s with the revelation by Robert Kennedy that over 100,000 poor Blacks, Native Americans, and mental patients had been sterilized without their knowledge or consent, as doctors in thirty states doing the sterilizations told their unwitting patients that they were performing 'a slightly painful pelvic examination' or 'routine surgery to prevent later disease.'

The field of behavioural genetics (the linking of behaviours to particular genes in a not dissimilar way to what Davenport, discussed above, was doing at the turn of the twentieth century) has been discussing with great optimism the findings of the 'Human Genome Project', suggesting that in the not too distant future we will be able to test children's genes before they are born and provide so called gene therapy to correct any genes that are considered undesirable. Do we not already offer abortions for children with known genetic abnormalities? New screening methods mean we can test for hundreds of possible genetic abnormalities or mutations that *may* result in the carrier being afflicted with known diseases. If we discover genes or perhaps a group of genes that contribute towards lets say hyperactivity, which is now defined as a medical disorder, is it beyond the realms of possibility in our current culture that we would then start offering abortions on medical grounds for children found to be carrying these genes? And what of the children already born with those genes. If we have already medicalized this problem to what extent would we go to in order to 'treat' and otherwise control these children (as children and then as adults)?

A telling example comes from the government funded violence initiative in the United States. Back in the seventies Mednick and Christiansen proposed a bio-medical screening programme, including screening approaches based on teacher ratings, to take place at elementary (primary) schools for early detection of future criminals. This proposal came out at a time when government agencies were indeed funding psychiatrists and neuro-surgeons who claimed that urban riots that had occurred were caused by genetic defects and brain disease in individual African Americans. Some of these doctors were advocating psychiatric brain surgery for selected rioters and even their leaders. One independent project in Mississippi was actually performing psycho-surgical operations on the brains of African American children deemed to be hyperactive and aggressive.

Fortunately, critics at the time compared these so-called treatment programmes to measures used in Nazi Germany and many of the programmes were abandoned under pressure, or took on other guises. For a time bio-psychiatrists were then discouraged from publicizing their efforts towards finding biological forms of control for urban violence.

Then, at the beginning of the nineteen nineties, Dr Goodwin, who was chief scientist at the National Institute of Mental Health in the United States and one of the Government's top research psychiatrists, feeling that public attitudes were more favourable again, re-publicized the idea that the violence prone individual was suffering from a physical brain ailment that could be diagnosed and treated. Indeed, in one of his speeches Goodwin went on to compare inner city youth to monkeys who live in the jungle who just want to kill each other and have sex. Goodwin not only re-proposed the idea of developing screening programmes to be administered to school children to discover potential violent offenders, but in addition proposed that many might then be treated from an early age with psychiatric medication.

Goodwin's ideas soon found favour in Government circles leading the national research council in the United States to publish the report *Understanding and Preventing Violence* in 1992, which provided a blueprint for a national violence initiative sympathetic to Goodwin's ideas and suggesting an important role for finding bio-medical causes and treating them. During the same year a review of violence research taking place at the National Institute of Health in the United States found that violence research was very much alive in the United States with over three hundred research projects, totalling forty two million dollars being funded in 1992 and with the bulk of the work taking place at the National Institute of Mental Health. Many projects were funded by Government agencies as well as private foundations and included many prominent psychiatrists, including a professor of child psychiatry at Harvard Medical School (Felton Earls). Earls' vision, like Goodwin's, was based on 'disease' prevention with the aim of screening and identifying individual children as potential offenders in need of preventative treatment or control. As with many in similar projects, Earls hoped the research he was involved in would link key biological, as well as environmental factors that play a role in the development of criminal behaviour with a particular emphasis on searching for bio-medical markers such as neurotransmitter problems and genetic abnormalities that can then be targeted for 'preventative' treatment.

In 1995 *The Bell Curve* was published. Since then it has become safer and more popular for those who believe there are evolutionarily superior and inferior humans to go public with their opinions. For example, citing race as proof of evolutionary status, Michael Levin, in his 1997 book *Why Race Matters*, says, "*Not one of the 1500 discoveries listed in Asimov's Chronology of Science and Discovery (1989) was made by a Negroid people.*"

Nobel Prize winner and driving force behind the Human Genome Project, James Watson, clearly feels that science in the shape of manipulating genes should be left to get on with it and should ignore any of the moral or ethical implications, "*My view is that despite the risks, we should give serious consideration to germ-line therapy. I only hope that the many biologists who share my opinion will stand tall in the debates to come and not be intimidated by the inevitable criticism. Some of us already know the pain of being tarred with the brush once reserved for eugenicists. But that is ultimately a small price to pay to redress genetic injustice. If such work be called eugenics, then I am a eugenicist"*[28] In his book *DNA the Secret of Life* Watson completely ignores any discussion about what makes one person somehow more valuable or important than another and is eager that we start exploring how biotechnology could eliminate 'mental illness', 'violence' and 'learning difficulties'. All the same fundamental philosophical mistakes, that inspired the original eugenicists to try and biologically engineer a society free of genetic 'misfits' and that led eventually to such unimaginable human tragedy, are made. Watson's main criticism of the eugenics movement is that they were poor scientists (not that their goals were so abhorrent) *"There is no legitimate rationale for modern genetics to avoid certain questions simply because they were of interest to the discredited eugenics movement. The critical difference is this: Davenport and his like simply had no scientific tools with which to uncover the genetic basis for any behavioural trait they studied. Their science was not equipped to reveal any material realities that would have confirmed or refuted their speculations"*[29].

As we move increasingly from the realm of difference to the realm of disorder, some physicians have now come forward to suggest that people with ADHD should be encouraged not to have children, lest their 'genetic weaknesses' or lower evolutionary status be passed on to future generations. One such voice is Dr. David Comings. The thesis of his book, *The Gene Bomb*, is that people with 'undesirable behaviour' tend to have less education and to produce children at an earlier age (interpreted as a sign of impulsivity of course) than well-educated persons, and therefore have more children. This produces a surplus of 'undesirable' people, carrying 'undesirable' genes, among our population (In his writings, ADHD is explicitly deemed 'undesirable').

The revival of the impulse to medicalise social issues, has led to a revival of interest in dangerous and brain damaging so-called treatments, with children increasingly seen as a primary target for such 'preventative' interventions. Methods such as electroconvulsive therapy and using high doses of toxic, often unlicensed psychotropic drugs normally used in adults with severe and chronic 'mental illness' are increasingly advocated for 'treating' young children with a variety of problems including aggression. The world's second largest industry – the pharmaceutical industry- realising huge profits can be made, are seizing their opportunity to contribute to the development of this worrying trend. Influenced by drug company lobbying the most recent development has been the adoption by the United Sates government of the longed for ideal of many biological psychiatrists, to develop a mental health screening programme for all school children. Teen screen- is the scheme developed by the pharmaceutical industry and pushed forward by the Bush administration to screen the entire nation's public school population for psychiatric disorders.

Although at this stage 'Teen Screen' and other screening programmes are meant to be voluntary, there are already examples of the screen being used without parent's knowledge or consent. Critics are claiming that if a teenager doesn't like doing maths assignments, 'TeenScreen' may determine that the child has a psychiatric illness called 'developmental-arithmetic disorder'. 'Oppositional-defiant disorder' could be diagnosed if the teenager argues with their parents, and, claim the critics, if anybody is critical of the above two disorders, they may be suffering from 'noncompliance-with-treatment disorder'!

Evidence is already emerging that an unusually high number of those who take the 'TeenScreen' questionnaire end up with a diagnosis and prescribed medication. The new eugenics seems well underway.

Some Concluding Thoughts:

What meanings we choose to give to behaviours has consequences. This means that we have to take into account the impact not only on the individuals but also more broadly on our cultural ideas. This in turn means we have to consider moral and ethical dimensions, in other words our values. How important is it for us to control behaviours we consider troublesome? How important is it for children to have these differences tolerated? What effect will viewing their behaviour as abnormal or disordered have on children's self esteem and on how all of us respond to them? Clearly deciding on what we choose to privilege (in other words which value system we choose) has a big impact on how we decide to deal with an issue like active and inattentive behaviours in children. For example (remembering these are not exclusive categories), if we decide to put the first (controlling the child's behaviour) as our primary focus- then we will focus on the individual child. If we decide to focus on the second (increasing tolerance for childish behaviours) - then we will focus on those around the child, and so on.

CHAPTER 3

ADHD as a medical condition

In this chapter I will explore the development of the current conventional view in Western medicine of ADHD and explain how it came to be socially constructed. Firstly I briefly describe the history of ADHD. I show how the idea that hyperactivity might be caused by some sort of brain damage can be traced back to the turn of the twentieth century. This eventually led to a diagnosis of 'minimal brain damage' coming into existence as a diagnosis that could be used for some children who were presenting as hyperactive. It was however, a rare diagnosis that did not stimulate much interest in the medical community. By the 1960's the minimal brain damage theories were losing credibility, as there was no evidence being found to suggest that minimal brain damage causes hyperactivity (what was being found was that minimal brain damage causes a wide variety of psychiatric problems rather than specifically hyperactivity). However, during the 1980's, Attention deficit disorder (ADD) and then ADHD began to take off as changes took place in how it was diagnosed, rather than as a result of any breakthrough in the scientific evidence.

After looking at the history of ADHD, I then try to outline the cultural conditions from which these ideas developed. To do this I will explore our changing understanding of childhood and child rearing in Western culture from a social constructionist (see chapter 2) perspective (in other words through understanding what cultural, social and political processes were occurring that may have caused changes in the way we view children's behaviour). I will look at the history of childhood in Western culture to help explain how we have come to view children's behaviour in the way that we do in the West. Our vision and understanding of what makes a normal childhood and normal family, changes over time as a result of changing cultural, social and political circumstances. When looking at the history of childhood we often find that times in which most change in the way we understand childhood occurs is when there is a perceived sense of crisis with regard to children and childhood. Thus we find that quite dramatic changes can take place over a short period of time after a period of relative stability. Furthermore, each successive change does not occur out of the blue but tends to build on ideas already present within the culture of the time. I hope to show through this, that the idea that children's behaviour problems are caused by medical conditions such as ADHD has occurred during one of these periods of perceived crises with regards children and at a time when Western culture was ready to accept such an explanation on such a large scale.

After this I look further into this medicalisation of children's behaviour and show how this is causing not only a change in the way we think about childhood problems, but also a narrowing of our idea of what a 'normal' childhood is, and is possibly also negatively affecting children and their parent's experience and view of themselves. Western psychology and medicine has developed an increasingly narrow idea of normal child development. Children have age-defined developmental checks from the moment they are born, leaving many parents anxiously comparing their offspring to others. This trend, I propose, is associated with a fear of diversity and difference, mother blame, ignoring of other cultures' perspectives, and the obscuring of social, political, cultural, familial, educational and psychological problems through the medicalisation (using a medical explanation) of such issues[30].

The labelling of children with 'genetic' diseases as the cause of their emotional and behavioural problems, is not only changing our ideas about disability, but, also disconnecting people from their own free will and responsibility for their behaviour (the idea that genes cause disorders like ADHD, could be seen as a modern version of 'possession' by bad spirits. Here we have something invisible that no one is able to find or measure that apparently erupts from deep in our biology and takes possession of our body so that we are unable to control our behaviour. The one- and crucial- difference is that in possession by an evil spirit, the possessing force comes from outside the body and is therefore potentially temporary, whereas possession by a bad gene is from inside the body and therefore potentially life-long).

A Brief History Of ADHD:

Over-activity, poor concentration and impulsivity in children were first thought of as a medical phenomenon early in the last century. The first recorded interest in children with poor attention and hyperactivity dates back to the turn of the century when a paediatrician, Frederick Still, described a group of children whom he believed showed poor attention, restlessness and fidgetiness, and went on to argue that these children had some sort of brain deficiency, but offered no treatment other than good discipline.

Hyperactivity and poor attention in children then came to be viewed as linked when the diagnosis of minimal brain damage (MBD) was first developed. The idea of MBD had originally come about following epidemics of encephalitis (an infection of the brain) in the first decades of the 20th century. After recovering from encephalitis (which often causes brain damage) these children presented with restlessness, personality changes and learning difficulties. Then, in the 1930s, came a chance discovery that stimulant medication could reduce the restlessness, hyperactivity and behavioural problems in some of these children. The doctor who discovered this (Charles Bradley) believed that this calming effect he observed is likely to apply to anyone who took low dose stimulants, not just the hyperactive children he was treating.

Not long after this episode, a number of doctors began to wonder if children who presented as hyperactive might have some brain damage, that the technology they had could not yet detect, that was causing their hyperactivity. Dr. Strauss's writings in the 1940s strengthened this idea further by his suggestion that hyperactivity, in the absence of a family history of 'sub-normality', should be considered as sufficient evidence for a diagnosis of brain damage, believing that the damage was too minimal to be easily found.

By the 1960s, however, the term MBD was becoming unpopular as evidence for underlying brain damage in children who showed poor attention and over-activity was not being found. However, at this time psychiatry was showing a growing interest in defining psychiatric disorders using behavioural guidelines. In other words, psychiatrists were abandoning looking for physical tests to help diagnose psychiatric disorders and instead developing a 'tick list' approach where diagnosis was made by the patient having a certain number the emotional and behavioural 'symptoms', with the symptoms being descriptions presented in a list (see chapter 1 for a list of the typical symptoms used in ADHD tick lists). For MBD this meant abandoning the idea that there was 'brain damage' and instead concentrating on what behaviours were being reported by those looking after the child (usually a parent and a teacher). Thus Attention Deficit Disorder (ADD) and then ADHD would soon be born.

Despite abandoning the 'minimal brain damage' diagnosis the assumption that ADD (and then ADHD) does indeed have a specific and discoverable physical cause, related to some sort of brain problem, survived. Yet, studies have shown that when you find minimal brain damage due to a variety of causes, this predisposes the child to the development of a wide range of psychiatric disorders as opposed to a particular type, such as ADHD. One of the most prominent child psychiatrists, Sir Michael Rutter, reviewed the evidence on brain damage in children, a couple of decades ago, and concluded that the available evidence shows that over-activity is not usually a sign of brain damage and that brain damage does not usually lead to over-activity. I am not aware of any research since then that contradicts that conclusion[31].

So it was that in the mid sixties the North American psychiatrists bible- the Diagnostic Statistical Manual (DSM)- in its second edition (DSM-II) invented the label 'Hyperkinetic reaction of childhood', to replace the diagnosis of MBD (The DSM is produced by the American Psychiatric Association and provides a list of psychiatric categories and how to diagnose them). Over the following three decades this new, now behaviourally defined, condition changed from being something child psychiatry had only a small interest in, to become the most prominent and most researched child psychiatric condition.

DSM II was replaced in the early eighties by the third edition (DSM-III). In DSM-III, 'Hyperkinetic reaction of childhood' was replaced by 'Attention Deficit Disorder' (ADD). According to DSM-III, ADD could be diagnosed with or without hyperactivity and was defined using three dimensions (three separate lists of behaviours): one for attention, one for impulsivity and one for hyperactivity. This three-dimension approach was changed in the late eighties when DSM III was revised (DSM-III-R), as was the name for this disorder. In DSM-III-R we now had a one-dimension approach (combining all the symptoms into one list of behaviours). The new term for the disorder was Attention Deficit Hyperactivity Disorder (ADHD), with attention, hyperactivity and impulsiveness now thought of as being part of one disorder with no distinction to be made between attention deficits, impulsivity and hyperactivity. When the fourth edition of DSM (DSM-IV), reconsidered the diagnosis in the mid nineties, the criteria for making the diagnosis were again changed, this time in favour of a two-dimensional model (two lists of symptoms) with attention deficit symptoms being in one list and hyperactivity-impulsivity symptoms in the other.

Studies have shown that each time the criteria in the DSM for diagnosing ADHD, was changed, more children could be diagnosed as having ADHD. For example, changing from DSM-III to DSM-III-R, more than doubled the number of children who could be diagnosed with the disorder. Changing from DSM-III-R to DSM-IV increased the possible number of children who could get a diagnosis of ADHD by further two thirds, with the criteria now being able to diagnose the majority of children with academic or behavioural problems in a school setting. Indeed DSM-IV also has a new category that can be used. This is the diagnosis 'ADHD not otherwise specified' which can now be made if there are symptoms of inattention or hyperactivity-impulsivity, but that these are not enough to meet the full ADHD criteria. If we were to interpret this literally (as sadly doctors often do) it suggests that nearly all children (particularly boys) at some time in their lives could meet one of the definitions and be diagnosed with ADHD.

A confusing factor is that there are other diagnostic manuals like DSM that can be used to make a diagnosis. ADHD only exists in DSM, which is the main diagnostic manual for North America. In the United Kingdom, child psychiatrists have in the past usually used the diagnostic guidelines of the International Classification of Diseases (ICD) in preference to DSM. The latest edition of ICD, ICD-10, and the last ICD, ICD-9, uses a narrower definition and calls it 'hyperkinetic disorder' (which as the name suggests focuses more on activity than attention). Even here we can see that ICD-10's definition makes a diagnosis more likely than ICD-9. Centres that use ICD and have changed from using ICD-9 to ICD-10 criteria, also noticed that the diagnosis is being made more frequently when using ICD-10 compared to ICD-9. However, practice in the United Kingdom has moved towards using ADHD as the diagnosis of choice in rather than the narrower diagnosis of 'hyperkinetic syndrome' thereby following American terminology (Britain, after-all, has a reputation of being America's poodle!).

Just to muddy the waters further, there is another related diagnosis that of 'DAMP' (pun intended!). DAMP refers to 'Deficits in Attention, Motor control and Perception', and is a diagnosis invented and commonly used in Scandinavian countries to cover most of the children previously referred to as having MBD and is applied to many children who could get a diagnosis of ADHD.

The modern champion of the ADHD diagnosis and one of the strongest advocates for a brain disease model and the use of drugs to 'treat' these children is Professor Russell Barkley. Barkley's (1981) book *hyperactive Children: A Handbook for Diagnosis and Treatment*, received widespread attention from both the public and professional media. From there Barkley's campaign quickly caught the interest of the pharmaceutical industry and soon an avalanche of research to find more support for the disease theory and drug treatment ensued. Despite the volumes of research and publications there is still no good evidence that supports the conclusion that ADHD is a medical disorder or that drug treatment is safe and effective (see chapter 1).

Western Childhoods:

To help us understand the background that made it possible for ADHD to be invented and become popular, I believe we need to examine the cultural and political environment within which it developed. This means examining how our cultural beliefs on what constitutes a 'normal' childhood have changed in Western culture (Western culture being the culture that invented the idea of ADHD).

Whilst the immaturity of children is a biological fact, the ways in which we understand this immaturity and make it meaningful is a fact of culture. Members of any society carry within themselves a working idea about childhood and its nature. They may not openly talk about their ideas, or write about it, or even think of it as an issue, but they act upon their assumptions in all of their dealings with, fears for, and expectations of, their children. Our ideas about what makes a normal or disordered child can, therefore, be seen as connected to current political, economic, moral or indeed health concerns.

Each historical period creates its own ideas about what normal childhood and child-rearing methods should be like, in other words each historical period creates its own novel version of the child. The developing images of childhood are not simply abandoned over time but fragments from each period are included in the next period's ideas of childhood. Looking at the history of childhood in any culture (as well as between cultures) we can see that our ides about what makes a normal or abnormal child and/or child rearing practices are neither timeless nor universal but instead rooted in the past and reshaped in the present.

Philippe Aries's 1962 book *Centuries of Childhood*, had a major impact in developing a new understanding of how ideas about childhood have changed in Western culture over recent centuries, particularly because of the boldness of its basic conclusion- that in medieval society the idea of childhood did not exist. Norbert Elias had already anticipated Aries's arguments in his 1939 book *The Civilizing Process*, in which Elias argues that the visible difference between children and adults (psychologically and socially) increases in the course of the (as Elias saw it) 'civilizing' process. However, Aries went further and illustrated the great variability of human society's attitudes to children and child rearing practices, not just by examining non-Western cultures, but also by referring to the familiar Western European past.

Aries argued that the modern idea of childhood as a separate life stage emerged in Europe between the fifteenth and eighteenth centuries, at the same time as modern ideas of family, home, privacy and individuality were developing. Aries believed that before the fifteenth century children past the dependent age of infancy were seen simply as miniature adults. Aries was not saying that this is necessarily a bad thing, if anything he was suggesting the reverse, that modern Western culture insists on a period of quarantine (for example through education) before allowing young people to join society. Even if we modify Aries's bold idea and acknowledge that every known society has its own beliefs and practices that in some respect mark off children from adults, the importance of his book is the understanding that there are many forms of childhood and that they tend to be socially and historically specific.

When we look at the history of childhood in the West we can see changes occurring in all aspects of childhood and child rearing. For example, in medieval Europe, child rearing was seen as being a mother's responsibility for the first seven or so years of that child's life. However, during the Renaissance period in fifteenth century Italy, the emphasis began to change and the father-child relationship was now seen as the most important in child rearing. It was the father's responsibility to choose and hire a wet nurse, to watch over their children's development and to thoughtfully interpret their child's actions so as to understand and shape their future. An influential writer at this time was Dutchman Desiderius Erasmus. Erasmus placed considerable emphasis on early education and attacked those who, in his view, allowed children to be pampered by their mothers or wet nurses out of what he saw as a false spirit of tenderness. Instead he thought fathers had to take control of their children's (in particular their son's) upbringing, in order to develop their child's character in a way that would, in his view, bring them closer to reflecting the divine.

Then in the eighteenth century, the followers of Rousseau (see below) attacked the traditions of the time that encouraged fathers to take charge of child rearing, insisting that father's ambition and harshness were more harmful to a child than the blind affection of mothers. Rousseau asserted that children have a right to be happy in childhood and even went on to suggest that childhood may be the best time of life. With this Rousseau inspired 'romantic movement' gaining a foothold in popular culture by the end of the eighteenth century, mothers regained the predominance they held in the Middle Ages and child rearing once again became a predominantly female occupation.

So, in the example above, we can see that in the space of a few hundred years, the dominant belief about who should be the most important parent changed from mothers to fathers and then back to mothers again. There are many similar examples of beliefs switching from one pole to the other. But let me return now to following a rough time-line of Western history.

After the medieval period when, according to historians like Aries, children were viewed as miniature adults, a new attitude towards children began to emerge in the late seventeenth century and early eighteenth century in Europe. The story of European childhood in the eighteenth century is framed by the writings of John Locke at its beginning and Jean-Jack Rousseau and the 'romantic movement' toward its end. During this century more and more people began to see childhood not just in terms of preparation for something else, whether adulthood or heaven, but as a life stage to be valued in its own right.

Historians believe that modern, Western ideas about children can be traced to the late seventeenth century (1693) when Locke published his influential book *Some Thoughts Concerning Education*. In this book Locke proposed that children should be viewed as individuals waiting to be moulded into shape by adults. In the mid-eighteenth century (1762), Rousseau published his highly influential book *Emile* in which he argued that children were born with innate goodness that could be corrupted by certain kinds of education. These two books were crucial in paving the way for a new focus, in European culture, on childhood, which was now being viewed as requiring separate needs and expectations than adulthood. By the mid-nineteenth century, childhood was viewed as a distinct life-sage requiring protection and fostering through school education.

Through the second half of the nineteenth century, this growing idea- that all children need to be in schools began to take root for several reasons. Firstly, many children were at that time being forced to work long hours in poor conditions for little reward. The scale and intensity of exploitation of 'factory children' appalled many critics, and campaigners began to promote a new idea of childhood, where children were not herded into factories. Secondly, there was the development of the first mass working class political movements that were also complaining about the dehumanisation of their children. This resulted in the middle and upper classes becoming concerned about the potential for social unrest from these protests and keeping public order. Lively debates occurred with middle class campaigners voicing the fear that the natural order of parents, and particularly fathers in supporting their children, was being undermined by the demand for child labour in factories at the expense of adult males. This led to a fear in the ruling classes that the neglect of children could easily lead, not only to damnation of souls, but also to a social revolution. Thirdly, the growing economic success of industrial capitalism had resulted in a growing demand for a semi-skilled, skilled and educated work force, which lessened the economic need for child labour and increased the economic need for education.

So, for the reformers the idea of effective schooling now became important, not just for the new idea about what children 'need', but also for economic and political reasons. These changes also paved the way for an important new development; that of introducing the state into the parent/child relationship. Not only had the reformers put aside the financial hardships many working class families would suffer as a result of the ending of the child labourer, but in addition, by changing our ideas of what children were thought to 'need', the parents of families who continued to send children to work were now seen as exploiting of their own children. In other words, the message this produced is that if children were useful and produced money, they were not being properly loved.

By the beginning of the twentieth century children in Western, capitalist states were now seen as individuals on whom the state could have a bigger influence than their families. Now that children were all in schools they also became readily available to a variety of professionals for all sorts of 'scientific' surveys. Professional interest in the idea of child development grew and the scientific study of the individual child was encouraged so that 'guiding principles' could be offered to parents and teachers. Thus, the medical and psychological professions helped popularize the view that childhood is marked by stages in 'normal' development. Without realising they were doing this, doctors and psychologists made assumptions about what constituted normal childhood development and normal parenting. At the same time the state was becoming more powerful and more able to interfere in family life through new laws that followed a debate about children's rights and an assumption that only the state could enforce these rights.

Before the onset of the Second World War, Western society still viewed child-rearing mainly in terms of discipline and authority of the parents (particularly the father). This pre-war belief was grounded in behaviourism and stressed the importance of parents controlling their children's instincts (children's instincts were seen as dangerous to society if not properly controlled) in order for children to grow up with the 'good' habits of behaviour that was believed to be necessary for a pro-social and productive life. During the Second World War anxiety about the effect on children of discipline and authority began to be expressed, the concern being that authoritarian discipline could lead to the sort nightmare society that Nazi Germany represented. Medical and psychological professional groups that spoke about the child as an individual and which favoured a more open and sympathetic approach to child-rearing, encouraged humane discipline of the child through guidance and understanding, and so helped popularise new ideals for child rearing, eventually resulting in the birth of the 'permissive' culture.

The 'permissiveness' model saw parent-child relationships more in terms of pleasure and play than discipline and authority. Parents now had to give up their traditional authority in order for children to develop individuality, autonomy and self-esteem. In addition, whilst the pre-war model prepared children for the workplace within a society of rations and economic depressions, the post-war model prepared them to become pleasure-seeking consumers within a prosperous new economy.

Childhood had now become a key metaphor through which adults spoke about their own social and political concerns. Thus permissiveness with regards child rearing was allowing, not only, new identities to be given to children, but also to adults. Mothers and fathers were responding to these changing ideas about childhood and child rearing and seeing this as a way for them to 'express' themselves more fully. Parental obligations were now giving way to the culture of fun and permissiveness for all.

Changing economic circumstances was also leading to enormous changes in the organization of family life. More mothers were working and thus a renegotiation of power within the family was taking place. The economic demands of successful market economies were resulting in greater numbers of families moving, less time for family life and a breakdown of extended family networks. Many families (particularly those headed by young women) were now isolated from traditional sources of childrearing information (such as direct advice and support from older generations). As a result childrearing guides and books took on a greater importance, allowing for a more dramatic change in parenting styles than would have been likely in a more rooted and stable communities. This resulted in greater 'ownership' by professionals of the knowledge base for the task of parenting. For advice on how to bring up children, people were now turning to professionals (including books written by them) as often as their own families.

The new child-centred permissive culture was also good for consumer capitalism. An industry of children's toys, books, fun educational material and so on developed. With the expansion of the consumerism and a more affluent population, permissive beliefs about children and child-rearing embraced pleasure as a positive motivation for exploration and learning.

In the 1980's and 90's, the monetarist policies of Ronald Reagan and Margaret Thatcher had a big impact on many aspects of Western culture. Children and families were often the losers in the new policies that emphasised a more aggressive version of free-market capitalism at the same time as reducing and cutting back on social supports for those at the bottom end of the financial hierarchy. The new political ideology that has since affected not only Western culture but has been exported worldwide, was in service of capital (in other words had the aim of increasing profits for the private sector) following a period of decline in Western economies. More parents were now forced to work for longer hours, and state support, particularly for children and families, was harshly cut resulting in widespread child poverty and the creation of a new under-class.

With the increase in the number of divorces and two working parents, fathers and mothers are around their children for less of the day. As kids are forced to withdraw into their own culture the free market exploits this, praying on their boredom and desire for stimulation. In such an environment poor children are constantly confronted with their shortcomings by media that tells them they are deficient without this or that accessory. In this unhappy isolation Western children respond to the markets push to 'adultify' them (in other words turn them into miniature adults), at the same time as the culture of self-gratification can turn adults toward what some consider more 'childish' pursuits. Thus children respond to these new cultural conditions by entering into the world of adult entertainments earlier and often without adult supervision. This is confirmed by studies that find that the modern Western child (or some might say the post-modern Western child) is sexually knowledgeable and has early experience of drugs and alcohol.

Some commentators argue that as a result childhood in the West is being eroded, lost or indeed has suffered a strange death. Thus our traditional ideas about childhood are disappearing as children have gained access to the world of adult information resulting in a blurring of boundaries between what is considered adulthood and what is considered childhood, leading to children coming to be viewed as in effect miniature adults once again. For example, we now have a fashion industry of children's clothing modelled on adult ones and the gradual replacement of traditional street games by organized junior sport leagues such as football leagues starting with the under-7s.

One result of these changes in families and lifestyles has been the development of some core tensions and ambivalent feelings about children. The children's rights movements, see childhood as being at risk and needing safeguarding against 'abuse' by adults (often without noticing how much the children's rights movement has already blurred the boundaries between what is considered adulthood and childhood), at the same time as seeing childhood as needing strengthening by developing children's character and ability to reason. In other words, on the one hand childhood needs to be preserved and on the other hand children have to be made older than their years. This contradiction runs through our modern beliefs about childhood innocence, we desire to keep children 'innocent' and we want to help children to move beyond it, we want to 'coddle' the child and we want to 'discipline' the child.

At the same time there has been a growing concern that children themselves have become the danger with children being viewed as deviant and violent trouble makers, despite coming from a generation who are perceived to have been given the best of everything. Thus by the end of the twentieth century our vision of childhood in the West is a polarized one, in one pole we have victimized 'innocent' children who need rescuing, in the other pole we have impulsive, aggressive, sexual children who are a threat to society. Just as children are polarized, so are parents who are now set impossible standards by many professionals including the 'child savers', with many parents finding themselves afraid they will be viewed as potentially abusive parents, by child welfare professionals. Being viewed as a 'normal' child and a 'normal' parent has arguably, become, harder than ever to achieve.

The common thread through both these visions of 'childhood at risk' and 'children as the risk' is the suggestion that modern society has seen a collapse of adult authority (both morally and physically). This collapse is reflected in the growth in parental spending on children and the endless search by parents for emotional gratification for their children. As we repeatedly hear these increasing concerns about children's development in the media and from parents, teachers, doctors, and governments, so different targets are blamed. Fingers have pointed towards the role of the family, particularly mothers, the genetic make-up of the child, and the nature of schooling environments. Negative judgements about children and their families have become harsher; such that parents and children feel ever more closely observed and 'under the microscope'.

Whilst parents are feeling the pressure to constantly scrutinize their parenting in order to measure up to these high expectations, schools have also had to respond to these double pressures. The result at the individual child level has been a mushrooming of individual child explanations, locating the cause of these perceived problems with children's behaviour within individual children. This results in the development of a new belief about the cause of the worries we have about children- that they are caused, not by our changing ideas about childhood, parenting, schooling and a narrowing of what we consider to be a 'normal' childhood, but instead they are caused by something going wrong in the child's genes that causes a 'chemical imbalance' in the child's brain.

The Medicalisation Of Childhood:

As an inevitable consequence of Western obsession with child development our professional and everyday ways of understanding and making sense of when things go wrong is framed with reference to our Western beliefs about normal child development. My child and adolescent psychiatry training consisted of a four-year course in 'developmental psychopathology', which is the 'science' that studies mental disease processes (psychopathology) with reference to normal development (developmental).

In traditional writing on development and developmental psychopathology, a particular approach to knowledge is taken, which for historical and cultural reasons is based on Western beliefs regarding the 'knowability' of the physical world; a form of science that is modelled on the physical sciences (this is the 'positivist' framework I mentioned in chapter 2). This means that our knowledge base in child development is based on experimental research which is carried out under controlled conditions and where statistical analysis of samples is expected. An underlying assumption is that the general laws of developmental change are present in the world, are the same all over the world, and can be discovered by appropriate research. When directed towards issues of development, this positivism tends to be accompanied by the belief that developmental change is best thought of as a natural, biological process.

The line of argument is also a functionalist one; that is it treats the activity of children as an adaptation to a relatively stable environment. Thus Western theories of child development and developmental psychopathology can be said to be born out of a positivist, naturalist and functionalist view of children, a way of viewing that comes from the success of the physical sciences. Both child development and developmental psychopathology set themselves the tasks of uncovering what they see as universal and natural processes by which human infants are transformed into fully adapted adults (or not).

Developmental psychology was one of the first branches of psychology to be established, precisely because childhood was seen as the best place to investigate how nurture impinged on nature. The assumptions that have guided developmental psychology and psychopathology are those of Western philosophy and thought. The development of a science of psychology took place in an atmosphere where the natural sciences had already achieved some very compelling accounts of the inorganic world. It is hardly surprising therefore to find that psychological reasoning drew heavily upon ways of thinking already found to be so fruitful in other sciences.

However, unlike the natural scientists, psychologists and psychiatrists have never had any clear idea of how the processes they study actually happen and how the moulding together of nature and nurture actually takes place (this is similar to the problem of understanding subjective life by objective measures only, that I discussed in chapter 2). What we are left with is a metaphor for a process and not the process itself. Psychologists and psychiatrists therefore can only speculate in extremely vague terms about the way their theories actually operate. With the powerful assumption that child development follows some set of undiscovered biological rules; genetics came to play an ever-bigger role in developmental theories. Borrowing ideas from the natural sciences meant that genetic material was now thought to have the power to determine not only how things are made (for example, having blue eyes or being tall) but also behaviour (so-called behavioural genetics) and a whole host of experiences and beliefs.

One of the strongest ideas in our modern 'scientific' culture is that if we want to know about something all we need to do is measure it.

Guided by this recipe, developmental psychologists and psychiatrists have employed those direct means of investigation, for example by using psychological 'tests' (such as those used to measure a child's intelligence) and diagnostic questionnaires (for example, to diagnose anxiety or depression or ADHD). The answers to these questionnaires cannot tell us anything directly about any quality of the child, only about a hypothetical property of the child, for example, the child's intelligence- in other words what the designer of the test believes intelligence to be. Yet psychological tests are often seen as a direct measure of something 'in' the child (like intelligence or 'real' medical conditions such as autism or ADHD). The use of measurement has beguiled many into assuming that they are finding out some truth about what the child being tested is like. All such tests achieve is to replace one unknown (the child) with another set of unknowns (the traits out of which the child is assumed to be constituted). As soon as we probe further to find out about what these tests and traits mean, we find that they too are subjects about which more tests and scientific debates are written. What often happens is a movement further and further away from the original matter of concern – finding out about the child.

This can be illustrated with an example. A Sixteen-year-old girl, lets call her Sara is referred to me by her GP because the GP thinks that she is clinically depressed. I listen to Sara's story and ask her many questions to find out what symptoms she presents with. I administer a depression-screening questionnaire and find that Sara scores above the threshold for a diagnosis, thus confirming my and the GP's impression that Sara is suffering from clinical depression. By diagnosing clinical depression, had I discovered the cause or meaning of Sara's current problems? Did I have any physical, objective evidence to back my diagnosis? The answer to both questions is no. Therefore, far from discovering the cause or meaning of Sara's problems I had *created* a new meaning for them- a story to explain the story she had given me. When I administered the depression questionnaire I created another story about my story about her story- that this questionnaire objectively measures something called depression. This questionnaire claimed to have validity and reliability from being 'tested' on samples of depressed subjects- another story saying that this questionnaire has been adequately tested to prove that it measures what it is supposed to measure. I could go on to talk about the literature on reliability and validity, the different sorts of reliability and validity there are, how useful each is and what they each mean- a story about a story about a story about my story about her story. With each layer of story I move one step further away from Sara's original story and from attempting to understanding and give meaning to her story in a more human way.

In the same way that the inability of psychiatry to prove the material reality of the diagnoses it uses, has left it open to justifiable and continued criticism of not only its concepts but the way it uses them; so developmental psychology and psychiatry too is having to face up to some powerful criticism. In this brief summary of some of the criticisms of the naturalistic, pre-determined theories of development, I have tried to illustrate why developmental ideology and developmental psychopathology are simply this cultures way of interpreting how children should be, rather than a scientific endeavour that is leading us ever closer to the 'truth' about the nature of childhood. For within the developmental story there is a constant subtext that is saying there is a superior and inferior position. Development says to the child, the parent and the teacher this is your future and if you do not reach it you are, in some senses, inferior. It is not just children who are said to develop but also peoples and economies. Development is about modern hierarchies of superiority and inferiority, it is about dismissing diversity. Developmental explanations instil the notion of individual competitiveness; from the moment you are born you will have developmental milestones thrust upon you. As parents we are desperate to see our children achieve these age bound expectations. Development of our children is under constant professional surveillance starting with health visitors and community paediatricians and moving on to general practitioners, nursery nurses, teachers and a whole range of specialists. We are concerned when our children seem to be falling behind and we are constantly encouraging them to achieve these expectations. If we are not concerned and not encouraging, then does that mean we are neglecting?

And what does this mean for the children themselves? If there is a belief that these are natural, unfolding processes for which professionals must be involved in helping children achieve, does this not encourage competitiveness from a very early age? How much do the children get caught in these parental and professional anxieties? How relaxed can children, from the moment they are born be, to just be, as opposed to having to do and achieve something to ease these anxieties? When these anxieties cannot be comforted and there is a perception that a child has strayed from their pre-destined development path, whom is to blame? In this blame ridden culture that needs an explanation for everything, much of the developmental psychopathology literature has generally pointed toward the mother for blame and more recently toward the child's genes. In a culture where families have shrunk and fathers seem to disappear and relinquish duty and responsibility in ever increasing numbers, mothers have to shoulder not only the responsibility for caring for their family (a role given much lower status in Western culture than many non-Western cultures), but also has to shoulder responsibility for things going wrong. In a final stab from 'developmentalism' mothers are then denied credit for their work when things do go well as children are then simply seen as achieving their biological destiny.

Why is it boys who consistently outnumber girls by somewhere between 2 to 1 and 10 to 1 in most of these apparently developmental disorders? Why does our view of development appear to discover such massive genetic fault in boys as opposed to girls? It would seem that modern, Western society has developed a set of beliefs and expectations about development and its problems that girls are better able to live up to than boys. Perhaps part of the modern 'naughty boy' problem is the inevitable outcome of a developmental story that our culture insists on telling, which sees many aspects of 'boyhood' and 'boisterousness' as undesirable.

These beliefs about children's development have a big influence on the education system our children grow up in. For example, special needs resources in schools go to a much higher proportion of boys than girls. Furthermore, the defining of a disability requiring special needs help at school is shaped by the disciplines of medicine and psychology. These two fields, as I have mentioned above, like to measure mental characteristics in order to determine normality. This means that in special needs, these measures reflect a belief that children identified with special needs have failed to develop properly. These labels then become attached to both individuals and groups of children who are now categorised as having failed to measure up/conform.

With the medical profession having played a central role in developing modern, Western ideas about child development and child rearing, it has been ideally placed both socially and politically, to respond to the growing anxiety about children and their development (that I discussed above). Using its status and position of power to further increase its own influence over children and families, paediatricians, child psychiatrists and psychologists, have chosen popular European enlightenment philosophical ideals that focus on logic, scientific reason (positivism in other words) and the individual. At the same time these professions exists in a market economy and so are affected by demands of increasing personal profitability. As a result, approaches that focuses on the individual child as the place to try and solve this modern anxiety about children, with the idea that a chemical imbalance or neurological delay in development is the cause of a child's perceived problems, has become commonplace practice in the West. As with adult psychiatry no evidence of physical abnormalities that confirm this belief has been found, and there are no psychological, neurological, or other physical tests available to help the clinician in making childhood and adolescent psychiatric disorder diagnosis (see chapter 1 for a discussion of this in relation to ADHD).

Market economies need to continually expand markets, has allowed drug companies to exploit these new, vague and broadly defined childhood psychiatric diagnoses. This has resulted in a rapid increase in the amount of psychotropic medication being prescribed to children and adolescents in the West (see chapter 1 in relation to the increase in prescriptions for ADHD).

With enormous profits to be made for the drug industry, the combination of doctors carving out new roles for themselves together with aggressive marketing by the drug industry, a very powerful and difficult to resist combination has arisen. Privileged social groups, who hold important and influential positions, have a powerful effect on our common cultural beliefs, attitudes and practices. Child psychiatry in the UK does appear to have re-invented itself in the last 10 years. Powerful child psychiatrists successfully influenced the UK child psychiatry trainings by convincing it that there were more personal rewards for the profession by it adopting a more medicalised American style. This has encouraged not only the creation and widespread 'recognition' for new child psychiatric diagnoses, but also the construction of whole new classes of disorder- such as 'neurodevelopmental psychiatry', which the public, trusting such high status opinions, has come to view as real.

Modern child psychiatric practice in North America has become based around symptom based, context deprived (in other words not looking at wider environmental factors) assessments, using multiple screening questionnaires, aggressive use of psychiatric medication and the use of multiple prescriptions often with little information about safety or long-term consequences. As with adult psychiatry, this places child psychiatry in a situation where the political establishment can use the profession for social policing purposes. Not only do child psychiatrists continue to make fundamental contributions to everyday thinking about what is normal and abnormal for children and parenting, but, without realising it, the profession volunteers itself as a powerful agent of social control (for example through using medication to manage behaviours schools are not being equipped to manage).

Much of the current popularity of this- child's genes as the problem- explanation may well be a reaction to the previous dominance, in child and adolescent mental health services, of the belief that nurture- in other words bad parenting- causes the emotional and behavioural problems of children. That approach seems to have targeted mothers in particular for an extraordinary amount of blame (often letting the uninvolved fathers off the hook). In a culture where mothers are expected to shoulder the responsibility for their children's behaviour, the judgement of schools and other parents that a child is beyond control becomes a direct reflection on that mother's parenting. Mothers can then experience a profound sense of self-blame, along with a sense of failure, guilt, helplessness and perhaps frustration or anger with their child. Since the growth of the idea that the difficulties are caused by an abnormality in the child's brain, a way out of guilt and blame for the beleaguered mother appears to become available. By viewing the problems she is having with her child as being due to a genetic condition, the mother can not only have renewed sympathy for her child, but also, she is freed from mother blaming- she is no longer a failed mother but a mother battling against the odds with a disabled child.

Whilst this may appear to solve one source of stress, anxiety and blame, the problem is that it simply shifts all of these feelings sideways without addressing them. The approach of seeing children's problems as being caused by some invisible medical disease is equally guilty in its simplistic theoretical assumptions, and in denying alternative possibilities. Furthermore, in my experience, it never solves the nagging doubt in the back of a parent's mind that it is their fault, leads to perfectly healthy children coming to believe that they have lifelong disability (this disconnects a person from their own free will, psychological problem solving skills, and ability to take responsibility for their actions), and exposes children to a all sorts of possibly harmful, psychiatric medications unnecessarily.

As we emerge from the so-called decade of the brain and the Human Genome Project the obsession with genetics and in particular behavioural genetics (the idea that certain genes code for certain behaviours) is obsessing psychiatry. Hardly a week seems to go by without some television documentary suggesting a whole host of social and health problems can best be understood through the lens of a persons DNA. It seems criminality, obesity, your choice of sexual partner, the number of sexual partners, your political beliefs and, of course, naughty children (which often boil down to naughty boys) are the result of bad genes. This is good for drug companies as it continues to give the message that we cannot be held responsible for our behaviour, thoughts and beliefs and are incapable of making choices in life because the power of our genes means that we have little control over these deeper biological impulses (not a new idea of course). It is a short step from there to a society where social control and social harmony is then maintained by medications and eventually the new eugenics (see chapter 2).

Chapter 4

Alternative theories of ADHD

In the last chapter I explored the social and cultural origins in Western medicine of the concept of ADHD. I briefly described the history of the development of ideas about ADHD, and outlined the cultural conditions from which these ideas developed. I explored our changing understanding of childhood and child rearing in Western culture and how the idea that children's behaviour problems are caused by medical conditions such as ADHD has occurred during a very recent period in Western history. I also explained how it relates to an anxiety and a sense of there being a crisis with regards children and their development. I then looked further into the impact this recent medicalisation of children's behaviour has had, and how this is causing not only a change in the way we think about childhood problems, but also a narrowing of our idea of what a 'normal' childhood (and normal child rearing) is, which in turn leads to changes in children and their parent's experience and view of themselves.

In this chapter I start to look at alternative ideas about ADHD-type behaviours, and how to view them. The current evidence base needs theoretical frameworks to make conclusions possible. As I have been arguing, the type of theoretical framework you choose will effect how you interpret the evidence- So, for example, you may interpret evidence that shows a rapid rise in rates of diagnosis over the last decade differently depending on your theoretical model: Thus if you chose the 'ADHD as a genetic illness' model, you may view such evidence as confirmation that we are now better at recognising ADHD; whereas if you chose the 'ADHD as a cultural construct' model, you may view this as evidence that our cultural beliefs about children's behaviour is changing; alternatively, if you chose the 'ADHD as caused by environmental factors such as poor diet' model you may view such evidence as confirmation that more ADHD is happening in children because their diet (or whatever other environmental factor you are concerned with) is getting worse.

I hope you can see from the example above that your theoretical framework will have a big influence not only on how you interpret the evidence, but also on what you might then do to help a child and their family. Thus looking at other theoretical frameworks that have been suggested in the literature on ADHD can have real practical benefits, helping us develop alternative solutions. This is particularly so, I think, if we can hold on to some healthy scepticism and resist the temptation to view any one idea as the 'truth' about ADHD and instead view the different ideas as all having something that might be useful in particular circumstances and with particular children.

In looking at different theoretical frameworks I will first refer back to our current sense of crises about children and their development and discuss some of the social changes that have affected children and their families. I outline some theories from neurobiology that suggest that some ADHD-type behaviours are indeed biologically based, but due to environmental causes such as early exposure to stress and trauma. I will present ideas from research on children's temperament, which offer another alternative biological model for ADHD- a model that assumes ADHD type behaviours can be viewed as part of the normal spectrum of behaviours that children have (in other words that ADHD can be viewed as being on a continuum rather than as a discreet disease state).

Following this I discuss a philosophical/psychological model (that has some aspects in common with models used in some Eastern traditional medicine) that changes the focus of thinking about problems from that of noticing things that are wrong to that of noticing and building on strengths.

Then I look at some of the theories around that suggest that changes in our culture and environment may be causing more ADHD-type behaviours in children. This includes theories that examine our changing concept of time and the increasingly 'hyperactive-inattentive' pastimes for children available in modern Western culture. These might be changing children's ability and desire to maintain attention and motivation as a result of the increasing use of media like television and computer games. Other theories discuss how changes in our beliefs about acceptable child rearing methods, have led to a verbal/intellectual style of parenting that may cause an emotional distancing from our children. Finally I discuss the impact of changes in our education system, changes in children's diet, changes in family lifestyles, and the role of consumerism in changing children's identities, beliefs and values[32].

A Crisis For Children?

Life got tougher for many families and their children in the West in the last few decades. From the mid to late 1970's, a marked shift in social welfare policies took place. American businesses became less profitable and so began cutting wages, speeding up production, increasing automation, weakening unions and curtailing welfare programmes. Economically, efforts turned to lowering taxes to boost businesses. This resulted in a re-distribution of income upwards by providing tax cuts for those in the highest income brackets (in other words the rich got richer) and there has been a steady widening of the gap between the highest and lowest earners in most Western countries. Losses in government revenues were partly offset by cuts in social welfare programmes. With the gap between rich and poor increasing, families bore the brunt of the worsening social protections.

Being a parent in many Western countries has become more and more difficult. Issues such as violence, poverty and the breakdown of the family unit have been affecting ever-increasing numbers of families. At the same time as successive American governments were introducing policies to favour the business sector at the expense of a welfare safety net, an ideological shift was taking place in order to justify these actions. Social programmes were no longer viewed as humane or necessary, but as something counter-productive as they cause dependence and poor motivation amongst its recipients. An increased hostility developed toward the notion of dependence on the state. This helped create a new marginalized 'under-class', crowded into no-go urban areas where underground economies (such as the drug trade) developed.

American right wing policies of a similar nature were imported into the UK in the early 1980's by the then British Prime Minister, Margaret Thatcher. The sense of social breakdown in the lives of children in this country (the UK) is also evident in the daily media reports and debates about school crises, discipline problems, expulsion, violence in the young, crime in the young, bullying, drug abuse, binge drinking, break up of the family, and breakdown in parent-teacher relationships. A study on what was loosely termed psychosocial disorders amongst the young (such as suicide attempts, alcohol and drug abuse, and criminality) concluded that there has been a sudden and sharp rise in these disorders throughout Europe and North America in the last two decades of the last century[33]. In the United Kingdom this has been occurring within the continuing widening of the social inequality/income gap, with by far the biggest group negatively effected being lower income families with children, although there has been a reduction in the number of children deemed to be living in poverty since the Labour government came into power. Nonetheless, a recent survey (conducted in 2004) by the UK Office for National Statistics found evidence that rates of 'mental health problems' amongst children are continuing to increase, and are more common amongst the poorer sections of society[34].

Changes in social, political and economic circumstances are closely connected with our common cultural beliefs and value systems. The last couple of decades of the twentieth century saw North America lead the way in promoting a 'masculine' competitive free market ideology and placing this at the centre of our value system. Socialism has become a bad word, and dependence (on the state for example) has come to be viewed as promoting passive helpless individuals who were of no use to society. The 'cult' of individualism has blossomed. The values of social responsibility as a guiding value system for the young has diminished, and has been replaced by worship at the mantle of the individual, Margaret Thatcher once famously saying, "There is no such thing as society". Social mobility was encouraged as the best way to defeat the massive levels of unemployment, with Norman Tebbit (a member of Margaret Thatcher's government) telling people they should "get on your bikes" to go to where the work is. As in the

United States, an underclass developed in the United Kingdom, with areas of urban deprivation that attracted an underground economy that often revolves around drugs and gangs.

The knock on effect for children and families of the triumph of this right wing capitalist ideology has, in my opinion, been appalling. These social stressors are likely to have contributed to the sadly negative experiences so many children in the West experience from the moment they are born. Children are growing up in families with no fathers, looked after by mothers who have diminishing support networks and whom the state believes should be working (there seems little importance attached to the work of a mother in Western society these days), in communities where drugs are sold at the school gates, in schools under increasing pressure to demonstrate higher academic achievement in their pupils, and where rival gangs shoot at each other in next door flats.

Could these increased life stressors for the young cause an increase in ADHD behaviours such as impulsivity, hyperactivity and distractibility? A number of scientists pursuing a neurobiological approach (in other words scientists who study the biological development of the brain), note how the symptoms of ADD/ADHD closely parallel those that occur during trauma, such as hyper-alertness, the need to act quickly, the need to be on the go at all times in the expectation of danger, and the inability to turn attention to matters other than those of potential threat. Their hypothesis is that, in a critical period in infancy some children experience trauma (they note that what is traumatic for infants may not be the same as what is traumatic for adults and vice versa), which sets in motion an automatic response, as though to some external threat. This impulsive psychological defence eventually becomes a habit that is 'hardwired' into children's developing brains. When older, such children are sensitive to threat to a much greater extent than other children are and revert back, as it were, to a state of 'red alert' very easily. Thus as with post-traumatic stress, such children react quickly, over-actively, and not so much to their ordinary life as to an anticipated threat.

Other 'brain development' researchers agree with this idea as more evidence is accumulating that shows that experience has physical/biological effects on the brain which is now seen as an organ capable of undergoing great changes in response to experiences, particularly in childhood but right up into adulthood. This model is not intended as a parent blame model, at the same time it doesn't set out to avoid the complex realities of family life and relationships.

Support for the idea that ADHD behaviours can be caused by childhood trauma can be found in the increasingly large body of literature that shows a link between childhood trauma or abuse and subsequent behaviour problems including ADHD-type behaviours, violence and aggression. For example, in a chapter a colleague of mine, Charles Whitfield, wrote for a book that I co-edited, he points out that there is a large body of literature showing a link between childhood trauma or abuse and subsequent behaviour problems including ADHD-type behaviours, violence and aggression[35]. In his literature search he found 77 published reports of a significantly higher incidence of ADHD type behaviours and ADHD among abused children and found only one study that looked for it that reported a negative association of ADHD with trauma. Charles Whitfield concludes that childhood trauma can lead to a multitude of health and social problems including those that result from disrupted development of the brain and nervous system as a result of the physical effects of chronic stress on the developing brain.

ADHD And Children's Temperament:

A related area of research takes as its starting point the assumption that behaviours such as levels of activity, attention and impulsivity are normal temperamental characteristics, and that children will biologically have different levels of these (in the same way children will grow to different heights). Viewing these behaviours as temperamental characteristics as opposed to signs of a medical condition, allows more attention to how these behaviours interact with the environment.

Research on children's temperament has shown that problems usually result from a 'mismatch' between a child's temperament and their environment, rather than temperament alone causing future problems for a child. Thus temperament theory research has shown that even children who are highly difficult temperamentally can become well adjusted behaviourally if their family, school and other social circumstances are positive, containing and supportive. Thus what temperament theory research has been suggesting is that the behaviours we call ADHD are probably inherited in much the same way as other personality traits, whether these behaviours come to be a problem is probably due to psychological and social factors in that child's environment.

Attachment To Fathers And Mothers:

Moving away from the possible biological effects on developing children of the modern stresses on children and families, some authors (such as Peter Breggin) have put forward a strong case for the missing role of absent fathers causing the ADHD type behaviours. In such cases, loving attention from their fathers is thought to be an effective curative factor for such children.

In a similar vein 'attachment theory' suggests that the modern stressful social situation is having a dire and negative effect on the ability of parents to provide the sort of strong, secure and positive relationships children need with their parents. An accumulation of stresses on a family (such as lack of support, unresolved loss, poor relationship with father, insufficiently positive relationship of parents with their own parents, pregnancy and birth complications and difficult infant temperament), in some families, it is suggested, causes increasingly negative interactions to develop between a child and their parent(s). What this leads to is exhaustion, frustration and irritability in the parent and challenging and hyperactive behaviour in the growing child. This eventually develops into viscous negative spiral of insecurity in the child and further exhaustion and frustration in the parent.

Indeed some attachment theorists argue that impulsivity, recklessness, negative attention seeking, hyperactivity, and poor concentration may be part of a psychological defence mechanism in the child that the child uses to cope with feeling insecure about their relationship with their parent. For example, It could be that hyperactive, impulsive and non-complaint behaviour by a young insecurely attached child is their way (probably unconsciously) of keeping their parent(s) close to them and constantly involved with them.

Reframing The Problem:

To reframe means to change the viewpoint in relation to a situation or object by placing it inside a different framework (in other words a different way of looking at the situation or object). This can then change the entire meaning that is given to that situation or object. Our experience of the world is based on the categorising of the objects of our perception into different categories. For example we may categorise driving in 'stressful experiences'. Once something is categorised as belonging to a particular class it is extremely difficult to see it as belonging to a different one. However, once we see that it is possible to categorise something as belonging to a completely different category (in other words, reframing) it becomes very difficult to go back to our previously limited view of reality (where it only belonged to one category). To use my example of driving, perhaps an experience of driving to a lovely hotel, full of anticipation could help re-categorise driving into 'exciting experiences', now that you have at least two categories into which you could put driving, it doesn't mean that driving can no longer be categorised as 'stressful experiences', but it does mean that you can no longer categorise it as *only* a stressful experience.

The process of reframing is a subtle one. It is a way of re-telling a story in such a way as to allow new possibilities and new ways of understanding the situation to unfold. The professional has to listen carefully, shift an emphasis here and question a conclusion there, in order to allow for the possibility that a new meaning could be offered.

In many ways all therapies offer a degree of reframing, asking the patient or the family to take on board a new way of looking at a problem.

So-called 'post-modern' theory is involved in re-examining power relationships that exist in our society, and that have big effects on shaping the way we think about the world around us. Thus, post-modern theory is constantly trying to re-frame our conclusions about the way things are, by questioning anyone who believes that life's experiences can only be viewed (categorised) in one or a few ways. A simple example might be that when the church had a powerful voice in our culture, understanding how the world worked was often with reference to god and the supernatural and this affected the way we behaved as well (for example, going to church, seeking advice from a priest for personal problems etc.). However, now that those who have power to influence are more likely to turn to science to explain the world, our common cultural ideas revolve around 'laws' of nature and the work of technology, which has changed the way we behave too (for example watching television to get information and seeking advice from a doctor for personal problems).

A 'post-modern' analysis of culture and power in relation to ADHD, suggests that a mother-blaming culture maybe an important factor in the rise of ADHD diagnoses. In this explanatory model mothers who constantly hear the negative comments about their child from school and other parents, experience a profound sense of self-blame, failure, guilt and helplessness as well as anger and frustration at the child. When put in contact with the 'ADHD industry' such a mother may, at least temporarily, feel freed from the mother blaming that has been so oppressive to her. She is now no longer a failed mother, but a mother battling against the odds with a disabled child. In this analysis, the primary problem is not seen as residing in the mother *or* the child, but in the effects of the dominant beliefs and powerful cultural position of the professional disciplines of psychology, psychiatry (as part of medicine) which cause both parent and child to become like helpless people whose identities are being shaped by these cultural beliefs and who then become separated from their abilities, competence and strengths.

'Normalising' boy behaviour is an example of reframing. In this case the approach is to re-frame the problem from one of 'abnormal' behaviour on the part of the child, to one of reinterpreting the child's behaviour as normal responses of a normal boy to particular environmental situations. Furthermore, by normalising you are also challenging the idea that the problem is with the child, to that of the problem being that of the way others (be they parents, relatives, neighbours, teachers or doctors) view the child's behaviour.

Another important and useful way to re-frame a problem is to change your area of focus. It is usual when we experience difficulties for us to focus on the difficulty (in the case of ADHD, this being the child's behaviour) or our own feelings of failure (in other words on the negative aspects of the situation). However, instead of focussing on the negative, the re-frame can be that of noticing and trying to strengthen the positive. Thus many children who could be diagnosed as ADHD, can be viewed as 'relentlessly curious' wanting to discover and full of enthusiasm for trying to do as much as they can. Indeed, wouldn't it be wonderful if we were able (as some children who get diagnosed with ADHD seem to be) to wake up full of energy, with each new day as a new adventure with so many unexplored, undiscovered things waiting to be found out! Wouldn't it be great to just live absorbed by the moment, not consumed by planning for the future and always living for the future (this is after-all the aim in many Eastern philosophies and religions, such as Buddhism- to be able to live in the moment).

Taking a positive view of these traits means seeing the potential creative and change inducing value that ADHD-type behaviours posses. On the go adventure seeking risk takers can be viewed as individuals who have the potential to push the boundaries of possibility, to invent through lateral thinking, and to produce social change.

What theorists who examine problems in families point out is the importance of not just describing and giving negative labels to problematic behaviours (in the child and/or their parents), but also trying to understand the intention behind them, which can often be allot more positive. For example, the mother who owns up to often 'giving in' to her child's demands because she feels guilty and mean if she acts towards him/her in such a way, can be reframed as being positively motivated by noticing that she is showing how powerful her love towards her child is and how important his/her happiness is to her.

In mainstream Western psychiatry and psychology the professional language revolves around notions of 'deficit' (in other words ideas that something is missing from/wrong with people diagnosed with psychiatric disorder). As professionals we are trained to search for deficit, to uncover 'psychopathology' to diagnose anything that doesn't fit our cultural opinion of 'normal'. This is not just an academic point. These cultural beliefs have consequences- huge consequences. They make us professionals act in certain ways and pass on powerful messages to children and their families. This can take our (the professional, the child, their family, their teachers etc) attention away from functional stories, from noticing the exceptions, from seeing strength, courage and resilience.

Post- modern therapies such as narrative therapy and solution-focused therapy challenge this narrow way of looking at things. By searching for exceptions to the problem (those bits in the child's life that don't fit the idea that they have a deficit), finding strengths and building on them, a form of therapy can be constructed that can create new, more positive and hopeful versions of the child. Such a 'building health' (as opposed to 'getting rid of illness') orientated approach is not only potentially empowering, but also, avoids the trap of the 'self-fulfilling' prophecy focussing on a deficit can produce. If you're told that your child has a permanent genetic disease called ADHD, the child, parents, teacher etc. will come to expect a certain degree of 'disability' to remain present for many years, and all will act according to that expectation, and end up perhaps not noticing those bits of the child that doesn't fit the ADHD story.

This brings me to another important and final issue to discuss in this section on re-framing- the dangers of becoming dependent on professionals. Our traditional understanding of the doctor/ patient relationship is that the doctor is a healthy 'expert' whose job is to diagnose illness and then prescribe treatment to cure or manage this illness. With chronic (long-lasting) diseases this means carrying on seeing the 'expert' regularly for many years, possibly lifelong. In mental health all too often this traditional doctor/patient 'script' creates unnecessary dependence on the doctor. With diagnoses such as ADHD and everyday life tasks such as parenting, the idea that a professional is needed long-term to manage children's behaviour can distance us from our own experience and knowledge base.

More often than not we, as parents, already know allot more than we may believe we know. This calls for a different sort of knowledge or expertise, one that is more subtle and grounded in an understanding of the culturally scripted nature (or to use an earlier phrase I introduced you to- the socially constructed nature) of our perceptions. Whilst a professional may have the knowledge, it is you, the parents/carers/child, who *know* the child. Thus there is a whole branch of theory that comes from philosophy, psychology, sociology, psychotherapy, and cultural studies (to name but a few disciplines) that is involved in questioning our excessive reliance on professionals for 'the problems of living' (which will always be there), at the same time as noting that there is a large variety of good local knowledge about issues such as parenting and children's behaviour that has always existed in various forms in communities around the world.

Modern Lifestyles:

Another culture specific set of ideas relates to our modern lifestyle. The increasingly centre stage role of electronic media that are fast paced, don't require mastering language skills, are visually distracting, and that young children spend so many hours sat in front of, may literally have changed children's minds. Sustained attention to the slower paced verbal inputs such as reading or listening is far less appealing than these faster paced stimuli.

Exposure to TV and computer games from a young age could then lead to a form of sensory addiction, leading to problems when children are asked to adapt to less stimulating environments such as school. Interestingly, among the Amish, who are well known for their rejection of most modern indulgences such as computers and television, symptoms of ADHD appear to be uncommon. Recently, researchers at the University of Washington have discovered a strong association between the amount of early exposure to TV and subsequent attention span in early childhood, supporting previous research that showed an association between amounts of TV watching and reduced reading ability and attention span[36].

Other modern lifestyle issues may also contribute to more ADHD type behaviours in our children. Advertising not only creates young consumers who pressure their parents, but by its short, snapshot nature could be training our children to have a short attention span. Children are not being taught to control their impulses in the same way as just a few decades ago. In the past with parents having limited disposable income and there being fewer readily available sources of instant gratification, children had to learn through necessity to control their impulses. Nowadays, with instant gratification being such a big feature of the consumer culture, children are no longer being forced to learn early self-control of their impulses, a problem made worse by the belief that a diagnosis of ADHD means the child can't learn self-control.

Fears about children's safety, together with more 'in-house' entertainments such as computers and TV, has also led to many children growing up with a lack of fresh air and exercise, leaving those more active boys to behave like 'caged animals' (this phenomena is sometimes referred to as 'the domestication of childhood' by some academics). Indeed there is evidence from animal experiments to show that access to what the authors call 'rough-and-tumble' play promotes brain maturation and reduces levels of hyperactivity and impulsiveness in later life[37].

Children's diets have changed. They are now high in sugar, salt, and additives and low and in fresh fruit and vegetables, and seafood. Patterns of food consumption and the make up of the Western diet have changed enormously in the last few decades. In the 1950s and 1960s ideas about farming began to change in the West and horticulturists began working to develop high productivity strains of our most common food crops, such as wheat and rice. As a result of these new strains, grain production rose by 75 per cent. However, the new varieties were very demanding of fertilizer, water, and pesticides. Many rural farmers could not afford the added costs to produce the new grains. In addition, much genetic diversity was lost because native strains were abandoned in favor of the new crops. So, in the 1970s Western farming moved from having many varieties to only a few and from small family farms to large corporate agriculture. At the same time new food processing methods (such as freeze-drying) which added many more artificial chemicals into the foods sold at supermarkets, was leading to mass production methods to process food, one aspect of which was the growth of highly processed convenience (or fast) foods to fit in with the faster and more frenetic lifestyles of 'consumers'.

Thus the modern Western child's diet contains a variety of foods or additives that may produce food intolerances (a milder form of food allergy), are low in proteins and high in carbohydrates, sugars, and fats, often show mineral imbalances, heavy metal toxicity, essential fatty acid deficiency, amino acid deficiency, and essential vitamin deficiencies. All these nutritional problems may result in ADHD-type behaviours.

Changes In The Way We Parent:

Life has become difficult for many parents who are often caught in a double pressure particularly when it comes to discipline. On the one hand there are increased expectations for children to show restraint and self-control from an early age. On the other hand there is considerable social fear in parents generated by a culture of children's rights that often stigmatises normal, well-intentioned parents' attempts to discipline their children. Parents are left fearing a visit from Social Services and the whole area of discipline becomes loaded with anxiety. This argument holds equally true for schools. Parents often criticise schools for lack of discipline. Schools often criticise parents for lack of discipline. This 'double bind' or 'Catch-22' situation has resulted in more power going to children. Thus, for some children with ADHD-type behaviours the basic problem may be a breakdown of their relationship to authority.

Parents are being given the message that their children are more like adults and should always be talked to, reasoned with, allowed to make choices, and so on. This line of argument says that kids can't be kids in the way we used to think about them- that is dependent, in need of rules, protection, values and authority. The question is then whether we inadvertently end up giving a child more power, responsibility and independence than they are capable of handling.

There is also a lack of common ownership of rules and values with regards to upbringing of children, therefore children learn that only certain individuals have any right to make demands and have expectations with regards their behaviour. Thus children can more easily play adults off against each other these days (for example mum against dad or teachers against parents). The basic problem here relates to the way in which the task of parenting has come to be viewed in Western culture, as one that needs childcare experts' advice in order to get it right. This has resulted in a form of parenting that some academics refer to as 'cognitive parenting' becoming more common. Cognitive parenting refers to an approach to parenting that stresses reasoning and verbal communication (talking) in preference to action. This results in parents being encouraged to give explanation and avoid conflicts. This 'hands-off', verbal model of parenting is more taxing, time-consuming and arguably *less* child friendly as children have a more 'action-based' view of the world than adults.

Changes In Our Education System:

School is another big part of children's life where considerable changes have occurred that could promote or sustain ADHD-type behaviours. Modern teaching methods emphasise self-regulation, autonomy of the child and reject spoon feeding (dependency). This can result in a poor environment for children who have problems with organising, ordering and learning. In classroom environments that are, for them, over-stimulating and offer too much choice and therefore encourage distraction and poor concentration, restlessness can be worsened.

Emphasis has changed in schools in North America and in the United Kingdom. Schools are now expected to demonstrate better levels of academic achievement amongst their pupils and often have to compete with other schools in national performance league tables. As a result much of the curriculum is being pushed downward from older to younger children, with less time being set aside for more energetic and creative activities such as physical education and music. Schools are anyway better set up for girl's development. There is now a large body of evidence that attests to the fact that educational methods currently used in most Western schools (such as continuous assessment and socially orientated work sheets) are favoured more by girls than boys. This is then mirrored in national exam results where girls are now consistently achieving higher grades than boys, even in some traditionally 'male' subjects like Maths and Science.

Special needs support in schools is four times more likely to be given to boys who lag behind girls in development of core school adaptive abilities such as reading and social skills. These latter two factors put together- more emphasis on academic achievement and differential rates of development- has put young-for-grade boys at a particular disadvantage with as many as four fifths of young-for-grade boys being diagnosed with ADHD and prescribed stimulant medication in some areas of North America.

Interestingly, research in the United States has found a clear relationship between boys' lack of educational achievement relative to girls' and the amount medication (stimulants) prescribed for ADHD. What this research found is that stimulant use in the United States is highest in prosperous white communities where education is a high priority, where the educational achievement of both sexes is above the national average and, most importantly, where the gender gap in educational achievement favouring females is at its highest. This suggests that ADHD (in the USA) is a diagnosis often driven by anxiety about boys' relative lack of educational achievement, in communities where educational achievement is highly valued[38].

The Influence Of Living In A Market Economy And Consumerism:

Children and then adults come to acquire their sense of self, in part, through incorporation of values, beliefs, and practices that sustain the desired social relationships of the cultural group they live with. So how does the ideology of modern market economies influence the way children and their parents see themselves, their roles and subsequently the values that shape the way they behave? This involves a somewhat complicated argument but I think it is worth mentioning.

One of the dominant themes used by advocates of capitalist market economy ideology is that of 'freedom'. Freedom is of course a value that, taken at face value few of us would argue against. However, 'freedom' is word used to mean many different things to different people, including those who are using it for opposite purposes. Thus, for example, the Palestinians may argue that they are struggling against Israel to achieve 'freedom' for their people; whilst at the same time Israeli's may justify their policies against Palestinians as being motivated by their desire to keep their own population 'free'.

All cultures have a mixture of laws and beliefs designed to curtail personal freedom, as one person's freedom can be another's oppression.

A rather un-important example might be that of neighbour who argues that they should be 'free' to play their music as loud as they want. However, affording such a freedom to that person may be affecting the neighbours right to live a life 'free' from noise pollution. This means that in practice all cultures have to develop systems (rules, written and unspoken) that balance personal freedom against social responsibility. The process of 'growing-up' involves learning how to curtail your individual desires so that they do not cause suffering to those around you (in other words to develop social responsibility). Of course where we see that point of balance between individual desire and social responsibility varies from culture to culture, as well as within any culture over time.

So when those who promote the idea of 'freedom' as being a central value to modern Western market economy, we need to understand what they mean by that. At an emotional level the appeal to 'freedom' can be understood as an appeal to rid us of the restrictions imposed by authority (such as parents, communities and governments)- in other words to prevent us from having to think about how our actions affect others; to by-pass thinking about social responsibility. This value system provides a set of beliefs that can sustain the economic basis of a successful market economy. In a fully 'free' market economy, companies should concentrate on maximising their profitability (looking after number one) without thinking about the effect their products and working practices, have on the rest of the population (in other words they should be free from having to think about social responsibility).

Such a value system is necessary to sustain the 'driven' nature of free-market economies, and the most ardent supporters of free-market ideology constantly argue that governments should not interfere in businesses, and reduce the amount of regulation they have.

The result in economic terms has been the creation of 'cut-throat' competitiveness and rampant consumerism. Competitiveness, because in a system that is based on individual desires (of the company) and that rejects a need to consider social responsibility, companies think nothing of driving you out of business or swallowing you up into their business. Consumerism, because, in order to sustain profit levels new markets need to continuously develop to stimulate constant growth.

If such a value system is driving the economic system we live in, how will it affect our behaviour at the individual level? By implication this value system is built around the idea of looking after the desires of the individual, who should despise any form of dependency or need for responsibility in relationships with others.

Taking this a step further, once the individual is freed from the limitations of social responsibility, they are (in fantasy at least) free to pursue their own individual self-gratification desires, free from the impingements, infringements and limitations that other people represent. Thus at the heart of this modern freedom loving, free market, value system, is an individual freed from the need to think about others in order to pursue self gratification. The effect of this on society is to 'atomise' the individual and insulate their private spaces- in other words it changes our ideas about the self and privacy, by setting the balance between the desires of the individual and social responsibility very definitely toward the desires of the individual. Whilst not wishing to overstate this case and make unsupportable generalisations, I think it does mean that to some degree obligations to others and harmony with the wider community, have become obstacles rather than objectives in Western culture. In this 'look after number one' value system, other individuals are there to be competed against as they too chase after their personal desires.

As I mentioned in Chapter 3 this post second world war shift to a more 'fun based morality' was already being noted by commentators in the USA in the mid-1950's, who saw that Western culture was now putting having fun (individual desires) as of greater importance than social responsibility; having fun was becoming obligatory (the cultural message becoming that you should be ashamed if you weren't having fun). Indeed it could be argued that with the increase in new possibilities for excitement being presented, experiencing intense excitement was becoming more difficult, thus opening the doors to the mass use of drugs (legal and illegal) in pursuit of the ultimate 'high' (this in a sense parallels, at the level of the individual, the process outlined above where economies need to grow endlessly in pursuit of continued profitability).

In this value system others can become objects to be used and manipulated wherever possible for personal goals and social exchanges become difficult to trust as the better you are at manipulating others the more financial rewards you will get. Dependence still occurs, but is more likely to happen with professionals thereby reinforcing the idea and status of the expert. A number of commentators have pointed out that this free-market ideology has necessarily led to the domination of market values in all spheres of life. This philosophy pushes to the limit an opposition between humankind and nature. The goal of finding an ecological harmony with nature disappears as nature comes to be viewed as a thing to be similarly manipulated for selfish ends.

In a capitalist, market driven economy, mass consumption is vital to maintenance of the system and therefore becomes an important part of our self and consciousness. Even personal relations and the self become like consumer items, for example just like the stereotype consumer wife who is comparing the whiteness of her sheets with those of her neighbours; people in consumer societies constantly compare themselves (and their own inadequacies) with others. This practice of self-examination causes a cult of self-awareness. In doing so it actually creates inner qualities, including whatever passes for personal growth with every day one seeking to make oneself a better product - new, improved, best and brightest yet. Yet, despite several decades of sustained economic growth, we are no happier; in fact population surveys show that levels of unhappiness and stress have been steadily increasing in Western societies in the past few decades[39].

Thus, growth not only fails to make people contented; it destroys many of the things that do through weakening the sort of social cohesion that comes when social responsibility is put ahead of personal freedom. Like the rest of our culture, psychiatry too is gripped by an ideology of growth, as we are encouraged to produce more and more 'knowledge' and diagnostic categories, endlessly researching, and yet seem powerless to do anything about the apparently deteriorating state of the mental health of Western populations.

There is another interesting consequence of having a value system that stresses the importance of personal desires at the expense of that of social responsibility. Such a value system, cannot sustain itself without the moral conscience beginning to feel guilty. As social animals we cannot eradicate our psychological tendency for experiencing remorse if (or when) we realise we are doing harm to others. Thus, I think, it is no coincidence that those right wing politicians who are the most enthusiastic advocates of free market ideology tend also to advocate the most aggressive and punitive forms of social control. Whereas some of the guilt-induced policy proposals are aimed at putting some restraint on unfettered competitiveness, greed and self seeking (most notably in more centre and left wing capitalist governments), amongst those more fanatical believers in the sacredness of market ideology, the most common psychological defence used to try and deal with the anxiety produced by this guilt is through finding target scapegoats for this anxiety.

Like a child who doesn't want to feel guilty at having done something they know is 'naughty', they try to blame someone else for the damage that has happened as a result of their naughtiness. This is the basis of the knee-jerk 'something must be done about it' ethos that leads to poorly thought out policies in response to media hysteria following high profile incidents. It reflects an inability in our culture to tolerate risk and anxiety and the constant need to find target groups to carry our collective burden of guilt. As a result the institutions which deal with our children from education, health and through to social services are ruled by faceless, emotionless technical procedures and policies designed to maintain distance, boundaries and regulate levels of human contact between the people who work in these agencies and the people they are meant to serve.

In order to keep this self-seeking individualistic value system intact, Western governments thus needs 'baddies' to blame for the personal suffering that is occurring as a result of its encouragement of selfishness. In other words instead of facing up to the suffering the encouragement of manipulation of people that greed brings to the world, our leaders need to convince us that our problems are due to other evils (like fundamentalist Islam, asylum seekers, homosexuals, single parents, bad genes etc.). As a result another hallmark of Western culture is the so called 'blame culture', which fills the media and contemporary beliefs and systems more generally.

The attention given to individual cases of child abusers whom society can disown as not belonging to or being (at least in part) the product of our culture, masks Western governments implementation of national and international policies that place children at great risk and the extent to which in many aspects we are a culture that is abusive to children. Right wing policies of the 80's and 90's cut health, social, welfare and education programmes as well as enforcing similar 'austerity' measures on developing countries, policies that had a particularly bad effect on children and families.

This also has a class specific character with the plight of poor children being viewed as self-inflicted and the more insidious problem of neglect of their children by middle class parents passing unnoticed. With the increase in the number of divorces and two working parents, fathers and mothers are around their children for less of the day. A generation of 'home aloners' are growing up. Since the late 1960's the amount of time children in the USA have with their parents has dropped, from an average of 30 hours per week to 17 hours per week by the early 1990's. As kids withdraw into their own culture, the free market exploits this, praying on their boredom and desire for stimulation. In this environment poor children are constantly confronted with their shortcomings by media that tells them they are incomplete without this or that latest accessory. As I mentioned earlier, in this unhappy isolation Western children respond to the markets push to 'adultify' (turn them into consumer adults) them by entering into the world of adult entertainments earlier and often without adult supervision. Thus the modern Western child is sexually knowledgeable and has early experience of drugs and alcohol. Turning children into miniature adults may also be exposing them to greater risk of sexual abuse through consumer culture's eroticization of the young as seen in popular images (for example in advertising) that presents highly eroticized, alluring little girls with make-up and beauty pageants who no longer look like little girls but like miniature versions of young women who are encouraged to walk suggestively across the stage.

With the goal of self-fulfilment, gratification and competitive manipulation of relationships to suit the individual's own selfish ends, together with the discouragement of the development of deep interpersonal attachments, it is not difficult to see why so-called 'narcissistic' (or self-concerned/centred) psychiatric disorders (such as anti-social behaviour, substance misuse and eating disorders) are on the increase.

Children are cultured into this value system by virtue of living within its institutions and being exposed daily to its values and beliefs (most notably through media such as television). Through this they are socialized into a system that embraces this free-market idea of freedom through promoting individualism, competitiveness and becoming consumers. Ultimately this is a system of winners and losers, a kind of survival of the fittest where compassion and concern for social harmony contradicts the basic goal of the value system. As this system is showing itself to be bad for children's happiness a similar process as above works to try and distance us from the anxiety arising from the guilt this produces in us. Many of us are aware at some level that children are at the margins of our culture, are not welcome in many places, and are the social group suffering the most from our frantic lifestyles with two working parents, lack of extended family support, parental conflict, separation, and divorce.

We also now have that generation that first experienced the impact of these changing family forms on them, grown up as parents. My consulting room is full of parents who experienced such unhappy childhoods and felt insecure in their relationships with their own parents, and are now struggling to know how to be with their own children. Instead of asking ourselves painful questions about the role we (as a culture including us professionals and parents) may be playing in producing this unhappiness, we can view our children's difficulties as being the result of biological diseases that require medical treatment (we can blame their genes).

These social dynamics also get projected directly onto children. Children come to be viewed as both victims (through adults using and manipulating them for their own gratification) and potentially 'evil' scapegoats (as if it is these nasty children's bad behaviour that is causing so many of our social problems). This reflects a profound ambivalence that exists toward children in the West. With adults busily pursuing the goals of self-realization and self-expression (these being the polite middle class versions of self-gratification), having unconsciously absorbed the free-market ethic, children when they come along 'get in the way'. A human being, who is so utterly dependent on others, will inevitably cause a contradiction in the goals of self seeking that individuals who have grown up in this society will hold to a greater or lesser degree. Children cannot be welcomed into the world in an ordinary way. They will make the dominant goals of modern life more difficult. They will to some degree be a burden.

The process of having a child can also be viewed through the prism of a consumer value system. Thus the desire to have a child can be seen as linked to a personal desire, many feeling that they are only 'complete' once they have had, the latest accessory- a child. In this way of viewing the nature of childhood in Western culture, adults sometimes have children for their own emotional gratification (compared to other cultures that may have very practical reasons for having children related to family rather than personal needs, such as helping with the upkeep of a farm or to complete religious duties). This causes a cultural shift in relation to gender, with girls being more highly prized for this purpose than boys, as girls are more likely to provide displays of emotional affection to their parents. For some boys these dynamics leave them in a lonely place, where they feel unwelcome, unvalued and caught in cycles of progressive alienation, jealousy and guilt with few male role models to turn to and find a healthy way out of their situation.

Why So Many Boys?

Despite the argument of some feminists that we now have a more equitable society, with women having greater freedoms and rights, another view (which I share) see the developments in our culture that I describe above as part of Western culture becoming more 'masculine' than ever. Major world-views are usually reflections of the interests and experiences of the most powerful social groups. In gender terms this is undoubtedly man. Men in the West are the main beneficiaries of the contemporary world order that has delivered great wealth to them; with the worlds richest fifth in 1990 receiving 83% of the world's income compared to the 1.4% that the world's poorest fifth received.

Western history of empire, conquest and in its most nakedly and violently masculine form- fascism; was made by men. Classical Western philosophy of reason and science through its oppositions with the natural world and emotions led to Western science and technology becoming dominated by 'masculine' metaphors (particularly in comparison with Eastern philosophies). In the West our idea about 'masculinity' emphasizes physical strength, adventurousness, emotional neutrality, certainty, control, assertiveness, self-reliance, individuality, competitiveness, skills, public knowledge, discipline, reason, objectivity and rationality- all things that are valued in our 'free-market' economies.

These attributes become important aspects of growing boys developing gender identities. With a narrowing of the emotional range allowed of our masculine heroes and a distancing from displays of tenderness, compassion and dependence being culturally prescribed for boys, it is no surprise that many boys grow up feeling isolated, misunderstood and with fathers with whom they wish to have closer relationships.

As growing boys absorb these masculine values, the absence of responsibility and the pursuit of self-gratification are then often bragged about in the adolescent playground (Where boys compete to drink the most pints and sleep with the most women etc.). The impact this masculine value system has on family and community life is, I think, profound. The Western free-market value system seems to have been designed for men. Men can follow the central goal of this 'look after number one' value system to its logical conclusion. Having brought children into the world, responsibility for child rearing and for maintaining family life then usually falls on the mother. If the going gets too tough then many fathers in the West choose to leave the family in order to have 'freedom' to pursue self-gratification, their sense social responsibility often disappearing with them. Guilt is often dealt with by displacing this through blaming the child's mother ("She tried to control me, wouldn't let me have my freedom") or their child ("he has chosen not to see me").

Although I should again remind the reader that everything I am arguing should be viewed with caution, I am simply exploring trends rather than trying to make unsupportable generalisations, the price I believe some boys may be paying for this 'masculinisation' of our culture is likely to be high in terms of their emotional well-being. Not only are some boys denied secure, stable and nurturing homes to whom they can feel the sense of loyalty that comes through belonging, but, in addition they are given a model of masculinity to aspire towards that devalues social responsibility, duty, love, and emotionally intimate relationships based on mutual dependency.

The institutions that work with children and parents reflect various aspects of this masculinized freedom/guilt dynamic. Schools in the United Kingdom have been colonised by free market managerial style, with the encouragement of greater competitiveness between schools and with each school's success being measured by the exam grades of their pupils. We see more and more winners and losers both for schools as a whole and for the individuals within them. You have to be pretty thick skinned to survive as a loser in this system without this affecting your view of yourself and your behaviour in some way.

Particular groups end up at particular risk. Thus many black and ethnic minority pupils in Western schools, feeling like humiliated 'loser' outsiders turn to a macho subculture that shows both defiance toward the authority of the system that is hurting them as well as embracing a culturally congruent solution that is 'hyper-masculine'- in other words a system that still relies on the values of free-market ideology and the pursuit of personal desires. For many working class boys the change in educational demands that has shifted toward an expectation that more and more pupils should go on to complete higher education degrees (reflecting the decline in manufacturing and a rise in demand for a more skilled labour force) has made experience of educational failure even more problematic, as many of the 'traditional' jobs for males, are no longer there.

Within a value system that promotes freedom to pursue your wishes/instincts a number of common escape routes are available to those who feel like they are the losers/failures/rejects of this culture. Within adolescent and increasingly younger childhood sub-culture there is a powerful culture of cruelty in existence. If you perceive yourself to be a failure within the school system then there are other ways to rebuild your sense of self worth and personal power such as a hyper-masculine sub-culture of cruelty that encourages you to seek gratification through alternative routes, including theft, drugs, alcohol and violence. This is often done through gangs (which operate like mini capitalist free-market cultures where those who can be the most self serving are to be most admired). These dynamics start in school where it has been found that those students who are most likely to develop an anti-school value system that includes asserting their masculinity through physical strength are boys who are failing academically.

Since the introduction of the national curriculum into United Kingdom schools the rate of children being excluded from schools has been raised at least six fold. The national curriculum introduced routine testing of children at various ages and the production of national league tables' that rate school performance as assessed by the academic performance in these tests of the children in their schools. The vast majority of children excluded are boys. Consequently, in this education free-market, where school examination performance is increasingly tied to reputation and recruitment, girls become a valuable and sought after resource. The belief in the perspective that girls are successful and boys are failing is reinforced by statistics on girls' achievement in all girl settings, across school type and across social class, which all show girls are consistently out-performing boys in the current exam system. As well as their lesser contribution to performance league tables, boys in general absorb the larger proportion of resources for additional support and special needs.

With boys becoming the more visible problem gender for schools it is likely that some of the behavioural problems displayed by boys in school settings reflects this problem/failure/disabled/naughty/stupid type labels being applied to them and their subsequent reaction to this.

Some critics have argued that traditional masculinity exists in a state of contradiction and crisis in which every new generation rediscovers the problem of young men. Others have argued that although models of masculinity are always changing there are specific historical times when a sense of crises and uncertainty about gender roles develops. In this respect, it is argued that modern, Western society is experiencing one of these disorientating, historical moments and what many boys are left feeling is a bitter sense of the pointlessness about what they do and the lack of social value and lack of positive attitude shown toward them. Culturally congruent alternative of an aggressive sub-culture of 'hyper-masculinity' can be seen as a strategy some boys use to fill in these despairing gaps.

Within male students, a sorting and sifting into an academic hierarchy increases the gap between 'failed' students and 'successful' students. Successful students construct their masculinity through an emphasis on rationality and are rewarded by social power giving them access to higher education and entry into higher status occupations. Failed students look to other sources of power and other ways of defining their masculinity- in other words other ways of being a man. Thus, sporting prowess, physical aggression and sexual conquest may become the avenues by which failed schoolboys find their sense self worth. A sub culture then develops where rejection of academic success is supported by a view of school and learning as an 'effeminate' activity to be rejected- real men don't care about school. An image of reluctant involvement is cultivated among many boys, resulting in many boys managing their academic careers carefully by avoiding an open commitment to work. In such schools where an anti-school masculinity has developed, boys who are openly committed to academic success, or who are poor at 'cussing' or who show their emotions easily, become targets for ridicule and bullying. Within these sub cultures boys are often very aware of their vulnerability, and try hard to live up to a more masculine 'laddishness'. Thus, some boys are caught in a conflict between defending themselves from their perceived failure in school at the same time as trying to gain the approval of the anti school peer group (characterised by one writer as the 'fighting, fucking and football' culture[40]).

Although this system may be a good training ground for many of the future participants in the capitalist, market economy, where it is desirable for individuals to be competitive, self seeking and able to use relationships for the purpose of manipulating others to serve their own needs, this leaves the problem of how to deal with the failures that this system inevitably produces.

Whilst you may feel, correctly, that the above arguments don't relate directly to ADHD, what I was hoping to illustrate, or at the very least to consider, are some of the reasons why some academics like myself feel that there is something of a cultural crises surrounding boys and boyhood. In this ADHD, as a diagnosis predominantly given to boys, may be a viewed as a bit like the proverbial 'canary in the mine', with the rising numbers being diagnosed with ADHD being a sign that should warn us that something is going wrong culturally that we need to examine, rather than being a sign that something has gone wrong in the brains of all these children with the diagnosis.

The Role Of Governments:

Some academics make the claim that as groups of children become the new dangerous classes then governments perceive that the task of bringing up children can longer be trusted to families, but has to be taken over by the state and its agencies. As a result there is a growing 'army' of professionals operating in the medical, psychological, educational and social sphere. These professionals essentially act on behalf of the state to maintain power of the state, often through the parent, by educating the parents, carers and other professionals about the professional's world view and are ultimately aiming to produce ways of living and thinking consistent with that of the dominant culture. Thus, it is argued that many professionals are themselves 'tricked' into thinking that the what they do is for the common good only and the means of achieving this common good is rational.

So, on the one hand children and their families are cultured through institutions such as media and education into high competitiveness, individualistic and low dependency beliefs and practices which produces winners and losers, and on the other hand the system deals with its guilt and anxiety through the development of 'cultural defence mechanisms' such as social services, child and adolescent mental health services and compulsory parenting classes which targets blame for failure and its consequences on individual children (who are then deemed disabled and suffering from a medical condition) or their parents (who are then deemed incompetent). We can only wonder about the cost to children's mental health and emotional well-being of this value system.

CHAPTER 5

Developing a multi-perspective approach

These days' children (particularly boys) are attracting psychiatric labels like ADHD, autism, aspergers and childhood depression, and receiving psychiatric drugs (often a cocktail of them) in ever-greater numbers. As I have outlined there are physical dangers for individual children in exposing them to potentially toxic side effects of drugs that maybe addictive and where there remains a black hole in our knowledge of the long term effects these drugs have on the developing brain. But there are also public health dangers, which though subtler, are just as real.

The emergence of these childhood psychiatric epidemics is, I believe, telling us something about what we in the West think of children. It's telling us that our idea of what makes a 'normal' childhood is narrowing. It's telling us that we are getting less tolerant of children's behaviours, thoughts and feelings. Instead of welcoming joyfully the diversity that children bring, we are demanding stricter conformity (at the same time as telling parents and teachers that traditional ways of achieving this are not allowed), and panicking when we feel our children are not conforming to these often contradictory societal expectations. Children are now put under intense, critical surveillance from the day they are born; by doctors, psychologists, social workers, teachers, in fact a whole army of professionals. We are told we have to do developmental checks from younger and younger ages to identify future psychiatric disorders.

In this chapter I wish to discuss how different theories and different systems of knowledge produce different consequences and how we might apply this understanding to the practical task of helping children and families without needing to use drugs. Although it is in the second half of this book that I present practical ideas on the how to do it this way, this concluding chapter of the first half of the book lays the ethical case for why to do it this way.

Thus in this chapter I discuss the importance of values and ethics. I do this at least partly through a personal account of how my developing ideas around what values should guide my practice, influences the focus of my approach. One of the things we learn in medicine is that our first duty is to do no harm. It is in this spirit that I am saying that we should do everything we can to avoid exposing children to drugs that we know can be harmful and where there is little evidence supporting their long-term effectiveness.

The Power Of Language:

Think of vacuum cleaner and you're likely to think 'Hoover'. Children nowadays know fast food brands by their logos but are unable to name most vegetables. Advertising 'burns' company names into your unconscious, like a farmer who brands their initials into animals using a hot poker. This then becomes as much a part of how we describe our world as country names and currency. How many in today's world could go shopping without thinking in terms of 'Nike', 'Gap', or 'Next'? What was the world of shopping like before they existed? When we buy trainers these days, do we buy them for their practical function or because it possesses a brand image. Furthermore, how far has the function of these trainers become primarily the brand image rather than their function as a particular sort of footwear? Indeed how far has the function of trainers become detached from that of protective footwear, and toward signifying your allegiance to a brand?

Language is a system of signs that reflects meaning like a mirror but can also create meaning like the light shining onto the mirror. As soon as I use words like 'mental health', 'mental illness' 'ADHD', I've entered a particular system of signs and constructed particular meanings, like the advertising billboard it comes to represent something more than just the word. What are the alternatives? Who benefits from this language? What are the implications of this system? How does this system influence our everyday thoughts, feelings, and actions?

All science develops in particular cultural conditions. As different disciplines develop their knowledge base, they move through a tunnel whose boundaries are partly the result of the social and political belief system of the societies in which they exist and partly the result of the history of that discipline. Members of the discipline often guard these boundaries jealously. The scientist working at the frontier of the discipline crawls up through this historical tunnel and sees only what is immediately ahead, blind to what is outside this tunnel. The boundaries of this tunnel are made up by a set of fundamental assumptions about the nature and purpose of the subject being studied and these assumptions are often derived from the social history of that discipline and the culture that allowed that discipline to develop.

Science, Bias, And Globalisation:

Putting science into its social and cultural context has allowed feminist thinkers to argue that because most scientists are male, masculine metaphors dominate much of the scientific analysis of reality. According to this view the dominant 'scientific' view on any subject focuses on 'masculine' matters such as the exploitation of nature and the stigmatization of motherhood. In this, 'scientific' beliefs have replaced religious ones as the new source of authority for patriarchal power. These unspoken and unconscious gender dynamics have then become ingrained into the history and belief system of modern, Western science. Science's masculine bias has usually favoured biological explanations for inequalities in factors such as gender, class and race. A masculine worldview emphasises controlling nature more than understanding and finding harmony with it. Masculine science rests heavily on linear thinking, quantification (measurement), and reductionism (trying to work out 'root' causes) in preference to the many other ways there are of obtaining and organizing information (such as interactive models).

Gender bias means that the knowledge we take for granted as being apparently objective is deeply influenced by masculine ideas and therefore can only ever be partial. The social position of the 'producer' of knowledge (in this case the scientist) affects how knowledge is constructed and investigated, thus all science can be thought of as having developed in a social field consisting of struggles, forces and relationships. These relationships determine what will be considered important problems, acceptable methods and correct knowledge that then govern the practices and results of that science.

Just as knowledge is constructed from a primarily masculine perspective so it is also constructed from a primarily Western cultural perspective. Thus psychiatric ideology and its system of classification reflect Western values. Western concepts of mental health tend to emphasise a focus on individualism, autonomy, scientific rationality, and consumerist orientations with a strong preference for using biological models and empirical methods (measurement) to build up the knowledge base. Such an approach to knowledge in mental health fits the economic interests of Western, market economies (for example, the pharmaceutical industry) as well as confirming to the knowledge producers (in this case the psychiatrists) the perceived cultural superiority of Western culture. As a result, mainstream psychiatric ideology assumes that Western definitions of good mental health are the standards by which to compare other cultures.

Similarly, class as a factor that influences our mental health and understanding of mental health has all but disappeared from psychiatric literature. The predominance of the middle classes amongst psychiatrists and therapists make it easier for them to ignore the psychological effects of living in more insecure social circumstances and also the strengths and resilience of working class communities, with the effects of class dynamics often trivialized or dismissed. Issues such as the increased incidence of 'mental illness' amongst those suffering adversity is usually put down to the biological effect of the illness causing the person to suffer greater adversity, despite considerable evidence that the reverse is also true, suggesting that more interactive models would take theory and practice further and that psychiatrists need to understand and have ideas on how to tackle the politics of social inequality.

The result of all of this class, culture and gender dynamics, is that the dominant professional mental health theories and practices promote a masculine, white, Western, middle class, heterosexual view of the world, and other systems of potentially helpful knowledge are marginalized.

On a global scale the problems go deeper. Since the end of the cold war Western civilization has been in a triumphant mood with some even suggesting 'the end of history' has occurred with the accompanying belief that all countries will have to embrace and accept Western capitalist democracies. A number of developments since then, such as global terrorism, the anti-globalisation movement, and the increasingly popular environmental campaigns and 'sustainable' development, all suggest this conclusion to be pre-mature.

Western neo-liberal democracy has at its heart a political project, which is that of the homogenization of the rest of the world- in other words it wants the rest of the world to copy Western society. The developing world is told to open their countries to 'free' markets, thus allowing multi-nationals to grow and develop a power base that crosses political boundaries to the extent that many 'brands'(representing multi-national corporations) are now more powerful than governments.

The global, political aims of the West are simply unrealizable. The extension of the Western way of life with its huge appetite for consumerism, to the six billion plus inhabitants of the planet runs into ecological obstacles. The people of the world could not benefit from the high standards of living seen in the West without gigantic transformations at every level that would require us, particularly in the West, to make significant sacrifices to our standards (materially) of living. The present Western value system based around free markets has absolutely no chance of equalizing the economic conditions in which different people live. Four centuries of capitalist expansion has already demonstrated this fact. The last half a century, during which the ideology of development (based on a Western vision of what development means) has not brought about even the smallest reduction of the North/South divide, rather the opposite.

Likewise, the wholesale export of Western concepts of childhood and childrearing (and their problems) will not work for other cultures. What we need instead of the colonial export of Western ideology is a more productive exchange of knowledge and ideology that is likely to bring benefits to both North and South.

The value system of current mainstream child and adolescent mental health theory and practice is in danger, I believe, of having a deeply negative impact on societies around the world and arguably on the world as a whole. Psychiatry's status and power as a professional group, means that, through popularizing the idea that up to 20% of children have a brain disorder called ADHD, we are actively changing the way childhood and its problems are viewed. By divorcing children from their context and stifling diversity through insistence on narrow, biomedical models, our cultural expectations of children have been transformed (in my opinion for the worse).

Developing A Value System:

It is not my place to provide a prescription of what values you should hold, only to get you to think about it.

For my part, as I have moved away from holding on to the exclusively Western, middle class, masculine ideologies I was trained with, I have turned toward post-modern philosophy and non-Western psychologies. Eastern psychologies are less concerned with mind body splits and more with concepts such as mindfulness, balance and harmony. Eastern cultures have, in my view, a more mature attitude to the nature of our existence. They reflect on the sacredness of our relationships to each other, to the earth and indeed to the universe. In contrast, Western culture revolves around power, control, wants of the individual and conquest (for example, of nature) at the expense of an interest in relationships. With global warming, we are now paying the cost of our wish to tame nature and focus on matter as a thing rather than a dynamic.

My value system means that I can no longer collude with what I see as the West's cultural hostility and ambivalence towards children. Western values of freedom and looking after number one, together with an economic system that demands mobility has led to a breakdown of family ties resulting in separations, divorce, absent fathers and the death of the extended family. Likewise, local communities have become dispirited and fractured, leading to a loss of good social support networks. Despite many non-Western cultures suffering from similar problems, the values of duty and responsibility that override those of individual aims and self-gratification has helped keep extended families and local communities together (despite the often negative impact of globalisation) giving a much more secure base for children to grow up in.

One of the most hopeful things I have gained from re-evaluating my stance toward psychiatry and psychotherapy is the importance of noticing and amplifying people's strengths. By sticking to the dominant model of focusing on illness and 'what's wrong', we lose our chance to discover everyone's strengths and abilities, and become unnecessarily dependent on 'experts' to sort out the problems that life inevitably throws at us. In other words we distance people from their own knowledge, their own ways of solving problems because we wrongly believe that the professionals' technical knowledge must be superior.

Professionally I can no longer subscribe to a value system that (as enshrined in the application of a traditional medical model to mental health) privileges notions of deficit and pathology. Professor Kenneth Gergen puts the problem like this "*The vocabulary of human deficit has undergone enormous expansion within the present century [last century]. We have countless ways of locating faults within ourselves and others that were unavailable to even our great-grandfathers.*"[41] Or as professor Thomas Szasz states, the impact on personal identity of the practice of pathologizing is most obvious in that of psychiatric diagnoses; "*The diagnostic label imparts a defective personal identity to the patient; it will henceforth identify him to others and govern their conduct toward him, and his toward them. The psychiatric nosologist thus not only describes his patient's so-called illness, but also prescribes his future conduct*".[42] Some have called this labelling process 'therapeutic violence' to patients who then experience the debilitating effects of diagnostic labels in terms of self-blame, self-loathing and intense self-monitoring[43].

I carry values of duty and responsibility into my work. I am no longer interested in how to classify children's behaviour, but am more interested in understanding children's context and how to help families develop their relationships more positively. I value diversity. This allows me to find genuinely positive aspects about the vast majority of clients and families I see. Of course, I do see families where there is an issue of persistent rejection or other forms of maltreatment that need to be confronted. However, my attitude and belief is that the vast majority of families I see are there because of a genuine concern from a parent(s) or carer(s) about their child and as a result this is indeed what I find.

Celebrating diversity does not mean condoning anti-social behaviour. Indeed, on this score I again look to non-Western cultures where expectations with regards social behaviour are lower during the early years but often higher following this, when compared to Western culture, with greater expectation of a community responsibility to provide firm discipline. In my opinion, much of popular Western culture has increasingly shied away from the question of enforcing effective discipline. We have competing arguments, one telling us that children are not given enough boundaries, the other that adults are routinely abusing and violating children's rights by smacking them or being too harsh on them in other ways. Both of these beliefs are, in my opinion, unhelpful. The 'Children's rights' movement can be accused of distorting power relationships within the family and thus inadvertently undermining parents. Smart children understand this and may unjustly complain to teachers or the police about their parents, resulting in further undermining of parents' authority. We need to understand parents' intentions before judging their actions. Sometimes parents' actions are making the situation worse (just as professionals' actions may make the situation worse) despite the best intentions. I believe we should support parents in finding effective ways to enforce discipline in their children using their own parental value system providing there is a good level of security and love for that child in their family.

When dealing with problems of children's behaviour, I believe we need to see the whole picture. For example, school life is a very important part of a child's growing years, given the amount of time she/he will spend there. There has been an on-going debate within education about school environments and educational programmes and how good they are for boys or girls. Feminist perspectives influenced education in Western schools of the past couple of decades, which led to the introduction of alternative and non-sexist images into teaching. More recently, however, the growing concern is about boys' failure, leading men's rights movements to describe schools as 'feminine' institutions because of day to day practices that favour girls, low expectations of boys, the absence of male role models and a curriculum that favours girls learning style. Evidence that backs this up, shows that girls prefer open-ended tasks that are related to real situations (as is popular in current school curricula), whereas boys prefer memorization of rules and abstract facts.

'Making sense' is a social process; it is an activity that is always situated within a cultural and historical framework. Through their social interactions with adults' children create accounts of their lives that become their world view- a sort of social map of the world. When adults bring attention to children's failures and the ways they don't measure up to educational and/or behavioural expectations, children then enter into a worldview and 'self-narrative' of incompetence. The impact this then has on our every-day ideas of childhood, boyhood, parenthood and mother-boy relationships in particular, are very powerful. As doctors/therapists we can strengthen these ideas or practice with a value system that challenges it.

As I have tried to show, Western culture has an individualist orientation to selfhood. For me however, the metaphor of 'connection' is a better one than the metaphor of 'separation/individuation' (so prevalent in the psychotherapy literature), particularly in relation to the experiences of marginalized groups such as women, children, and ethnic minorities. I strive to place a positive value on caring and concern for others. Paradoxically, even this metaphor can become problematic when mothers are influenced by the belief that they are only valuable through the extent to which they show concern for others. 'Looking after number one' is then viewed as pathological when a woman does it, with men who do it seemingly praised by peers for their 'laddishness'. Similarly men who show an attitude that places the family/group interests over their individual ones are often seen as somehow 'special' or worthy of the sort of extra praise that a women who carries such a sense of social responsibility rarely receives.

The metaphor of separation/individuation may also support depression in mothers. Parents can fall victim to parent blaming (particularly mother blaming) if they do not push their children to becoming independent. Boys may be particularly aware of their ambivalent position with regards 'connection' in Western society and internalize the cultural messages that say <u>'boys don't cry' and 'don't be a mummy's boy/sissy'</u>. Thus boys may be particularly vulnerable to the powerful effects of a culture that invites them and their parents to stigmatize feelings of dependence, belonging and connection. In my work I do give value to the desire for autonomy and separation/individuation in certain circumstance but also value children feeling connected to their families. This does not mean that there are no situations in which a close loving relationship between a parent and child becomes part of the problem- indeed there are. But changing what I view as important and meaningful has resulted in shifting my gaze in a new direction, and finding a new position from which to discover a 'balance' on this issue.

Striving toward a way of practicing that challenges the notion that professional knowledge is the 'truth', or at least a good reflection of it, means finding new ways of conceptualizing clinical problems.

The claim that there is no politically or socially neutral, objective way of giving meaning to a psychiatric problem, is not the same as saying there is no way to find solutions to these problems. On the contrary, by being mindful of our value system we can through conversation and discussion arrive at pragmatically helpful ways forward that is not dependent on pre-existing concrete therapist/doctor derived notions of normality, progress and good outcome. This value challenges the notion of the doctor/therapist as the ultimate or only arbiter of the therapeutic process.

We can start importing some of the value systems of developing world cultures, value systems that have served their children probably better than Western ones. Childhood, motherhood and fatherhood can begin to be understood as having a central place in social and economic arrangements. Connection to each other rather than power, control and mastery can become guiding principles. Macho working practices can be challenged as bad for society. Free market thinking as a value system can be challenged as bad for society. We can promote Eastern ideals such as balance and harmony, such as learning to live with sequential rhythms of life that takes you through light and darkness, through suffering and joy, through humiliation and mastery. Governments' ideas on education can be challenged to provide more boy-friendly activity-based curricula and to enforce discipline without the use of medical labels or washing of hands from the problem through exclusion. Doctors can be challenged to stop their addiction to medical labels and drug prescriptions. Parents can be urged to challenge such stigmatizing practice and to insist on non-drug based solutions. The cultural resistance of objectors can be fostered. Our professional trainings and mental health services can be challenged; there needs to be debate, openness and transparency.

The voice of protest (despite the overwhelming odds against it) can make itself heard however dimly. For medical professionals like myself to carry on blindly colluding with the instutionalization of our cultural hostility toward children is simply not acceptable.

Sami Timimi

PART 2

PRACTICAL ALTERNATIVES TO DRUGS

Sami Timimi

Chapter 6

On using this section

In the first section of the book I provided an overview of current thinking in ADHD and the various challenges to this. I hope that has helped you think about some of the problems you may be experiencing in a different way and helped you see some of the 'big picture' dynamics. In this section I will present a collection of ideas and strategies that come from a variety of different and well established perspectives, which you might find helpful to use with your child, children, or family more generally. I will discuss a variety of different approaches in the knowledge that different things work for different people. You will have realised by now that I do not believe that a <u>'one size fits all' approach is either necessary or useful</u>. Therefore, the ideas and strategies contained in this section try to examine different aspects of a child's and family's lives that could be changed. It may prove helpful for all the aspects I cover to change or it may be that only one of them needs to change for you to make a positive difference in your children's lives.

Of course this book can't cover every unique problem. For example, it may be that your child has a physical condition that needs accurate diagnosis and treatment. A wide variety of physical conditions can present with similar behaviours to those described for ADHD (in other words, impulsivity, poor attention, restlessness and hyperactivity). These include conditions such as hypothyroidism, anaemia, hearing impairment or a visual impairment, petit mal epilepsy and a number of long lasting conditions which can cause a general discomfort to the child and which may present as a poor behaviour such constipation, asthma, eczema and celiac disease. Things in general to look out for in excluding a diagnosable physical include: changes in your child's behaviour and personality (which might indicate the onset of a medical problem), and the presence of other physical symptoms (such as a recurrent skin problems, recurrent infections, frequent diarrhoea, shortness of breath and so on). Most of these conditions can be diagnosed with relatively simple blood or other tests together with good history taking from a doctor. Therefore, if you are concerned about your child having a physical condition please consult with your doctor.

There are also circumstances where some children and/or their families may require more intensive psychotherapy. For example, there may have been a history of sexual abuse or other forms of abuse (in either your child or his/her parents) and other traumatic experiences (such as domestic violence) whose effects may require help from an experienced and competent therapist. There is much research that has established a clear link between children experiencing traumatic experiences and them then displaying ADHD type behaviours. Whilst finding a good therapist to help with this can be difficult, if this is your situation and your child is diagnosed with ADHD and you are offered treatment with drugs, my advise is to politely turn this down as this may do no more than mask the problem that needs to be addressed.

There are other more common family issues that this book should be able to help with, but some families may also need some extra professional help as well. For example, ongoing conflict between parents will make a consistent approach to a problem more difficult to achieve, will give opportunities for your children to play one off against the other, and can lead to children feeling insecure and unhappy with home life which in turn often leads to behavioural problems in the children. Of course if you are often in conflict with each other this also provides children with a model of how to deal with different opinions and if you, as parents, stubbornly refuse to listen to each other, you should not be surprised if your children stubbornly refuse to listen to you!

I am not saying that differences of opinion between parents are unhealthy or that parents should never argue in front of their children. Differences of opinion are healthy, however, it is the ability to show that you can find a way to resolve them, as well as showing that arguments from time to time between people who are committed to each other are a normal part of relationships, that makes the difference between healthy conflicts and unhealthy ones. If such conflicts are occurring continuously and there is a break down of the parents' relationship, this is more likely to cause harm to children and whilst this book may be able to help with some of the problems you are experiencing with your children if this is your situation (particularly if both of you are willing to give some of the ideas in this book a go) it may be that you first need to seek some help for yourselves to improve your relationship and your ability to work together as parents.

Some similar comments could also be made if you are separated or if you are living in a 'reconstituted family' (in other words families with step parents). These families have their own particular dynamics which you need to bear in mind when using this book. For example, in reconstituted families it is usual for the relationship between the biological parent and their biological children to be more intense than in ordinary, nuclear families. This is because a parent may feel guilty about the effects that the break up of the biological parent's relationship has had on their children, at the same time as their children may have turned to them for reassurance and comfort whilst going through the difficult period surrounding the break up of their original family. At the same time, the step parent may find it difficult to develop a close emotional bond with her/his new partner's children, partly because they have missed out on the emotional bonding phase that happens early in a child's life and partly because the new children may reject the new partner as a poor replacement for the one they have lost. Step children often also target some of their, inevitable, anger at that new step parent. Add to that cocktail, the powerful emotions commonly associated with a grieving reaction which are frequently present following the break up of even the most fragile families, resulting in feelings of sadness, despair, anger, hopelessness, fear, and insecurity and one can see that considerable psychological skills are required in order to be able to negotiate your way through the emotional maze that reconstituted families often present.

Having said all of this, I have been repeatedly surprised and impressed by the resilience, creativity and resources that the families I see in my clinical work show in the face of very difficult circumstances. I am often pleasantly surprised by the ability of individuals and families, even those who appear to be in the most desperate situations, to find solutions that work for them and make meaningful differences to their lives. Indeed, it has become very rare for me these days to have to carry out prolonged and in depth therapeutic work with most of the children and families I see. Sometimes it is simply a matter of helping people re-examine their own expectations of what is reasonable for them to expect from their children. Sometimes it is putting in new strategies to change children's behaviour, sometimes it is changing diets and sometimes it is understanding the emotional dynamics within the family and changing these. The principles, on which these successful approaches are based, are outlined in these chapters so I am confident that, whether you will need extra professional help or not, you should find something of use and value to you in the following pages.

How To Use This Section:

I have structured this section of the book to be read in sequence, almost as if you were attending a weekly or fortnightly appointment. Chapter 7 discusses some of the common pitfalls which are worth keeping in mind as you go through the subsequent chapters, which give the practical suggestions. Whilst I expect that at least some of you will be too curious to stick to it as a week by week course, it is my belief that if you concentrate on one thing at a time it is much more likely to yield results than trying to do all of the things at the same time. Consequently, by all means go ahead and read this in what ever order you like and as fast or as slow as you would like, but whatever you decide to do, bear in mind that maximising your chances of success is going to happen through trying one thing at a time and concentrating on one area at a time and gradually building up from there.

It is also worth bearing in mind the importance of being patient. This is because, although most of these areas are likely to bring some improvements, it is quite possible that only one of these areas is going to make a major difference to you and your children's particular situation and therefore please persevere with the suggestions before deciding the approach of this book is not for you.

It goes without saying that the biggest factor by far in the success or failure of using this book is going to be the amount of effort you are prepared to put into implementing the suggested interventions. There are no magic bullets, and as much as most of us would like life to be made much easier, with a simple, safe and effective pill that we and our children could take to smooth away life's ups and downs, the reality is (as I have indicated in the first section) that there is no such thing. In that respect, what I have discovered repeatedly through clinical experience is that the families who get the most out of the approaches I use are the families who are prepared to put the most into it.

Finally, I would like to encourage you to be open, honest and self-reflective. Whilst you should trust in yourself and your own knowledge, beware of the temptation to try and change others (like your husband or wife), it is always easier than looking at ourselves and taking responsibility to change what we do.

Chapter 7

Common pitfalls

The two most common pitfalls that I experience in my clinical work are:
1. Giving up on an intervention too quickly, and
2. Allowing hopelessness to seep in when the inevitable setback occurs.

Giving Up Too Quickly:

It is important that you make a commitment to see through whatever intervention or strategy you have decided to try and not give up on the strategy if you feel that you are not getting anywhere after a few days or a few weeks. In each section I will explain how long you should try before you can expect changes. This is particularly so for food supplements where you may have to wait for as long as two or three months whilst the supplement is working repairing and improving the functioning of cells before changes are observed. With some of the interventions like the behavioural interventions, the use of negative consequences for unwanted behaviour usually means that unwanted behaviours actually get worse before they start to improve. This is because if you are putting boundaries around negative behaviour and the child does not like this, then they may feel they have to go even further than usual in their negative behaviour in order to get you to give in.

Becoming Hopeless Following A Setback:

The other common pitfall is to do with setbacks. Setbacks are an inevitable part of any recovery process. There are many reasons why people experience setbacks. This can include the normal ups and downs of life, 'taking your eye off the ball' resulting in a slackening off of the strategies that you were using, and upsetting experiences that cause deterioration in behaviour. Whatever the reason, setbacks are so common that they inevitably occur at some point. What often happens when a setback occurs is that parents, the child, the teacher (or whoever it is effecting) feel demoralised, and think something like "what was the point of all of the things that we just did as we are back at square one now". At this point, hopelessness creeps in and with it a sense of failure and a loss of confidence in the ability to bring about lasting change. When the inevitable setback occurs, therefore, it is important to remember that your reaction of demoralisation and despair are perfectly normal, that what is happening is what usually happens and that, far from being back at square one, whatever improvement had occurred is a fact that cannot be taken away. If there has been a period of improved behaviour then this means you have already learnt new skills. These skills will help you deal with new situations and setbacks as they arrive. When the inevitable setback occurs have a think about what might be happening, talk to someone close about them, and return to those strategies that have been successful in the past, or adjust them to suit better the new circumstances.

Although the above are the two most common and troublesome setbacks there are others worth keeping in mind. These include unrealistic expectations, lack of commitment to the strategies, inconsistent application of the strategies, guilt and other emotional obstacles, unresolved marital/parental relationships, 'scapegoating', cross generational alliances, not using the strategies for all your children, poor bonding and hostility towards the child, the anger—guilt—reparation cycle, inadvertently supporting the creation of a 'safe zone' (over-protection), fear of change, lack of support, lack of time, and unresolved trauma. I will now discuss each of these briefly:

Unrealistic Expectations:

If we have unrealistic expectations of our children's behaviour, then we will continue to feel disappointed with them. Your disappointment may be felt by your child through the various ways your frustration and disappointment is shown. This can include negative comments towards your child about them. In addition, the emotional upset your disappointment may cause you is often noticed by children. A difficult question to answer is "how do I know if my expectations are unreasonable?" Of course, this is never going to be a straightforward question with a straightforward answer, and will vary from individual to individual. Our relationships are always multi-dimensional and there are always likely to be bits of our expectations (in any relationship, not just with our children) that are a mixture of reasonable and unreasonable. In helping you try and 'unpack' whether there are particular areas of unreasonable expectation that may be hindering your relationship with your children here are a few things to consider:

- Are you expecting your child to stop expressing their emotions? The emotion we find hardest as parents is that of anger. Anger, however, is a strong and, indeed, energising emotion. It can be unhealthy to suppress it. What would be better to try and achieve is helping our children to find ways to express anger in a way that is not going to harm people around them. This is hard for any adult to do, let only children (I'm sure a moment's reflection will confirm this). Therefore, whilst becoming calm, having total control over anger, and not getting angry is an unreasonable expectation, encouraging your child to express anger (and other emotions) in ways that are non-harmful to others, is a reasonable expectation. Note how well you yourself are able to control anger and whether at times you are expecting your child to do something you find difficult. This can be a good guide as to whether your expectations are unreasonable.

- Are you expecting to get rid of negative emotion? Whilst it is a reasonable expectation and, indeed I would argue, a vital necessity, to have a relationship with your child which is underpinned by positive emotion and love towards them, it is unreasonable to expect an absence of negative feelings, such as anger, hostility and, indeed, shame in that relationship. A mixture of positive and negative feelings is present in any meaningful relationship and the presence of negative feelings does not mean your relationship is in trouble. It is very common for children when they are angry and upset with you to say 'nasty' things about you or themselves such as "you are the worst mummy/daddy in the world" or "I wish I was never born".
- Can you separate behaviour which is the result of poor comprehension or misunderstanding from that which is simply due to disobedience? Questions to ask here are: does your child have a particular learning disability, or has your child not been listening to your instructions (for example, have you been getting them to repeat what you say to insure that they have understood what you are asking). If your child does not understand your instructions, then they cannot follow through

what you are asking of them. Over long periods this may become a source of frustration and unfulfilled expectations.
- Are you expecting a boy to stop being boisterous? Boys and girls are different. Fathers may find it hard to relate to girl's behaviour and mothers may find it hard to relate to typical boy behaviour. The latter one is particularly relevant in ADHD as it is a diagnosis given mainly to boys. Boys, as I have mentioned before, are naturally more impulsive, physically active, and aggressive than girls. Of course, this does not mean that all boys are like this or that all girls aren't. However, if you are trying to eliminate the impulsiveness, levels of activity and aggression of some children who are naturally more boisterous, then you will be likely to feel disappointed. This is just part of the natural personality traits of many children, particularly boys, and, as I have mentioned previously, these are all personality traits that can be to that child's advantage in later life.

Inconsistency:

Most parents know about this but it is worth restating. Children are often clever enough to spot opportunities to further their own desires. If mum tells their child they are not allowed to, lets say, meet their friend because they have misbehaved, then it is a common strategy for them to go to the other parent and ask them if they can go and see their friend, particularly if they know that this dad is more likely to say yes. Therefore, before trying to apply any of the strategies in this book please ask your partner or any other person who is important and involved in the care of your child to also read this book, or at least discuss what you're doing with them. Discuss any strategies you are thinking of implementing with them to make sure that you are in agreement and that you will support each other and back each other up as you work through your problems. Of course 100% consistency is very rare and a degree of inconsistency is part of life, indeed, it would be very boring if all our relationships existed with people who were just like us (as much as sometimes we wish this in fantasy)! This brings me to my next common pitfall.

Unresolved Parental Relationship Difficulties:

If there are unresolved difficulties of a serious nature between parents and/or carers of the child (whether they are together or separated) then this will often show themselves through the behaviour of their children. This is where issues such inconsistency can become a potentially serious obstacle to progress. Furthermore, it is not just serious, unresolved difficulties between parents, but also between you and others involved extensively in the care of that child, for example an unresolved difficulty between a parent and a grandparent who also does a lot of caring for the child. Although it is beyond the scope of this book to deal with all the different types of problems that carers may have in their relationships with each other, the key to establishing working solutions to these types of problems is for decisions to rest with the immediate parents or carers of the child, communication, and compromise.

In a situation where the parental couple have separated it is vital to put any continuing animosity towards one another to one side, to keep the child out of any arguments, and not use the child in any way as a tool to express hostility towards a partner. Sometimes when there are disputes in the parental relationship, parents may recruit one of their children as an ally against the other. This can happen whether the parents are still together or separated. In this situation the parent will say negative things about the other parent to their child, which can result in split loyalties for the child. In this situation you should try to arrive at business like agreements on what common strategies to use and what ways of communicating with each other about the child that there will be. This may require a third party (an outsider to the relationship) to help you negotiate this, whether this be a professional or a trusted acquaintance.

I have sometimes heard it said in my clinical sessions that it is the child's behaviour that has caused the marriage to split or problems in the parent's relationship. Whilst I accept that some behaviour problems make parents feel ill, I think that such a conclusion should be avoided. As parents we have, and should have, a more powerful position in the relationship with our children. In typical family systems, the parents should be in charge- they have to be the boss. With this power comes responsibility. In the same way that we, as parents, are trying to teach our children to take responsibility for their behaviour, we too have to take responsibility for our actions and decisions. Not only is it unreasonable to pass the burden on to our children through blaming them for causing any difficulties we are experiencing in our parental relationships, but also expecting to solve our parental relationships by getting rid of behaviours which we don't want to see in our children, sets everyone up for failure. Its also worth keeping in mind that sometimes children misbehave as a (unconscious) way of keeping parents together when there is a fear that they may separate (as parents then focus their attention on the problems that the child is having rather than on the problems between themselves).

Unresolved Issues From Your Own Childhood:

All parents were children once, and I certainly know from my clinical experience that many parents I see had difficult childhoods or are carrying issues from their past that, for whatever reason, remain unresolved. By itself this is not a reason why any of the suggestions in this book would not work however; it is worth reflecting on this, as it may help you identify emotional obstacles that prevent you from carrying out strategies that may prove to be effective. For example, if you had a poor relationship with your parents, you may, once you became a parent yourself, have decided that you were going to make sure your children never grow up to have the same poor image of you, that you had of your parents. This may, without you necessarily realising this, have led you to avoid 'upsetting' your children, because of a fear that this will lead them to hate you (which is the very thing you're trying to avoid). In turn this means that you might get stuck when it comes to strategies (like some of the strategies in the consequences chapter) that involve being able to tolerate upsetting your children and them saying horrible things like they 'hate you'. Search within yourself to try and identify whether your own childhood experiences may make some things difficult because of the emotions they provoke. Ask yourself some questions like: Do I feel my parents loved and valued me? Were my parents interested in me and did they take me seriously? Did my parents show encouragement and support? Did my parents set a good role model for me? Did my parents give me boundaries and encourage me to take responsibility for my actions? Did other things happen outside the family that had a major impact on my childhood, for the better or worse? Once you've reflected on these questions ask yourself if you (or other people) have notice that you act just like your mum or dad? If not have you gone to the other extreme in an effort to be the opposite of your mum or dad?

Scapegoating:

I often liken families to a drama or play. In most families we find that, over time, people establish their role and position in that family. It is as if we each have a script and for the family system to function everybody has a different script and always uses their own particular script or role in that play. Upset is created in a family if somebody steps out of their usual script as everyone else then becomes unsure of what their lines are. This seems to be true whether a family has got a good, well functioning script or a terrible and problematic one. This is where the phenomena of 'scapegoating' can happen without anyone being aware that that's what is going on. There is a humorous example of this in a series of children's books that my children have enjoyed for some years. The books are about a boy called *Horrid Henry*, who is always badly behaved. *Horrid Henry* has a brother who is called *Perfect Peter* because he is, in contrast to *Horrid Henry*, always so well behaved. The script in this particular family is that *Horrid Henry* is always naughty and gets told off and *Perfect Peter* is always, in contrast to this, good and used to being told good things about his behaviour. Generally, of course, both children live up to these expectations. In this particular story *Horrid Henry* decided not to follow his usual 'script' and to try his best to be good for the day. As the day goes on *Perfect Peter* finds it harder and harder to cope with the fact that *Horrid Henry* is not being told off. *Perfect Peter* finds this change of script very difficult. As the day wears on *Perfect Peter* tries to keep provoking *Horrid Henry* into being 'nasty' towards him (an attempt if you like to return this family to its usual 'script'). *Horrid Henry* refuses to rise to the bait as he is being good that day and eventually *Perfect Peter* is so frustrated by this he ends up doing something very obviously naughty so that he ends up being told off and *Horrid Henry* praised.

This story is certainly familiar for many families where there tends to be one sibling who is the 'naughty' one. However, if it becomes another sibling's turn to be the naughty one, then the sibling who is usually naughty often becomes good. So it is useful to ask yourself whether the child you are most concerned about is playing the part of the 'naughty' child in the family system and this has become his or her script. As you might find in many school playgrounds, other siblings may use various strategies (such as winding them up, or always telling on them) to keep them in that familiar role. If you think this may be the case then keep a keen eye out for how other siblings may be provoking the one you are most concerned about to stay in the role of the 'naughty' one, and put in some negative consequences for that provocative behaviour.

The Anger-guilt-reparation Cycle:

See if you recognise this pattern. You are infuriated with your child's behaviour and in your anger you scold him or her and impose some sort of punishment. Later you calm down and feel guilty for what you have done and so feel you have acted unfairly and that your punishments where unduly harsh. As a result you try to repair some of the damage that you feel you have done in your anger and therefore give the child that you have felt you have treated badly some sort of treat, essentially to make yourself feel better. It is worth noting here that this cycle can also occur in your children, who may similarly go through an anger-guilt-reparation cycle. Whilst, in itself, this is a perfectly normal and, in some ways, a healthy thing to be able to do, it can become a problem when this becomes the usual pattern with which conflicts with your child are dealt with and the way in which consequences are imposed. The child learns that any consequences imposed may be withdrawn and, indeed, may be followed by some sort of reward, thus, commonly behaviour deteriorates again after the special treat, you feel furious with the child again for not responding positively to your 'treat' and you go back into the anger-guilt-reparation cycle.

If you recognise this cycle, then my advice is that you have ready to hand, simple consequences that you know you will be able to stick to (see chapter 10), and if you feel that your behaviour towards your child when you are angry was unacceptable, then the healthy way to do the 'reparation' is to make a sincere apology to your child explaining carefully what aspects of your behaviour towards the child you felt was unacceptable, but not minimising whatever behaviour you felt was unacceptable from your child. By doing this, you are also modelling the ability to take responsibility for our behaviour.

Not Using The Strategies For All Of Your Children:

Whilst some of the strategies suggested may be specific to one of your children with whom you are having difficulties (for example, some dietary interventions), others should be used for all of your children (such as behavioural consequences strategies) as otherwise you risk the child with the problems feeling that they are being unfairly picked on.

Hostility Towards Your Child:

In some situations the predominant feeling towards your child may have become that of hostility, rejection and anger (in other words a predominantly negative and rejecting emotion towards your child). There are many reasons why this may have become so. Maybe you had an unhappy childhood and the behaviours of your child remind you of painful, unhappy things in your own childhood- things that you are trying to forget. It could be that your child's behaviour reminds of you of an unhappy and painful relationship in your adult life, such as a child reminds you of his or her father who was aggressive and bullying towards you. Or it may be that years of difficulty with your child's behaviour have 'soured' your relationship with your child.

Whatever the reason, if there is a predominantly negative and hostile set of feelings towards your child, it is highly likely that your child will know this and feel insecure in their relationship with you. This can have many consequences. The child can come to view themselves as bad, unlovable, or unlikeable, resulting in poor behaviour. At the same time, because you have mainly negative feelings towards this child, it will become increasingly difficult to come to notice positive aspects of your child and so your attention will be routinely drawn to those things that confirm your negative view of your child. This can quickly become a mutually reinforcing, negative cycle- in other words, your child feels rejected and becomes angry and poorly behaved, and thus confirming your negative impression of your child, leading to you having hostile and rejecting feelings to them, and so on. If you recognise this situation then use the strategies in this book but pay particular attention to finding opportunities to build a more positive relationship and a more loving relationship with your child, making a particular effort to start noticing the positives.

Inadvertently Supporting The Creation Of A 'Safe Zone':

We are exposed to constant messages telling us how dangerous the outside world is, particularly for children. It is a very normal response to then try to protect our children as much as we can from exposure to unpleasant and traumatic experiences such as bullying and drug abuse. The result has been something that some call 'the domestication of children', where it has been observed that children are increasingly confined to the home environment or indoor settings at school where their behaviour and actions can be monitored much more closely. This desire to wrap our children in cotton wool and protect them from the dangers of the world 'out there', is completely understandable, but not necessarily very helpful in allowing children to develop the 'resilience' that they may need to cope with the reality of the world they find themselves in. Learn to let your children go and cope with the anxiety it causes you (see chapter 8).

Fear Of Change:

As I mentioned above under scapegoating, families have a tendency towards repeating a particular script where everybody has their own role (whether people like their role or not). When somebody starts changing their role it challenges the whole family script, leaving other individuals in the family feeling uncertain about how the new script works. In these circumstances there is a natural tendency to want to return back to the familiar script (even unhappy ones – it is a kind of 'better the devil you know than the devil you don't'). It is a familiar experience for many of us in clinical practice that with some families the advice given is not acted upon by them – or only half-heartedly or incompletely acted upon. There are many reasons for this including some of the ones outlined above. However, one important reason worth thinking about is whether you fear change. This can be change in how you think, what you do, how you manage time in your family's lifestyles, in personal ambitions and so on. Change always includes a certain amount of anxiety and fear of the unknown, not just for the individual but also the other family members as the usual 'family script' is disturbed. Be aware of this and embrace the excitement that can accompany reaching into the unknown and the new possibilities for your life that may be opened up by this.

Lack of Support:

As the old African saying reminds us 'it takes a village to raise a child'. Life as a parent seems harder than ever these days, not only are there higher expectations with regards our children's behaviour and a close watch kept on our behaviour as parents by various agencies of the state, but also our family and community support networks have dwindled. Raising children demands a lot from us, both physically and mentally and given the pressures on us to behave in particular ways as parents, more than ever we now need trusted partners, friends and other family members to provide us with both emotional and practical support to share the burden of responsibility. I discuss social support further in chapter 11.

Lack Of Time:

Another feature of modern life is how busy and time stretched we are. Working hours have increased over the past few decades and it is the norm now in two parent households for both parents to work. When we are not working we are often busy trying to complete the necessary household chores, like cleaning and shopping, leaving less and less time for us to spend with our children and to give them the sort of attention they need. With trying to complete so many things with such little time we have more and more reasons to feel stressed.

This pattern may have been less of a problem in times gone by and in other cultures, where children grew up surrounded by other children. Having regular, easily available playmates (as I did as a child growing up in Iraq) means that there is less need for the adults to be available as the providers of fun time. Sadly, the way our culture in the West has developed means that a decrease in the amount of time parents are spending in their families is coinciding with the increasing domestication of children (in other words children increasingly being confined to places where there is constant adult supervision, such as schools, clubs and home, due to the fears I mentioned above). I deal further with the issues of time for family life in chapter 11.

Unresolved Trauma:

As I discussed in chapter 4, sometimes being exposed to trauma can cause very similar symptoms to ADHD. I am using the term trauma here in a very general way to refer to painful experiences that a child has suffered. These include child abuse, witnessing domestic violence, parental separation and severe bullying. Traumatic experiences can leave a child preoccupied with issues such as their own personal safety, the safety of others they care about, what is going to happen to them and their family, and coping with certain things that may remind them of their traumatic experience.

Of course, everybody reacts differently to trauma and each particular person's circumstances have different features. For some trauma may lead them to feel preoccupied, constantly worrying about their safety and the safety of others and therefore they will present with poor concentration and matters such as school work will be of limited importance to them. Others may have developed the psychological defence of 'being on the go', that is by constantly doing things it keeps their minds away from thinking and worrying about what has happened and what may happen to them in the future. Others still may find the school a sanctuary, away from whatever unhappy situation they are experiencing, and their difficulties only become obvious in the home setting.

The most important factor to help children who have experienced trauma is having a secure, stable and loving social environment. It is not, contrary to what some may believe, the provision of special therapy for a child who has been traumatised (though this is certainly helpful for some children). Therefore, much of what this book says is just as relevant to helping a child who has been traumatised. What I cannot agree with on a moral level is to diagnose children who have been traumatised who are presenting with symptoms of poor concentration and impulsivity as having a 'neuro-developmental' disorder, such as ADHD, and prescribing medication for this. To me this is simply re-victimising the victim.

Coming Off Medication:

Some of you reading this book will have a child who is taking psychiatric medication for ADHD. Having read this book thus far, some of you may decide that you wish to take your child off this medication. Although it's advisable to consult a doctor before coming off medication, your decision on whether to withdraw your child's medication rests with you. Many people find that their doctor won't agree with their decision. A study for the UK national mental health charity 'MIND' (the study was with adults who wished to discontinue their psychiatric medications) found that, in practice, doctors were often unhelpful. Many thus decided to come off medication against the advice of their doctors, or without involving them in the decision. Furthermore, when coming off their medications, the most helpful people were those who had no role in prescribing their medication such as other service users, self-help groups, and complementary therapists. Doctors seemed to be less concerned than service-users about the side effects of medication, less understanding of their desire to live without drugs, and more likely to doubt their ability to do so successfully[44]. So if you have taken the decision to take your child off medication, don't let your doctor disagreeing with you necessarily put you off.

When weaning a child off any psychiatric medication, you should bear in mind that some withdrawal symptoms are likely. This is because psychiatric medicines act at the nerve endings of brain cells, and the result of their action is to increase or decrease the amount of a certain chemical involved in relaying signals from one brain cell to another (a neurotransmitter). What often then happens after a while of this change in the amount of neurotransmitter, is that brain cells start changing to adjust to the new levels of neurotransmitter. For example, if a drug has caused an increase in neurotransmitter levels, then, over time, the brain cell receiving this neurotransmitter will start reducing the number of receptors (that receive the signal from this neurotransmitter) that it has, in reaction to the increase in this chemical. This is why for many people the psychological effects of psychiatric drugs tend to ware off over time, often leading to gradually increasing doses being given. It also means that withdrawing the drug suddenly is not recommended.

The general 'rule of thumb' is that if your child has been taking a psychiatric drug for over 3 months then wean them off gradually over a period of 8 to 10 weeks. Below 3 months this can be done quicker. If your child is taking a long acting preparation (such as Concerta), then ask your doctor to switch your child to the equivalent dose of a short acting preparation (In Concerta's case this will be Ritalin or Equasym), which will then be easier to adjust.

For example, let's suppose your child is taking 40mg a day of Ritalin. A 'weaning off' regime may then look like this (it will involve using a sharp knife to cut the 10mg tablets):

- Week 1: Go to 35mg per day in divided doses, starting with reducing the last dose of the day.
- Week 2: Now go to 30mg per day in divided doses.
- Week 3: Now go to 25mg per day in divided doses.
- Week 4: Now go to 20mg per day in divided doses.
- Week 5 and 6: Now go to 15mg per day in divided doses.
- Week 7 and 8: Now go to 10mg per day in divided doses.
- Week 9 and 10: Now go to 5mg per day (morning only).
- Week 11: Discontinue.

If your child is taking more than one medication then work out a weaning off regime for each one, and then do the withdrawal programme for each one by one, rather than at the same time. If one drug has been prescribed for the side effects of another, then start with the original drug. For example, if an anti-depressant has been prescribed after a stimulant (which may have caused the low mood), start by first withdrawing the original drug, in this case the stimulant, and then the subsequent drug, in this case the anti-depressant.

The Structure Of The Next Chapters:

The next six chapters describe practical strategies that you can try. Each chapter contains a short discussion around a topic followed by suggested interventions. They are structured as if each chapter represents a therapeutic session and therefore the suggested way of using this section of the book is to try each chapter's interventions for a week or two before moving on to the next chapter and then trying that intervention in addition for the next week or two and so on.

It is structured in this way in order to give you a logical set of building blocks to look at the suggested ideas one after another with plenty of time between each intervention. I would also like to encourage you not to stop doing an intervention when you move on to the next chapter. When carrying out each intervention remember that you are looking for the smallest changes. It is small changes that eventually lead to bigger ones and it is also this eye for detail and ability to notice, apparently, little or insignificant things that make the best therapists (as in effect you are going to be for your children).

Chapter 8

Stress and assertiveness

In this chapter you are asked to take a step back, take stock of your lives and the place of your children in it. I will ask you to reflect on these issues and to think about what you would <u>like to see change, not just with your children, but also your relationship with your children.</u> In the intervention you will be asked to reflect on the role of stress and the impact this has on your relationships, the importance of authoritative assertiveness and to reflect on the emotional patterns in your relationships with your children.

There is an old African saying that it takes a village to raise a child. Raising children has always been a complicated business that demands much effort, time and commitment. In modern Britain this task seems harder than ever. The pace of life is faster than at any time in the past and we barely have enough time to catch our breath before moving on to the next task that we have to do. Children are expected to behave better than ever before and many of us no longer feel it is safe for our children to be allowed to run off their energy and explore the world in their own way as we all listen to terrible stories of children being victimised or becoming bullies themselves.

It has also become harder to know how we should act as parents. In the same way that day after day we hear reports that eating this food or that food is bad for you or behaving in this way or that way is bad for you, so it is easy to get confused by the different messages we hear about how to be a good parent. It seems that the days where you were allowed to trust your instincts and turn to family and friends for support are long gone and these days we are told that it is 'experts' who can tell you how to be a parent. Unfortunately these experts sometimes come up with different opinions and cannot seem to agree amongst themselves as to what the problem is and how to remedy it. Some experts tell you in what way to change your style of parenting and others may tell you that there is something wrong with your child.

In my opinion there is no one right or wrong way to solve a problem of difficult behaviour in a child. What I have learnt is that every child is different and that every family is different. I value these differences highly and appreciate that what needs to change in one relationship maybe very different to what needs to change in another parent/child relationship.

Whilst the emphasis in this part is about a positive outlet, problem solving and using positive feelings to help achieve what you want, it is worth saying that a whole range of negative feelings such as anger (blaming the child or other people), self doubt (feeling that you cannot do what is required and are not capable of working through these problems), guilt (such as self blame and feeling that the difficulties are of your own making), and despair (a sense of pointlessness and hopelessness about things ever changing) are all entirely normal and indeed expected emotions when anyone is going through a process of trying to bring about changes in their lives. Indeed, I would say that you should expect such feelings and when they do occur, try to accept them and not let them distract you from your continuing effort and commitment to making changes.

It is also worth remembering that what keeps a problem alive and unresolved is more important to understand than what causes the problem in the first place. This means that not understanding 'the root cause' of the problem is not as important as knowing you can make a difference whether you understand it or not. In this chapter therefore, you are asked to start concentrating on making changes, to now move beyond thoughtful reflection (as I have been encouraging in this book up until now) and into action mode.

If I were to come up with a motto or mantra of the most important ingredient to help you make lasting changes, it would be this *"Keep Calm, stay firm"*. This is why I have put dealing with stress and then assertiveness in this first chapter. I recognise how hard this is to do, but if you can achieve this and avoid raising your voice or getting into arguments and manage not to give in when provoked, then all the other interventions will become so much more effective and so much easier to implement.

Dealing With Stress:

Stress causes biological changes in the body. Stress is part of our 'fight' or 'flight' mechanism, evolutionarily designed to protect us from danger in our environments. These dangers that get our body aroused ready for 'fight/flight' have largely moved from physical threats to psychological threats and there is much evidence to suggest that modern culture is more psychologically stressful, at the same time as having less social support available to help modify that stress.

Furthermore, the more we have transferred stress from the physical to the mental sphere, the less we seem to have opportunities to process the physical effects of stress on the body (and mind).

One of the tasks of this chapter is to look at the relationship between how you feel and how your children subsequently behave (and your perception of how they are behaving). One of the most important factors to understand here is the role of stress. As I explained in the first section of this book there are many reasons why we are living more stressful lives and it would be very surprising indeed if these increased demands that we all have did not lead to increased levels of stress.

When a person is stressed they are more emotionally aroused and more likely to see things in black and white extremes ("you *never* do as you are told, you are *always* fidgeting") and more likely to see events in catastrophic terms ("you're driving me *crazy*", "I *can't cope* with looking after you anymore"). That way of thinking can easily lead you to doing and saying things to others that you later regret and can easily get you to lose your sense of proportion.

It is also worth remembering that we are most likely to take out that stress on those closest to us and, particularly, those less powerful than us. As a result it is no surprise that children often bear the brunt of many adult stresses and without realising and indeed without meaning to do it, we often take out our stresses on our children. This is entirely normal - I know that I do it from time to time- but it rarely leads to an improvement in stress levels, indeed, quite the opposite as taking out your stress on your children leads to them becoming angry, upset and stressed too, which may lead them to behave badly which in turn leads to further stress for you and a deterioration in your relationship with that child and so on.

So learning how to cope with stress to help protect your children from having stress being taken out on them can be very useful. Here are a few ideas you can try:

Breathing exercises: Breathing is one of the things often emphasised in Eastern religions and philosophies as breathing is the first thing we do when we enter out of the womb and into this world and the last thing we do before we leave it. Furthermore, stress hormones and the way the nervous system works means there is a direct relationship between your breathing and your levels of stress. For many people the more stressed they are, the faster and shallower their breathing becomes. Just as your nervousness can affect breathing so you can do the opposite- by changing your breathing you can affect how stressed you feel and actually calm your body down. A simple method is outlined below.

First settle yourself comfortably in an easy chair or bed with your arms by your side and your legs uncrossed. Now close your eyes and allow your attention to turn towards the sensations in your body. Notice the sensations in your hands, where they are resting against the chair or bed and follow the sensations up your arms into your shoulders, down your back and down the backs of your legs, right into your feet. After allowing yourself to be absorbed in noticing how your body feels, move your attention to your breathing. The aim here is going to be to take slow, deep breaths in and out (the out breath lasting a bit longer than the in breath) so that your lungs fully expand in each breath. A good way to get used to this exercise is to count silently in your head up to 7 on the in breath and then up to 11 on the out breath. Try to make the in breath and out breath as smooth as possible and while you are breathing in and out and silently counting, focus on the sensation of the air as it enters and exits through your nose and the sensation in the chest of the lungs fully expanding. If the 7/11 count is too much then try 3/5 or 5/8, whatever feels most comfortable to you but trying to keep the out breath longer than the in breath (the out breath is more likely to stimulate the relaxation response in the nervous system). Try to keep all the worrying thoughts out of your mind and focus as purely as you can on your breath and the sensations it causes. After you have done this for about five minutes (or even just doing it ten times) you will feel much calmer and more energised.

By practicing this exercise e a few times every day, until you have got the hang of it, you will eventually get to the point where you don't need to sit down, lie down or close your eyes in order to be able to achieve a similar effect simply by taking a few moments away from the situation and making a deliberate choice to slow down your breathing in the way that you have practiced. Simply using breathing you can learn to calm yourself down relatively quickly. Like most things in life, for most people this won't come naturally and will need to be practiced regularly until you've got the hang of it.

Using visualisations: As in the breathing exercise first create a nice, safe place, by settling yourself comfortably in an easy chair or bed with your arms by your side and your legs uncrossed. As before close your eyes and allow your attention to turn towards the sensations in your body. Once you have done this imagine that you are at a favourite place, a place that makes you feel positive, healthy, energised and calm (such as a nice beauty spot, or a beach on a warm sunny day- places that make you feel energised, healthy and calm are often natural places as one of the things that help us feel calm in the busy, modern world is a closer connection with nature). Now 'fill in' the scene that you have: What can you hear? Is there any wind, or a nostalgic pleasant smell in the air? How does the ground feel under your feet? Are there any other people or animals? What else can you see, hear or feel?

Some Common Visualisations Used For Relaxation Include The Following:

A walk by the sea: As above focus in on details, what is the weather like? What's the ground like underfoot? Are there waves rolling in? Are there seagulls in the air? And so on. Others include a walk in the woods, climbing up a mountain, by a mountain stream or, indeed anywhere you personally associate with feeling more relaxed and energised.

The visualisation and the breathing exercise can be combined, for example, start with the breathing exercise, moving on to visualisation. Unlike the breathing exercise which you can learn to do at any time of the day and in most settings, the visualisation exercise does require you to put a bit of time aside (ten to fifteen minutes) when you know you are going to get a bit of peace and quiet to carry this out.

You can, however, combine a simpler visualisation with the breathing which, done together, after practice can help you calm down quickly in most situations. First you need to think of a colour that you most associate with calm. Suppose you picked blue. Start by doing the breathing exercise then imagine a blue waterfall falling slowly inside you from the top of your head right down to the tip of your toes. As this waterfall gradually spreads through your head, into your neck, down your shoulders, into your arms, into your hands and fingers, down your chest and stomach, into your legs and right up to the tips of your toes, you are likely to feel a calmness spreading with it. Again practice makes perfect and once you've 'trained' your mind and body to associate this colour with a calm feeling, you will hopefully be able to imagine this coloured waterfall inside with your eyes open and thus feel calmer quite quickly. Don't worry if you have trouble with this, it is more difficult than the breathing exercise, but worth persisting with as this can be a powerful technique.

Regular exercise: Strong evidence shows that exercise relieves stress and depression. If you are not getting regular exercise, then start with a simple walk every day – it does not have to be vigorous. It could be combined with other things like walking round to visit a friend or waking your children to school. You should try to get a minimum of twenty to thirty minutes exercise per day. Think about going to the gym, or swimming, or whatever you might enjoy sports-wise, regularly.

Affection: Don't forget others have the power to soothe us and us them. A good, long hug and kiss from a loved one or to a loved one will say a lot more than words at the end of a heavy day. Better to do this than increase one another's burdens.

Being Assertive And Authoritative:

Assertiveness is another important skill, particularly for those living in the West, where the demands of modern parenting make it indispensable. Assertiveness can be thought of as a set of behaviours that help us to indicate clearly and confidently what we believe, want, and feel to other people, without abusing their rights. Being assertive means being authoritative (not authoritarian) without resorting to aggression/violence or passivity (withdrawing and giving up) to get what you want (providing of course this is not riding roughshod over someone else's rights). Children need their parents to be authoritative. They need to know their parents are strong and wise enough to be effective in enforcing whatever rules or routines are necessary in the family. There are two important areas to work on when becoming authoritative through assertiveness: persistence and negotiation.

Persistence: If you are not assertive you may give in to your children's unreasonable demands far too readily or take 'No' for an answer far too easily. The main technique to practice the art of persistence is called the 'broken record'. When a record is scratched we hear the same track over and over again. Broken record is the skill of being able to repeat over and over again in an assertive and relaxed manner, what it is you want to say and want to see done, until your child (or another person if your being assertive elsewhere in your life) provides it or agrees to negotiate with you. The main benefit is that once you have prepared your 'lines' (in other words what you are going to say), you can relax knowing all you have to do is repeat this. You merely repeat your script, no matter how abusive or manipulative your child tries to be (for example the line might be in response to a persistent request from your child for a packet of sweets, in which case you could say

'No, you are not getting any sweets today' and keep repeating that, but most importantly stick to your guns, don't buy the sweets!). This is one way of avoiding descending into arguments with your child.

Negotiation: For many situations persistence will be the more important aspect of becoming authoritative, particularly in the early stages of becoming assertive. Once your children know that you can be persistent without giving up or becoming violent, space for negotiation begins to emerge. Once your child is showing a desire to communicate without being abusive or manipulative then the most important skill is being able to listen carefully and then give your understanding of what is being said in order to gain clarification, whilst keeping calm. Keep to the point, using broken record if necessary, but once you see your children are ready to communicate nicely and with reasonable requests, try to model for them negotiating differences of opinion. Avoid being stubborn and be prepared to offer a compromise. Test this out by having practice negotiations with your partner or friend playing the role of your child. Acknowledge how your child says they think and feel (try to see their point of view) and then say how you feel and think, so that you can model the process of taking other peoples feelings into account (without being manipulated).

Relationship Patterns:

It stands to reason that if we, the parents, are unhappy and our family ship starts sinking that the children will sink with us. Once we become parents we have to make large adjustments in our understanding of who we are, and what we want from life. One of those adjustments is that of lessening the importance of our own individual desires in exchange for promoting our duty to our family and our social responsibility for our children. In cultures where your sense of self is intimately tied up with being part of a family then this transition is relatively easy as your social standing (and therefore self esteem) is enhanced by having children. It is more difficulty in modern, Western culture to make this transition from looking after your own needs and wishes to being responsible for others. Social esteem in the West seems to rest much more on factors such as academic achievement, successful career, how much money you can make, and what consumer objects (like a brand of car) you own. Unfortunately, there seems only a limited amount of esteem attached to becoming a parent, particularly if it means giving up on your career or interfering with it.

This, however, is the reality and if you are somebody feeling down and defeated by what children and family life has brought you then I hope you are reassured to know that you are in the same boat as many (if not most) parents having to deal with what family life means in the West. The good news is that there are lots of things you can do to improve your own circumstances, and I hope you will find a lot of them in this book.

Changing the emotional patterns in your relationship with your children: Try noticing what is different about the times when the behaviours you want to see your child doing are happening. What were you doing? How were you feeling? What else had happened that day? Who else was with you? How did you respond? Write a few of these observations in a diary. Keep this daily diary for a couple of weeks. Try to concentrate your observations on the periods where your child shows good behaviour, and resist the temptation to turn the diary into a place to vent your frustrations and make a long list of complaints. Read your entries to your partner or a friend, this may help you reflect on what was happening at those times when your child was well behaved. Providing you are making plenty of entries of observations of when your child was being well behaved, then also make notes observing similar areas for when your child is behaving poorly. Now read through your notes (again with a partner or friend) to compare what was happening when the behaviours you don't want were occurring, to when the ones that you do want occurred.

CHAPTER 9

Separating the Child from the Problem

We are all aware of how problems can take over anybody's life. We find ourselves thinking about whatever this problem is throughout the day and it feels as if we can't escape its effects and stress levels start to rise. When a child is the centre of a particular problem it can also feel a bit like that to them. They expect to get into trouble, they expect to be told off, they realise they are seen as trouble and naughty and eventually this becomes their identity. Once a child believes they are trouble and naughty and this becomes their idea of who they are, they often start to behave in a way that confirms this identity. In other words if they believe 'I am naughty' then they come to expect that they should behave as a naughty child. Children, all children I believe, need a secure sense of belonging and need attention in order to achieve this. If they experience that they can get attention when they misbehave, soon this will become woven into their idea of themselves and how they fit into their family, school, or indeed their place in the world more generally.

It is worth reminding ourselves, however, about how other problems in our lives affect us. We have all had experiences of being stressed by a particular problem and I am sure we have all noticed that when we are stressed we act in a different way to when we are relaxed. In other words when a problem is around it does something to us – to how we feel, to how we behave, to how we respond to others.

Thus I find it very helpful to separate the child from the problem. It is the problem you are trying to defeat. It is the problem you are trying to find a solution to and you all know that there is a lot more to your child than the problem. Sometimes even the simple phrase "it is your behaviour that I don't like (or find unacceptable) and that has nothing to do with how much I love you", if repeated often enough can get that message through to your child. Perhaps, more importantly than what you actually say is having this idea as a way of thinking about the problems you have in your relationship with your children. This can help to prevent the problem taking over your thoughts and feelings about your children, so that you can carry on noticing all the positive aspects, positive behaviours and positive things that you love about your children.

It can help in this process to give a name to the problem and once this problem has been named to develop its 'persona'. I sometimes develop different names for the 'problem' with families I work with, depending on what they have already told me. Some examples of names we've given for difficult behaviour include 'the red mist', 'Mr Temper', 'the bully monster', 'nasty man', and sometimes even bad or manipulative characters from stories that a child identifies such as 'Voldamort'. Sometimes a more light-hearted name works well like 'Fred', 'Silly-man', or 'Professor Nutty'.

The idea behind this is to capture the children's imagination and help them and yourself view the problem as being down to forces that are not firmly rooted just in the child. Therefore, to do this properly means taking a much broader view of the problem and seeing how it acts, not just on the child but also on you and the rest of the family.

In other words when 'red mist', 'bully monster', or 'professor Nutty' is around, it is not necessarily just the child who is being effected and behaving 'out of character' but it could also be others including yourself who are losing your temper and behaving 'badly' as well.

Once a problem is framed in this way then your task as a family is to work as a team together to get rid of, or minimise the influence of this unwanted guest. This can lead you to starting to ask some very different questions about the influence of the problem and can change the dynamics from one where you are trying to control what you see as a problem firmly rooted within your child, towards that of understanding how the unwanted guest is upsetting your family.

Who Is Mr Temper And What Is He Like?

To work in this way you have to start observing things a little differently and asking some different sort of questions. For example, when is 'Mr Temper' (if this is your name for the problem) most likely to be around? Does he follow you home from school? Does he keep popping up at bed time? When 'Mr Temper' is around, how does it affect what you feel, what you do, and what you say? What sort of pattern of responses do you find various members of your family are pushed into when 'Mr Temper' is around? Is 'Mr Temper' more likely to show himself when you are feeling in a particular way such as stressed? Does 'Mr Temper' leave you feeling desperate, hopeless and embarrassed; if so, is this exactly what 'Mr Temper' is trying to do? And so on.

Just as important as understanding what happens when 'Mr Temper' is around, is also understanding the times when 'Mr Temper' is not around. This can be very difficult to start with. If you are always on the lookout for 'Mr Temper' your attention will, naturally, be drawn to those times. To start with you may need to make a particular effort to understand what is going on when 'Mr Temper' is not around and make a particular effort to notice these times and build on them for within them are potential solutions. Are there particular times when 'Mr Temper' is not about? What are we doing at those times? Is 'Mr Temper' less likely to want to stay when we are all having fun? Does 'Mr Temper' find it hard to get a look in if we are out doing something? Does 'Mr Temper' find it hard to get a look in when my partner and I are getting on and supporting each other? Does 'Mr Temper' eventually go away if I stick to my guns and don't give in to his demands? Does 'Mr Temper' get confused on those days where I praise, hug and pour affection onto my children? And so on.

To use this strategy, you are trying to harness the observational skills of all members of the family as you pull together to analyse, then understand and then develop from this understanding new and creative ways to start defeating the unwanted guest. Again you may find keeping a diary helpful, but this time one that you do together as a family project, that involves all of you making entries. It could be a bit like your 'battle diary' against 'Mr. Temper' where you note your strategies together. The more playful you make it the more your kids will like it.

CHAPTER 10

Consequences

Articles and books about child rearing for thousands of years from many different cultures around the world, have talked about the importance of rewards and punishments in helping children learn that particular culture's ideas of right or wrong (in other words that particular culture's moral code). Modern psychology books are no different, what does change over time and place is each cultures ideas about what sort of behaviours are felt to be desirable and acceptable and what sort of rewards and punishments are felt to be desirable and acceptable and what sort of balance there should be between rewards and punishments (some cultures emphasise punishments more, other cultures emphasise rewards more).

It is, in my opinion, up to each of you, as individual families, to make your own decisions about what behaviours you see as desirable and acceptable in your children, what punishments and rewards you feel are appropriate and works for your children and what balance between punishments and rewards you feel works for you. What I believe does need to happen, however, is for you to take some time to think about this and compromise on any disagreements you may have within your family about consequences. Once you have agreed, in principle, what your boundaries are, work out a firm system of consequences and try to be as consistent as you can with this system.

There is no magic involved in devising a set of strategies to deal with consequences. However, do read the section on common pitfalls in particular, before attempting to put a strategy into place. In many ways what is more important than the actual strategy you use, is knowing that the main adults who are going to need to use these strategies are in agreement with them and that whatever strategy you choose you are going to give it a good thorough go, of at least a month's duration, before deciding whether it is going to be useful to you or not.

When you are carrying out any consequence strategy, please remember that there is a natural tendency within any family to pull it back to its usual way of functioning (or the usually family script as I have called it above in chapter 7). So, when you start such a programme remember: the forces acting on you, that are pushing you to give it up, will be considerable. Now you have to put this together with the knowledge that when you are trying to change difficult behaviour, using a behavioural consequences programme, what usually happens is that behaviour gets worse before it gets better. This means that you will be very likely to consider giving up the programme in the early days and weeks, as it may feel like it is making the situation worse and everybody around you unhappy. It is absolutely vital that you remain aware that this is exactly what you expect to happen and that you do not give up on the programme at this point.

Below I have outlined two types of behavioural consequences strategies that I have been using with success in my clinical practice. There are plenty of other variations and the two examples below are by no means the only ones. However, I think it is true to say that the various programmes and books out there describing behavioural consequence strategies (such as the many books on parenting) are basically different variations on the same theme of promoting positive behaviour through positive consequences for good behaviour (such as attention, praise and rewards) and various strategies to reduce unwanted behaviour through negative consequences for this (such as time out or removal of privileges).

This is not rocket science, however, what can make a difference when there is a problem is being more systematic and consistent in your approach- in other words producing a system with clear rules, expectations and guidelines. The two examples below are geared to different age groups. Initially, I have adapted some of the ideas from David Stein's book *Unravelling the ADHD Fiasco, Successful Parenting Without Drugs* [45] and these approaches are suitable for primary school age children. In the second part I have adapted ideas from Scott Sell's book *Parenting your out of Control Teenager: Seven Steps to Re-establishing Authority and Reclaim Love* [46] which is more suitable for secondary school age children.

Learn to talk and find time to communicate with your child. Use this as a guide to help you focus on how to implement consequences. Remember that every family is different and every child is different and you can learn by trial and error what works best for your family and your child. Please also remember that whatever system you use it takes time, hard work and persistence before you begin to see results. Finally remember that whatever system you use it will require troubleshooting, lots of thinking, lots of action, lots of practice and is likely to test you emotionally to your limit (and beyond). This is where the mantra I introduced in chapter 8 is particularly important, **"Keep calm, stay firm"**. If you can do this then you are much more likely to produce appropriate consequences, and less likely to produce 'knee-jerk' more extreme consequences (like "You'll be grounded for a month" or "I'm sending you to a children's home") that would be unfair and that you are unlikely to complete.

Primary School Aged Children:

Positive consequences (rewards): Children usually need incentives and things to aim for to help motivate them to achieve. Whilst material incentives, such as money, sweets and toys are often useful, the types of rewards that are most likely to build a child's self-esteem are social ones. These range from simple and immediate displays of positive affection and pleasure at them behaving in the ways you want them to behave, such as praise and physical affection (such as hugs and kisses), to longer and more time consuming social rewards such as outings together and other ways of spending time together. As with negative consequences this needs to be worked on and worked on so that the child can hear good things about themselves and experience positive feelings towards them. At the same time be careful not to overdo this – you do not want to praise your child for a brief bit of good behaviour in the middle of lots of bad behaviour for which you are using negative consequences. Also, if a child receives too much praise, hugs and outings, it could become too easy for that child to get these and so their effectiveness will then start to diminish. Try to avoid the temptation to praise your child continuously, linking your praise with definite acts where your child has demonstrated effort to do something positive, this is what you are trying to pick up on.

Negative consequences (punishments): The main principle here is to find a way to 'bore' your child into doing as they're told. Boredom tends to be an effective technique as children hate having nothing to do and you don't have to expose your child to the potential negative effects of fear as a method of control (fear can sometimes cause some children to become unnecessarily anxious and inhibited). Here are a few suggestions as to how you might achieve boredom. These can be used as tricks up your sleeve, which you can implement. Having more than one idea can help in terms of having backup plans if one method isn't achieving the result you desire, but please remember that whatever technique you use it is important to stick to your guns and not give in (you want your child to get the message that there are consequences for his/her actions, that these consequences will be enforced, that you are strong and determined enough to do what ever you need to do to enforce those consequences and that you will get the message through to your child about what you consider to be acceptable and unacceptable behaviours).

Please also remember that when you start using any particular strategy your child's behaviour is likely to get worse before it gets better and it is especially important at these times to really stick to your guns and stay calm but determined, even though the 'button pushing' on the part of your child may feel like it is driving you, emotionally, to an intolerable position. In fact, it is especially important not to give in when this is happening as if you give in now your child will learn that they have to go to even greater extremes to get their own way. This period of things getting worse before they get better can sometimes last a week or two, so be prepared.

- **Time-Out** Find a place in your house where your child can 'serve' their time-out in a position that is particularly boring and where you can monitor, to some extent, their behaviour during the time-out. The place you find should be free of anything that is likely to interest the child (bedrooms tend to be a bad place for time-out as there are usually toys to play with or interesting things to look at, similarly having a view through a window can be a bad place for time-out as there may well be things to look at going on outside). The position of the time-out place that you find should be one that is as uninteresting as possible for the child so that he/she experiences boredom. Set a time limit for the time-out such as 10 minutes or 15 minutes and explain the procedure to your child before you need to use the time-out. The time-out has to be served in complete silence. If your child moves from their time-out position, says anything, whines or cries during the time-out then the 10 or 15 minutes will have to start from scratch again. Remember the time-out is only finished when your child has sat there for the allocated time in complete silence. At the end of the time-out your child has to apologise if the time out was for doing something that they shouldn't have done and/or do the task that they were not doing that caused you to implement the time-out. If they do not apologise or the bad behaviour starts again or they do not do the task they were set, then the time-out procedure starts from scratch again. If your child is refusing to go and serve their time-out, then, until they do so, they should not be allowed to do anything else, whether this is watching television, playing with toys, going out with friends or even having their dinner. It is only if your child is refusing to go to time-out and is starting instead to do one of the things that they are not allowed to do until they have served their time-out (such as watching television or playing with toys) that you may have to become involved in physically restraining them to prevent them from engaging in any activity until they have served their time-out. Use the 'broken record' technique if necessary (see chapter 8). Remember you want them to get the message that you are very serious about this consequence and what you say will be done. Try as hard as you can to avoid any arguments, fights or eye contact as all of these are forms of attention and you are trying to withdraw all stimulation from your child for the period of the time out. Remember it takes as long as it takes and if it takes your child 5 or 6 hours before they finally do their allotted time in silence so be it.

- **Other back up ideas**: As well as implementing the time-out above you can also add, if necessary, other negative consequences in the same minimal fuss manner. Other strategies can include:
- Grounding a child and not allowing them to see their friends for an evening or a weekend.
- Giving them extra tasks that they do not wish to do around the house.
- Giving them extra homework or other schoolwork that they do not wish to do.
- Withdrawing objects that they enjoy playing with from their room for a specified period of time.
- Banning them from doing things that they enjoy doing (such as watching television or playing on the computer).
- Using a money chart/pot, that starts each day as full and then you lose some money (get a fine) each time you misbehave. Get plenty of small change so money earned can be handed out at the end of each day. For example if you have decided your child can earn up to 20 pence per day, then you could fine 1p for minor misbehaviour and 2p for more serious misbehaviour.

The beauty of the above system is that it is simple; it does not require you to think about what has happened before, it simply focuses on consequences and this is one of the best ways of helping children start to take responsibility for their own actions. When trying a system like this please give yourself at least a month (treat it as an experiment for a month) before deciding whether it is going to be helpful for you or not. Keep in mind your other children and use the same or a similar (age appropriate) system as you are using with the child you are most concerned about.

Secondary School Children/ Teenagers:

The principles behind this are similar. The aim is for your adolescent to understand clearly that there are consequences to their behaviour and thus learn to take responsibility for their actions. The skills discussed in chapter 8 particularly those of managing stress and being assertive/ authoritative are vital if you are going to help your adolescent develop a clear idea about boundaries and what you consider acceptable or not. Compared to the younger age group, however, there are some differences in emphasis with adolescents. Adolescents are older, peer pressures are different, and therefore their tastes and desires will have changed. Nonetheless, as with the younger children, you should first aim to establish your rules/boundaries (being persistent) before getting into negotiations. Remember too that adolescents just like younger children need to feel loved and valued, so make sure that you tell them this and do things with them to make them feel valued and appreciated by you.

To help you think about devising consequences that are more likely to 'hit the spot' with an adolescent, fill in the following table. Take your time to think carefully about each consequence. As before, discuss this with your partner or any significant other who is involved in looking after your child.

The table contains some typical motivating factors for adolescents living within modern Western cultures. With each consequence, think about how much it can be either a positive motivator or a negative one. Let's take money for example. Money can be a positive consequence if your adolescent likes earning extra money. It can be a negative consequence if your adolescent hates having money taken away. It can also be both a positive and negative motivator if your adolescent loves earning extra money and hates having money taken away.

Give each positive and negative consequence a score out of 10, based on your judgement of how likely that particular consequence is to affect your child, where 0 is not at all and 10 is extremely likely. So to return to my example of money, your adolescent may be strongly motivated to earn money (perhaps an 8 out of 10 as a positive consequence), but, although not liking the idea of money being taken away, can cope easily without it (perhaps a 5 out of 10 as a negative).

Consequence	Positive motivator (out of 10)	Negative motivator (out of 10)
Money		
Use of telephone/ mobile phone		
Personal freedom		
Clothes		
Transport (taken places)		
Trust (to do things)		
Appearance (to dress as they like/ want)		
Personal possessions (be specific)		
Time (with family)		
Time (with friends)		
Use of computer/ game console		
Others (that you can think of- be specific)		
Others (that you can think of- be specific)		

Once you have completed the table, draw up an action plan of consequences, that can be put in place if your adolescent continues to misbehave. Start with some of the lower scoring consequences. Try to aim at having at least 3 levels of consequences, so you have a plan A, B and C for both positive and negative consequences. Let your adolescent know about plans A and B, but keep plan C a secret.

For example, let's say that your 'top 3' negative consequences in reverse order were: transport (scoring 7), clothes (scoring 8), and credits for their mobile phone (scoring 9). Let's say that your 'top 3' positive consequences in reverse order were: money (scoring 7), transport (scoring 8), and credits for their mobile phone (scoring 9).

Plan A (which you would explain to your adolescent) would then involve the lowest of your 'top 3' in each of the negative and positive. Thus in my example 'Plan A' would be withdrawing transport (you taking them places) if the adolescent's behaviour was unacceptable (of course I am assuming here that you have already worked out what you mean by unacceptable behaviour, and explained this clearly to your adolescent) and giving them extra weekly 'allowance' (money) if they are well behaved.

Plan B (which you would explain to your adolescent) would then involve the second of your 'top 3' in each of the positive and negative columns. Thus in my example 'Plan B' would be taking away some favourite clothes if the adolescent's behaviour was unacceptable and giving them extra transport (you taking them places- for example to school or to friends) if they are well behaved.

Plan C (which you keep secret) would then involve the top of your 'top 3' in each of the negative and positive columns. Thus in my example 'Plan C' would be taking away (confiscating) credits for their mobile phone, if the adolescent's behaviour was unacceptable and giving extra credits for their mobile phone if they are well behaved.

With both the negative and positive consequences, work out a reasonable period of time for that consequence to stay in place. In the example above, for example, with negative consequences you could have withdrawing transport for one week (in Plan A), taking favourite clothes away for one week (in Plan B), and taking credits from mobile phone away for 2 weeks (in Plan C); with positive consequences you could have extra weekly 'allowance' (money) for 1 week (in Plan A), giving them extra transport for two weeks (in Plan B), and giving them extra credits for their mobile phone for two weeks (in Plan C).

You then basically work through starting with negative consequences in Plan A if they are misbehaving, onto Plan B if they misbehave again during the time that the negative consequence for Plan A was in place, and then onto Plan C if they misbehave again during the time Plan B's consequence is in place.

Resist the temptation to launch straight from Plan A to Plan B to Plan C during a single episode of behaviour. Misbehaviour straight after giving a negative consequence is most likely to be related to you giving them a consequence that they don't like. Wait until they have calmed down from that episode and have accepted their consequence. If they then misbehave again during the time the negative consequence is in place (for example, in the example above on Plan A, this would be one week of not transporting the adolescent), in a totally separate and unrelated incident, then go into Plan B, and so on. Make sure you stick to the consequence and see it through. Avoid the temptation to give something back during the time scale you have specified, however good (or bad) they are behaving. You want your adolescent to know that you will enforce boundaries.

If your adolescent has now appreciated that you are serious about the consequences you impose, or if they are responding more easily to positive approaches and encouragement, then go through the positive consequences in your Plans, starting with positive consequences in Plan A, if they are still behaving well by the end of the time for Plan A, then onto the positive consequences for Plan B, and if they are still behaving well by the end of the time for Plan B, then onto Plan C's positive consequences (which will have remained secret and so be a pleasant surprise for them).

Chapter 11

Lifestyle and Family Life

How often in this day and age do we have time just to do nothing, just to enjoy each others company? Lifestyles have changed enormously over the past few decades. About thirty years ago there was lots of talk around about preparing ourselves for a culture in which leisure time was going to be plentiful and working hours shorter, with more labour saving devices being invented (like robots to take over manual work in factories and washing machines and dishwashers to save time with housework). Instead what seems to have happened is that we have to work longer and longer hours and have shorter and shorter holidays. As we have become a more mobile culture people move around and loose touch with the immediate support from family and friends in their local community.

We have also been taken over by a consumer culture, which tells us that happiness is linked to having more things. One effect of this culture has been that many of us now live our lives planning for the future all the time – trying to accumulate more things and trying to keep away the debt that many of us develop as a result of chasing after a better future. This is a big contrast to cultural attitudes that are very much more centred on the here and now and where enjoying each others company and feeling connected to your extended family and broader community is more valued.

Changing Your Family Lifestyle:

Have a think about these issues:

- Diet
- Family time.
- Fresh air and exercise.
- TV and computer games.
- Bedtime routines.
- Chores, responsibilities and independence.
- Support.

Are you getting enough time where you as a family can simply enjoy each other's company – just spending time together, getting to know each other? Do your children have enough opportunities for regular (daily) fresh air and exercise? Could you improve your children's diet so that they are taking less sugars and artificial additives, flavourings and colourings and instead more fresh fruit and vegetables and fish? Might you consider adding some supplements to your children's diet? Do your children spend a lot of time playing computer games or watching TV? If so would you consider limiting the amount of daily time they spend doing these activities? Do you have a bedtime routine including some time doing calming non-stimulating activities before bedtime? This chapter helps you to think about these and the many other related questions this topic produces.

Dietary Intervention:

As I have already mentioned (chapter 4), Western diets have changed enormously in the past twenty to thirty years. There are many more chemicals in our diet as food production has switched into bigger roles for large corporations with the liberal use of preservatives, colourings and flavourings so that we have greater availability of cheap, easy to prepare but often poor quality foods. Indeed, the situation has become so bad that many doctors have been warning that because of the current generation's diet and lifestyle (such as lack of exercise), they will be the first generation since the end of the second world war who are likely, on average, to live shorter lives than the previous generation. And it's not just the increase in chemicals in our children's diets that's proving to be a problem. There has been a substantial increase in the amount of sugar, saturated fat and salt in children's diet at the same time as a marked decrease in vegetables and fish. In other words the diets of children in the Western world have become poorer.

The second thing to bear in mind is that there is now a large scientific literature which claims to demonstrate a clear connection between our diet and our subsequent behaviour. In other words, the concern that many have voiced for a while that our poor dietary habits may be causing some of the behavioural problems we are seeing in many children has the support of many research studies. For example, a well known study carried out on the Isle of Wight recently involved a large number of pre-school children. Their parents had to keep these children on a diet carefully chosen to be free of any additives. In certain weeks the children were given a daily drink that either contained additives (in typical amounts that would be found in children's modern diet) or an identical looking or tasting fruit drink. Neither the parents nor the children knew which type of drink was being given. It was found that parents reported significantly more disruptive and inattentive behaviour on those weeks the children were receiving drinks with the additives, even though the parents or their children did not know which drink was being taken[47]. Thus careful attention to diet may prove vital in changing the behaviour of some children.

There are three main elements to a complete dietary intervention: eliminating irritants, adding missing nutrients, and getting an overall balance in the diet.

Eliminating irritants: The first place to start is to eliminate, as far as you can, all artificial (that is synthetic) colouring, flavouring, preservatives and pesticides. This does take some adjusting to and will often mean a big change in the way you shop. It means trying to buy 'natural' as far as possible, in other words getting unprocessed ingredients and using them to prepare meals. Where you are buying processed foods or tinned foods you will need to be looking at the label to check for 'e-numbers'/other additives, or looking out for products that are labelled as free from artificial colouring, flavouring and preservatives and free from monosodium glutamate. To minimise the effects of pesticides buy organic whenever possible and make sure you wash fruit and vegetables before eating or cooking them. If eliminating additives does result in improved behaviour or concentration, then this can usually be seen within anything from a few days to a week.

Eliminating all additives from the diet is certainly a good starting point for developing a healthy diet that can promote good behaviour and concentration. However, there are other potential irritants that you may need to consider eliminating from your child's diet. Whilst eliminating additives is generally good for promoting healthy diets anyway (whether or not there are obvious, noticeable effects on behaviour and learning) eliminating these other potential irritants can be done on a trial basis and there is no need to stick to them if no benefits are observed.

One thing that is sometimes helpful to do while you are trying to work out whether there are particular foods that appear to cause behavioural problems in your child is to keep a food diary. In the food diary you keep a note of what food your child eats on a day by day basis and then write down your observation of your child's behaviour, particularly during the period that starts around twenty minutes to one hour after they consume the drink or food. By keeping a food diary for a number of weeks you may be able to pick up particular patterns of behaviour that appear to relate to specific categories or types of food.

One thing to consider eliminating from the diet is lactose. Lactose is mainly found in dairy produce and so this is essentially a dairy product free diet (although it is found in other products such as some types of bread and of course chocolate so please look carefully at the labels). Dairy products are common in the Western diet. However, protein from cows' milk is generally not that compatible with the human body and is quite dissimilar in form to human milk. Many countries of the world, particularly Eastern Asian countries, have not had dairy products as an important part of their diets during their history and so you will find many people from such non-Western populations are particularly sensitive to dairy products.

Lactose sensitivity can present in many different ways including poor behaviour, and difficulty concentrating, but also frequent bowel problems (such as recurrent diarrhoea or/and stomach cramps) and ear, nose and throat infections. If your child has a history of other conditions from the family of allergies, such as asthma or eczema or had a history of cows' milk intolerance when they were a baby, then you should seriously consider a dairy-free trial period.

To do this you must eliminate all dairy products (and any other products containing lactose) for a period of one month. This should allow ample time for any lactose that has accumulated in body tissue to have been completely eliminated by the body. During this time you will obviously be observing for improvements in your child's behaviour and any other symptoms you may be concerned about. At the end of the month reintroduce dairy produce for a period of a week and observe to see if there is any change (in particular deterioration) in your child's behaviour or other symptoms. This is the simplest way to establish whether there is lactose sensitivity and whether you should consequently move on to a diary free diet for your child.

Another potential irritant worth considering is Salicilates. Salicilates are a group of chemicals related to aspirin. There are several kinds of salicilates which plants make as a natural pesticide to protect themselves. Some people are sensitive to salicilates, in which case their behaviour may deteriorate following consuming foods containing them. Foods that have high levels of salicilate include apricots, blackberries, blackcurrants, cranberries, dates, grapes, oranges, pineapple, plums, strawberries, sultanas, peppers, radish, chilli peppers, almonds, raspberries, redcurrants, prunes and cordials and fruit flavoured drinks. Thus to try a salicilate free diet means eliminating those foods (particularly citrus fruits, berries and fruit drinks) from the diet for a month followed by a week reintroducing them as with the dairy free diet above. A food diary may help you identify whether eliminating high levels of salicilates in the diet may be worth trying.

Finally it may also be worth considering eliminating gluten. Gluten is a protein found in wheat, rye, barley and oat products. A gluten free diet means eliminating many common foods that children have, for example most cereals, most commercially available bread, any products containing flour or thickening agents and many other sources of starch, such as regular noodles and pasta. If you are wishing to try a gluten free diet then, be warned. This is one of the hardest diets to do as so many of the foods that children like contain gluten. However, with the right child the results can be dramatic. As gluten is stored in the body tissue much longer than either salicilates or lactose this means that if you are to undertake a gluten free diet you should allow a period of three months completely gluten free before trying a week with gluten products again, before you can conclude that the gluten free period made a difference or not.

Adding missing nutrients: Western diets are well known to be very low in certain types of essential fatty acids that are vital for the healthy functioning of brain cells. These essential fatty acids line the brain cells and are necessary for efficient functioning of the brain cell membrane. They are commonly found in certain types of fish, particularly carnivorous fish (such as fresh tuna, salmon and mackerel) and certain types of seeds (such as flaxseed, linseed and sesame seeds). Fortunately, there are now a number of preparations available with the right balance of essential fatty acids which can be simply added to your child's diet. Whether or not they make a difference to your child's behaviour and concentration, they will still be a healthy addition to any diet (although caution should be used if your child has a diagnosis of epilepsy or any other neurological disorder, in which case please discuss this with your doctor before commencing your child on these supplements).

The products that I have used with success with children in my care include *Efalex* and *Eye Q*, both available at most large pharmacy/supermarkets. A more recent product which claims to have the oils in purer form is *Vegepa*, which is available over the internet (at www.vegepa.com). My usual advice is to give three times the recommended daily intake for the first two months to bring the stores of the body up to normal levels.

Many children also have diets which are low in fresh fruit and raw vegetables and thus are deficient in certain vital vitamins and minerals. If your child has a poor intake of fruits and raw vegetables then I would recommend adding to the diet a daily multivitamin and mineral tablet.

Balancing the diet: As a general rule Western diets, particularly those of children, are too high in sugars, saturated fats and salt, and do not contain enough fibre. Apart from the general health problems that such diets can cause, these imbalances in, particularly the sugar and carbohydrate content of a diet, means that blood sugar levels can have constant fluctuations throughout the day, leading to energy bursts followed by energy dips. In order to try and rebalance children's diets my advice is simply to re-establish the principles of a healthy diet. This usually means cutting out all processed sugar, as far as possible, and that includes the majority of sweets and chocolates (of course exceptions can and should be made on special occasions or at particular times where you are not too concerned about the sudden burst of energy that high sugars will cause). It means reducing the amount of red meats in the diet and, as far as possible, getting protein from white meat (particularly fish) and pulses. It also means trying to increase the amount of fruit and vegetables in the diet. With regards to vegetables, raw vegetables are the best source of nutrients and fibre and when cooked it is best to cook vegetables by steaming for no longer than ten minutes (so that they still maintain some of their crunchiness) and this way they maintain most of their goodness.

Having three good meals throughout the day with each meal having some source of complex carbohydrates (such as pasta, brown rice, potatoes, wholegrain cereals, porridge oats, wholemeal breads, root vegetables, pulses) can help regulate blood sugar levels throughout the day – complex carbohydrates release their sugar and energy more slowly thereby avoiding the highs and lows in the blood sugar level. This is particularly important with breakfasts so that your children can have a good nutritional start to the day, particularly before they go to school. With regards to drinks, this means cutting out fizzy drinks and squashes and replacing them with water and fresh fruit juice (although caution may need to be shown here if your child turns out to be sensitive to Salicilates).

Whilst for some this may seem like quite a difficult dietary plan to follow, it should be remembered that this was the diet that most of us followed up until twenty or thirty years ago when the nature of food processing began to go through radical changes and much more sugar and salt was added to food products in order to get us 'addicted' to the taste of the product so that we would keep buying it. Treats like sweets, chocolates and fizzy drinks, once they become part of your everyday diet stop being treats. Taking them out of your everyday diet means that they can once again become treats if your children get used to only having them on particular or special occasions.

Family Time:

Many families I meet in clinical practice have found that the demands of modern life have put so much time pressures on them that they have little opportunity to spend positive time together as a family. For others time together has become a source of stress, arguments, and disagreements and so it is avoided. Indeed when family life has become dominated by problems and tensions, fun times together seem to slip away and disappear.

If positive family time together does not seem to be happening, then it is time to do something about this. Of course it's less of an issue for those who still live in a supportive, extended family system where there is regular contact with family members both within and outside the immediate nuclear family. However, the reality is that for the majority of us in modern Western culture, we live in nuclear families and rely on our immediate family for social and emotional support. Like adults, children need to feel that they belong and that they are important, valuable and loved within the unit they belong to. If positive times together are not happening very often, most children will feel a degree of insecurity. They may fear that they don't belong anymore, or that the family in which they belong is going to break down.

This insecurity is not going to disappear after one or two good times together. However, the more they can experience positive family time together the greater the likelihood that, over time, they will develop a better sense of belonging and emotional security. Furthermore, any changes you make will challenge your family 'script' (see chapter 7), so to start with there is going to have to be a degree of 'fake it until you make it'. Here are some questions you might ask yourselves to help you think about how you might go about developing more family time and more fun times together:

Review your working hours: Can you change your working hours to a more family friendly pattern? Can you afford to reduce your hours if you are spending long times away from home?

Have meals together: What happens at mealtimes? Are you having regular mealtimes together? Can you aim to have one meal together every day?

Going out together as a family regularly: Do you have a day of the week that you can spend together, doing something together? When was the last time you all went out together, or had a holiday together? This need not be expensive – a walk in the park or a local playground is better than sitting in front of the television.

Do fun things together at home: How often do you play games together? How often do you all talk to each other and find out about each other's day?

In a book by Catherine Bateson, called *Full Circles, Overlapping Lives*,[48] she argues that culture in modern, Western society has been changing so quickly that generations have become strangers to each other. In other words our ideas, values and beliefs and how we go about the task of living in the world are changing so radically, and so quickly, that each new generation of parents, are finding it harder and harder to relate to the sorts of things their children do, believe, value, and are interested in. If there is some truth in this (and I for one think there is) then there is a real need for us as parents to find ways to communicate and be with our children, to build bridges into their world so that we don't simply map our own beliefs about what is right and what is wrong and how to live straight on to them (although, of course, it remains important to provide our children with a model of the values that we want them to grow up with).

Fresh Air And Exercise:

Another feature of modern life in the West, is that young children are getting less exercise than they used to, and are spending more time following indoor pursuits and in settings where they can be watched over by adults (and therefore have less freedom to take risks). Indeed, these days physical education is getting less time in the school curriculum and many schools have sold off their playing fields. Against this, there is evidence that children in general, and boys in particular, need regular exercise and 'rough and tumble' play.

Try and make sure your child is getting exercise on a daily basis (aim for at least an hour a day of active play). If they are the 'outdoor' type, are they getting enough opportunities to play freely outside? Are there any organised sport activities or clubs locally that your child could join? Martial arts classes can be particularly useful, as they not only provide a forum for exercise and a place to learning self protection, but they also teach self discipline.

Television And Computer Games:

At the same time as there has been a decrease in the amount of time children spend doing exercise and active things, there has been an increase in the amount of time children spend with more passive pastimes like computers and television. There are a number of studies that have shown an association between the numbers of hours spent watching television or doing computer games and the likelihood of having problems with concentration and hyperactivity once the children are at school (see chapter 4).

Therefore, my suggestion is to monitor the amount of time your children spend watching television or doing computer games and have a time limit on these activities, as well as some rules about appropriate content and times of day when they are allowed to watch television or play computer games. For example, it is usually a bad idea to allow your children to watch television or play computer games just before bedtime, as bright, visual media have an arousing effect on the brain. This brings me nicely to my next point.

Bedtime Routines:

There is also accumulating evidence that our children are sleeping less than previous generations and it is well known that lack of sleep causes poor concentration and in some children can cause hyperactivity. Establishing a good sleeping pattern is therefore important if your children don't have one.

There are many ways to establish a routine that you are happy with and I am not a great believer in there being only one way to do any of the things suggested in this book, including bedtime routines. What I think is important is to establish some sort of regular routine so that you and your kids know roughly when bedtime is, and what is going to happen then. The following is just my set of suggestions that can hopefully guide you to set up your own routine which will work for you and your children.

Set a regular bedtime for your children and this can be different on schooldays from non schooldays, and vary according to the age of the child. About half an hour before the set bedtime begin your routine. Try to include relaxing activities before going to bed. In my family when it comes to bedtime with my 8 year old daughter and 9 year old son we often play for a short time, perhaps a board game, sometimes a bit of rough and tumble play. Then my children go and brush their teeth, put their pyjamas on and on alternate nights they will have a nice, warm bath before they do this. Once they are ready for bed they snuggle up to either my wife or I, in our bed and we read them each a chapter from a story they have chosen. After this they are tucked up in their own beds and left to go to sleep.

Of course there are enormous variations in bedtime routines across the world. In many South Asian cultures a regular bedtime is uncommon. Children spend their time around extended family members, some falling asleep in their mothers' laps, others taking themselves off to sleep when they are tired. Children there are more generally trusted to develop their own natural waking and sleeping rhythms. In such a system sleep is not an issue that adults feel they need to control in their children and therefore there is little tension around sleeping patterns. However, the situation is very different in modern, Western culture with the demands of long school days for children and work timetables for adults; sleeping routines for children have become important and often a battle ground when a child refuses to sleep.

In helping you establish a good bedtime routine with children who refuse to sleep, in my experience two important factors need to be looked at: dealing with children who get out of bed after they have been put into their bed, and creating a non stimulating bedroom environment.

With regards children who get out of their bed once they have been put into it, what often happens is that bedtimes become an extended game between the child and the adult and therefore a way for the child to stay up longer. The child's complaints (such as appearing distressed and crying, or that they are thirsty, hungry, or scared) is rarely more than clever attempts to keep you engaged in delaying their bedtime. Putting a stop to this sort of behaviour can happen very quickly providing you have the courage and emotional energy to see any strategy through and to mentally cope with the apparent distress and upset your child may well demonstrate when you put such a strategy into action (here again, managing stress and maintaining an assertive/authoritative stance will be important-see chapter 8). Breaking the cycle of long, disruptive bedtime routines can sometimes happen very quickly- within a few days. However, you constantly need to be on your guard in the first few weeks of establishing such a new approach, against the temptation to slip back into the old routine.

Here is my suggestion: Agree on a reasonable bedtime (meaning a time in which you expect your child to be tucked in bed ready for sleep) and a relaxing bedtime routine as described above. Deal with any of their usual complaints at bedtime during your bedtime routine. For example, if "I'm hungry" is a frequent complaint when they go to bed; then make sure your bedtime routine includes a snack before they go to get ready for bed. If the complaint is that they are frightened, then a nightlight in their room or leaving a light on in the hallway outside their room may be helpful.

Once they are tucked into their bed and the bedtime routine is finished, leave them in their bed and leave the room with the clear instruction that you expect them to stay in their bed whether or not they are asleep. Now that they are in their beds, your task is a simple one (although emotionally and physically very demanding). From now on every time they leave their beds, however distressed they become, you do not speak to them, you do not interact with them, and you do not give in to their demands, but simply return them to their bed. If they come into your bed in the middle of the night when you are asleep, you wake up and return them back to their own bed. If you want to do this effectively you need to be strong, persistent and you will need some support. If there are two of you at home then it makes sense that the parent who finds it easiest to do this (from an emotional point of view this is often, though not always, the father) should be the one who takes responsibility for the doing the task. The basic message you are trying to get through to your child is that once they are in bed you expect them to stay there. Expecting them to go to sleep on demand is, of course, unreasonable. Therefore, the aim is to get them to stay in their bed and sleep will usually follow once the routine becomes established.

With regards the second point (making bedrooms into a non-stimulant environment); this usually means that things like televisions and computers should be kept out of the bedroom. These are stimulating to the brain and the temptation to turn the television on once mum or dad thinks you have gone to sleep is strong. Use soft colours and soft lighting, make sure they are not getting too warm or too cold in their beds and sometimes some soft, new age style or lullaby style music playing in the background can help some children get to sleep.

Finally, also ask yourself if your child is getting enough exercise and running off enough energy to feel physically tired when it comes to sleep time.

Responsibility, Trust and Independence:

Have a think about the current level of input your children have toward your household. Do you feel they are making enough of a contribution? If not, think about adding a simple chore/responsibility, which they have to do regularly as a contribution towards the running of the household. You may even decide to reward this with a small amount of money. Think about opportunities to treat them with trust and responsibility – have a system in place of rewarding them for showing that they are trustworthy and withdrawing any privileges for showing that they are not. You may also want to have a think about homework – do you have a regular amount of time set aside for homework? Do you think that enough homework is being done? If not, think about making regular homework times and a system of rewards/punishments to make sure that this happens.

Support:

Being a parent is one of the most important and demanding jobs any of us will have to do. Most non-Western cultures recognise this and give parenthood (particularly motherhood) a high social status with a lot of esteem attached to it. In addition they promote family structures which make for rich sources of support for parents, particular mothers.

As I have discussed in this book, in modern, Western culture the task of parenting has become so much more difficult and there are so much more pressures on parents. One of the factors that has contributed to this is our increasing isolation and disappearance of traditional sources of support. Even modern nuclear families where there are two parents around, are struggling to support themselves. When moving away in search of better jobs (or any job) we often leave our usual circle of support. For many families, an increasingly common pattern is for fathers (in particular) to have to travel long distances to get to their jobs, and so they are away from the family for extended periods of time, whether this is through daily travelling or having to stay elsewhere for several nights a week. Whilst I am continually amazed at the ability of families to show great resilience and cope psychologically with these very modern pressures on family life, it would take a miracle if this was not having an effect even if just in terms of having so much less time to discuss and talk about bringing up a child (or indeed the fear of talking about the complexities of bringing up a child as the parents may want to avoid talking about things that could cause upset or other difficult emotions in the short time they get together).

To try and counteract some of this cultural (and economic) pressure, we have to become good at creating our own social support networks. Try this: make a list of all the different people who may be a source of support to you (whether this is family, friends, work colleagues, professionals and whether this is from a practical point of view, such as looking after the children for a little while, or an emotional point of view, such as someone to talk to). Make sure you have this list to hand with telephone numbers in an easily accessible place. Once you have this list try deepening some of the relationships with the people on this list. Call a meeting for people on this list if you are really struggling with your child and are in urgent need of some emotional and/or practical support. You may be surprised at how generous people are prepared to be. When I have suggested this to a number of families whom I've worked with, and who were in 'crisis', many have come back to me pleased to report how surprised they were that their neighbour, friend or particular family member came forward and made some radical and unexpected suggestions to try and help (such as they would take over the school run, they would have the child for a week, or they would come to stay in their house to provide direct support).

Another way to try to improve your social support network is to join a local group. This does not have to be around parenting but could be anything in which you have an interest (such as further education or a particular hobby or coffee mornings).

CHAPTER 12

Working with schools

There is a sense around that schools in the West are in something of an ongoing crisis. Although this sense of panic about education is somewhat exaggerated and exploited by the media, there are many aspects of school life in the West that seem to be causing problems for our children. The driver behind many of the diagnosis of ADHD seem to be motivated by schools' inability to deal with boisterous behaviour and the consequent temptation to turn such behaviour into a medical condition (such as ADHD) that doctors will sort out. This is something I and many colleagues I have spoken to and worked with have experienced. Colleagues of mine who regularly go into schools often report feeling exasperated by how frequently they are coming across situations where schools are putting labels on children when they are unable to cope with their behaviour. This is particularly noticeable in schools that are, for whatever reason, struggling- having had a poor report or a poor showing in the league tables, or a high staff turnover, and so on.

However, it is easy to be judgmental about schools without appreciating the particular pressures that schools and teachers are under to produce ever higher standards of achievement in their pupils and the threats to them (including job security) if they do not. As I have explained earlier in the book the outcome of this has been rocketing numbers of exclusions of boys and a similar increase in numbers of children (again mainly boys) who are described as having 'special needs'. In a peculiar way the increase in the amount of funding for special needs has become the 'backdoor' way of getting more money into a poorly funded education system. This does raise the question however, of whether we would be better off, instead of attaching this money to individual children, to use this money to improve the school experience across the board.

As a result of these dynamics individual children getting labelled with psychiatric disorders such as ADHD can be viewed as (and indeed this is the way that I view this) part of exploiting children to cover up the failings of schools and the government. If you are experiencing pressure from a school to have your child labelled and put on medication then I urge you to resist this. Teachers are not qualified to make such diagnosis, have little knowledge about the alternatives, and what is apparently the easiest way to solve school based difficulties, is not necessarily the best for your child. Schools also need to do their bit and you have every right as a parent to expect them to join you in a search for other solutions.

In dealing with problems at school my first suggestion is to try out the other strategies suggested in this book. For many children, once you have gained control of the problems at home, the problems at school then begin to improve. However, for a number of children even after improvement of the behaviour at home, problems at school still persist and if, after a good stretch of time with improvement in the behaviour at home (say a couple of months), the behaviour at school has not similarly improved, then consider trying some of the following suggestions.

Improving The Learning Environment At Home:

Children learn what is important and what they value from what is important and valued by their parents. Ask yourself whether your child is not particularly interested in school and learning because this is not something that you are particularly interested in at home. If this is the case you can create a more positive value towards learning and academic endeavours through promoting this in your daily life at home. Show your own interest in learning through reading books, papers and further education. Introduce your children to reading from a young age (and if you have not it is never too late to get them interested in this).

Get The Right Assessment And Help:

Does your child have learning difficulties or behaviour problems (or both) at school? Ask your school what strategies they have in place to deal with either the learning difficulties or behaviour problems. If there are learning difficulties, has your child had an assessment for these, for example from an educational psychologist? Does your school have an individual education plan for your child and have you been consulted in drawing up this plan so that you can include your own ideas from how you are dealing with the problems at home? Does your child need a statement of special educational needs? Do they need extra assistance at school, such as a learning mentor or classroom assistant to help them with particular areas of either behaviour or learning? Are there any medical tests that need to be done, for example, does your child need a hearing test or test of their eyesight? Is there a problem with your child being bullied? If so, ask to see the school's anti-bullying policy and find out what they are doing about it. Teachers (like many other professionals these days) are busy with complicated paperwork, bureaucracy, high expectations and many children to manage. As a result they are not always in a position to pay particular attention to individual children. Consequently you may need to make sure that teachers and other professionals have examined your child's circumstances and identified things that could be changed and done differently. Don't accept being persuaded to go down the simplest (for them) route of labelling and medicating your child.

Working With School To Close The Home/school Loop:

Clever children are particularly talented at working out how different systems work and playing one bit of the system off against the other. So, for example, a child may complain to his parents about being unfairly treated by teachers at school in order to get out of facing consequences or homework or to get certain teachers they dislike into trouble (This can be a very difficult one to call as some of the complaints may be true and need to be listened to and understood from the child's perspective). When this happens you can get into a situation of parents blaming the school and school blaming the parents with the child falling through the gap in between (regardless whether the child enjoys this or not).

Closing this- what I am calling the home/school loop- becomes relatively simple once you have got past any of the emotional blocks to this (such as those described in chapter 7) and you have a sympathetic and approachable school. Closing the home/school loop basically relies on setting up a good, robust system of communication.

What you decide to do is not as important as having a good system agreed between you and the school, where you feel listened to and your ideas are taken seriously by the school and you take the school's ideas seriously too. The simplest form is a daily home/school diary in which the teacher writes a few comments on your child's behaviour at the end of each lesson. Many schools have their own system of a daily report card which teachers have to sign and make a brief comment on the child's behaviour at the end of each lesson. Once you are getting this regular feedback about your child's behaviour throughout the school day, you can implement a system of consequences (positive and negative, as described in chapter 10) depending on the reports that you get. For some of the negative consequences you may choose to have school based ones such as extra homework over and above what is expected, or your own 'detention' at home (grounding and withdrawal of privileges).

However, I would like to mention a few problems with home/school diaries or report cards. Although the majority of schools I have worked with quickly appreciate and understand the idea behind something like a home/school diary, I have experienced situations where some schools or teachers have, for whatever reason, used these only to put in negative comments about the child and to write down episodes of bad behaviour only, seemingly not noticing when the child is behaving well. Similarly, I have also experienced the situation where children quite like having a home/school diary and have come to realise that most gets written into it when they misbehave with days when they are being good only getting a couple of words like 'good today' as an entry. Therefore, if the diary is being used by the school only to note or particularly to highlight negative behaviour then it is unlikely to work and should be reviewed with the school.

The home/school diary idea is not the only way to improve communication. For some parents this is not what they are looking for and what they need are regular opportunities to sit down with a teacher and talk about how their child is doing and to be alerted to any issues, positive or negative. In this case an alternative way is a weekly meeting at the end of each week between the parents and the child's teachers. This need not be as difficult time wise as it may sound for teachers; a five minute conversation on a Friday in the playground with the teacher can be an arrangement which satisfies some.

For some children it is the idea that school know more about how they are at home and visa versa, which seems to make the difference in their behaviour. Sometimes closing the home/school loop is about setting up meetings between parents and teachers where the children are present and involved in the discussions whether they are hearing things they want to hear or not. Involving children in regular meetings between parents and school not only helps children see that the adults are working together and therefore less easy to play off against each other, but also gives an opportunity for the child's voice to be heard and for their perception of what is happening to be taken seriously.

Teaching Your Child Social Skills:

As with everything else in this book I am not putting forward any earth shattering new ideas that have been developed by men in white coats running around laboratories with clip boards carefully studying how children behave! Some children have more difficulty making and sustaining friendships, some children get themselves into difficulty by losing their temper and becoming aggressive towards other children if things are not going their way, some are not particularly interested in making friends and are quite happy getting on doing their own thing, some have grown up surrounded by adults and are quite comfortable interacting with adults but have had little opportunity to develop the social skills to interact with children their own age, and yet others have grown up in cultures that have different ideas and ways for children to interact and are simply inexperienced in interacting with children from a different culture.

There are many reasons why children may have difficulty in making and keeping friends, indeed is it not possible to accept that some children aren't particularly interested in having many (or any) friends? However, for some not being able to make and keep friends can affect their experience at school where they may feel isolated and unhappy. However, there are potentially endless ways to help your child gain a better circle of friends, and sometimes this will happen by itself once you allow yourself to feel less anxious about this issue and let your child sort this one out themselves.

Contributing to helping your children develop better social skills is really about spending a bit of time and effort talking to your children, giving them some tips, dealing with poor behaviour using good consequences, and trying to keep your anxiety, about things changing for your child, at bay. The following are just a few ideas and suggestions.

Talk to your child about making friends and give them some useful tips, particularly on how to deal with conflicts (resist the temptation to sort out their conflicts for them). When going through a particularly difficult situation with a friend give them an idea on what they could do about it. For example, if there is a friend whom the child feels is being 'nasty' to them, talk to your child on how they might ignore that, walk away from it or even have a humorous remark or two which they might say back to this child. Talk to your child about being assertive. If somebody is getting them to do things which get your child in trouble, your child needs to learn to say 'no' to these friends (just as with assertiveness more generally which I discussed in chapter 8). Use stories from your own childhood about situations where maybe you had problems with friends and how you dealt with them. Children love to hear stories about their own parents' childhoods and getting a message through to your child like this often works much better than a telling off or instructions which the child may not want to listen to. If your child is starting from scratch, talk to them about tactful ways of making that first approach, for example asking the new potential friend something about themselves or their own hobbies or what they like to play. Most people (including children) like people who show an interest in them.

Create opportunities for your children to make new friends or strengthen their existing friendships. For example, make time for your children to invite friends to come and visit them at your home. Encourage them to ask somebody and then sort the arrangement out with that person's parents. If you have friends with children of a similar age invite them all round. Find clubs which offer structured activities for your child to attend which will give him/her an opportunity to mix with others their own age whilst doing structured activities. Organisations such as scouts and brownies, and clubs such as martial arts, are good in this respect as they not only have a structure to their activities but also have codes of conduct and discipline for the children who attend.

If Necessary Change Schools:

Sometimes the situation between a school and a child has got to the point where your child has a particular reputation and the school are scaptgoating your child. If this has happened, then sometimes, no matter what you do, their view of your child will not shift. Alternatively, it may be that you have got to such loggerheads with the teachers that communication between you and the teachers has broken down and cannot be mended. When it reaches this point it is likely to be best for everyone to try for a fresh start. In this case, find a new school and meet with them before your child starts there to try and put in place some positive measures such as the ones suggested above to help your child start at the new school in a positive way.

A few very brave parents that I have met have actually taken the decision to give up on the mainstream system altogether and opt for teaching their children themselves. If you have decided to go for this option try to make sure your child is still having plenty of opportunity for mixing with other children and that you have plenty of support yourself through one of the organisations that support parents who have decided to teach their children at home.

CHAPTER 13

Helping others with your Expertise

Building a First Aid Kit:

Have a look over what you have done over the past few weeks and months since starting this book (and before). What ideas have you found helpful? What things did you try out that you felt made a difference - even just a minor or temporary one? Think about your social network – what people do you know who you think you could turn to for help at times of crisis (whether this is simply talking things through or people who could offer more practical help)? Make a list of all the things that you have found useful and then make a list of all the people you know who could be of help, together with their telephone numbers. Now put these ideas and lists into a box or container, ready to be taken out again when you need it. At times of crisis use this 'first aid kit' and try contacting people on your list to see what help or ideas they may have or be able to offer.

Helping Others With Your Expertise:

If you have the time, I would now like to ask you a favour. It would be of great benefit to other children and parents to know what has worked or made a difference for you with your own child or children (whether it was something in this book or completely unrelated to what you've read in this book). Different things work for different people and the more professionals like myself can find out about real people and the challenges they face in their real lives, the better able we are to understand the issues and the more ideas we have that might be useful to other children and their families. So my final entry into this book is in the form of a request. Please could you write to me outlining your experience with your child/children, explaining which way of conceptualising their problems made sense to you and what intervention (if anything) has made a difference. If your son or daughter can be persuaded to write about this from their perspective, then this is even better. You can choose whether to include your name/address or stay anonymous and please indicate whether you would be happy or not for me to refer to, or reprint your story in any of my future writings. You can write to me at:

Dr Sami Timimi
Consultant Child and Adolescent Psychiatrist
Child and Adolescent Mental Health Services,
Ash Villa,
Willoughby Road,
Sleaford,
Lincolnshire, NG34 8QA
UK

Or send an e-mail to

stimimi@talk21.com

NOTES

(Endnotes)

[1] These are questions taken from the Diagnostic Statistical Manual IV (DSM-IV): American Psychiatric Association. (1994) *Diagnostic and Statistical Manual of Mental Disorders, Fourth Edition (DSM-IV)*. Washington DC: APA.

[2] You can find detailed arguments and full references in my previous books (written for an academic and professional audience): Timimi, S. (2002) *Pathological Child Psychiatry and the Medicalization of Childhood*. London: Routledge-Brunner; Timimi, S. (2005) *Naughty Boys: Anti-Social Behaviour, ADHD and the Role of Culture*. Basingstoke: Palgrave MacMillan; and Timimi, S. and Begum, R. (eds.) (2006) *Critical Voices in Child and Adolescent Mental Health*. London: Free Association Books.

[3] For example: Battle, E.S. and Lacey, B. (1972) A context for hyperactivity in children over time. *Child Development* 43, 757-773.

[4] For a summary, see Taylor, E. (1994) Syndromes of attention deficit and overactivity. In M. Rutter, E. Taylor and L. Hersov (eds.) *Child And Adolescent Psychiatry, Modern Approaches: Third Edition*. Oxford: Blackwell Scientific Publications.

[5] Rappley, M.D., Gardiner, J.C., Jetton, J.R. and Howang, R.T. (1995) The use of Methylphenidate in Michigan. *Archives of Paediatric and Adolescent Medicine* 149, 675-679.

[6] Brewis, A. and Schmidt, K. (2003) Gender variation in the identification of Mexican children's psychiatric symptoms. *Medical Anthropology Quarterly* 17, 376-393.

[7] See http://www.adhdrelief.com/famous.html.

[8] For further discussion, see Leo, J.L. and Cohen, D.A. (2003) Broken brains or flawed studies? A critical review of ADHD neuroimaging research. *The Journal of Mind and Behavior* 24, 29-56.

[9] See discussion in Preface. The potential mistakes that we make in conclusions about differences in brain size/shape/function is very similar to that the phrenologists made. Thus our conclusions about psychiatric disorders based on vague and often non-specific brain differences have been referred to as the 'new Phrenology'.

[10] For further discussion, see Carey, W.B. and McDevitt, S.C. (1995) *Coping With Children's Temperament: A Guide for Professionals.* New York: Basic Books.

[11] Barkley, R. et al (2002) International Consensus Statement on ADHD. *Clinical Child and Family Psychology Review* 5, 89- 111.

[12] For all the update research on ADHD genetics see Joseph, J. (2006). *The Missing Gene: Psychiatry, Heredity, and the Fruitless Search for Genes.* New York: Algora.

[13] See for example Schachter, H., Pham, B., King, J., Langford, S. and Moher, D. (2001) How efficacious and safe is short-acting methylphenidate for the treatment of attention-deficit disorder in children and adolescents? A meta-analysis. *Canadian Medical Association Journal* 165, 1475-1488.

[14] MTA Co-operative Group (1999) A 14 month randomized clinical trial of treatment strategies for attention deficit/hyperactivity disorder. *Archives of General Psychiatry* 56, 1073-1086.

[15] MTA Co-operative Group (2004) National Institute of Mental Health Multimodal Treatment Study of ADHD follow-up: 24-month outcomes of treatment strategies for attention-deficit/hyperactivity disorder. *Pediatrics* 113, 754-761.

[16] Qouted from Hearn, K. (2004) Here kiddie, kiddie. Available at http://alternet.org/drugreporter/20594/

[17] See Hart, N., Grand, N. and Riley, K. (2006) Making the grade: The gender gap, ADHD, and the medicalization of boyhood. In D. Rosenfeld, and C. Faircloth (eds.) *Medicalized Masculinities.* Philadelphia: Temple University Press.

[18] See for example Babcock, Q. and Byrne, T. (2000) Student perceptions of methylphenidate abuse at a public liberal arts college. *Journal of American College Health* 49,143-5; and Teter, C. et al (2003) Illicit Methylphenidate Use in an Undergraduate Student Sample: Prevalence and Risk Factors. *Pharmacotherapy* 23, 609-617.

[19] For further discussion of the research in this area, see Jackson, G. (2005). *Rethinking Psychiatric Drugs*. Bloomington: Author House.

[20] Lambert, N.M., and Hartsough, C.S. (1998) Prospective study of tobacco smoking and substance dependence among samples of ADHD and non-ADHD participants. *Journal of Learning Disabilities* 31, 533-544.

[21] See for example P. Bracken and P. Thomas (2005) *Postpsychiatry*. Oxford: Oxford University Press.

[22] Page 10 in Clarke, J., Hall, S., Jefferson, T. and Roberts, B. (1975) Subcultures, culture and subcultures. In S. Hall and T. Jefferson (eds.) *Resistance Through Rituals: Youth Subcultures in Post-War Britain*. London: Hutchinson.

[23] See Thom Hartmann's website http://www.thomhartmann.com

[24] Please see page 10 and http://www.adhdrelief.com/famous.html

[25] Harrell, W. (1999) *For Entrepreneurs Only*. Franklin Lakes: Career Press.

[26] Quoted in http://www.thomhartmann.com/whosorder.shtml

[27] I have summarised the eugenic movements relevance to psychiatry in general and ADHD in particular in my book Timimi, S. (2005) *Naughty Boys: Anti-Social Behaviour, ADHD and the Role of Culture*. Basingstoke: Palgrave MacMillan; other useful summaries can be found in Breggin, P. and Breggin, G. (1998) *The War Against Children of Color*. Maine: Common Courage Press, and Whitaker, R. (2002) *Mad in America*. Cambridge MA: Perseus, and at http://www.thomhartmann.com/whosorder.shtml

[28] Page 401 in Watson, J. (2003) *DNA: The Secret of Life*. London: William Heinemann.

[29] Page 365 in Watson, J. (2003) *DNA: The Secret of Life*. London: William Heinemann.

[30] All the issues explored in this chapter are covered in greater detail in my book Timimi, S. (2005) *Naughty Boys: Anti-Social Behaviour, ADHD and the Role of Culture*. Basingstoke: Palgrave MacMillan

[31] Rutter, M. (1982) Syndromes attributed to minimal brain dysfunction in childhood. *American Journal of Psychiatry* 139: 21-33.

[32] More detailed discussion and full references can be found in the books I have written for an academic audience including: Timimi, S. (2002) *Pathological Child Psychiatry and the Medicalization of Childhood*. London: Routledge-Brunner; Timimi, S. (2005) *Naughty Boys: Anti-Social Behaviour, ADHD and the Role of Culture*. Basingstoke: Palgrave MacMillan; and Timimi, S. and Begum, R. (eds.) (2006) *Critical Voices in Child and Adolescent Mental Health*. London: Free Association Books.

[33] Summarised in Rutter, M. and Smith, D. (1995) *Psychosocial Disorders in the Young: Time Trends and their causes*. Chichester: John Wiley and Sons.

[34] Hitchen, L. (2006) Address poverty to reduce mental health problems among children, says BMA. *British Medical Journal* 332, 1471.

[35] Whitfield, C. (2006) Childhood trauma as a cause of ADHD, aggression, violence and ant-social behaviour. In S. Timimi and B. Maitra (eds.) *Critical Voices in Child and Adolescent Mental*. London: Free Association Books.

[36] Christakis, D., Zimmerman, F., DiGiuseppe, D. and McCarty, C. (2004) Early Television exposure and subsequent attentional problems in children. *Pediatrics* 113, 708-713

[37] See for example Gordon, N., Burke, S., Akil, H., Watson, S. and Panksepp, J. (2003) Socially-induced brain 'fertilization':

Play promotes brain derived neurotrophic factor transcription in the amygdale and dorsolateral frontal cortex in juvenile rats. *Neuroscience Letters* 341, 17-20; and Panksepp, J., Burgdorf, J., Turner, C. and Gordon, N. (2003) Modeling ADHD-type arousal with unilateral frontal cortex damage in rats and beneficial effects of play therapy. *Brain and Cognition* 52, 97-105.

[38] See Hart, N., Grand, N. and Riley, K. (2006) Making the grade: The gender gap, ADHD, and the medicalization of boyhood. In D. Rosenfeld, and C. Faircloth (eds.) *Medicalized Masculinities*. Philadelphia: Temple University Press.

[39] For further discussion of this issue, see Hamilton, C. (2003) *Growth Fetish*. Crows Nest: Allen and Unwin.

[40] Mac An Ghaill, M. (1994) *The Making Of Men: Masculinities, Sexualities And Schooling*. Buckingham: Open University Press.

[41] Page 13 in Gergen, K. (1991) *The Saturated Self: Dilemmas Of Identity In Contemporary Life*. New York: Basic Books.

[42] Page 203 in Szasz, T. (1970) *Ideology and Insanity*. New York: Doubleday-Anchor.

[43] Tomm, K. (1990) A critique of DSM. *Dulwich Center Newsletter* 3, 5-8.

⁴⁴ See MIND's publication "Making sense of coming off psychiatric drugs" available at http://www.mind.org.uk/Information/Booklets/Making+sense/Making+sense+of+coming+off+psychiatric+drugs.htm

⁴⁵ Stein, D.B. (2001) *Unravelling the ADD/ADHD Fiasco: Successful Parenting Without Drugs*. Kansas City: Andrews McMeel.

⁴⁶ Sells, S. (2001) *Parenting your out of control teenager: Seven steps to re-establishing authority and reclaim love*. New York: St Martin's Press.

⁴⁷ Bateman, B., Warner, J.O., Hutchinson, E., et al (2004) The effects of a double blind, placebo controlled, artificial food colourings and benzoate preservative challenge on hyperactivity in a general population sample of preschool children. *Archives of Disorder of Childhood* 89, 506-11.

⁴⁸ Bateson, C. (2000) *Full Circles, Overlapping Lives*. New York: Random House.

About the Author

Dr Sami Timimi is a consultant child and adolescent psychiatrist who works in the National Health Service in Lincolnshire, UK. He writes from a critical psychiatry perspective on topics relating to child and adolescent mental health and has published many articles on many topics including eating disorders, psychotherapy, behavioural disorders and cross-cultural psychiatry. He has authored two books, Pathological Child Psychiatry and the Medicalization of Childhood, published in 2002 and Naughty Boys: Anti-Social Behaviour, ADHD and the Role of Culture, published in 2005, and co-edited with Begum Maitra Critical Voices in Child and Adolescent Mental Health published in 2006.

Lightning Source UK Ltd.
Milton Keynes UK
10 January 2011

165435UK00002B/206/A

9 781425 988296